Birthday Girl

NIKO WOLF

Birthday Girl

HODDER studio

First published in Great Britain in 2022 by Hodder Studio
An Imprint of Hodder & Stoughton
An Hachette UK company

1

A CIP catalogue record for this title is available from the British Library

Hardback ISBN 9781529366655
eBook ISBN 9781529366662

Typeset in Plantin Light by Hewer Text UK Ltd, Edinburgh
Printed and bound in Great Britain by Clays Ltd, Elcograf S.p.A.

Hodder & Stoughton policy is to use papers that are natural, renewable
and recyclable products and made from wood grown in sustainable
forests. The logging and manufacturing processes are expected to
conform to the environmental regulations of the country of origin.

Hodder & Stoughton Ltd
Carmelite House
50 Victoria Embankment
London EC4Y 0DZ

www.hodder-studio.com

For Violet
2005–2019

"Never say you know the last word about any human heart."

Henry James

1996

Afterward, he would wonder how anyone got through life without dying. People got on and off planes. They crossed streets without looking. And, once in a while, someone would disappear, leaving no clue as to where they had gone and no trace of themselves behind.

They have pooled their money and rented a house out east. Not a grand house, it's true, more like a small cottage in the almost-Hamptons. The first night, they had all been up late doing tequila shots. The next morning, Maddie is up early and announces that she's going down to the ocean, "for a paddle." He hears these words through a fog of sleep and alcohol.

"What?" He opens his eyes. "*Now?*"

The pillow smells unpleasantly of mildew. Does it matter that he's been breathing this in all night?

"Yes!" she is saying. "Come on, it'll be *brilliant*."

She is standing in the doorway in a green summer dress and the shirt he had planned to wear at dinner tonight. Her blonde hair falls messily around her face. Her eyes have that mischievous glint.

He hauls himself up onto his elbows and peers out of the window. The September skies are gray and unpromising. A spreading circle of damp sits on the ceiling above. Could it be any more obvious they've been ripped off?

There is no sign of the others. They will be sleeping off their hangovers in peace. Once he and Maddie set off, the air is fresh and invigorating, and his head begins to clear. They cycle the few miles to the bridge, cross to the long spit of land that forms the ocean road, and park their bikes next to the dunes. The red flags are out along the beach, and the Atlantic rolls in high and cold. It's early. No surprise that there is not a single other person to be seen. Maddie is running ahead, already halfway through the dunes. She has so much energy.

"Don't go in!" he calls, out of breath, sure that he just felt a few drops of rain on his face. "Be careful!"

But his wife is not the sort of woman who cares.

"Pussy!" she yells back, sprinting down the sand. He isn't complaining. His gorgeous wife . . . He loves this about her. How bold she is. How fearless. If this makes her a challenge, occasionally hard to keep up with, he is a lucky man, and she is so worth it.

"Coming!" he shouts back and jogs after her.

A crumbling concrete jetty extends out into the water, the far end sitting just under the waves. As Maddie runs lightly along it, it is as if she's hovering right above the water, which would hardly surprise him. Is she planning on diving in? The tide is going out, the water too shallow, he realizes, as helplessly he watches her kick off her flip-flops, leap up, and with a joyous "*Whoop!*" jump in—feet first, thank God—*splash!*

The jetty is slippery, so he picks his way along it carefully. Not as far as the end, though. He takes off his sneakers and sets them down a safe distance from the edge, then sits with his legs dangling over the side. Cautiously, he dips a toe in, and the waves wash over his feet. The water is even colder than he expected. It's like stepping into a bucket of ice. How can she stand it? As his feet start to go numb, he sees that even Maddie knows better than to venture in too far. Knee-deep in the surf, she stands with her arms outstretched, as if to welcome the waves. He squints toward the horizon. Large expanses of water have always made him uncomfortable.

"How is it . . .?" he calls weakly.

"Amazing!" she shouts, beckoning to him. "Get *over* here!" He grins, thinks how good it is to see her looking so happy again.

As another wave crashes into her, she staggers a little. Is she going to make him go all the way in? Farther out, the ocean is violently circling and churning. And, though he hates to be a party pooper, could that be a rip current? Just in case, he takes off his glasses, folds and stashes them carefully in his jacket pocket. There is something else in there—*the plane tickets.* How could he forget? He's been saving in secret for over a year, his plan being to surprise his wife at her birthday party tonight. Then, on impulse, as they'd left the house just now, he'd decided to bring them with him.

She's wading back toward him, lithely pulling herself up onto the jetty, dress soaked, hair damp.

"Wow, that woke me up! C'mon, let's get breakfast." She jumps up, slips into her flip-flops. *Breakfast?* As he heaves himself up, it occurs to him that the party is hours away. And the idea of presenting the tickets in front of their friends strikes him as kind of showy and cheesy. Maddie is always telling him to let go; to be less uptight, more spontaneous. Feeling reckless and just a tiny bit insane, he tells her to wait a second.

"Close your eyes . . ." He takes the tickets from his jacket with a "Surprise!" and presents them to her with a flourish.

"Happy Birthday, Mads," he says, as they stand, crazily (spontaneously!) out in the Atlantic Ocean—or as good as.

He is proud of himself. Maddie looks down at the tickets, mystified. She has no idea. And then he sees the recognition dawn in her face, and the tears spring up in her eyes. "Oh!" she says. "Oh, Jon . . . Oh, you shouldn't have . . ."

Sharpie

2019

The line that a half hour ago snaked all through the bookstore has finally dwindled to zero. A five-Sharpie night—in other words, an excellent turnout. In a little over two hours, Jonathan has signed more than 150 books and spoken to twice as many people. He loves his readers—loves talking to them, loves answering their questions, loves getting their take on his work. "Your first book," one reader had said, "it was like you wrote it just for me. Like you were speaking *just* to me." As he makes sure to say at events like this one, his readers see all kinds of things and make all manner of interesting connections that he, the author, may have missed.

He packs up his things and thinks about dinner. Both his agent and publicist have taken off already, which is fine. It's good to have a few minutes to himself. Tossing his phone and a handful of the remaining pens into his bag, he makes for the first set of escalators. 8:30 p.m. Is there time for a quick beer at Tavern on Jane before he heads home? After all these years, there is still an adrenaline rush that comes with public speaking, and he feels the need to decompress. But they are having a late supper. And a good bottle of Chassagne-Montrachet waits, picked up during their last trip to Europe.

At the top of the escalator, he sends a quick message.

Hey you . . . might stop by the bar first. Okay?

Within seconds, her reply flashes back.

Right back atcha. Still working on supper, enjoy your drink.
XOX

At the entrance to the subway, groups stand chatting or waiting for friends. A steady stream of students and couples emerge from beneath Union Square, dressed to the nines for a night in the big city. Crossing 14th, he heads down University Place, feeling buoyant and relaxed. He relishes these late-summer evenings, the buzz and honk of Friday-night traffic, the sight of his fellow New Yorkers out for a good time. He makes a right along 11th Street, aware of being at that delicious, addictive stage of writing a new book, when the story seems to simply pour out of him. Like sitting on the floor untangling a huge ball of string, it isn't everyone's idea of fun, but for him it is totally absorbing. Resolving the knots, finding the loose ends, the holes getting smaller and smaller as the various threads of the story come together. Laura says it's easy to tell when he's "on the scent"—door to his study closed, internet disabled, phone off and locked in a drawer. The sense of compulsion and single-minded purpose is the most incredible high. The heady sense of achievement when he gets his characters' thoughts out onto the page. Predictably, by the time he reaches the fringes of the West Village, the idea of cozying up to the bar at his local tavern feels kind of contrived. One of those clichéd things male writers are supposed to enjoy, when actually, he'd much rather be home. Besides, one or two plot points came to mind during his talk earlier. After dinner, he'll need to jot them down and then pin them up on his sticky-note wall, or he'll be up at some crazy hour unable to go back to sleep. Naturally, he keeps a notebook on the nightstand for exactly this purpose. As he tells his readers, inspiration can strike at all hours—in dreams, in the shower, on the subway—the danger being that, by the time you get back to your desk, you'll have forgotten them all.

He walks in to find Laura in a close grapple with the salad spinner. Three pans are simmering on the stove. The air is fragrant with the smell of sage, lemon, and butter, while the promised bottle of wine sits ready on the counter.

"Couldn't stay away, huh?" Laura laughs, and turns to kiss him. "How was your thing?"

"Oh, you know . . ." he says, drawing her into a clinch. "*Mobbed.*"

Her dark hair is gathered into a neat braid. She feels sturdy and solid in his arms. Adorably, she is wearing one of his old button-ups—a look he loves on her, but which Laura has pronounced "too undone" for outside the house.

"*So* jaded." She clicks her tongue and neatly disentangles herself to go check on supper. "I'm sure you can handle it."

"You know me." This idea of himself as the jaded writer is an old joke between them. "Is this ready to go?" he asks, indicating the bottle.

"All yours."

He takes a couple of glasses down from the cabinet and pulls up a stool to the island. With their respective careers being so busy, they frequently find themselves eating after midnight. There is a childlike appeal to being awake in the darkest hours, like an echo of Christmas Eve. The feeling of cosseted security, he imagines, when a parent who cares about you whips up a snack when you are supposed to be in bed. As an adult, the activity is intimate, companionable. Something they've always done together. Laura might get home after a crazy evening at the restaurant, and he'll wake to the smell of

7

an omelet or fresh waffles. Sitting around the island in his pajamas, watching Laura cook, is just about his favorite thing in the world. Just one of the myriad pleasures of sharing a home with someone.

"So . . ." Jonathan says. "How was *your* evening? Did you figure out what it's all costing me yet?"

Laura turns, wooden spoon in hand, and cocks an amused eyebrow.

"Good try, lover. I think you mean, what it's costing *us*?"

He's teasing, and she knows it. In sheer dollars, he is the main breadwinner, though Laura is chef and owner of her own restaurant. "Actually, you'll be *extremely* relieved to hear we're at fifty guests."

"Seriously?" She dips a spoon into the sauce and brings it over for him to taste. "Yum!" he says.

"Yep." She grins. "And yep."

"You're amazing, you know that?"

"So they tell me."

Jonathan isn't the only one impatient for supper. The cat jumps up on the island, nudges at him with her face. He finds her food and dispenses a generous portion into her bowl. Sitting back down he wonders which annoying relative or tiresome associate Laura has managed to cull from the list. Between his book contacts and her network of connections in the restaurant world, they know an awful lot of people. If previous family events are anything to go by, various nieces, nephews, and third cousins will be lining up to corner him about how to publish the novel they haven't yet started. And that, he reminds himself, is perfectly OK. Because not so long ago he was exactly where they are now. He holds off asking Laura for more details. "Plausible deniability," as their friend Jay would put it. Their wedding was originally planned for September, but after his son pointed out the issue of the awkward timing, this had been hastily revised. Though he is happily, *finally*, tying the knot with Laura, planning a wedding is not his idea of a good time. His role is to demonstrate enthusiasm, veto anything outrageous, and, last but not least, show gratitude. He takes his glass and swirls the wine around for a few seconds, enjoying the anticipation of the first sip.

"Hon? I was thinking," Laura says, chopping a small pile of sage with the alarming speed of a professional, "that for the reception we could take Heather and Saul up on their offer of the orchard upstate. What do you think? I'm seeing Heather for lunch tomorrow. I know she'd be thrilled."

"You wouldn't rather just do it at the lake house? Or have something here . . .?" Privately, he's been hoping she will agree to the latter. There's plenty of space in their backyard, and it'd be way less hassle to have it in the city than have all their guests trek elsewhere. As for Heather and Saul's orchard, for reasons that should be obvious to everyone, it is hardly his first choice for a celebration. Even now, he can conjure the scene in his mind—the half-empty rows of chairs, the paltry collection of mourners, the odor of wilting flowers.

"But, Jon, it's so gorgeous there in the fall." Laura sighs.

"Yes, but if we have the ceremony and the reception here, we can all get drunk in one place," he jokes.

As she turns back to the stove, he can't see her expression. He takes a first sip of the wine. "Wow, this really is amazing. Remember when we found it?" Italy, 2010. After he wound up the last leg of his European tour for *A Knack for Killing*, which had spent months on multiple bestseller lists. Jay had flown out, and the three of them had celebrated in Rome.

"I picked up your jacket from the tailor," Laura says.

"Sorry?"

"For the wedding. It's upstairs if you want to check it fits."

"Oh, yes. *Definitely.* I'll do it first thing tomorrow. And we're not doing gifts, right?"

Laura lowers the heat on the stove, neatly repositions two of the pans, adds a generous amount of butter to the other. His stomach rumbles in anticipation.

"Gosh, no. It's not like we actually *need* anything." They're not exactly spring chickens in their twenties or thirties, he thinks to himself, so this is kind of a no-brainer. *And*, though no one would be tactless enough to say it out loud, this will, after all, be his second marriage.

He gets up and goes to the stove, lifts the lid on the nearest saucepan, dips a finger in the sauce. Linguine with lemon and sage brown butter—another favorite. As Laura laughs and gently slaps his hand away, he gets the strangest sensation—a surreal sense of observing his own life through the eyes of an onlooker. Presumably a lot of writers share this experience, Jonathan thinks, but for a second or two he'd felt like one of those couples. One of those annoying, overly cute rom-com couples that you see in date-night movies. Laura rolls out fresh pasta dough and cuts it into perfect strips.

Outside it is raining softly. Beyond the French doors, past the dripping trees at the far end of their huge backyard, other windows, other lives, look out onto theirs. New Yorkers like themselves, eating dinner, gossiping on the phone, watching porn, getting dressed and undressed. Going about their lives. Each window like a TV screening its own reality show. As Laura plates their starters, he wonders how their lives appear to these anonymous neighbors. Privileged?

Certainly. But do they seem like good people? Do they look happy?

He gets up to open a second bottle. It's true, he decides, as the cork emerges cleanly with a soft "pop." There really is nothing that they need. After all the ups and downs, life is kind of perfect.

Lift

1996

At first, they think Jonathan's reporting an abduction.

"Hold up," says the female cop, who has introduced herself as Detective Ragione. "You're telling us your wife *got into* some guy's car of *her own free will?*"

It was only when they made their way off the beach, he repeats, that they saw they were not alone. There was a car in the parking lot. Sporty and expensive-looking. An E-type Jaguar, according to his wife.

"A what?" The detective asks him to spell it. "Fancy . . ." she murmurs, writing it down. Jonathan is trying so hard to control his emotions. To cast his mind back and answer all their questions correctly. But his heart is filled with such a terrible sense of foreboding that this is far from easy.

"And then what happened?" says Mahoney. So far, the male cop has been observing, saying very little. It's unclear which of the two is in charge.

Jonathan hesitates, knowing exactly what comes next— Maddie, eyes shining, gesturing toward the car—and how terrible it will sound.

"She asked if . . . if I thought he could give her a lift," he replies.

"A ride?"

"Yes."

"The driver of this car?"

"Yes."

"And what did you say?"

He is silent for a moment, his eyes on the floor.

"I . . ." he says, finally. "I said, 'I dare you.'"

The detectives exchange a look.

"Wait, you dared your *wife* . . . to get in some . . . random vehicle?" Ragione says. "With a *stranger*. Did I hear that right?"

He swallows hard, nods. He knows how crazy it sounds. "It's her thing, that she's always done," he explains. Over their four and a half years together.

"Her *thing*, huh?" says Ragione. A quizzical look at her partner. A dismissive flick of her pen as she makes another note. If it's possible for someone to write in a hostile manner, he thinks bitterly, this person has mastered it. And the way she repeats his words back to him, what does it mean? Is she trying to bait him?

"You're saying she's done this before?" Mahoney says.

The cop appears not that much older than himself, Jonathan thinks, yet his whole demeanor suggests someone far more mature. The eyes are dark, the gaze interrogative and penetrating. Missing nothing. Giving nothing away. Relaxed in his plastic seat, legs akimbo, feet flat on the floor, Mahoney reminds him of John Wayne, or one of those Delta Force types you see in films. You hear a lot about domestic violence among cops, but he can't imagine Mahoney beating his wife. What he can imagine, though, is that if the detective encountered a violent criminal, he would not hesitate to take out his gun and shoot the guy straight through the heart.

"Maddie loves vintage cars," Jonathan answers. "And she can be a bit impulsive, but their owners always seem happy to show them off." He can only imagine what the cops think of all this. And of him. But it happens to be the truth. He's already told them that he's out here with his friends Laura and Jay, and either would back him up on this point. "*Is she out of her mind?*" his sister Heather had once remarked. "*Who does that?*" He'd had no answer then, either. To others, Maddie's behavior wasn't cute or endearing, but downright dangerous.

"So you weren't worried?" Mahoney says.

"No, not at first."

"No?" Ragione cuts in.

"Well, no. It's not like she hasn't done it before and been totally fine."

"First time for everything . . ." she says.

He's never dealt with the police before, and being questioned like this gives him a sick, panicky feeling. The more they fire questions at him, the more he finds himself stumbling through the answers. As the sweat collects under his T-shirt, Ragione keeps writing, doesn't bother looking up. He feels the tears pricking at his eyes, but he won't give her the satisfaction of breaking down. Somehow, they have traced the telephone number of the house they're renting and have let him call. No one is picking up, and there's no answering machine. Over the past year almost everyone they know has gotten a cell phone, but it's a luxury he and Maddie can't afford. And not anytime soon, either, he remembers, after blowing months of pay on plane tickets.

He'd watched Maddie briefly speak to someone through the driver's side window, he tells the detectives. Then she'd gotten in the passenger side and the car reversed and drove off. The scene is so vivid in his mind—the sand dusting the road, the cascade of grit sent up by the tires as the vehicle skidded slightly and disappeared around the corner like a scene in a movie. And how he—her husband—stood there and did nothing to stop her.

"You said it was a foreign car?" Mahoney says. "Right-hand drive. Could your wife have been driving?"

He hadn't thought of that.

"It's happened before," he admits, "that someone has actually let her take the wheel." He thinks of telling them that he had wished he'd brought his camera, because he'd have loved to take a picture as the car came back and rounded the corner. A souvenir for his beautiful wife. Of her daring spirit. It's unlikely they'd care.

"It's kind of her thing," he repeats hopelessly. It's important that they understand this.

"Yeah, you said." Ragione raises an overly plucked eyebrow at Mahoney. She isn't buying it. He doesn't blame her, but it's not as if he's under arrest . . . *is it?*

"How many people in the car?" Ragione again.

"I told you . . . one. I mean, I can't imagine—"

"You can leave the speculation to us, Mr. Dainty. Just answer the question."

Was there space in that kind of car, he thinks, for a third person? It would have to be someone fairly small.

"You said it was raining," Ragione goes on. "You were cold. She abandoned you. Left you there to wait."

He'd been unsure how long he should give it. What was reasonable? Twenty minutes? Thirty? *Where was she?* As it began to rain, he'd tried to stay calm and come up with some rational explanation.

"Isn't it true that you were angry, knowing that Ms. Morgan—your *wife*—had taken off with some guy and left you?"

He feels his stomach lurch. "I was worried," he replies. "And annoyed," he admits. "A little."

"So you were angry. What happened when she got back?"

"What?" He looks up, confused. "I told you. She never

came back. That's . . . that's why I'm here." Aren't they listening?

"You sure about that? Maybe you guys got in a fight? Things got out of hand. It happens."

"*No,*" he says indignantly, his voice breaking. "I love her. Maddie's my wife. She's the best thing that ever happened to me."

Another "uh-huh" from Ragione. As if his wife has not just vanished into thin air. Or as if finding her is not a priority. Are she and Mahoney partners, or whatever the term is? *Partners in crime.* Even to him, in his wretched, beaten-down state, it's pathetically obvious that she is trying to impress Mahoney who, judging by the ring on his finger, is a married man.

"I just don't understand why she would do this," Jonathan says. The experience is unreal in the worst way. As if he's not actually sitting here, but observing himself in a nightmare, helpless to stop it. *How could Maddie do this to him? How could she put him in this position?* "It makes no sense for her to just . . . leave like that . . . It's not who she is. Not who *we* are," he says. It is hateful having to utter these private things to such a cruel and unsympathetic person.

"So how long did you wait around for her?"

"I'm not sure. I'm sorry . . ." He has to fight hard to hold back tears. "It must have been about an hour."

"'About' an hour? You're wearing a watch, Mr. Dainty. And yet you say you have no idea how long you were waiting for your wife, a woman who'd just stepped into a vehicle belonging to a complete stranger?"

The wait had been agonizing. Alone on the beach, on the lookout for any sign of his wife, he'd felt utterly powerless, with no clue what to do for the best. Of course the sensible thing was to go right to the police. But that felt like an enormous choice because it would make everything feel real.

And what if Maddie reappeared and he wasn't there? But Jay always said that almost any decision was better than none. Which is how he had managed, somehow, to get himself back on his bike and pedal to the police station.

"I can't be sure," he says uncertainly. "I must have looked at my watch, but I don't remember what time it was." He's finding it hard to focus, to keep his mind on one thing. For a third time, Ragione makes him describe the car. *Red. An E-type Jag. From 1961.* "That's what my wife thought it was," he says. The barely concealed sneer on Ragione's face lets him know how unmanly or "less than" she sees him as. But then he remembers something.

"One of the front headlights was busted out," he tells her, "and covered in black duct tape."

"Which side, left or right?"

He thinks for a moment. "The right side," he answers.

"*Right side*, huh?"

"I think so . . ." he says. "Why?"

"You're not sure?"

"I couldn't say for sure." Does it matter which light it was? He has described the car, isn't that enough for them to start looking? The woman just wants to give him a hard time, he's convinced of it.

"Sounds like he was waiting for you . . ."

"What?"

"The driver. Like he was waiting for you guys. Or one of you."

Jonathan has not considered this. And yet, in light of everything else he has told them, the idea possesses a hideous kind of logic. Without explanation, both cops abruptly stand, gather up their notes and leave the room. Ragione returns fifteen minutes later holding a cup of coffee in her hand. She doesn't offer him one, instead casually mentioning something about a lie-detector test. He asks her what she means, but she ignores him. She is no better than a school bully, he decides. As she takes him back over his story again, his thoughts seem to form in slow motion. One particularly intense volley of questions leaves him so shaken that he feels on the edge of hysteria.

Mahoney returns and hands him a paper cup.

"How you holding up?" he says kindly. Jonathan takes the coffee, more grateful for this one small act of kindness than the cop can possibly imagine. "I get that these questions are tough," Mahoney says, sitting down. "But it's our job to ask. It's possible you remember more than you realize, so we need you to think back, because the first two hours are critical. Do you understand what I'm telling you?"

Jonathan nods. The detective pauses, as if waiting for him to say something. "Jon, if it helps you any, most cases like this, someone gets carried away, ends up in a bar, has a few beers . . . You get the picture. They show up sooner or later," he adds as a hideous picture floats into Jonathan's mind. "Anything else you need? Water?"

"No. Thank you."

"Speak up if you need a break."

"I want to keep going," Jonathan replies, taking a sip of the bitter, lukewarm liquid.

For the next hour, he does his best to give the right answers as they take him over and over what happened. Mahoney nods, listens intently. The questions turn intense and repetitive, running forward, backward, until his head spins. Did he and Maddie see anyone or anything suspicious on the way down? Did they talk to anyone? Ask for directions? How about on the beach? At one point they have him recall the sequence of events in reverse, from his arrival at the station back to their all leaving the city the day before. Are the police actually out searching for her? he thinks. Or is the sum of their manpower right here, in this prison cell of a room, focused solely on him? Once or twice Ragione's stance appears to soften toward him, only for the rapid-fire questions to start up once more as she attempts to pick apart his story.

"You said the taillight was broken."

"One of the headlights . . ."

"You could see the headlight, but you couldn't see the driver?"

He shakes his head no.

"I'm sorry," he says. "Maybe the sun was in my eyes."

"You said it was raining."

"I . . . I can't remember." The sun had emerged very briefly at some point, but he can't for the life of him recall precisely when.

"Did your wife make a habit of this?" That hateful smirk.

"A habit of what?"

"You know," Ragione says. "Getting into cars with strangers." The woman is some kind of sadist, he decides, who has found her vocation in law enforcement. He returns her gaze with the stony expression it deserves. Or he attempts to. She makes him feel extremely ill at ease.

From somewhere outside comes a woman's voice—"Where is he?"—and for the craziest second he thinks it's her, Maddie. *Of course!* It's all been a stupid misunderstanding and she's here to rescue him, is demanding to know what the hell they're doing. A few seconds later, the owner of the voice pokes her head around the door . . . Not her. His heart sinks. "Chief's looking for you guys," she says.

"Have to wait," Mahoney tells her. As he turns his attention back to Jonathan, the gimlet-eyed Ragione is relegated to the sidelines.

"Jon, we're gonna keep bugging you on this stuff," he says, "while your memory is still fresh. Is there anything else that stands out for you? Any detail, however small? Anything we could've missed?"

He thinks of his sister, trained as a lawyer, fearsome in her way. If only she were here to speak up for him.

"What we need for you to help us understand," Mahoney says, "is why your wife—why Maddie—would get into a vehicle belonging to someone neither of you know."

Aren't they listening? Jonathan hangs his head. Even to his own ears, his words have begun to sound bizarre and made-up.

Fireworks

1991

Eyes tightly closed, he feels around under the sink for the object he stashed soon after moving in. It's dark in the apartment, which is an illegally let storefront—small bedroom in back, bathroom and kitchen in the middle, railroad style. In the tiny front room, a padlocked metal shutter blocks all but the merest sliver of sunlight. He can feel the familiar outlines of under-the-sink kitchen clutter—bleach, sink plunger, cans of something toxic. Maddie has a last-minute rehearsal and won't be done until 9:30 p.m. Which couldn't be more perfect, because it gives him more time to prepare. As his fingers skitter away from a dusty, years-old roach motel and close around what feels like a dead water bug, he almost screams. *God, if she could hear me*, he thinks, *squealing like a girl*. At last, right at the very back, he finds what he's looking for—an empty paint can.

After scrubbing his hands with hot water and soap, he goes out to search the tiny backyard. Or rather, the filthy tangle of weeds and old mattresses that's home to rats and who knows what other horrors. Maddie had suggested making it into a real yard. The problem with that, he'd explained, was that once it became a pleasant place to hang out, all the other tenants would want in—bringing noise and guests and loud parties full of strangers, and so forth. *"Sounds cool ..."* she had replied wistfully. The yard yields some useful scraps of wood that he drops in the empty paint can and takes up to the roof.

Maddie shows up around ten forty-five and asks to "borrow" his shower. "It's November 5th," she calls from the bathroom.

"Oh, right," he calls back with deliberate nonchalance. "What is that again? I forgot . . ."

"*Bonfire Night!*" she yells back. "I *told* you." She has often talked about the British beach resort where she was born, and the traditions that she grew up with, and they sound almost as exotic as she does. Almost—but not quite. It was impossible to imagine anything or anyone that could compete with her.

She emerges from the bathroom, his towel wrapped around her body, wet hair streaming. "Seriously," she says, "it's a big deal there. Everyone has a bonfire and they light sparklers and let off fireworks all night." The whole country set alight? Oil-soaked rags wrapped around stakes, set on fire, and marched through dark, cobbled streets? In America, he thinks to himself, there would be deaths and lawsuits.

"There's this one town," she goes on, "where they build an effigy of the Pope, set it on fire, and chuck it in the river. It's so brilliant." His Catholic parents would have a fit. Though as with so many of her tales, he's not sure whether to believe it or not.

"So . . . it's kinda like the Fourth of July," he teases.

"*What!*" She shakes her head furiously. "I told you, it's the total opposite of all that crap!" She wrinkles her nose in disgust. "Ugh, I mean, that whole 'Mom and apple pie' obsession you have over here." Her lip curls derisively, and he kind of loves this too. How passionate she is about life. That her likes and dislikes loom larger than other people's. While other people, he has discovered, totally bore him.

She sits down next to him on the couch and rests her head on his shoulder. "It's just . . . different," she says softly.

"I wish I could see what it's like," he says. "Where you grew up . . ." They are silent for a moment. She reminds him of a Rubik's Cube. How does she work? How does she think? How to get all her different facets to line up in the same direction at the same time? He loves that she's so intriguing, and so complex to figure out. He wants—*needs*—to know every single thing about her. To solve the puzzle of her. It's essential, like food and air to him. Or a drug; delicious and forbidden. His parents would call this a sin of lust.

"Hey," he says, pretending to have a sudden idea. "Maybe someone's letting off fireworks in the city tonight. How about we go up to the roof and keep a lookout?"

Maddie looks so doubtfully at him that, for one heart-stopping moment, he is certain she's going to say no and tell him she has plans already . . . Why hadn't he thought this part through?

"Sure." Sulkily, she gets up and tosses the towel on the sofa. "There won't be any, though."

"I'm sure you're right," he agrees, watching her disappear into the bedroom. He is still in awe of the way she can pad around the apartment so unself-consciously naked. Not that he minds, obviously. A minute later, she comes out wearing the shirt he saves for special occasions. They take blankets and beer and climb the stairs to the roof. A mere six floors above the ground, the city is transformed. The sky is cloudless and darkest blue. The Empire State Building glitters silently.

"Close your eyes," he instructs.

"Why?"

"Just trust me." Stepping out of sight behind the wall, he lights the miniature bonfire-in-a-can he prepared earlier. "Okay, you can open them now!"

She can't believe it. How did he keep it a secret for so long? As she gasps and claps, he feels himself glowing with pride.

"There's more." He grins.

Last week, he'd gone down to Chinatown before class and bought a bunch of fireworks. They've been right here on the roof for days, wrapped, waterproofed, and taped in layers of trash bags. There are firecrackers and Roman candles, delicate showers of yellow and electric blue sparks. He is so absorbed in her pleasure, as she hugs herself and exclaims in delight, that he barely sees them. She leaps up and dances wildly around the little fire, a stick figure glowing in the dark, his glamorous scarecrow. For the next hour, they sit together cross-legged, feeding it bits of trash and old newspaper they find scattered across the roof. Gazing out at the city, Maddie wants to know which is his favorite building.

"The Empire State Building?" he replies. He's never really thought about it. Maddie says she prefers the Chrysler because it's "not as obvious" and it possesses more glamour.

She tells him about going to the vintage car rally with her dad. Cars aren't really his thing, but he eats it up, ravenous for every scrap of information. Every scrap of her. More beer plus the dregs from an old bottle of vodka Maddie discovered at the back of the fridge, and when the air turns cold, he barely notices this either. The city is theirs, she tells him, and theirs only. "Fuck everyone else," she says. They locate the Brooklyn Bridge, lights just visible, twinkling faintly to the south-east. It grows late. Saturday night seethes below. Traffic and sirens and crackheads screaming in the street. The bass rumble of music floats across from the clubs and dive bars that crowd Avenue A. Maddie offers to get him a fake ID so they can go check out some bands one night.

"You have a fake ID?" he asks.

"Of course!" She laughs.

This is their third date and, though neither has said it out loud, he is struck by the certainty that they are going to spend the rest of their lives together. He asks if she'll ever go back to England. Maddie shrugs. England is cool and everything, she says. But her dad died a few years ago. And she's never had the best relationship with her mom. Besides, its Europe. And everyone knows Europe is old and dead. What she really wants is to move to Los Angeles ("Los Angeleeez," she pronounces it).

"Really? Why?" This is news to him.

"Why not?" she replies. She "adores" cinema. She will live at Chateau Marmont. And she will keep two Siamese cats on red leashes and walk them on the boardwalk in . . . "What's that place by the beach called again?" she asks. He can't remember either, he fibs, feeling slightly out of his depth, and making a mental note to look it up.

"It'll be brilliant," she goes on. "Pineapples for breakfast and peaches for lunch." She will wear a green silk dress by Yves Saint Laurent, like the one that actress wore to the Oscars. "And I'll sleep all day and write all night."

"You're a writer?" He'd thought she was an actress.

"Yes, of course." Before he can ask more, she's already on to the next thing. "Seafoam . . . chartreuse . . . *eau de nil* . . ." she intones, as if speaking from a trance. Closing her eyes, she rocks gently back and forth, like one of those hippy girls that hang out in the park. "Don't you think that there are more beautiful names for shades of green than for any other color?" she says. He nods stupidly.

Your eyes, he dares not tell her, *your eyes . . . are the craziest, most hypnotic, entrancing shade of green*. Her confidence, and attitude of all-knowingness—it's because she's from Europe, he decides, then. *Europe*—he's read about it. Well, obviously, who hasn't? He has yet to actually go there, though. As a child, the farthest they'd traveled as a family was Disney World. He doesn't even own a passport.

In LA, Maddie continues, she will drink health shakes and do yoga and meditate every morning, because that's what everyone does.

"You're not allowed to get fat there," she explains, and he thinks of the little roll of skin around his middle. And his thighs, which, unlike hers, are not as well-muscled as he'd like. As for his sloping shoulders . . .

"I'll write in cafés and eat lunch on the beach," she is saying, warming to her theme. She will discuss life and love with writers, actors, directors. "I'll write a movie. Or maybe I'll act in one."

Even from her, Jonathan thinks, this should sound like a pipe dream. Naive and verging on the ridiculous. Yet for some reason he can totally see her doing all of these things. And on the weekends, she continues, she'll go hiking in the hills and visit Griffith Observatory.

"I want to be a writer as well," he blurts, and is taken aback to hear the words come out of his mouth. It's an ambition he hasn't shared with a soul, not even Jay. "And win the Booker Prize," he adds.

She throws her head back and laughs.

He's unsure how to take this. Did his confession sound arrogant? In this area, too, he's not half as sophisticated as he'd like to be. But she is . . . *dazzling*. There is no other word for it. He has never in his life met anyone like her. She is everything he wants . . . and everything he wishes he could be.

Hours pass before he at last gathers the courage to lean in toward her. They exchange a drunken kiss. And then another. Leaving the roof, they clutch each other for support, giggling as they take the stairs down to the apartment.

Afterward, he lies in the dark—ecstatic, terrified. He has a paper due tomorrow, but it'll have to wait. Their relationship is weeks old, but he would move heaven and earth for this girl. Would gladly kill for her. If anyone ever harms her, he decides, no matter who it is, he will go out, and he will get them. This feeling must be what love is. If you didn't have it, it wasn't love. His life feels thrilling and dangerous. As if he's stepping around the edge of a huge ravine . . . being pulled over a waterfall . . . hovering on the edge of a black hole. His mind is brimful of metaphors. Does she feel it too? And who will jump first?

In the early hours, lying next to her, he can't seem to stop smiling. His face hurts with the effort of trying not to. He wants to wake her and confess his love. But he can't. Not yet. Because she is even more lovely in repose. She is all beauty and all mystery, and he wants to look at her forever. He is barely twenty years old, and his glorious future, with this amazing woman that he cannot possibly deserve, stretches out like the promise of a million Christmases.

Damaged

1996

They let him call the house again. Filled with anxiety, his palms are so sweaty he can barely keep hold of the phone. This time—*thank God*—Laura picks up. She, too, is full of questions. "There you are . . . Why didn't you tell me you guys were going out early? I'd have cooked breakfast. Are you with Jay? I called his cell, but he's not picking up."

Her voice sounds like a recording from a former life—the house, waking up this morning, cycling to the beach. She has found "the most gorgeous" tomatoes at the vegetable stand "and this *amazing* pie shop . . . Oh, and I already picked up candles for the birthday girl," she adds, "so that's one thing you can cross off your list!"

Feeling the detectives' eyes on him, he manages to cut in. Laura is shocked, but composed. She tells him to sit tight and not to jump to conclusions. "You know how she is. She'll have gotten distracted, be off on some crazy adventure somewhere, and lost track of the time."

Laura will call his sister, Heather, to check on Ben. She'll let Jay know what's going on the minute he gets back. And they have the cottage for one more day, she reminds him, so they can easily have the party tomorrow. Or even one evening next week, when they're all back in the city.

"It's all going to be fine," Laura says. "I just know it."

Yet again, he is asked to go through that morning's events. Mahoney nods reassuringly. Ragione looks by turns amused and appalled.

"What about Maddie's relationships?" Mahoney asks. "Any problems?"

"No, of course not. She's popular with everyone."

Ragione throws her partner an amused "Aren't they always?" look. As if excavating Maddie's friendships or private life could possibly help, Jonathan thinks grimly.

"No problems with her . . . *relationships*," Ragione says, with a meaningful leer, "or none that you know of," she adds.

Is it an act? Jonathan wonders. Some special technique known only to cops? Does she genuinely not believe what he's saying? *Good cop, bad cop.* Real cops, aping the ones you see in the movies.

No. He won't take the bait. He refuses to look at her. Instead, he takes an interest in the ugly poster taped to the wall opposite—a washed-out image of a sandy beach shaded by palm trees, bizarre and incongruous in the stuffy little room. They have taken down details of where he and Maddie live, together with those of where he works and the name of Maddie's acting school. Ragione looks hard at him. Her skin is faintly pockmarked with traces of adolescent acne. And a part of him is surprised that, despite the stressful situation, he is still able to observe and take in such a trivial detail. Perhaps it's an after-effect of the shock.

He asks whether they've managed to get hold of his friend Jay.

"Not your concern," Ragione replies.

"We're sending someone over to the house," Mahoney says. Maybe this is what Mahoney is up to during his long absences, Jonathan thinks. That, or he's just addicted to coffee.

When it's her turn again, Ragione glances down at her notes for a moment, then holds his gaze for a few seconds.

"Did you kill your wife?" she says.

"Wait, what? Of *course* I didn't!"

"You're lying."

"What?" He looks wildly at Mahoney. "No! I'm not," he says, his voice rising. "I'm telling you everything I know."

"Then what do you think happened?"

"I . . . I don't know," Jonathan stammers. What's going on? He feels completely out of control. There is a moment of silence. "It's my fault," he tells Mahoney. And it is, he thinks. It *is* all his fault. He can be mad at his wife all he likes, but he let it happen.

"Relax," Mahoney says. "We're just havin' a conversation, right?" With a look of distaste he fishes what looks like some kind of instant coffee bag out of the cup, then without looking tosses it clean across the room and lands it in the trash can. "Let's talk about your wife's state of mind," he says. "How would you describe that?"

"Happy. I told you. She seemed really happy."

"Not upset for any reason?"

"No."

Mahoney takes a slug from the cup, winces.

"Would you say, in your opinion, that her behavior has been erratic recently? Has she seemed different to you in any way?" More than once they have asked whether Maddie has a history of mental health issues.

"No . . . I don't think so. Not that I've noticed."

They bring up the plane tickets again, have him go through the details. The extended tour through Asia, Europe, Africa. Flying west to east, as far as you can travel, arriving back where they started two months later. At least, that was the plan.

"You guys got a nice life, huh?" Ragione again.

"I ... I guess so ..." Dropping off their child with his grandmother in England, before swanning around the world together for a couple of months—to someone like Ragione, he and Maddie must sound rich and spoiled.

"You're not sure? Some problem you're not telling us about?"

"Yes. I mean *no*. You're confusing me."

"Sure sounds like it."

What will it take, Jonathan thinks desperately, for them to believe him? For them to understand that they are wasting their time and need to get out there and look for his wife?

"I told you, she was fine," he says. The detectives exchange an indecipherable look, and with a terrible jolt he realizes that he has just spoken of Maddie in the past tense. *Seemed* happy. *Was* fine. He tries to think of the grammatically correct term—is it "is" or "was"? They are talking about the past, so either is correct—isn't it? Both cops look blankly at him as, from the darkest recess of his mind, an even worse idea emerges: it is always the husband ... In books, TV shows, films, news reports, isn't it always the husband who's guilty? *Always the husband.* Not sometimes. Not occasionally. *Always.* Movies and books are the sum total of his experience with policing and murder. Like the good-cop, bad-cop routine, he has always assumed this was some cliché found only in fiction.

"*Is* fine," he corrects. "My wife is fine. I'm sorry. I misspoke."

Mahoney regards him levelly for a moment, slowly draws a ring around something on the sheet of paper in front of him.

"No problem," he drawls. Wherever Maddie is, Jonathan thinks, all these hours later she could be miles away. *Lost.* He takes a breath, looks directly at Ragione. "Why aren't you out there," he says, "trying to find my wife?"

As Mahoney takes over and calmly continues with questions Jonathan has already answered, his own words reverberate in his mind. *My wife is fine . . . My wife is fine . . .*

But this isn't quite true, is it? His wife. His beautiful, damaged, impossible wife. She was—*is*—not fine. And she hasn't been for some while.

Style

2019

After an early-morning trip to the Greenmarket, and an unsuccessful search for yellow alpine sea salt, Jonathan arrives back at the house to find Ben in the laundry room. What looks to be several weeks' worth of dirty clothing is spread in fetid piles across the floor. He stands in the doorway for a moment and watches as Ben pushes jeans, shirts, and socks into the washing machine.

"Hey, careful there, buddy," he says, "you're gonna break it."

"Oh. Hi, Dad." Ben looks up and grins. "I thought I'd come visit with you and Laura."

"Great, well, it's good to see you."

Ben turns back to the machine and continues stuffing things in.

"You know, you can always call and give us the heads-up. I mean, this is your home, obviously," Jonathan adds. As ever with Ben, he is not getting his point across too clearly. "I just meant it'd be great if you let us know when you're heading over. That way we can make sure to be here, or whatever."

His son's back stiffens for a moment. Then he turns, eyes wide. "Sure, Dad. *Definitely.*"

They don't have such a bad relationship, he decides, as Ben returns to his task. Some of their friends' kids, far younger than Ben, are just entering their troubled teen years. As parents do, he'd waited for his son to turn into the inevitable sullen, difficult teenage specimen he'd so often heard about. But aside from a few isolated incidents, this had never happened. That said, in the past year, he's found himself having to overly explain things. And in trying to get across some point of conduct, he has a sense that his son is silently judging him. He bends to gather up some of the clothes and is surprised to see one of his own shirts, one wrinkled arm hanging limply from the pile. Laura had bought it for him this past Christmas. And though writers are supposed to scorn fashion, and it's perhaps a tad colorful for his taste, a nice Etro shirt is his one concession to style. He seems to recall Ben admiring it as well.

"Actually, Dad?" Ben turns.

Hastily, Jonathan tucks the shirt back into the pile, feeling inexplicably guilty. "What is it, bud?"

"I was wondering, like would it be cool if I stayed with you? With you guys, I mean. Just for a couple weeks."

"Sure, I should think so." A few seconds tick by. "Why, what's going on?"

"Nothing major. Stuff with the apartment. You know."

On the contrary, Jonathan doesn't know. And, as usual, Ben isn't saying.

"Like what?"

"So, like the management company still hasn't fixed the shower. So we can't really use it. And there's all these other repairs and just dumb whatever stuff they haven't done."

Ben's apartment is in a brand-new building, but there have been a slew of problems. Most recently, a non-draining sink. Or was it a slow-running toilet? What with the wedding plans and his European tour coming up, it's not easy for Jonathan to keep track. After a year out—which, to Ben's credit, he'd spent traveling through Latin America to hone his Spanish—they had all agreed that if he returned to college, Jonathan and Laura would take care of tuition and rent. Money is deposited into Ben's account in a lump sum each semester because it was felt he was adult enough to administer rent and payment details himself. Ben's side of the bargain entailed finding a little job during the weekends or evenings to pay for his day-to-day expenses. But this hasn't happened.

"How many times have you asked them to make the repairs?" he asks Ben.

"A bunch of times."

"And you've put it in writing? Like Aunt Heather said?"

"Of course, Dad. I told you."

"Okay, so legally they need to fix the problem, or we stop paying rent." Jonathan likes to think of himself as well-informed on tenants' rights and the like, though really, who is he kidding? At this point, wealth insulates him from such problems.

"You and your roommates need to stop payment," he says, "and put the money in Etro . . ." He clears his throat. ". . . in *escrow.*" If his son registers the slip, he doesn't say.

"Sure." Ben shrugs. Ben must either have asked to borrow the shirt and has forgotten, or Ben meant to ask and it just slipped his mind. His son has always been a tad spacey, at times downright careless. He can't count the number of computers and iPhones Ben has either dropped or left on the subway. And with job hunting and full-time school, his son has a lot on his mind. He watches Ben fiddle with the controls, turning dials and pressing buttons.

"Want some help?" he offers. If only his son would look him in the eye when they talk. Not that they ever properly talk . . .

"Nuh-uh, I got it."

"How about your roommates? Where are they staying?"

"Dunno. Like with their parents?" Ben kicks the washer door closed. With one knee wedged up against it, as if to prevent everything from bursting out, he punches in the washing cycle selection with his fingers.

"OK. Let me speak to Laura and we'll figure it out. By the way, she's cooking dinner tonight if you'd like to join?" The machine starts up with an unfamiliar jolt, the clothes whirling tightly through the little window. "If you don't already have plans, I mean?" Jonathan adds.

"Maybe. I have class in a few. And I might be meeting a friend for cocktails."

A friend? Cocktails? Jesus, it all sounds so grown-up. His son has a right to his own life, but don't these friends have names? As Laura has pointed out, so long as Ben depends on them for expenses and a roof over his head, they have a right to know what he's up to.

Ben sidles past him, slides his hoodie off the counter and pulls it over his head. Blond hair askew and, under this light, his face looks thin and drawn, his eyes red-rimmed.

"You doing OK, buddy? Not studying too hard, are you?"

"Sure, Dad, I'm doing great."

Jonathan recalls his own time at college—the drunken parties, the weed hanging in the air, the all-nighters pulled in the library right before finals.

"Okay." He stands there uselessly for a second, unsure what to say. "Well, I'll let you get on. Make sure to let Laura know if you'll be here for dinner, OK?"

"Absolutely. Thanks, Dad!" Ben goes upstairs.

A short while later, the front door slams. Jonathan stands at the living-room window and watches his son reach the bottom of the steps, and make a right—in the opposite direction to school.

Swanky

2019

Jay strides toward Jonathan with his usual air of exaggerated purpose—phone pressed to one ear, eyes trained skyward, as if ready to call in an air strike.

"Traffic," he says, sliding into the booth and tossing his phone on the table.

His friend is six minutes late to their favorite restaurant. Six minutes which Jonathan could have used at his desk, instead of tearing himself away at a crucial point in his story. But pointing this out will solve nothing, and Jay can lose his temper when pressured. Jay asks about the upcoming book tour to promote *The Sinking Pool*.

"I'll have a few days in London," Jonathan replies as his friend runs his eyes down the drinks list. "Then Europe, East Coast Crime Fest, Hamptons Crime Fest."

"The Hamptons . . . ?"

"I know." There's a beat. "I expect it's an oversight."

They're saved by the arrival of the waiter.

"Tito's and soda, ice, no lemon. Jon?" Jay says.

Drinking during the day makes Jonathan sleepy nowadays, so reluctantly he orders a grapefruit and soda. The waiter has a slight stutter and, after he's delivered their drinks, Jay makes a face.

"*Be nice* . . ." Jonathan warns. Jay laughs.

"So you're all good on the next book. You're into it, right?"

"Yes," he replies. "It needs some work, but I'm feeling pretty good about it."

Jay makes a joke about how, with every new book, Ocean Falls acquires more murder victims. It's true, he thinks. His latest features no less than seven unlucky young women. "I'm like a serial killer." He laughs. "Soon there'll be no one left."

"That's why they pay you the big bucks. So what's up with the TED people? Still bugging you?"

"*TEDx*," Jonathan replies, letting out a sigh worthy of a teenager. "Not TED." TED's less talented little brother, he thinks to himself. They've asked him to deliver a talk about crime and human psychology, he tells Jay. Except their whole preachy, earnest, quasi-religious, motivational self-help thing makes him feel rather queasy.

"Hey, don't hold back . . ."

"I'd just feel weird being a part of something so phony and dishonest," Jonathan says.

"Suck it and see?" Jay narrows his eyes. "TED's a big deal."

"*TEDx*," he says. "So it's really not." In matters like this, though, he tends to defer to Jay. Not only because he's a superb salesman—a real-estate investor with an impressive track record of "wins" (as Jay will insist on phrasing it). Time and time again his friend has either nixed or pushed him hard on a particular engagement—and it has always ended up being the right call.

The waiter drops off a basket of bread that neither of them has ordered. Wrapped lovingly in a rustic-looking piece of navy-and-white striped linen, accompanied by a miniature dish of unsalted butter that is neither too hard nor too soft, the bread still warm . . .

"You with me?"

"Sorry?" Jonathan has briefly lost track of the conversation.

"I said, what have you got going on next week?" Jay repeats. "Got some clients in town. Fun guys. Wanna hang out? How's Thursday look?"

His friend has retained the blue-eyed handsomeness of his youth. Unfortunately, he still talks, acts and thinks like some late-twentieth-century frat boy. Invariably a night out will involve a steak house or a strip club, neither of which is particularly appealing. Jonathan pauses to take a sip of his drink.

"Love to," he replies. "But I have to prep for an interview."

"Oh yeah? Cool. Who with?"

"Just one of the newspapers."

"*The* newspaper? You're in the mix for that? That's awesome, dude."

"No. *A* newspaper," he sighs. "Just the *New York Times*." They've been over this before, the thing he'd never admit to anyone but Jay. That what he dreams of is landing the prestigious "Brunch in Depth" interview which runs in the weekend edition of his favorite newspaper. The tone can verge on a little fawning, but they always have it somewhere swanky and exclusive. Cindy, his agent, has yet to snag it for him, though.

"C'mon. The *New York Times*, that's a cool gig, right?"

It is and it isn't, he replies testily. Some years ago, one of their writers gave him a decidedly lukewarm book review. Or so he'd heard.

"I get it. With your schedule you gotta consider the cost-benefit ratio, or you'll be up to your tits in shit," Jay replies, and then wisely changes the subject. "Hey, so Laura's definitely opening that new place in LA?"

"Samphire? Indeed, she is. We're both super excited."
Though this means they'll both be doing a lot of traveling, he
explains, and in completely opposite directions.

For the next few minutes, they catch up on other news as
Jay scrolls intermittently through his phone and then takes a
brief call with a client. As Jay discusses his latest deal, Jonathan
takes in the painting that hangs above their booth—the mysterious nude, her face obscured, body outstretched in seductive
chiaroscuro along a deep blue couch. Lunch here is a regular
and pleasurable occurrence, and this is the booth where they
always sit. Today, however, he finds himself weirdly depressed
by it all. 2:15 p.m. already. A few more hours' work and he'll
at least have earned a couple glasses of wine. Their food
arrives. Jay attacks his steak with gusto.

"Fuck me. I am so fucking *hungry,* you don't even know . . ."
Jonathan, yet to start on his goat cheese and arugula salad,
inspects his fork for smudges, surreptitiously wiping it under
the table on his napkin. "Gotta boogie in fifteen," Jay
announces through a mouthful of steak. "So, what's new?
What else is going on with you?"

"Nothing much. Had a nice turnout for the event up at
Union Square the other day. And we're headed up to the
house one weekend soon, if you want to join?"

Jay's phone vibrates again. He glances briefly at it, hits
ignore.

"Yeah, sure, lemme check my schedule," he says, with a
nervous glance at the bread basket. Like Jonathan, Jay attends
the gym and tries to stick to a healthy diet. Unlike Jay, he
thinks uncharitably, he himself is mostly successful. Baked
goods are Jay's Achilles' heel, bread having played a leading
role in his frequent tumbles off the diet wagon. Now, having
studiously ignored the bread basket for almost twenty minutes,
Jonathan gestures toward it.

"Are you going to eat that?" he asks.

"Have the waiter take it back if it's bugging you ..." Jay counters with a shrug of pure indifference. Sending the bread back to the kitchen will involve committing multiple infractions—bothering the waitstaff, acting like food neurotics, being weird ... As a busboy cruises slowly past the table, neither man says a thing. *Game on.*

"Meeting this girl in fifteen," Jay says, with another fraught glance at the bread basket, as if it's a bomb about to explode. "This girl" will be merely the latest in an endless string of women to whom Jay has refused to commit, Jonathan thinks. Laura has attempted to fix him up with various friends over the years, but Jay has always preferred the bachelor's life.

"How're you doing with all the other stuff?" Jay asks. One hand strays toward the butter dish, the other to the basket, lifts a corner of the napkin. *Victory!* Today, Jonathan will get to win the battle of the bread basket.

"The wedding?" he replies innocently as, not for the first time, he worries that his outside self doesn't match his inside. Jay can act brash and gung ho, but he looks out for Jonathan and keeps a steady eye on his emotional life, and always has. Naturally, nothing is ever said—that would be deeply uncool—but his old friend has been known to drop the tough questions when he thinks Jonathan requires a nudge.

"Yep." Jay tears off a hunk of bread, slathers on a sizable wedge of butter. "That's the one."

The *wedding*. As the smell of fresh bread wafts invitingly across the table, Jonathan makes a big deal of coaxing a last squeeze of lemon onto his salad. The wedding. Like the bread basket, the word seems to crouch like a hand grenade on the table between them. He's not going to be the one to pick it up.

"Laura has it all under control," he replies finally. "You know how she is."

"Figured," Jay nods approvingly. "She's a good 'un, that woman. You're a lucky man." Too late, Jay catches Jonathan gazing longingly at the bread basket, and, smiling, pushes it toward him. As Jay resumes hacking at his steak, it's unclear whether his smile is down to Jonathan's impending wedding, or his soon-to-have-failed willpower.

Nuisance

1996

Thirty-six hours, and Jonathan has gone from suspect to nuisance.

There are no leads, and the cops are clearly bored with him.

Mahoney gives him a ride back to the house. Jay and Laura took the bus back to the city this morning. Laura had offered to pack Maddie's things and take them with her so that Jonathan wouldn't have to face seeing them, and he had checked himself into a fleabag motel off the highway.

Restless and anxious, by the afternoon he finds himself making his way back to the station. No one appears surprised to see him, and the building's signature reek of stale coffee, bleach, and old paper is by now familiar and strangely comforting. They sit in a room that has Mahoney's name on the door. Tall metal shelves stuffed with manilla folders line the walls. Atop a beaten-up file cabinet sits an ancient—and clearly broken—coffee machine. In one corner, a precarious tower of cardboard boxes is marked *Case Files*. He recalls Ragione's manic note-taking and wonders whether his name is among them.

"—But I just don't understand. A car like that can't just disappear," he is telling Mahoney. Is it helping, he wonders, showing up at the station to pester the police like this? The cop patiently answers his questions, but he looks tired. A couple of local people remember seeing them both, Mahoney says.

"Said you guys looked pretty happy . . ." Ragione pipes up, with an expression he can't begin to decipher. *And so we were*, he thinks numbly. Happy and carefree, with no clue what would happen next.

"Funny thing," Ragione adds nastily. "No one remembers seeing the car. Like you said, car like that . . . you think it'd get noticed."

"Then why can't you trace it?" Jonathan snaps.

Mahoney steps in. The DMV has one blue E-type registered in the area, he says, but no red ones. Elsewhere on Long Island there are a couple of red E-types on record, but it'll take time to check them all out.

"What about in the city? A lot of people drive out here at weekends," Jonathan says, ignoring Ragione's "tell me about it" face. Does she never take a day off? All night he had sat up with Jay and Laura, trying to think of "rational explanations"—where to look, who to call. It was hopeless. Now his head feels fuzzy and thick. Some coffee might help, but no one is offering.

"Unclear," Mahoney replies. "Ragione?"

"We found another one out in"—her mouth twists— "Greenwich Village, or someplace." Evidently, Jonathan thinks, she takes great pride in pretending to be vague about the geography of Manhattan. Maddie once told him there was a name for that—reverse-snobbery.

"One yellow, two blue ones, a bunch of reds . . ." Ragione goes on as a memory comes to him, of himself and Heather as children, squabbling over a family-size bag of M&M's.

With the filing of the official missing person report, the incident has begun to filter out into the wider world. By the evening, people begin calling in to the station. On the local TV station, a reporter interviews various people who report having seen the car. Their accounts are conflicting. The driver was blond, dark, tall, short, old, young, male, female . . . The images flicker on the tiny motel TV as Jonathan paces back and forth. Every minute fills him with more anxiety. By the evening, the story has made the national news.

"The young woman's husband claims . . ."

". . . the husband reportedly . . ."

". . . simply vanished. In this day and age, it's hard to believe . . ."

On CNN, passersby appear to be stopped at random and asked to speculate. Some express surprise or doubt when they're told that a young woman had gotten into a car with a complete stranger. One laughs. An elderly woman walking her dog says she may have seen a younger, athletic-looking man leaving the beach yesterday. Her eyes aren't what they used to be, though, so she really couldn't say what he looked like or how old he was. Or even if he was there in the first place. A bearded man in his thirties claims to have seen a woman driving at speed across the bridge. Like the car in that video, he tells the interviewer, the one from the mafia when they killed JFK? The picture cuts abruptly to a couple with a colossal baby in a stroller. They might have heard a scream, the husband says, as his wife wipes ice cream from the child's chin. "I think it was a deer," the wife says. "They're out of control." People are practically lining up to get on TV and contribute their two cents' worth. Almost beside himself, Jonathan turns it off and calls Mahoney.

"Look," Mahoney says. "We're doing all we can. We're talking to anyone we think might have real information, but most people aren't as observant as you'd think." The detective asks whether anything has come to Jonathan, any recollection of the driver, what he looked like or what he was wearing.

He understands that these details are important, but honestly couldn't say if he even got a look at the guy in the first place, he replies. And it's true. The driver's identity remains a perfect blank, like a face cut out of a photograph.

Heather calls again. Ben is doing just fine. And no, *of course* she hasn't told him anything. Why would she do that? Though a couple of detectives have been to the apartment.

"What?" Jonathan says in alarm. "What did they want?" His sister is over a hundred miles away, looking after his son for the weekend—why on earth would the police think she had anything to do with it?

"They wanted to know whether you guys had been fighting," she says. "I expect it's standard for them to check."

She calls out to Ben, who comes on the line and says that he has invented something called a "tank-copter" out of Lego.

"Wow. A tank-copter? That's great, buddy." It's heartbreaking.

Heather comes back on the line.

"I can't believe this is happening," Jonathan tells her. His sister can be controlling and interfering, but for the first time in his life he is grateful to have her on his side. Now, he waits for her to say that everything will be all right.

"I know," Heather replies. And, after another long pause: "Me either."

Escalator

2019

Jonathan opens the dishwasher and thinks about murder.

Someone—it can only be Ben—has neglected to run the machine, and there are no clean plates. He finds a bag of mixed greens in the fridge, throws in some of last night's left-over salmon, and gives it a shake, then eats standing up while reading over the plotline for *Gold-Plated Murder,* the new book he's working on:

> *When a young Manhattan property heiress is found dead at the summer's most important charity ball, Detectives Connor and Caleffi are first on the scene. But what first appears as death by natural causes is soon discovered to be something altogether more sinister. Then six more young women go missing, and as Ocean Falls' dedicated crime-fighting duo find themselves caught up in a tale of jealousy, revenge, and cold-blooded murder, they are forced to grapple with a few of their own personal demons . . .*

So far, so good. The killer could be any one of four or five candidates. And soon—*today*—he needs to figure out whom.

The cat appears and winds itself around his legs, meowing furiously. He takes a tiny chunk of the expensive fish—"Shhh. Don't tell chef!"—and places it on the floor in front of her.

She gazes steadily up at him. "What?" he says, "what can I do for you?" One sniff at the fish and she stalks off, tail in the air. *Another reason to prefer dogs.*

With Laura at the restaurant and Ben still sleeping, he feels like he has the house to himself. He flicks on the radio—Heather's husband, Saul, speaking in patronizing tones to some reformed member of the criminal underclass—and turns it right off again. Why is it that whenever he goes to listen to NPR, he always manages to catch Saul's show, *Making Waves*? Was it some unconscious form of self-torture? Pinned to the fridge, he notices now, is a note in Laura's neat handwriting: *Try me*, it says, next to a cheery arrow pointing toward the laundry room. He finds the jacket hanging on the back of the door, concealed inside a thick plastic cover that resembles a body bag. For over a week it has been making its way from closet to dressing room to study, to various doors and hooks all over the house. He unzips it and runs the fabric under his fingers. Linen, chosen by Laura, of some substantial yet impeccably fine quality. As a piece of clothing, it really is quite beautiful, one of the most luxurious things he has ever owned. Then again, he did just eat breakfast, so perhaps it's not the ideal time to try on such an important item. And—he remembers—the poor manager at Barnes & Noble has already left several messages to say that he has Jonathan's iPad, left behind after his event. Jonathan replaces the jacket on its hanger, grabs his keys and phone, leaves the dishwasher to go through its cycle, and walks up toward Union Square.

At the new café on University Place, he orders a to-go cup of green tea that tastes like stewed pond water. What he yearns for is an *espresso con panna*—two shots of shitty Starbucks coffee with a generous helping of whipped cream. What he actually *needs* is that blissful sense of completeness he gets after putting in a good day's work, when he can look forward to a guilt-free evening unwinding with some trashy TV. Like the feeling he gets after a good workout. Or sex. Well, kind of. Sex has never been the main draw with him and Laura. Unlike Jay (to take a standout example) he hasn't exactly "sport fucked" his way through life. And that's OK. After eighteen years, he and Laura have a mature relationship with a moderately active sex life. All perfectly normal.

Though his trainer has forbidden it, at the cash register he treats himself to a small bar of milk chocolate. Outside, he unwraps the gold foil wrapper, breaks off one square. And then, on impulse, breaks off another and pops both pieces into his mouth. *Delicious*. It's one of those bright blue days you get in the city, and he feels his mood lift. *Simpsons* clouds, high and fluffy, float between the buildings. He stops off at the Greenmarket—butcher, cheese guy, fresh catnip—then heads across to the bookstore and rides the escalator to the top level.

"Thank you so much," he says as with both hands the manager reverently passes Jonathan's iPad to him across the counter. "I've been lost without it."

The man looks mortified. "I'm so sorry! I should have had it messengered over."

"Not at all!" he replies jauntily. "It got me out of the house, and I could use the exercise."

The truth is, he hadn't even noticed the thing was missing. He keeps three iPads, all synced and ready. One for travel, one under the TV, and another in the study, or floating around wherever. They chat for a few minutes, the usual stuff about Amazon and the shuttering of the smaller, independent bookstores across the city.

"I'm a huge fan," the manager says. "Your event? It sold out in, oh my gosh, fifteen minutes."

"That's great to hear." Jonathan smiles, mirroring the guy's sincerity. "It was a fun night."

At the top of the store's escalator, he remembers he has an appointment with his trainer. Annoyingly, this means dumping his bags at home before schlepping all the way back uptown. Directly in front of him, two women stand stock still and side-by-side, chatting animatedly. He finds himself thinking of a comment of Maddie's, that Americans don't know how to use escalators. He lets out a pointed little sigh.

One of the women turns to glare at him and this, he will remember afterward, is the moment when he sees her. Below him on the main floor, among a knot of people moving toward the exit. It's like an electric shock, his body registering it almost before his mind can take it in. *Maddie. It can't be.* He tries to get past the women, but they won't budge. The blonde one tsk-tsks at him, actually shoves out an elbow, and mutters something about what a "rude man" he is.

"Please!" he begs. "*My wife.* It's an emergency!" In a matter of seconds, she will be through the exit and out on the street. As the women step grudgingly to one side, he sprints down the escalator, throws his bags on the floor, and dashes outside. Pedestrians, delivery people, hot-dog sellers. Frantically, he runs up and down the sidewalk. At the end of the block, he races across the street, narrowly misses being hit by a cyclist, and back into the Greenmarket. More crowds, people and dogs, nameless faces. Strangers.

For the second time in his life, his wife has vanished into thin air.

He makes his way home in a daze, turning all the while to look behind and around him, searching faces, doorways, looking in store windows. *Maddie*—it wasn't a close-up view, but he'd know that profile anywhere. Head up, chin jutting in just that way she had. *Used* to have. Is he losing his mind?

He finds himself in Washington Square with no memory of how he got there or why. Passing under the archway, through the students and pot sellers, his body seems to float. He has become so used to thinking of her in the past tense, he realizes, that he has almost forgotten what she looked like. The way she held herself. The way she was . . .

Feeling like he's about to be sick, he has to sit down on a nearby bench and close his eyes for a minute. His whole body is shaking. In the dusty concrete bowl of the empty fountain, three students play hacky-sack, keeping the little bag aloft as a crowd looks on, mesmerized. Was it her? Or just someone who looked or moved like her? What, exactly, had he seen? The ground floor was busy, buzzing with people. He had glimpsed her from behind and from above. And also, from a good sixty feet away. His phone buzzes. His trainer.

"Really sorry . . ." he says. "I had a family emergency. Please charge me the session and I'll see you next time."

Was it her? He calls Mahoney's number. Keeps it brief, asks as casually as possible when he's next planning to be in the city. As it turns out, Mahoney will be here tomorrow, volunteering for some EDP training event ("Emotionally Disturbed Persons," the cop explains). There's a pause. Jonathan's mind is once more running over what he saw, or didn't see.

"Everything OK . . .?" Mahoney asks.

"Sorry, yes," he fibs. "All good. I'll see you tomorrow."

Laura calls, he hits ignore. He needs some time to absorb what just happened and get his thoughts in order. He manages to stand, continues slowly through the park. His body feels insubstantial and strange, as if moving under the ocean. All the while a jittery thread of excitement runs through his limbs. Turning up Sixth, he remembers the groceries discarded at the bottom of the escalator. Nothing to be done. He certainly isn't going all the way back there at this point. Instead, he continues home, forcing his addled brain to go through the different scenarios and explanations: Being tired and distracted. Being a little anxious about forgetting his appointment at the gym. And the woman herself being, it's true, a fair distance away. *The woman*—because with this thought Jonathan understands that in his mind she is, in fact, back to being a random lookalike, not his missing wife at all. God, how ridiculous he was being. Honestly, how likely was it that in an apparently random coincidence, on a perfectly ordinary Monday, he should just happen to catch a glimpse of his dead wife in his local bookstore? By the time he gets home, he's convinced himself he imagined the whole thing.

Worry

1996

Twice, Mahoney has them all drive back to the beach, has Jonathan "walk the scene" and point out exactly where he and Maddie were. The second time around Ragione is mercifully absent. Paperwork to catch up on, Mahoney explains as they drive past the coast-guard station and onto the bridge.

"Don't take it personally," he adds, as if reading Jonathan's thoughts. "Gets ahead of herself sometimes. Saw her interrogate a guy once, accomplice in a robbery down the block. Had him squealin' like a rat in a blender." He grins. "She's sharp, that one."

They are off the bridge, turning onto the beach road. "Intuitive," he goes on. "Got that women's intuition. Women are smarter than us. She loves nothing better than catching someone out in a lie. And don't even get her started with the pink handcuffs."

"Sorry?"

"When she was a patrol officer, she used to carry these pink handcuffs. Some perp gave her a hard time for being a female? She'd whip out those babies."

He shudders. Why is Mahoney telling him all this? Is it a joke? A dig? Something said to frighten him? Whether a hardened professional, or merely unprofessional, the woman is terrifying. Who knows what she will try to pin on him.

As Mahoney steers the car along the beach road, Jonathan's stomach twists into even tighter knots. Through the window the ocean looks gray and vast, and it's all he can do not to be sick. Mahoney asks him about the driver again.

"I can't remember," Jonathan replies miserably.

"But you can describe the car pretty well . . ."

"Well, yes," he says, unsure where this is going. Mahoney's right, though. It is strange how perfectly he's able to recall the car's details—the Jag's inexplicably beaten-up appearance, the dented fender, the one front headlamp covered in peeling black electrical tape. "I can't tell if it's that I didn't see who was driving, or if I just can't remember," he says.

Mahoney shrugs. "Gotcha. We see it all the time." Mugging victims get a clear look at their assailant, he explains, but can only describe the gun, frequently in minute detail.

Mahoney, Jonathan decides, is the kind of man women love, and men secretly want to be like. The kind of guy who walks away from explosions, from marriages, from complications of any sort, and never looks back. He admires men like this, but can only dream of being one. As they arrive in the parking area, he almost expects to see the car waiting for them. But the lot is empty, appearing more desolate than before. *Pointless*, he thinks bitterly, this whole exercise is totally pointless.

The wind is sharp, blowing out toward the dark ocean with an edge that feels merciless and cruel. Mahoney paces the parking area for ten minutes, peering at the ground. They trudge down through the dunes to the beach itself, likewise empty. Just the regular pounding of the surf, and the wind whistling in their ears. Jonathan fastens his jacket around him as Mahoney squats down, appears to sift through a handful of sand, then squints out to sea for what feels like many minutes.

They return to the car, where Mahoney suggests Jonathan go back to the city.

"There's nothing for you to do here," he says. "You've just got to let us do our job."

Shaken by their visit to the beach, Jonathan finds himself agreeing.

After driving to the motel and waiting for him to pack his few things, Mahoney drops him at the bus stop.

"Wanna make sure you leave!" he says, as the bus rumbles up, and Jonathan can tell he is only half joking. "Get some rest. I'll be in touch."

It feels so utterly wrong to be going back to the city without her. Listening to the few other passengers recount their inane weekends, and the nausea-inducing throb of the engine, the whole journey is agonizing.

He takes the subway up to Heather's on 108th to pick up Ben. As he gathers up Ben's toys and books, he can't seem to stop his hands trembling and keeps dropping things. His sister stands in the living-room doorway with a concerned look on her face.

"Jon, why don't you leave him with us for a few days?" Heather says for the third time. "Saul's away, and I have a bunch of sick days I need to use. It's really no trouble."

Jonathan doesn't respond.

"Just until you get yourself organized . . ." she adds, as he scrabbles around under the couch for one of Ben's trucks.

"Meaning what, exactly?" Does she think he can't take care of his own son?

"*Jon* . . . come on. Don't be like that."

"Is there something you think I should be doing," he says, standing up, "that I'm *not* doing?" They've been here before, and this is an old argument with them—Heather, the responsible older sibling, Jonathan, the younger, with his unrealistic dreams of fame and fortune, forever trying to wriggle out from under her shadow.

"Of course not. I'm simply saying that you'll have things you need to take care of." *Like what?* he wants to snap, as the word *funeral* rises up from some dark and terrible place to anchor itself at the very center of his mind.

"Jon . . ." She comes toward him. Jesus, is she going to try and hug him? He shakes his head.

Does it not occur to her that he might want to keep his son close? he says, bundling a whimpering Ben into his padded jacket. She and Saul don't have any children, he goes on, how can she possibly understand?

His sister takes a step back, looks hurt. He hurries Ben out of the apartment, punches the down button on the elevator. Heather hovers at the apartment door, arms wrapped tightly around her body, that same look on her face—worried, uncertain . . . *Patronizing*, he decides.

"Call me when you get home," she says. "Okay?" The doors slide open. He helps Ben step inside, doesn't bother to answer her.

In the cab, he turns his attention to his son. He tells him his mom had to go away for a bit. Saying this is painful, but what choice does he have? Face turned into the seat, Ben cries softly to himself like a wounded animal, as if he senses what has happened. Surely this is all a huge mistake, Jonathan thinks. Maddie will come home. May already be there, waiting for them at the apartment with one of her crazy stories. "Seriously, you will never *believe* what happened . . ." He can almost hear her voice saying this. The minute he puts the key in the door, he will smell her perfume, hear her call out and ask where they've been. "What's the big deal? Honestly, you just love to worry about nothing." She'll laugh. And this time he won't mind in the slightest.

Ben has school tomorrow. Normally, Maddie watches him in the evenings, and Jonathan has him during the day when she's rehearsing or in class. He has a bar shift tomorrow night; what will he do about Ben? And why didn't he take Heather up on her offer? He tries to consider his options, but days spent glued to the TV news seem to have scrambled his brain. On the phone last night, attempting to describe to Laura what was happening, he had found it difficult to piece together his days in any logical manner. The whole ordeal seemed to exist in his mind out of sequence, like a series of disjointed scenes in a movie, with himself as the bad actor, dumbly reciting his lines. And yet, he decides, there is still hope. Still a chance that none of this is real. That, in some twist before the end, it will turn out to be "all a bad dream."

Twenty minutes later, he and Ben arrive at the apartment—silent and empty and smelling of nothing.

Hanging up his coat, he goes to empty its pockets and finds his birthday card to Maddie, still sealed in its plastic wrapper: *On your birthday, wishing you a day to remember, and many more! Here's hoping you get everything you deserve!* He had bought it only last week, at great expense, from the fancy Alphabets store on Avenue A. He opens the desk drawer and places the card inside. All he had wished for was a happy day. One that, in years to come, they could look back on with their kids and grandkids. *A day to remember*, he thinks, closing the drawer. *But not like this.*

Drama

1992

"It's for class," Maddie answers breezily when Jonathan asks what she's doing.

It's his first night off in a month—no class, no bar shift, no plans. Writing out some ideas for his novel, he'd been wondering where all the noise was coming from. In the backyard he discovers Maddie with some object wrapped in a towel, smashing it against the ground. Now, she unrolls it for him to inspect. "See?" She grins. His Eeyore mug. Shattered into tiny pieces. He doesn't see at all.

"My mom gave me that . . ." he says before he can stop himself. She looks genuinely surprised.

"I'm really sorry. I didn't realize. It looked sort of old . . ."

"It's OK." Easier just to pick up a new one at Pottery Barn, he decides, than make a big deal of it. They are silent for a moment.

"Sorry, Jon." She puts her arms around his neck, kisses his face. "I grabbed it without thinking. Don't be cross!"

She has always been impulsive, he thinks, and since this is one of the million reasons he fell in love with her, he can't very well be "cross" with her, can he?

"Really don't worry," he sighs, "but I don't get it. What has my kitchenware got to do with your acting class?"

"It's for my 'activity,'" she replies, as if this explains everything. "We're learning how to say our lines while doing something completely different. You have to do both at the same time. Like walk and chew gum." She settles into the rickety plastic lawn chair, wraps one long leg over and around the other. "In real life, people often do two things at the same time, right?"

He nods.

"For instance, I'm doing the dishes and we're also having an argument." They've never had an argument. And he can't actually recall the last time Maddie did any dishes, either. But never mind.

"So, in class that's called your 'activity.' And for *my* activity, I was going to glue your cup back together." He tries not to stare at the shards of china scattered on the ground.

"I see," he says.

"I know, right?" she says, misreading his expression. "I didn't get it at first either."

She goes on to tell him about "finding the emotional truth" of a character. "Even for people who use 'the Method'— which *we* don't, obviously—there are loads of similarities between acting and writing."

Curious, he asks whether she can give him an example. She has often said that acting helped nurture her creative process as a writer, but never really explained why. In weeks they can afford it, movies are their thing. Even more than sitting in the dark with her, it's the conversations they have afterward, about the actors and their "craft," that he looks forward to the most. With her writing, though, she is more reticent, bordering on secretive.

"Hmm . . ." She closes her eyes for a second, wrinkles her brow. "I suppose it's . . . taking something that isn't actually true, and imagining it for yourself? And then, if you do it well, for your audience it *appears* true." She pauses. "Or something like that." She laughs.

"No . . ." he says, "I mean, yes, I totally get what you mean." But he doesn't. Not really. Once again, her grasp of a subject is so much more advanced than his own. And the fact that rather than *talk* about something, she just goes ahead and *does* it is what makes her a real artist, he decides. The other night he'd woken to find her sitting up in bed, furiously writing in one of her notebooks.

"Ideas . . . they come to me in the middle of the night . . ." she had explained. She must have filled a whole bunch of notebooks by now. None of which she has ever let him see. Sometimes this can feel as if she is shutting him out, or doesn't trust him.

"The key is to work your *what-if*s," she is saying, as if speaking about a life-or-death situation. "To really push them. When I'm working on a part, I ask myself, what if such and such a thing happened? How would I feel about that? What would I *do?* And then what? And what next . . .? And what happens after *that*?" She leans forward intently in her seat. "This one time," she continues, "my character had to be sad about her husband dying. But in my head, I'm thinking, that's not something that resonates with me. That's when I thought about my mum's dog, Tilly. How would I feel if something happened to her? I mean, the audience doesn't know if you're crying about your dead husband or your dead dog, right? To them the result looks the same. If you believe it, so do they."

He nods, tries not to feel hurt.

"And I got an A." She grins.

"It's like telling lies for a living," he says. "Which sounds kind of—"

"Kind of what?"

"Nothing. It was just an observation."

"Yes, but what were you going to say?"

"Just that I love animals and all of that, but . . . it's just . . ."

She looks curiously at him.

"What? Just *what?*"

"It just seems . . . a little manipulative is all." He's teasing. Kind of.

"Well, of course it is! That's what I've been telling you. That's the whole *art* of it."

Jonathan has other questions, but it's too late for that. He's blown it and now she's pissed at him. Still, as he follows her inside, he makes a mental note to add this to all the other intriguing snippets he has picked up from her. In the tiny galley kitchen, he makes them hot tea, and they discuss their plans for later. He asks whether, if she has time, she might be interested in hearing an excerpt from the novel he's writing. Maddie may not care about anyone else's approval, but in his own case, reading out his work to someone is a decision he's been wrestling with for weeks. It feels daunting, knowing how readily she expresses her views on things. ("Ugh, I *despise* the royal family," she'd declared on an early date. "You Yanks love them so much, you can take them!" He'd never mentioned Princess Diana again.)

But it has to be done eventually, and she's the person whose opinion he values the most.

"Sure," she says, settling herself on the couch with an expectant air. How he envies her self-contained confidence.

"Actually," he says nervously, "it'll be good to read it out to someone who's not me for a change."

"Go on, then." She grins—and he does. Barely three paragraphs in, it's so obvious that she's not interested. That she's trying—not very convincingly for an actress—to stifle her boredom.

"Should I stop . . .?"

The question brings to mind his inexpert fumbling in bed the other night. Not that she'd *said* anything . . . but the experience had left him painfully aware of his ignorance, his lack of experience in that area.

"No, silly, it's interesting." *Interesting . . .?* "But I *really* have to pee. Can you wait a mo?"

As she disappears into the bathroom, he recalls the one time Maddie met his mother.

"Johnny's problem," his mother had said during dinner, "is that he's too ambitious for his own good." The implication being that his girlfriend might rein in his unrealistic expectations.

Of course, it's hardly Maddie's fault, if around her he feels like a total rube. Like one of those small-minded, provincial Americans she makes fun of. Though as he's explained over and over, he finds those people just as lame and annoying as she does, if not more so. Meanwhile, he has let her teach him chess and made time to read all her favorite writers and poets. Would it hurt her to return the favor? Hemingway, Fitzgerald, Salinger, Steinbeck, all his own favorites, suggested and rejected.

"I just can't get into them," she had groaned. "And why are they all *men*?"

Just the other night, she'd insisted on reading aloud an extremely long British poem he's fairly sure was written by a man. After a ten-hour bar shift, he had little appetite for hearing about some old guy who kept a picture of his wife hidden behind a curtain, or whatever. But for her sake, he'd at least tried to appear interested. She comes out of the bathroom, takes her place on the couch. He resumes where he left off, attempting to vary the tone here and there to capture her interest. Four lines in she interrupts to ask about the title, wonders aloud whether it could be seen as "a bit pretentious."

Does she do it on purpose, he wonders then—reject the things that are important to him? Somehow, he makes it to the bottom of the first page and manages to stumble over the last sentence—at which point, Maddie yawns. Not just a regular yawn, either, but a yawn like a theater actor making sure to reach the people in the nosebleed seats. It arrives right at the section he's the most proud of, as well. Where his young protagonist reminisces about the long summers he spent as a boy with his grandfather, and the wonderful tales the old man used to tell, all described in loving detail.

"That bad . . .?" No sooner are the words out of his mouth than he knows he's not ready to hear the answer. Worse, it has made him sound needy and insecure—the very thing that makes her crazy.

"Not at all. It's great, seriously!" She sounds like she means it, he thinks to himself, but now she's explained how acting works, it's hard to know whether to believe her or not. Several pages slip from his hands onto the floor. In their life together, he often finds himself using one or other of her British phrases. Friends tease him about it, but they've rubbed off on him, and Maddie has told him it's cute. He'd managed to weave a number of them into his story—had she even noticed?

"Completely fine," he mumbles, getting down on his hands and knees to pick them up. He gathers the pages into their elastic band and shoves them roughly into the desk drawer.

"Suit yourself," she sighs, rising from the couch. Lifting her arms above her head, she moves them rapidly from side to side like an athlete warming up for a race.

"Hey, Fluffer are playing Brownies tonight," she says.

Maddie has accused him of being too much of an "indoor cat," but he'd thought they agreed to stay home for once. At least, that's what he'd taken from the slightly tense exchange they'd had earlier. He'd been hoping to get some writing done. Perhaps submit his stuff to a few magazines . . .

"It's kind of late," he says. "Aren't you hungry? I could make us something?"

Maddie rolls her eyes, flops back down on the sofa.

"You are *sooo* predictable sometimes. Anyway, I already told Laura we'd meet up."

At gigs, Maddie and Jay joke that Jonathan behaves like an old person, standing at the back with a pained expression on his face. Brownies, he thinks, with its puddles of beer on the floor and the girls "bopping" along at the front, was the worst one of all. Aside from himself, Laura is the only person among their friends who seems able to break away and go home at a reasonable hour.

"I guess I wouldn't *mind* seeing Laura," he offers. An amused half-smile from Maddie.

"I'm perfectly capable of going out on my own, you know." She kicks off her shoes, heads to the bathroom.

Outdoor cat—how can he tempt her to stay home? From here he can just about see her reflection in the mirror. Brushing her teeth with the faucet running, spilling water over the floor. On nights like this, he wishes he didn't love her as much as he does.

"Guess what?" she calls. "One of the guys is hooking me up with this producer later."

One of the guys. The intense, greasy-haired musician guys in filthy plaid shirts that she has insisted on making friends with. He has yet to see a single one of them pick up an instrument. She takes the nail scissors from the cabinet and starts twisting little sections of her hair, and snipping at them with expert swiftness. He watches as she applies lip gloss, puckers her lips, doing her "mirror" face.

"I might be back sort of late," she continues, rubbing at something on her teeth. "He's this really smart guy, just dynamic and cool. And he's putting together this independent film."

She is so busy, he thinks, so hard to pin down. Going out, "networking," rehearsing lines, jotting down stuff in her secret notebooks, swimming laps at the scary, germ-ridden public pool on 25th Street. He admires it, the way she'll hang out at the all-night diner to write and, fueled by endless coffee refills, set off walking at 3 a.m. She's walked the entire length of the island at this point, as far north as the Cloisters, all through Harlem, and down to Battery Park, and "has met loads of interesting people." Or so she says. Likely it's a bit of an exaggeration, but he's never seen the point of contradicting her. "It's good for my head," she likes to say. Meanwhile, there's something deeply comforting about waking up in the wee hours to hear her moving around in the kitchen. The smell of that weird Marmite toast she practically lives off, the sound of the kettle boiling, Maddie singing softly to herself. Bringing him coffee in bed, even if not precisely the way he likes it. They say the city is safer than it used to be, so he tries not to worry, but the other day they'd nearly gotten into their first fight over it. At least the mayor was cracking down on "antisocial behavior," he'd happened to remark. No more erratic-looking man brandishing a squeegee, lying in wait like a mugger for his terrified parents as they drove through the Lincoln Tunnel. No more murderous cannibals and homeless people, he'd added humorously. "Oh, *goody*!" Maddie had shot back. "No more going out and you wondering whether I'm going to get chopped up and made into soup and fed to all the nasty homeless people in the park, eh? No more dancing, no more *fun*."

This had seemed rather unfair. The tabloids might sensationalize the news, he'd replied, but it wasn't as if they were allowed to print lies. And it wasn't only the *Post* that ran the story. The cannibal thing was a real incident. That *actually happened*. And right in our neighborhood. Maddie had just laughed. He watches her as she buzzes around the room, pulling on black combat boots and some kind of slip that resembles a garment that his grandmother might wear to bed. Given the opportunity, he'd prefer them to move somewhere safer, like the Upper East Side. But Maddie maintained it was full of phonies and refused to even step foot there. Still, at the other end of their block, Tompkins Square Park is at least now an actual park. A place to relax, clean and pleasant to be in. He likes seeing the young families and the contented couples strolling arm-in-arm, even if Maddie prefers the drag queens at Wigstock and striking up conversations with pretend anarchists and random misfits. And at least the rent was cheap. Or cheap-ish. Not that Maddie pays any. When they first met, she was couch surfing her way around the city, staying with an assortment of very unsavory-sounding characters. His formerly neat and tidy apartment is now verging on the chaotic, but he'd feel like a heel bringing any of this up. *High maintenance, high performance,* he thinks, the rule Maddie applies to the fanciest of fancy cars. He ponders this as she stands in the center of the room and fixes a loose strand of hair.

"A girl like that . . ." Jay had observed early on, "a girl like that could really make you feel like someone." She really is stunning. Like a cat, Jonathan decides, moving quickly and fluidly about the little apartment—his own gorgeous, astonishing, inscrutable feline. And maybe she's right—he could at least *try* to be less predictable, couldn't he? Less of a stick-in-the-mud. A bit more spontaneous. As Maddie likes to say, you can sleep when you're dead.

"Maybe I will come out with you guys," he offers, going to stand up. She comes over, gently pushes him back down on the couch and plants a soft kiss on his forehead, ruffling his hair with such utter tenderness that it makes him blush. "Silly . . . You stay here and work on your memoirs."

"Okay, well tell Laura I said hi!" he says cheerily. "And *don't do anything I wouldn't do* . . ." Another of her phrases.

"Ha." She flashes her biggest movie-star smile. "*As if.*"

Every time she leaves, it is as if she takes with her a layer of his skin or some vital internal organ that's crucial to his survival—leaving him frightened, empty, vulnerable. He'll never completely understand her, but he does trust her. And she always comes back.

Shrink

2019

Mahoney takes a slug from his cup, grimaces, puts it down again.

"Jesus, this coffee is for shit."

"The bar around the corner does a pretty good one—we could go there?" Jonathan offers, before realizing how tactless this sounds. Mahoney grins.

"Yeah, don't I know it. What are you gonna do?" Unlike the fictional Detective Connor, Mahoney long ago won his battle with the booze. Now, where coffee is concerned, Mahoney goes for the upscale hipster independents at six dollars a pop. In contrast, Jonathan, the would-be guilty liberal, patronizes the diner around the block where the coffee tastes stewed and sour. It is a rare point of contention between them. That and the Yankees, whose progress Jonathan keeps only half an eye on. Sports don't interest him, but he feels obliged to have some kind of knowledge at hand.

Over the years, he and Mahoney have become good friends. When Jonathan had called yesterday, he hadn't mentioned wanting to discuss anything in particular, and Mahoney hadn't asked. Seeing your dead wife wandering through the local bookstore wasn't the easiest subject to broach. And though it can't possibly have been her, for some reason the experience has been nagging at him, and it seems prudent to get the cop's take. With some trepidation, he relates what happened. Mahoney listens to the whole story—the escalator, the crowd, his wild-eyed search—stopping him at intervals only to ask him to recall or repeat certain details.

"First off," he says, when Jonathan has finished, "sightings like this are pretty normal. They even got a name— 'bereavement hallucinations.' In World War Two, widows would swear up and down they saw their husbands and sons walkin' around alive." Mahoney, he remembers, is a longtime devotee of military documentaries on the History Channel.

"You sound like my shrink," Jonathan says.

"Yeah, except I'm tellin' you for free." Mahoney pauses, picks something off his doughnut. "My sister . . . her kid—my nephew—he went missing in the parking lot at the mall. She's loading groceries in the trunk, turns around, he's gone. Just like that. Vanished." At which point, he continues, his sister pretty much lost her mind.

"I'm so sorry," Jonathan says, "when was this?" He's attended baptisms, pool parties and Fourth of July cookouts at Mahoney's house. He would have met the sister at some point, but couldn't put a face to the name.

"Long time ago. Few months before your wife went missing."

"You never said . . ." Jonathan can't help feeling slighted.

"Yeah, well . . ." Mahoney shrugs, which is no answer at all. Instead, he takes a swig of his coffee, scowls as it goes down. "PTSD, they said it was. Stopped going out. Couldn't take care of herself. Doctors put her on medication, the whole nine." Mahoney had assured his sister that just because they hadn't found her son didn't mean he wasn't out there. "What I didn't say—and I guess I can say this to you now—is with a case like that, the odds are long. And the longer an individual is missing, the longer they get." A pause. "In your wife's case, as you know, we're talking decades." Another brief silence as they both pick up their drinks. *Displacement activity*, Jonathan thinks—the conversation veering into difficult territory.

Mahoney is like a father to him at this point. Other crime writers have accused him of being in the cops' pockets. With his privileged inside track, they joke, he never has to pay a speeding ticket. Except, as he enjoys pointing out, as a New Yorker he rarely uses a car. Sure, his books feature police officers who are noble and self-sacrificing. And yes (though Laura isn't happy about it) he donates to the Police Benevolent Association each year. Why on earth wouldn't he? The cops have been good to him. Mahoney in particular. In fact, when Maddie went missing, it was their friendship that had allowed him to imagine any kind of a future for himself.

"She 'saw' him once," Mahoney continues unexpectedly. "Her boy. With some guy who looked like Ronald McDonald or that clown from *It*." He laughs grimly.

Jonathan pictures the mother. Out of her mind with grief, not knowing whether her child was dead or chained up in some madman's basement. Does she ever think of her son and picture him alive? Growing up, living his adult life, oblivious and elsewhere?

"Do you think she actually did see him, though?" he asks. The cop shakes his head.

"Trauma, guilt, psychological stress," he replies. "That stuff works on your mind."

All the times Jonathan has pictured the scene—Maddie striding purposefully up to the car, pulling open the door, getting in, the car roaring off. All the things he'd wanted to say to her, but never got the chance to. Wondering how she must have felt at the very moment of her death. What had not occurred to him in some while, however, was that his wife might still be alive.

"Okay, but what if Maddie lost her memory?" When they first met, Jonathan explains, Maddie was waitressing, working for cash under-the-table, using made-up social security numbers or ones belonging to dead people. Until they were married, she didn't even have a driver's license or a bank account. "She was super smart and resourceful," he says. "Maybe she didn't know who she was. She could have had some lost years, worked random jobs, built a new identity." Mahoney is silent. "A blow to the head could cause that, couldn't it? What if she—"

"Let me stop you there, Jon," Mahoney cuts in. "You got it all figured out, but that's a lotta *could*s. It *could* happen, sure. But sooner or later she or someone else would have figured it out. That's a fact."

"I guess there was just something about her," he says. "This *person*. The way she looked. How she moved." He sighs. "I can't explain it."

Mahoney looks thoughtful.

"Is there some reason you think you're seeing her now?"

Jonathan shakes his head.

"None that I can think of." *How about marrying her best friend?* He bats the thought away.

"Jon. I'm gonna say something harsh. And you're gonna let me know if I'm speaking out of turn."

"Okay . . ."

"You ready?"

Jonathan nods, wonders what's coming next.

"If she is alive, why wouldn't she come find you and Ben?"

A pause.

"I've thought the same thing," Jonathan admits.

"Right. My other point is that we—the detectives assigned to the case—we always worked on the assumption that she didn't know the perpetrator, the driver of the car. Abduction, kidnapping, murder, possible suicide. That's what we were looking at."

Suicide. In all this time, whether or not an actual crime was committed has never been in question.

"I've been straight with you from the get-go, haven't I?" Mahoney says. Jonathan nods, realizes he's been holding his breath. "But some things need to be said."

It's not like Mahoney to beat around the bush, he thinks, watching the cop pick up his cup again. As the hairs on his forearms stand up, not for the first time he wonders whether Mahoney, like his fictional counterpart Connor, is like a two-way mirror, with the ability to see right through people.

"We weren't wrong to rely on what we knew," the cop continues. "Not wrong at all. It wouldn't have made a damn bit of difference with how we went about the investigation."

Does he think Jonathan is questioning his professionalism? Back when they first met, his ideas of policing were informed by TV and movies, where cops drank, and drank hard, and crossed the line in more ways than one. Whatever Mahoney's personal struggles, Jonathan has never once witnessed his friend do or say anything inappropriate.

"What I'm saying is . . . what if she did?" Mahoney asks.

Jonathan stares.

"Sorry, what if she did what?"

Mahoney sits back, folds his arms.

"You never saw the perpetrator, correct?"

"No . . ."

"You never saw his face. Coulda been more than one person. Coulda been a she for all we know."

Is this meant as some kind of joke?

"You told me that you were having a few issues, you and your wife?"

"What exactly are you getting at?" Jonathan has spoken sharply, and Mahoney looks at him in surprise.

"Jon, c'mon. Don't get defensive on me."

"Sorry, Matt. You're right." He sighs. "I guess I'm just feeling kind of . . . *freaked out* by everything."

"Understood." Mahoney appears to study him before continuing. "First, let's assume it was just the one person," he says. "It's possible that this . . . *guy*, the driver, was known to her." Another short silence, as if Mahoney is weighing up how to deliver his next words. "*Second*: either she was abducted by him or—*just maybe*—she went with him of her own free will."

"Set the whole thing up, you mean? Staged her own disappearance?" He wasn't expecting that.

"It's not illegal to go missing. We normally see it with men. Older white males with family they don't want the responsibility of. But some women, I guess they can get in a funk after having a kid and . . . Hey"—Mahoney raises his hands—"not sayin' it's right, but someone could want a do-over, a new start. Make a life for themselves someplace else."

"I thought you said that couldn't happen, someone being able to just vanish in that way."

"Like I said, if we're talking your memory-loss scenario, like in the movies, it's unlikely. But disappearing on purpose? Used to be people could fly under the radar. These days, you're looking at computers and ID checks, everything digital and networked. So no, it wouldn't be so easy. But if a person really set their mind to it, likely they could pull it off."

The cops aren't the only ones who'd made assumptions, Jonathan thinks to himself. Though in his own case, it had taken many years to properly accept that his wife was dead. In all this time, and for whatever reason, has he been doing Maddie a disservice? Has he underestimated her? She was an actress, after all.

"Like I said, it wouldn't have changed anything about our investigation," Mahoney repeats. "Bottom line up front, we ran a trace on the car and turned up zilch. We checked out everyone she had contact with and got that all squared away. Friends, classmates. Nothing worth bothering you with." Mahoney frowns into his coffee cup for a moment. "Jon. I'll be honest. I dunno if you want to go rehashing stuff at this point. Could do yourself more harm than good."

Jonathan looks questioningly at him.

"Sometimes, it's better to leave the past in the past is all," Mahoney says. They appear to be going in circles. Or perhaps circling around something Mahoney doesn't feel comfortable saying.

"You may be right," Jonathan says, too tired to figure it out. "So where does all this leave me?"

"Unclear. I'm not saying you saw her. And I'm not saying you didn't. I'm saying it's possible, but very unlikely. Sorry, Jon. I know you want to put a lid on this. That you need . . . *closure*. I wish I could tell you more."

Despite himself, Jonathan can't help smiling. Mahoney does not live in a world of "closure" and "processing" feelings. It must pain him to use these terms, but he does so out of simple human empathy.

"I totally understand," he replies. "And Matt, I appreciate your talking this through with me. I figured it was worth running by you."

"Sure thing. Anytime." And after an appropriate pause, "How you doing otherwise?"

"Pretty good. Busy. The new book's coming out, and I'm working on the next one." Mahoney grins, raises an eyebrow.

"Book sixteen, huh? So, what you got in store for me this time? You givin' me another divorce or what?"

Jonathan smiles. Detective Connor shares many of Mahoney's characteristics—the relaxed drawl, the ex-drinker and family man who hankers after his younger days. And occasionally, it had been not-so-subtly suggested, women who were not his wife. The police divorce rate hovered at 50 percent—and he'd spent enough time with Mahoney's old cop buddies at home in Queens to understand why.

"Hey, I gotta keep up with Ragione," he goes on. "All puffed up last time I talked to her. Got some writer on her tail, wanting to interview her for a book." Mahoney laughs. "Guess I'm not the only cop with fans, huh?"

"That's nice," Jonathan says tightly. Like he could care less what that dreadful woman is up to. Ragione, of course, makes an appearance in the world of Ocean Falls, only somewhat altered, as a suspicious, bullying schoolteacher. When he gets around to it, this person will likely be the victim of a painful and grisly murder. Mahoney looks expectant, so he feeds him the usual line: that a character, good or bad, may start out as a real person, but morph into someone else entirely. Mahoney looks skeptical, almost hurt. He's heard it all before, of course. Jonathan's coy denials and performative bemusement. They have become a little ridiculous. After all these years, maybe his friend deserves the truth.

"Hmm . . ." Jonathan says slowly.

Mahoney's expression is childlike, almost comical in its anticipation.

"Well . . . let's see." He pauses for dramatic effect. "I guess you'd know better than me," he says—and sees Mahoney's face light up, thrilled as a kid in a candy store.

"*Gotcha!*" the cop grins. "I goddamned knew it."

Sinking

1997

Jonathan's woken by a deafening ringing sound, like a fire alarm going off next to his head. He gropes for the phone, attempts to focus on the voice on the other end.

"I checked on your situation," it is saying, "but I need to get some more information." *Heather.* Glancing at the clock, he's shocked to see that it's 9:15 a.m. *Shit*—he's overslept the alarm. Ben should have been at day care thirty minutes ago.

"Heather," he starts, "I just don't have time right now—" The voice cuts him off.

"Hello?" Now fully awake, he can hear that the voice is nasal and whiny, nothing like Heather's commanding baritone. "Is this Mr. Dainty?"

"I'm sorry, who is this?"

"I'm calling about your wife's credit card. Sorry for your loss, but we need to get some information about what happened."

Heather has said he isn't liable for any of Maddie's debts, but the collection agencies keep calling anyway. Messages pile up on the answering machine. His sister has been doing her best to help, but like everything else, the situation has gotten a little on top of him.

"We understand that this is a difficult time for you," the voice says sympathetically. "But we need proof that your wife has passed away and that the cause of death has been established by a qualified medical professional."

Through the thick fog in his head, he tries to recall the correct response. The one Heather has coached him on to put callers like this in their place.

"Even if it's a suicide," the voice adds.

Suicide? He wants to jerk the phone from his ear and hang up. How dare she! His wife would have *never*. He sits up, shifts his legs over the side of the sofa, takes a breath. Has she been following his story in the papers? For the *New York Times*, it's old news, slipping off the pages within weeks. This hadn't stopped the tabloids, though, pondering aloud whether the wife had been murdered by her husband for some kind of insurance payout. As if he or Maddie could ever afford such luxuries.

As the voice talks on, Jonathan tunes out as best he can, takes the phone into the kitchen, finds a more or less clean glass, fills it up at the sink, and gulps down lukewarm water. If he doesn't get this call over with, they will only call back. He had a tiny bit too much to drink during his brunch shift yesterday. Heather's fault, pressuring him about some ridiculous "remembrance ceremony." It's not even been five months.

". . . and a copy of the police report," the voice is saying. "I'm sorry, I'm sure you're going through some tough times."

Heather has warned him about this as well—the debt collectors using fake sympathy, acting like your best friend so they can con their way into your bank account. In the other room, Ben is awake, chattering away to his toys. Jonathan positions himself in the bedroom doorway and tries in vain to signal him to start getting dressed. On the phone, the one-way conversation appears to have taken a bizarre turn.

"... I mean, it must be sooo difficult," the voice coos. "'Cause, like, if that was me who'd murd—"

"Excuse me? Excuse me, *what?*"

A giggle. Then a snort of laughter as a male voice comes on the line.

"Like, '*Boo-hoo! I murdered my wife!*'" A whoop of group laughter goes up on the other end—"Wooo! Hahaha!"—Jonathan can hear them high-fiving each other around the room.

He slams the phone down. It's not the first time—how could he not have caught it? He searches the kitchen for last night's bottle of vodka, finds it empty. Not so long ago, he had wondered how on earth he would get through it—the next week, the next hour, the next minute. And this is how, he thinks bitterly—with paperwork and exhaustion and fading hope. And hateful prank calls from bored students with nothing better to do. Shaken and humiliated, he goes into the bedroom and coaxes Ben into clothes, socks, shoes. Breakfast eaten, teeth brushed, he gets them out of the apartment only to realize that he's forgotten to prepare Ben's lunchbox. Back they go, spend fifteen more minutes trying to locate bread that doesn't appear too stale, plus something to put on it. More brain fog. More time wasted. Ben wails. Out the door for a second time, the wails go up a notch. He doesn't want to go to school, he sobs, he wants to go to Auntie Heather and Uncle Saul's.

"Ben, what would your aunt and uncle say if they knew you weren't in school?"

"Don't care," observes Ben tartly. Jonathan resorts to pleas and bargains, but Ben only cries louder.

Is he not giving him enough? Or enough of the right things? His son still cries for his mother, and in darker moments, Jonathan can't help wondering if Ben wishes it were his father who had disappeared instead. Everything seems to take twice as long as it should. Each day brings some new version of this morning's ordeal. In a bad building, on a bad block, in a worse neighborhood, as Ben screams, he now has to endure disapproving looks from the sketchy individuals that still line their street.

He practically has to drag his son up the steps to the facility, at last leaving him in the hands of the capable-looking woman inside. The East Village gets up late and as he heads back, the street feels tranquil, almost bucolic. What he'd love to be able to do more than anything right now, he thinks, is to head over to the new Starbucks on Astor Place and sit calmly with a cup of coffee. Watch the world go by, jot down some of his thoughts—*if only*. Every one of his credit cards is maxed out on groceries and bills. Each journey must be considered, every purchase weighed up. He hates himself for this . . . *lack*. For not being in charge of his own life. For feeling dependent on his dwindling group of friends and relatives. Well-meaning restaurant colleagues encourage him to go out after work. But the idea of people thinking him broke or desperate is unbearable, so when he does cave in to the pressure, he finds himself overcompensating by lunging for the check.

"It'll do you good to get out of the apartment," people say, not understanding that brunches and bar tabs or late movies are no longer within his means. *I have become one of those pathetic people,* he had thought to himself the last time, trapped amid a group of his raucous coworkers, ordering a Coke and a small green salad. When it came time to pay, the guy who had downed the most drinks suggested splitting the check five ways and Jonathan had left the place both hungry and $85 dollars poorer.

By the time he's been to the laundromat and walked the extra few blocks to the cheap, foul-smelling Gristedes supermarket on 14th Street, there's barely an hour left before he needs to pick up Ben. Back at the apartment, he inserts a fresh sheet of paper into the typewriter.

His fingers are just hovering over the keys, thoughts scattering away from him, when he's startled by the sound of a man's cough, followed by an odd shuffling noise. It's coming from outside, directly behind the old store doorway, which has become a shelter for crackheads and junkies. He looks up to see a long stream of dark yellow urine flowing under the door, snaking its way across the floor toward him. Ripping out the paper, he balls it up and throws it across the room, where it lands a good distance from the trash can. Who cares where it ends up? If it ends up in the trash, what does it matter? No one will miss it. In every way, he and Ben are sinking. And he hasn't a clue how to stop it.

Gossip

Kill me now, Jonathan thinks, as Heather leans over to affectionately rub Saul's arm.

"That interview was one of your best yet," she is saying. "So impactful and insightful." She looks across at Jonathan and Laura. "Guys? *Tell him.* We never miss a show, right?"

"Wouldn't dream of it," he agrees.

Heather and Saul have tickets to a new play and, without thinking, he had agreed to pretheater drinks at Valtameri. Saul has already knocked a jug of water into Jonathan's lap and delivered a lecture in his most pompous radio voice about the lack of minorities in popular fiction. As his brother-in-law meanders through another self-serving anecdote, Jonathan observes the spittle arcing into the air—not a good look on anyone. A very nice bottle of Riesling sits between them, but he doesn't feel in the mood. Exhausted but wide awake at 3 a.m., he'd found himself on his phone performing searches for *Maddie Morgan, Madeleine Morgan, Maddie + Morgan,* and even—hopefully—*Maddie Dainty* (his own name, which she had refused to take). Most references to her disappearance would have been summarized and archived twenty-three years ago, before the advent of the internet as the bottomless bowl of information it is now. Even knowing this, seeing zero search results offers the eerie suggestion that she never existed in the first place. As Mahoney had implied, all of Jonathan's hypotheses about her would-be reappearance are deeply stupid. The stuff of bad movies. Or, as Jay would phrase it, "crazytown." *Would*, that is, if he had shared any of this with his friend.

Around them the room is thick with gossipy, faintly hostile conversations. Reminiscent, he thinks now, of that Lou Reed song, whose name he's forgotten, that Maddie used to like. Since the moment they sat down, part of him has been listening through the restaurant's chatter for her voice. ". . . Economy . . . start-up . . . Oh my God, posted what?" Would she even understand what anyone was talking about? If she was alive and conscious in the twenty-first century, he supposed that she would. *But is she?* He pictures her walking through the city, firing off texts, lol'ing away—the notion both crazy and utterly plausible. Stealing a quick glance behind him, he feels Laura's eyes following his and senses her puzzlement. He can't help it, can't shake the feeling that *she's* somewhere nearby. Out of sight. Watching. All her old gang are here—older, if not wiser. All her friends, *still* friends, all these years on. They're successful and they look it. Saul—exhibit number one—with that ill-advised, questionable shirt stretched tight across his little paunch; he is literally bloated with success.

"Take Finland . . ." Saul is saying. *Let's not*, Jonathan thinks.

"Exactly," Heather murmurs huskily. "You're so right." The tips of her fingers perform a gruesome stroking motion on Saul's hand. *Gross*.

Why does his previously matter-of-fact sister feel the need to engage in these revolting public displays of affection? He tries to remember when it started. Actually, it would have been some while ago, shortly after Maddie's disappearance, when perhaps the reality had sunk in for Heather, who for the first time may have imagined what it would be like to lose her own spouse. He wonders what Maddie would make of their lives, with their luxury and choice. Or his and Laura's, for that matter, with their dinners out and carefree attitude to bill-paying. The travel and prizes and parties and casual taking of overseas vacations—would she be proud of him?

In the past week he has scanned each and every passerby, searched for her gait, her posture, her smile—some subpar version of which he has occasionally deployed at book signings. All the old feelings are back—the hopelessness, the powerlessness, the frustration. Mahoney had pointed out the obvious: why hadn't she come to find him? What could she be waiting for? he wonders as Saul continues on with his prim lecture. Likewise, if she has been out there all along, *why show up now?* Once again, that cold sense of unease shimmies up his spine.

A couple of nights ago, he'd told Laura he was off to the gym and had instead taken a walk across town to his and Maddie's old neighborhood. Featureless new buildings, trendy cocktail bars, elegant boutiques. Everything cleaner, safer, guarded by crews of twenty-four-hour doormen. The East Village gussied up like an aging tart, frayed at the edges but familiar all the same. After growing up in dreary, upstate New York, he'd arrived to a city that felt sexy, gritty, and open-ended. The crack epidemic was waning, but not quite enough to ruin the charged, dangerous thrill you got walking the city's streets. At least, that's how he remembered it. Junkies and murder and dancing in bars, crack vials crunching under-foot—who knew he'd find himself missing it all? *Die yuppie scum.* Maddie's failed musician friends had long since retreated to the suburbs of Jersey and Westchester—who's "sold out" now? Arriving on their old block, he'd thought he'd taken a wrong turn at first. But no. Their building was gone, replaced by a bland brick condo. The sight of it left him unnerved in some way he couldn't name.

A tap on his knee—Laura, with their secret signal—*time to go*. He signals back—two taps. If Saul isn't done in two minutes, it says, he'll make their excuses and they'll get out of here. What would Maddie make of her husband and her best friend, exchanging secret signals? Not to mention their impending marriage. *Impending*—he catches himself on the word. They certainly didn't plan for it to happen. It wasn't as if Laura were some consoling busybody or predatory spinster taking round casseroles to widowers. When Maddie went missing, Laura was devastated. When a few years later they had gotten together, it had taken them both by surprise.

"... Makes us all strangers to each other when we don't take responsibility for our actions ..." If it's even possible, Saul's voice appears to have grown louder. Were they still on the damn Scandis? Or was Saul preaching to the choir about some other social justice issue Jonathan tuned out ten minutes ago? He thinks instead about Mahoney's theory, that Maddie could have known the driver of the car. Ragione had implied something similar all those years ago, though Jonathan had chosen to forget most of what she had to say. Now, in his mind's eye, the car was indeed waiting for them. Elegant lines faintly menacing, engine patiently idling, ready to whisk its passenger into oblivion. Once more, that eerie sense of almost being able to see the driver's face, the witness's urge to conjure up or fill in the gaps.

As Saul ignores the check dropped in front of him, Jonathan mentally walks himself back through the scene from the other day—the main floor viewed from the vantage point of the escalator, the aisles dotted with browsers, the general herd moving through, the entrance also an exit. There was a slight bottleneck created by people standing around, jabbing desultorily at their phones as they waited on friends. Had any of them appeared physically affected by her presence? Had anyone moved out of the way to let her pass? Impossible to say.

Across the table, Saul pushes his glasses farther up onto the bridge of his nose. ". . . Exploiting and preying on . . ." he is saying. ". . . mental health issues . . . weaker," he intones, to a series of indulgent *uh-huh*s and *exactly*s from Heather. At which point, Jonathan finds himself bizarrely and unexpectedly assaulted by an image of Heather and Saul having sex. *Time to go,* indeed.

A busboy arrives to clear their table and Saul takes the opportunity to pull his minor celebrity act and make chitchat with him.

"The fact of the matter is, they're just kids waiting tables for exploitative wages," he informs the group afterward, casting a significant look at Laura, whose tolerant smile goes from thinning to distinctly strained. Heather looks embarrassed, but says nothing. Jonathan thinks about saying something, but doesn't. Meanwhile, their two minutes were up some time ago.

"I mean *really*," Saul says, pursing his lips.

Jonathan had had the bad luck of catching a brief snatch of *Making Waves* again this morning. "*You sayin' a rising tide raises all boats*," an aggrieved caller was complaining, seconds before Saul cut him off, "*but what if you don't got a boat?*" Now, clearing his throat, Jonathan can't resist recounting this exchange, and the caller's amusing riposte, with the table. In the difficult silence that follows, Saul's mouth, small and feminine, twitches and forms itself into a sour moue of annoyance. Heather glares at him. Laura frowns. *Seriously?* Jonathan thinks. Why *shouldn't* someone call out Saul on being a fraud? Laura taps at his knee again. *Double tap.* If *only* . . .

"Guys . . ." Jonathan reaches across the table and grabs the check. "You've got curtain up in twenty minutes. And we need to head out."

"Excuse me, uh, *Jonathan*?" Saul, doing his best to control his fury. "Has anyone ever told you that you're a very angry person?"

And has anyone ever told you you're a boorish, tiresome blowhard? Jonathan wants to laugh in the guy's face.

"Not recently," he replies, with an air of supreme nonchalance. He stands, sees Laura is already standing. Time to make their getaway.

"Always great to see you, Saul." He smiles.

Timing

1997

A Remembering Ceremony—that's the name Heather's settled on. "Why don't we all hunker down after lunch on Sunday?" she had said. "Just to check in."

"Check in on what?" Jonathan had replied.

Since almost the moment his wife went missing, Heather has been in full-on "efficient" mode. Meanwhile, her mealy-mouthed euphemisms aren't fooling anyone. Sitting around her kitchen table, even Saul looks worn out.

Both have been fantastic about Ben. As far as possible, Jonathan has sacrificed his more lucrative evening shifts in order to be with his son in the evenings. But when he does have to work, Saul will pick up Ben from daycare and Heather will drop him off before work the next day. Still, the child ends up staying here far more than he'd like. Which makes it hard to stand up to his sister when she's being like this, though a mean-spirited part of himself wonders whether this wasn't her intention all along.

"It's healthy to acknowledge the situation in some way," she is saying, as if recommending to a politician some kind of damage-control strategy. Ironic, he thinks, considering that these exchanges feel so dishonest, more so for what no one will say. He watches Saul meekly clear away their lunch things, loading them into the dishwasher before disappearing into his

95

study with the excuse of a pressing deadline. Heather has yet to lose someone close. And she has Saul, who is going out of his way to be as agreeable and helpful as possible. Just last month came the announcement that the two of them would be renewing their vows. A small ceremony in the orchard of their house upstate, Heather had said. "Then off to Nantucket for a whole week!" Their timing feels insensitive, even cruel.

Heather licks her fingers, leafs rapidly back and forth through her notes. What he wouldn't do for an upstate retreat of his own to escape to. It'll never happen, of course. In fact, any day now he expects to be fired from his job.

"It's an important milestone," she goes on. That's another thing—this weird, pop-psychological language his sister comes out with these days. Where does she get it from? It's not like her at all. He watches as she draws another thick black line through an item on her long list of them.

"Some kind of . . . *closure*," she says, as if thinking aloud, ". . . a *ceremony*."

No call from the police. No body found. Was it a good sign? A bad sign? Months spent not knowing how to feel. Feeling cheated and angry. Watching others' lives continue on as if nothing has happened. Every night his wife appears in his dreams—murdered, lying in a ditch, floating face down in the ocean. Every day he waits for the phone to ring, and to hear Mahoney's voice on the other end—"We've found her." But this hasn't happened. And as more and more time goes by, it has become obvious—even to Jonathan—that it likely never will. Through the large kitchen windows, he sees that a mist has rolled in from the Hudson—something comforting in the way it encloses them.

"It's good to send out cards. Gather friends together," Heather continues. "Maddie's friends, obviously," she adds.

"*Obviously*," he says.

He reaches across the table for the coffee pot, notes the grim, dogged way she's going down her list—*check, check, check*. His grief doesn't fit into his sister's neat black-and-white world. Could she make it any more obvious that she wants to draw one of her thick black lines under the last five months as well?

"You think about . . . all the things you wished you could have said or done," he'd told her early on. "And it seems impossible that you can't do things differently, or bring the person back and let them know exactly how you feel."

Heather's expression had been unreadable, but he'd gotten the strangest feeling. That she'd wanted to—or was about to— say something. And then Saul had come in, and the moment had passed. Since then, when he tries to talk to her about his wife, about the jumble of feelings her absence has stirred up, Heather's eyes glaze over and his words are interrupted with a rapid stream of "Yes . . . yah . . . yah . . . right . . . uh-huh . . ." It's as if they're in a competition to see who can finish his sentences first.

And as if she is itching to draw a line through Maddie herself, he decides, tipping the mushed-up dregs of coffee into his cup. And can't wait to have her buried and gone. Except that—inconveniently—there can be no burial. No funeral. No ashes. No grave. Which presumably is why Heather is being so very insistent on this hateful "remembering ceremony."

"This must all be terribly inconvenient for you," Jonathan says. And when she doesn't answer—"Heather?"

"What's that?" She looks up, glasses askew. "Jon, it's no trouble. I *want* to help. You know that."

"Uh-huh."

"I can't believe I'll never see her again," he'd told Laura when she'd taken him for coffee last week. *Literally, I can't believe it.* Twice a week he follows up with the cops out east. Makes sure to get Detective Mahoney (not Ragione) on the line. What choice does he have? The other night, seconds into a call with him, he had glanced at the clock and realized that it was past one in the morning.

"No sweat," the cop replied, when he'd apologized profusely. Then he'd asked Jonathan what was really on his mind.

"My wife," he had begun. "She wasn't a careful driver . . ." In so many ways, revealing this had felt like a betrayal. Complete strangers had been known to let her drive their priceless vintage vehicles, he had continued. "And some- times . . . she drove too fast. So, if she is . . ." It was hard to get the word out. "If Maddie is . . . *gone,* for my own peace of mind, I need you to find her."

"I understand," Mahoney had answered. They have built a lot of trust over the months, and the cop hears the terrible desperation in his voice. There had been similar conversa- tions. Possibly too many. But he is more grateful for them than Mahoney can ever know.

"We've searched all over, Jon. And we're gonna keep look- ing. We're not gonna give up on her."

Divers, fishing boats, helicopters, police. Local people turn- ing out, walking the highway and the smaller streets, checking cabbage fields and abandoned houses. Looking in ditches, God help them, combing the pine woods and the banks of the bay. The whole exercise was futile.

One phrase has been repeated to him over and over: *It gets easier.* And each day he does his best to believe it and put on what Jay terms his "game face." But it feels like living a lie and, some days, all he wants is to have it over with. For someone— anyone—to call out the whole thing as a sham.

". . . By the river or in the park?" Heather says. "What do you think?"

Out of the window, the mist has dissipated. A plane traces a high arc in the sky. Heather waits, pencil hovering—he can almost hear her impatience—before resuming her neat checking off of items. Scratch, scratch ... *scratch*. He can't bear it. He gets up and starts pacing the kitchen. He doesn't need anyone's pity. Doesn't need Heather to try and "fix" the situation—or him. And with it, he can't help feeling, his *inconvenient* grief.

"I wish you'd let me help," she says.

"Maybe I don't want your help."

"Oh, stop."

"*You* stop."

"Just take the damned help, Jon." Is this what he wanted all along? To get a reaction? *Check*. "God knows you could use it," she continues. "Trekking out to friggin' Long Island every two days—I'm sorry but you're acting like a crazy person. Someone needs to tell you. It's not healthy."

Once a week, depending on his schedule, he takes the Long Island Rail Road out east. He asks questions, tries to gather any precious nuggets of information, anything the cops may have missed. When he'd first been interviewed on local TV, the townspeople had admired his grit and determination. These days (according to Ragione), the general feeling is that he's out of his mind. A pest.

"You're not helping anyone," Heather says.

"Except Maddie," he shoots back. "You're forgetting about her."

"Anyone need anything?" Saul has come back to fumble noisily in one of the overhead cabinets. "More coffee?" He takes mugs down from the shelf, almost dropping one. Then loiters nervously by the espresso machine, eyes darting around the room, as if looking for cockroaches. Whose decision was it, Jonathan wonders, this renewing of the vows? Not Saul's, he's willing to bet. He knows how it feels, being pushed around by Heather.

"Thanks, Saul, we're fine," Heather replies shortly. Poor Saul. Maddie had labeled him "the poor man's Napoleon." And admittedly his brother-in-law is rather short. And he's losing his hair. But that's hardly his fault, and he certainly doesn't deserve Heather's contempt.

"More coffee would be great, Saul." He smiles. They have never been close, but he admires his brother-in-law immensely. Right out of college, he'd landed a coveted slot on public radio, with a show called *Making Waves*. Once a week, Saul interviews a selection of "the great and the good" about items in that week's news. Only two days ago he'd listened as Saul put a rather arrogant guest in their place: "Of course, therapy only works if you're completely honest . . . Doesn't it . . .?" Saul had remarked cleverly. The show is great and Jonathan makes sure never to miss it. Now, Saul puts down a fresh pot of coffee and scurries out of the room. Who can blame him?

Heather adjusts her glasses. "We could do a photo," she says. "Get it blown up. How would that be?"

Has she forgotten? There's already a fucking poster. Hundreds of them. Pasted over half the walls and telephone poles and store windows of Long Island. All show the same image—Maddie, posing on a bench in Tompkins Square Park, grinning from ear to ear. Does Heather really expect them all to go stand in the freezing cold next to the river or some other godawful cliché of a "scenic" city spot his wife would have totally despised? He knows exactly how that would play out. Someone—most likely the hapless, henpecked Saul—will make the trip down to Pearl Paint to purchase an easel. While someone—himself, probably—will be encouraged to say something confessional and moving. It occurs to him that

Heather had never liked his wife. And that they have never had this out in the open.

"Sure," he says agreeably. Heather, on the alert, narrows her eyes.

"What?"

"I said *sure*. If you were asking me. I mean, *why not*? I mean, I'm not gonna ask where you get off, thinking you can choose how and when I 'commemorate' my wife?"

"'Remember,' not 'commemorate.'"

"Whatever." He has made it crystal clear how he feels about this whole morbid project, but she doesn't listen. With each minute spent sitting in her stupid kitchen, he feels his sanity slipping away.

"It's an opportunity to share our memories, to help you—"

"*Move on?*" Heather looks away. "Is that what you're getting at? That I need to *move on*? Well, guess what, Heth? Maybe I don't want to move on. Maybe I'm not ready. But hey, don't worry about what I think. Blow up a photo. And while you're at it"—he takes a breath—"why not go all out and purchase an empty coffin? *How would that be?* A whole lot more economical, right? And, like"—he hears his own voice go up another notch—"and like, hold *auditions* and *hire a fucking actor* to play the body? How would *that* be!?"

Heather gazes at the wall with a tolerant expression, puts down her pencil.

"Jon, I am so very sorry for your loss," she says. "We all are. But it's been months, and you need to accept it. Not keep looking for things that'll only make you feel worse." *What is she talking about?*

"*Worse*? How could I feel fucking worse, Heth?"

"Forget it." She sighs, picks up her pencil. "Do what you want."

He's not letting her off the hook that easily.

"You think she walked out on us?" he says. "You think she ran off with someone else? Is that it?" In meetings with the police, in conversations with journalists, with work colleagues, he could almost hear what everyone was thinking. The explanation that dare not speak its name. Heather turns to him, her lips a tight white line, opens her mouth to speak.

"Hey . . ." Saul, coming toward them, hands outstretched. "Hey, *people*. Can we all calm down? Heather doesn't mean for you to get upset. She's just trying to help," he says, with a quick glance in her direction. "We both are." He receives a look from Heather, backs off with a hopeless little shrug, withdrawing to his study and quietly closing the door. Heather looks pissed.

"What the heck is wrong with you?"

"What do you think?"

"I think you're being childish." *Minimizing*, he thinks. A little trick she picked up from their mother. "Look. I get it. You've been going through the worst time." She takes off her glasses and places them on the table, rubs the little space at the bridge of her nose. "We all have."

Is she joking? What the hell does Heather have to complain about?

From the room along the hall, there is a small cry. They both listen for a moment—but it is just the one. Their raised voices have intruded on some dream or other, but Ben is still asleep.

"I need to get him home," Jonathan says. Standing, he takes his coat and scarf off the back of the chair.

"You won't stay for supper . . .?"

He thinks of Ben, curled up with his toys in the guest room. Of the empty fridge back at their apartment.

"I'm sorry if I've pressured you," Heather says. "It's been awful for you, a nightmare . . . I . . ."

"It's a school night," he says. "We'll eat at home." Heather looks abashed, and he feels bad. "Sorry . . ."

"Me too," she says.

Refusing Heather's offer of cab fare, he sets off with Ben to walk across Central Park. It's a fair distance, but the air is fresh and cool and he could use the exercise. With some luck, the journey will tire Ben out and they'll both be able to get some sleep tonight.

"We'll go past the Natural History Museum," he tells Ben, "and through the park. And the boating lake at 72nd. We love it there, don't we?"

He and Maddie used to take Ben to see the toy boats, he remembers. They used to laugh at the older fathers, their kids pestering them for a turn at the controls. As they zig-zag slowly toward Central Park West, he thinks about the afternoon he has just wasted. There have been so very few occasions when he's felt able to share his feelings with Heather. To tell her that Maddie had been his whole world. And that this world was now lost to him. Sympathy, he decides, but no empathy. As with so many do-gooders, there is an essential coldness at the heart of his sister that he will never get to the bottom of.

After a few blocks, Ben is tired. Without the strength to carry him, Jonathan ends up spending their last dollar-fifty on the subway.

Blindsight

2019

"*Yes,* I get that he talks too much . . ." Laura is saying.

Rain has been falling all day, but in the last hour it has stopped. Ninth Avenue is washed clean and teeming with people. Busboys put out chairs and wipe down tables, people are out walking their dogs. He should be enjoying the stroll, but he isn't.

"But honestly, why would you go out of your way to provoke him like that?"

"Me?" He looks at her in surprise. "All that stuff about restaurant staff and 'taking responsibility'?" *Come on.* "You don't think he was asking for it?"

Laura sighs.

"Maybe it is a bit hypocritical, considering . . ."

"Considering what . . .?" Not that Jonathan disagrees, but "hypocritical" is a strong word for Laura, who chooses her words carefully—if not as carefully as he does. "Because he's privileged?" he asks when she doesn't respond. "Not that we're not," he adds quickly.

"Sorry." She smiles. "I don't know what I meant by it. I'm tired, I guess." She links her arm through his. "And I had just a little too much wine. How about we just take Saul off the menu tonight?"

"Agreed," he says. They pass a bedraggled young woman sitting on the sidewalk cradling a small baby. "Shall we get the light?" he suggests as the green man flashes, and they both jog toward it.

There's no real hurry. The light, he realizes, merely provides the excuse to move quickly past something that perhaps they'd both rather not see. *Blindsight*—that seeing unseeing-ness, almost unconscious among city-dwellers. Maddie had made a point of talking to homeless people, he remembers. Asked them their story, gave them money, and maintained that it was none of her business what they spent it on. At the time, he'd felt almost embarrassed for her.

They linger briefly outside a collection of antique stores where Laura likes to window shop. Neither consults the other first, the likes and dislikes of each in this case being completely understood. Their route through the city may vary, but in this way their patterns are automatic and in sync. Laura has her eye on a rather beautiful Provençal daybed, asks whether he thinks they can find a place for it at the lake house upstate. The frame, she points out, is exactly the right amount of worn.

"Mmm, maybe for one of the guest rooms?" he suggests. In the window's reflection, he sees movement, a figure with something in its hand. Turning, he sees that it's just a teenage girl carrying a skateboard.

"Hon?" Laura searches his face.

"What?"

"You seem distracted. And you were kind of preoccupied at the restaurant earlier."

"I'm fine." He smiles. "Just book stuff on my mind." He'd woken in the night thinking about Mahoney and his opaque "past is past"-type comment. Not that he didn't appreciate his friend's concern. Or expect him not to question the notion of Jonathan's wife coming back from the dead. It was half the reason he'd approached him in the first place. But replaying the words in his head at 3 a.m., it sounded like more than that. Almost as if Mahoney were warning him off.

Laura takes out her phone, trains it on the bed in the window, and snaps a photo. He'd performed a search on Maddie's mother, Joyce, last night as well. No surprise he found nothing. No photos, no Facebook, not even an obit in her local newspaper. Like Maddie's, the majority of Joyce's life was lived pre-internet. Which prompts the shameful thought that, if the tragedy had to happen at all, better that it should happen then—and not now. Nowadays, doubtless a million conspiracy theory websites would spring up, with timelines and diagrams that detailed exactly how the famous crime writer had murdered his wife.

"By the way," Laura says. "You were talking in your sleep again last night."

"Was I?"

"I had to wake you up. You don't remember?"

"No . . ." He'd barely slept, so is faintly surprised he'd even had time for a dream. "What was I saying?" he asks, as they continue walking. "Anything interesting?" Does he talk in his sleep a lot? he wonders. It's never been mentioned before.

Laura appears to hesitate for a moment.

"I couldn't tell," she says, eyes moving back to her phone.

The air feels warm, and Jonathan loosens his collar. They pass a poster advertising a movie playing the midnight slot at the Metrograph—*In Cold Blood*.

"You and me . . ." he says, pointing to the poster. "We saw that in Bryant Park."

Now it's Laura's turn to not remember.

"Bryant Park? Huh. Did we?"

"Come on . . ." he says. "Honestly?" What a total disaster it all was, but also how hysterical and funny. "We took vodka in a flask, and some lady had a fit and said you were only allowed to bring wine," he says. "Oh, and we forgot to bring food, so we were starving!"

Laura regards him with a weird, sidelong expression. "Forgot the food? That doesn't sound like me . . ."

"I'm pretty sure it was you," he says—then realizes that he's not sure at all. Jonathan, Maddie, Jay, Laura—their group right after college. *The Fearsome Foursome.* Laura brought the food, Jonathan brought the beer, and Jay and Maddie brought the party. It was only the two of them that day, he is certain of that much, but could it have been Maddie? Somehow, in the minute or two since the memory had come to him, it has become cloudy and indistinct, soiled in some intangible way. How was it possible for something which had once felt so significant to become so misremembered?

"Bryant Park," Laura is saying. "All those people with their blankets and their crappy wine."

Everyone was a snob about something. And he gets that slumming it in the sweltering heat with a festering lump of shitty brie and a bunch of strangers would never be Laura's idea of a good time. Her restaurant life is so full of people, of noise and clatter and chaos that, when she doesn't have to be there, all she wants is to kick back at home or grab a quiet dinner someplace. As an averagely social writer, chained to his desk most days, Jonathan would like to think he was the opposite. He's not, of course. Not anymore. The city still had so much to offer. And they both talked a good game. Making plans to check out this well-reviewed event, or that cool new gallery. Yet all they seem to do, he realizes, is work and plot to leave town.

"Hey," he says, "speaking of crappy wine, how about cutting through Chelsea Market? I've been meaning to check out the new tasting room at the Wine Vault."

Laura agrees, and though he pretends not to notice, as they continue on, she keeps stealing glances at him, as if trying to see what he's thinking. As a couple, they have pledged to share everything. There are supposed to be no secrets between them. And he wants to share everything with her, he really does. *Maddie or Laura?* The question nags at him. He had promised himself one whole day that wasn't focused on Maddie. On where and how—and *if*—she was. One single day to concentrate on his current relationship and all the errands that were piling up on his to-do list. And—*God help him*—on his damn manuscript. They cross 23rd into Chelsea. Ugly new high-rises stand shoulder to shoulder with older buildings. Laura mentions a meeting with her partners to discuss Samphire.

"If there's time, we should take a trip up Highway 1."

"What?" He must have zoned out for a moment. The effects of his recent insomnia.

"LA. When we're out there. We always planned to, didn't we?" Laura says. "We'll have a few months, so it should be doable." *A few months?* What is she talking about? In the past, Laura has maybe mentioned . . . *something* along these lines. But he doesn't recall agreeing to anything definite. There's his schedule to think about. And the godforsaken place itself, bursting at the seams with priced-out New Yorkers who never shut up about how fantastic it is. That wasn't even counting the prevalence of yoga as some kind of quasi religion.

"Let me double-check with Cindy," he says, but Laura's not letting it go.

"I thought we'd agreed it was doable, Jon. I mean, you can work from anywhere, can't you?"

"For a long weekend, sure. But I can't swing it full-time. You know that."

Rain has started coming down again and they continue on in silence. This is the extent of their adventures these days, he decides, as they enter Chelsea Market. He used to think nothing of heading out at midnight to catch a late movie at the Angelika. Or two in a row, sneaking into the second as the credits rolled up on the first. He hasn't set foot in the place for years—was it even still there? As a proud New Yorker, not knowing the answer makes him feel ashamed.

Maddie or Laura? Of the four friends, it was Maddie with whom he used to seek out new things, gobbling up films, concerts and happenings all over the city. How had they managed to do so much on so little? Was it simply that he was older now? Richer? Less easily impressed? Or was it a case of less imagination? Not that, *surely* . . . It's as if he's catching his last breaths in the city. As if this is his last chance. But for what? Laura goes off in search of their wine guy while he checks out the new tasting room, but his heart isn't in it. As they near the house, he suggests grabbing a burger at Corner Bistro. It may not be the best burger in the city these days, but the place has a certain old-school charm. Laura makes a face.

"Sorry, hon. I'm wiped. Is it OK if we just eat at home?"

"Sure. Totally fine."

"Go another night?"

"Sounds good. Whatever works."

". . . Tuesday?"

"It's a plan." Their script, he thinks. It never varies. As an adventure, Corner Bistro was fairly sedate and unambitious. The whole appeal lay in the spontaneity because, come Tuesday, as Laura must also realize, one or both of them will have settled upon some other excuse.

"I was planning to throw together a *pasta al limone*," Laura announces as they take the steps up to the house. "Don't worry." She grins. "You can thank me later."

What would *she* make of their perfectly renovated West Village home? he is thinking. *Die yuppie scum.* A quick glance up and down their street—what is he looking for?

"Sound good . . .?" Laura asks.

"Sounds brilliant," he replies. And feels, more than sees, Laura pause, for the briefest second—before turning the key and pushing open the front door.

"Home at last," she says, somewhat too cheerily, as they enter the familiar-smelling hallway.

Brilliant? he is thinking. *Brilliant* was one of *her* words. He hasn't used it in years.

Kiss

1997

"*Who?*" Joyce is yelling so loudly that he has to hold the phone away from his ear. He has not spoken to his mother-in-law since Christmas. And before that—to his shame—not since the week her daughter went missing. There had seemed little point, considering. On the other end, the lightbulb finally goes on.

"Oh!" Joyce says. "It's you." *At last.* He asks how she's been.

"Fair to middling. You know . . . muddling along."

"Glad to hear it." He commences to update her in the simplest terms possible. No news yet, he says, but they are not giving up.

He and Joyce have met exactly twice. Once when he and Maddie first flew over to see her, then again after Ben was born. Both times Joyce had paid for the tickets and, though Maddie had insisted this was no big deal, it had left him feeling quite inadequate. On the other end of the line, there is silence.

"Joyce?"

"That's fine. *I told you.*" And after another long gap: "When is she bringing my grandson to see me? Put my daughter on the line!"

"Joyce . . .? I'm sorry, Ben needs to be in school right now and—"

"*Who?*" she barks. "Who is this?" And with growing hostility, "Who the hell are you when you're at home?"

He's about to hang up when another voice comes on the line. "Sorry about that, dear. Are you Mrs. Morgan's son-in-law?" She tells him that she's Joyce's carer.

"I understand that they did tell her," she says. "At the time. When it happened." She lowers her voice. "But Mrs. M, she keeps forgetting, poor love. If she even knew in the first place. Can't keep it all in her brain, if you know what I mean. Anyway, they thought it best to stop telling her. It's not right, making them live through it again and again, is it? Best not upset them. That's what they recommend now."

A memory comes to him, of Joyce's town—the pastel-painted houses and narrow crooked streets leading down to the ocean, the shabby, peeling grandeur of the buildings that line the boardwalk. Like Maddie herself, they had appeared singular and beautiful. You could see the ocean from the top of every hill and, each time you caught a glimpse of it, the color seemed to have changed, from green to gray to blue, and back again. The whole place had felt magical.

"Right. Of course," he replies. *Early onset dementia*—the disease already making itself known that second time, as they sat around on lawn chairs in Joyce's pristine backyard, surrounded by neat flower beds.

"Give Granny a kiss," he had instructed Ben and, as his son dutifully waddled over, he had watched the smile freeze on Joyce's face, and seen her coldly disentangle the child's arms from around her waist. By the time they had left, she seemed to have trouble remembering Ben's name.

"It's how they get," the carer is saying. "Refuses to wear her 'hearing bits,' as she calls them."

"I completely understand," he says. "Look, could you just tell Joyce that her son-in-law called to say hello?"

"I'll try, but I can't promise she'll remember you the next time. It's in one ear and out the other these days. Strong as a horse physically, but with her mind, she's on a bit of a downward slope, is Mrs. M." Is he imagining it, the tinge of blame in her voice? As if somehow Jonathan has had a hand in her patient's abrupt decline. It must be lonely, spending your days with the elderly and the frail. "She does talk about her daughter. Your wife. *Maddie*, wasn't it . . .?"

Wasn't. Unreal, he thinks, even now. He's touched that this person should remember, but hearing her name said like that causes him actual physical pain.

"Oh, yes, she does talk about her," the carer muses. "From when she was a little girl. Has all her photos. Such a cute little thing, wasn't she . . .?"

In the end, it had been Laura, his organizing angel, who had pushed him to call Joyce when Maddie went missing. And Laura who, later, had gently suggested that it was OK to let go of her belongings. With Ben safely in kindergarten one day, Laura had arrived at 7th Street armed with boxes, garbage bags, and two industrial-size tape dispensers.

"She wouldn't want you to blame yourself," she had said as they went through the closet . . . the drawers . . . the storage boxes under the bed.

Wouldn't she? he had thought. Surprisingly, the task had come as a relief. Trying to carve out a life surrounded by his wife's possessions—her dresses and T-shirts, her beloved, beaten-up motorcycle boots—had not been easy. (Or, in Heather's new touchy-feely language, "not healthy.") Maddie's absence was always present, and some days—*God help him*—it had felt like living with her corpse. He had asked Laura's advice on which items should be shipped to Joyce in England. In the end, they'd mailed a photo of Maddie holding Ben on her lap, along with some chocolates of the sort Joyce (who had a sweet tooth and the British teeth you'd expect) was fond of. Did she ever receive the chocolates? Or had Nurse Ratched and her cohorts gotten to them first? Having walked the last of Maddie's belongings up to the Salvation Army, he'd felt unexpectedly lighter. Days later, he realized Laura must have included all of Maddie's notebooks in Joyce's package as well. He had come across them only recently, in an old shoebox on a high shelf in the closet. But with his chance finally here, he couldn't bring himself to look at them. Some day in the future, he had decided, if and when he felt ready. Maybe it was a kindness that Laura had done him, to put an ocean between himself and his wife's private thoughts. And, if and when he ever feels OK about himself, he'll pay Joyce a visit and see if he can retrieve them.

"She has all her things round her," the carer is saying. "All her photo albums and her little knickknacks. Doing quite well, considering. I mean, poor dear . . . Well, she doesn't even know what day it is . . ." As the carer chatters away, he imagines Joyce in her timeless world, and he envies her.

Niche

1997

The moment he arrives, Jonathan knows it's a mistake.

One of his bar regulars had suggested he stop by, promising "a literary crowd." Flattered, but apprehensive, he had managed to rope in Jay as support, but he canceled right as Jonathan was leaving. It had taken all his strength not to simply stay home. But he'd already arranged for Ben to sleep at Heather's, and besides, he'd told himself, he *ought* to go . . . ought to get out of the apartment and socialize with adults for a change. He had pictured a ragtag gathering of aspiring writers and struggling actors glugging down cheap wine in some apartment much like his own. As if that wasn't scary enough, he finds himself in the lobby of a large townhouse, where an immense Christmas tree stands like a tinseled sentry. Tinsel, baubles and—he sees now—*actual candles*. From somewhere overhead, some lavish upper reach of the house, wafts a hubbub of voices. Music is playing. A piano, and someone singing in a high, warbling voice. A friendly looking girl asks to check his coat and, feeling flustered, he manages to hand it over. He climbs the grand spiral staircase up to the second floor. Guests stand with glasses in their hands as waiters glide easily between them with trays of elaborate hors d'oeuvres. The women are dressed in colorful arty dresses, the men relaxed in open-necked shirts or WASP-y sweater-over-shirt ensembles. Fighting the urge to flee, Jonathan stashes his bottle of cheap wine behind a bust of Emily Dickinson and makes for a nearby drinks table.

As it turns out, everyone is pleasant and friendly, introducing themselves to anyone who, like himself, appears to be at the party alone. On the next floor up, guests smoke on a terrace that overlooks a beautiful community garden. After a brief conversation with a war correspondent from *The Times* in London, Jonathan finds himself talking to an elderly, twinkling Belgian dominatrix. Bizarrely nun-like in a gray pinafore dress, she informs him that Katharine Hepburn lived a few doors down and used to sit in the backyard to rehearse her lines.

Another floor up, a fire blazes in the grate and a small band plays 1920s jazz classics. Guests lounge on tasseled couches, listening with rapt attention. The singer is petite and dark with red lipstick. She reminds him of a little bird. A man playing the clarinet has hair that's parted to one side and flattened in an old-fashioned way. Faces from another age, he decides, musicians emerging out of a time warp to play for them for this one night only. He has been almost nowhere, and done nothing to write home about, but outside of books and Woody Allen movies, he had not thought such a world existed. He thinks of the plane tickets pressed masochistically between the pages of a dog-eared copy of *On the Road*. There had been no time to tell her about the best part. That you got to choose— which countries, which cities, and in which order. Around the world. Travel was her thing, and he had been so excited to let her plan their route.

Later, the doors to the kitchen are flung open and dinner is served from a large buffet. Salmon, strips of rare beef, and mushroom risotto, served by the ever-smiling staff. If only she could be here to appreciate it all with him. He takes his plate into the dining room and notices a woman smiling in his direction—office-smart in a navy-blue pant suit.

"Is this chair free?" he asks. She waves a hand covered in a number of large, shiny rings.

"Sit, sit . . ."

He does, and she slides a pack of cigarettes toward him across the table.

"Thank you, but I don't smoke," he says.

"Aren't you a barrel of fun," she says dryly. And after a pause, "Good networking, huh?"

"I suppose so. Everyone certainly seems very pleased with themselves," he adds cleverly—and instantly regrets it because this makes him sound bitter. This person would already have taken the measure of him. Noted his disheveled appearance, the stained black bartender's pants, shiny at the knees from too much washing. Analyzed his yellowing shirt, frayed at the cuffs, and not in any stylish way. Earlier, he'd been excited to recognize a famous author. Until the man beckoned him over and asked, with devastating politeness, whether Jonathan could bring him another gin and tonic. When the woman flings back her head and laughs throatily, he feels almost faint with gratitude.

"Ain't that the truth!" she guffaws, and introduces herself as Cindy.

"I'm Jon," he says. "*Jonathan.*"

Shaking cigarette ash onto the table, Cindy proceeds to regale him with tidbits about the other guests. "Let me tell you a little sumthin' sumthin' about that one . . ." she'll say in a low voice, jabbing her cigarette in their direction.

He's not sure whether to believe half of what she's saying. To him, the other guests seem to positively vibrate with charm. Everyone seems about to launch their first novel, their debut a thrilling success, their bestseller optioned by Hollywood, the movie up for seven Oscars . . . and that's not even taking into account the journalists from the *NYT*, the writers from *Vanity Fair*, the *Paris Review*, the academics and war correspondents and Pulitzer Prize winners, and people with weirdly unplaceable accents who did obscure but glamorous-sounding things at the UN.

"And her?" Cindy is saying. "*Sheesh* . . . Let me tell you a little somethin' about that one." This, he decides, is where the city has been hiding the *real* city. Its real self. The Manhattan he has always dreamed of.

"And what do *you* do with yourself?" says Cindy, who appears to have run out of gossip.

"This and that," he replies. It's his standard answer nowadays. One that saves everyone the embarrassment of the truth. That he is a twenty-seven-year-old widower, lone parent, and failed novelist, tending bar four nights a week, toiling over the same unpublishable novel, and too broke to drink himself to death.

"But you *are* a writer, correct?" she says, squinting at him. He stares. This has to be one of the best things anyone has ever said to him.

"Is it that obvious?" he replies in a way he hopes comes across as cool.

"And? What do you write?"

He explains as best he can.

"Ah . . ." She shakes her head. "The *L-word* . . ." He looks blankly at her. "*Literary* fiction, darling. Impossible to publish these days. You should find a genre. You know . . ." she continues. Her fingers make an impatient waggling motion. ". . . A *niche*."

"Yes, I know what a *niche* is," he replies shortly. All of a sudden he feels angry, conned into some game where he's made to feel gauche or ashamed of his efforts.

"Sure you do," Cindy replies smoothly. "But have you thought about it? You could write something more commercial—thriller, spies, crime—whatever floats your boat. Then later, if you still want, you can write your Great American Novel or whatnot." He thinks about the only actual thing he has written and not torn up, *The Insistence of Mist*, his would-be first novel. He has sent it to sixty-seven agents and received more than enough rejections to paper his tiny bathroom with. Cindy studies him over the rim of her dirty martini.

"I'd highly recommend that you consider it," she says. "If you're interested in paying the bills, that is."

He's heard versions of this advice before, discouraging words from well-meaning friends. None of whom is actually *in* the publishing industry, he reminds himself. And Cindy will be no exception. As she drains her glass, it is as if all his hopes and dreams are draining away with it. The contrast with the grandeur of the room—its polished crimson walls glimmering seductively in the candlelight, the fireplaces blazing in every room, the educated, jocular tones of the men, and the assured, tinkling laughs of the women—it's like a knife in the gut. He pushes the thought away, wonders how to extricate himself from this humiliating conversation before she does. How were you supposed to make your excuses at these ... *soirees*, without seeming rude or abrupt? What was the etiquette? As Cindy glances over his shoulder, he doesn't feel surprised or even offended. A waiter swoops in with a fresh martini.

"Thank you, sweets," she tells the guy, handing over her empty glass. Cindy, he realizes, had simply been looking out for her next drink.

"Are you married?" she asks, twirling her olive around the glass. He's not sure he wants to discuss his personal life with her. She's not unattractive, but she's older, late thirties, at least.

"Kind of," he replies. "I have a son, Ben." As a single dad, he'd discovered, you were treated like a hero. As a *widowed* dad, you were a hero's hero, practically a god.

"How wonderful!" She smiles encouragingly.

"He's amazing, actually," he says. "A really sweet kid. Super bright, you know? Only just turned five, but always has his nose in a book. His mother . . ." he begins, and wonders why he's about to offer this complete stranger his life story. Cindy waits, head on one side. "My wife," he explains, "she's not around."

Cindy doesn't seem like the kind of person who has time for people's problems. He should take this opportunity to present himself as someone other than the grieving husband. "My wife, she went missing, almost a year ago now," he tells her. He looks around for his wine glass, but it's gone.

"Missing . . . ?"

"Is still missing, I mean."

"How awful. I'm so sorry." And without missing a beat, "So what's the plan for you now?"

"The plan?"

"Your plan. For you," she replies. "And for your kid."

No one has properly asked this question. Not in so many words. Heather had gotten her way and organized a sparsely attended memorial (for that, undeniably, is what it was) in the orchard at her house upstate. Saul absented himself for most of it. Meanwhile, friends have taken a step back, as if they're embarrassed for him or he's carrying a contagious disease. *What's the plan for you now?* Maddie was his plan, and without her, he feels adrift. But as Cindy discards her olive into a nearby ashtray, he considers her question, perhaps for the first time.

"I guess my plan is for people to read my writing," he says. "And to make a living."

Cindy bends down, rummages in a large leather handbag, bulging with papers and magazines.

"Jonathan, right?" He nods. "I need to go circulate, but it was great meeting you. And, like I said, if you decide to work on something else . . ." She holds out a business card. "So long as it's not any of that tortured-artist stuff"—she gives a short laugh—"you be sure to give me a call, OK?" She stands, tosses the pack of cigarettes in her bag.

"I mean it," she adds. "You seem like a guy with a story to tell." He looks at the name on the card. *Cindy Straub. Literary Agent.*

"OK?" She is looking down at him, imposing in her black patent pumps.

"Yes," he answers, stunned. Who wouldn't know *that* name? An agent at her level, he'd never even considered sending her his work. "Yes, I will. Thanks. *Thank you so much.*"

A curt "Good luck to you" and she moves off in the direction of someone more successful. Not difficult in this crowd, he thinks. *Just throw a brick,* as his wife used to say. He listens to the general "mwah-mwah" sound of air kisses behind him, wishing he could have made a better impression on Cindy, instead of pouring out his entire sad life story. He likes her. She seems cool. In her shrewd, straight-shooting way, she reminds him of his sister—before Heather got so weird, that is. Cindy, he decides, seems like someone who makes things happen.

Back at the apartment, he looks over his novel—overwritten, weighed down with extended metaphors and elaborate sentences. Instead of staring at the TV, he sits down at the typewriter and inserts a clean sheet of paper. He works all night and by the next morning has the first fifty pages of *Dark Tide*. And with it, on paper at least, justice will be restored.

Judged

2019

The week that follows is muggy with perpetual rain. He stays home with the AC turned up and applies himself to his new book. Sunday night, he's in the kitchen watching Laura construct an elaborate cheeseboard. A new dessert wine has been added to the list at her restaurant, and he's been looking forward to sampling it. Though she claims it's perfectly safe to drink, he's somewhat less excited about the raw milk she acquired yesterday in some shady hookup involving an Amish guy in a truck. On the plus side, he'd scored some excellent Honey Crisp apples at the Greenmarket and Laura now slices them thinly, arranging them alongside some fresh figs. The cat watches, ears pricked. The apples are a favorite treat and, after first removing any seeds, he bends down and offers her a small sliver. Delicately, she takes it from his fingers and scampers off, as if afraid he'll change his mind. This never fails to break his heart. He and Laura are about to sit down with their calendars when the front door slams, startling them both. Footsteps descend the stairs, and Ben appears. He looks a bit taken aback to see them.

"Hey, buddy," Jonathan says, noting the collection of shopping bags that—he also can't help noticing—Ben carefully places on the floor outside, just out of view. "Been shopping?"

"I thought you guys were going out," Ben says.

"Schedule night." Jonathan gestures to the food on the counter. "You're welcome to join us." Ben frowns, looks down at his phone. Laura raises an eyebrow and opens up her planner.

"Stop touring," Cindy had warned early on, "and you'll sink like a shark." As his agent likely intended, the words had put the fear of God into him. But he and Laura have made a monthly ritual of it—working out the hows, wheres, and whens, in order to carve out time together. And bribing themselves with copious amounts of food and wine certainly helps. As Ben rifles noisily through the kitchen cabinets, Jonathan tries to focus on the task at hand. This week they are unexpectedly in sync. They'll be able to snag some quality time together, Laura says—maybe take in an off-Broadway show.

With Laura shuttling to and fro from the West Coast, plus his book signings and his upcoming spell in Europe, they won't see so much of each other in the next couple months. After that, of course, is the wedding. He tops off both their glasses and keeps half an eye on Ben.

"Fall's right around the corner," she goes on. "You know how that is for the restaurant." Jonathan begins to read out a bunch of cities—London, Rome, Copenhagen. Arrivals and departures, venues, and dates. Ben interrupts sharply.

"That's Mom's birthday," he says. "In case you guys forgot."

So it is . . . he thinks to himself. The last day any of them saw her alive.

"I haven't forgotten, Ben," Laura says. Ben glares at her. "And neither has your dad."

Again, that sense of being resented. Of being judged harshly by his son. People said birthdays were more difficult than the anniversary of a death, but in Maddie's case they were one and the same. Until the disconcerting events in the bookstore, this was the first year he hadn't found himself counting down the days. A healthy sign, his therapist would say. A sign of progress.

Ben yanks open the fridge, starts pulling out various containers. He and Laura resume going through their schedules. As the would-be step-parent, Laura is in an impossible position. A "hands-off" approach, and you are cold and uncaring. Anything more proactive and you are interfering, risking another "You're not my *mother!*" outburst, like the one they had recently over the date of the wedding. As Ben's father, he should say or do something—anything—in support of his significant other. But what? Allegedly, the key to good parenting was to make firm boundaries. And stick with them. This has never been his strong suit, though. As Laura has pointed out, he's more comfortable being "the good guy."

"Why is there never any food in this house?" mutters Ben, going into the pantry. As Laura gets up and goes to close the fridge door, Jonathan shakes his head at her, mouths "Leave it." Stuyvesant, followed by Harvard or Yale—that was the plan. But somewhere along the way, his ambitions for Ben had gone awry. His son never got the grades, and made it into a third-tier college by the skin of his teeth, only because Laura had practically filled out the application for him. After crashing about in the pantry for a few minutes, Ben comes back with an armful of packages—cans, tomatoes, a bag of dry pasta—and dumps them next to the stove.

"Ben?" Jonathan says to Ben's back as his son fills a saucepan with water. "Obviously, we'll all be acknowledging your mom's birthday. When haven't we?"

"Yeah?" Ben turns. "You won't even be here." He scowls, slamming the cutting board onto the counter. As he begins loudly chopping, the smell of garlic fills the air.

"No," Jonathan replies. "Not this year, that's true. And I'm sorry about that. That I have to work, I mean. And that I can't be here, just this one time. We'll all do something when I get back, OK?"

"Right," Ben says, "your *book tour*." Laura, who's quietly loading things into the dishwasher, lets out a sigh. Jonathan gets up, takes over her glass of wine.

"Everything all right?" he murmurs.

"Not exactly . . ." She pushes a piece of hair out of her face, nods toward Ben, now plucking items off the cheeseboard with manic abandon—grapes, cheese biscuits, apples—popping them into his mouth while scrolling through his phone. "You *have* to talk to him, Jon."

The other night, expecting a takeout delivery, Laura had asked Ben whether he'd happened to see the three fifty-dollar bills she'd left on the counter. It was a perfectly harmless inquiry, but his reaction had left all their nerves in shreds for days. At Laura's insistence, he'd waited until Ben was out and gone through his room. He'd been hoping to find nothing. Instead, at the back of the closet he'd found a padlocked gym bag that contained what felt an awful lot like cash—and plenty of it. What did it mean? Concern, inquiry, "checking in," a generous allowance—has he not done all the right things? He'd put everything back exactly as he found it, and said nothing, not even to Laura.

"So, Ben?" he asks, brightly. "What did you get up to today? Anything fun?" Ben shoots him a sideways look. Quick and furtive, like an animal.

"Nothing," he replies through a mouthful of white truffle Moliterno sheep's cheese, priced at one hundred dollars a pound. "Just class."

"And how's that going?" No response from Ben, who spits an olive pip into the dish and continues to lay waste to their supper.

Is it his own fault? Has he given his son too much leeway? *Not enough?* After his first book came out, their lives had become calmer, their days acquiring a routine. He'd never let himself forget that his child had lost his mother, obviously. But since Ben arrived two weeks ago he's been acting like an overgrown teenager. Now, before Jonathan can make a second failed attempt at small talk, Ben abruptly goes upstairs, taking his shopping bags with him. The kitchen is a mess of basil leaves and garlic; their decimated cheeseboard and a half-eaten bag of chips lie discarded on the counter. Ben's bedroom door slams. As the sound reverberates through the house, Jonathan lets out a breath. Another evening ruined.

"Seriously?" Laura says.

"You're right," he tells her, getting up before she can launch them into another conversation about boundaries. "I'll take care of it."

He knocks gently on Ben's door. No answer. Faint sounds of voices from inside. He steels himself and walks in. Ben lounges on the bed wearing an oversized pair of headphones. He looks only mildly surprised to see his father standing there, and immediately closes his laptop.

"I . . ." Jonathan begins. "*Laura* and I have made a very disturbing discovery. I'm sure you know what I'm referring to and . . ." Ben looks back at him, wide-eyed. The contrast between this and the hostile Ben of five minutes ago is bizarre and disturbing. "We'd like to know what you have to say about it," he says.

"Dad, sorry but I don't know what you're talking about."

He nods toward the closet. "Do you need me to show you?"

A momentary flash of anger crosses Ben's face. Or did he imagine it? It was almost undetectable. A second later Ben has checked himself, returns to the same easy, conversational tone.

"You mean that money Laura said she lost? Dad, I told her, I didn't even see it." *Mr. Reasonable.* The shopping bags sit next to the bed, brands he doesn't recognize, but clearly expensive. *Supreme,* says one. *Off-White,* says another—whatever the hell that's all about.

"And *these?*" he says, pointing at them. "Where does all this come from?"

"They're, like, clothes?" Ben replies, as if his father is out of touch and irrelevant. *Uptalk,* he thinks to himself—ironic, because in his rare text messages, Ben seems incapable of using question marks when they were actually required. "They're my roommate's," Ben continues breezily. "His dad gave him a bunch of money for his birthday and his mom's kind of a bitch about that stuff, so, like, I'm looking after them for him. I'm pretty sure I told you."

Pretty sure you didn't. Nothing about this story holds up or makes any sense. Like so many of his son's excuses, it feels rehearsed. Veering close to the truth, without actually being true.

"Uh-huh," Jonathan says. *Give 'em enough rope*—Detective Connor's favorite technique. Let Ben incriminate himself. Let him fill the silence with his implausible excuses. If there was one thing he'd learned in therapy, it was that at some point you have to stop blaming your parents for everything. You have to take responsibility for your own actions.

But Ben just gazes steadily back at him. They appear to be in some kind of stand-off. Jonathan walks over to the closet, opens the door. Coat hangers, the usual tangle of clothes and magazines strewn across the floor, countless pairs of sneakers. Caleffi, he thinks, would choose this moment to start yanking open drawers, tossing their contents out onto the floor. Socks, underwear, T-shirts.

"Where is it?" Jonathan says, trying to stay calm. "The *bag*. Does that belong to your roommate as well?"

"My school bag?"

"Whichever one has all the money in it. It's a simple question, Ben."

"The one I use to carry my textbooks? It's in my locker, at school." And in a sulky tone: "I don't know what you want from me. You and Laura, you always act like I'm up to something."

An image comes into Jonathan's mind, superimposed over the one in front of him. A small boy, curled up in his pajamas in the bedroom on 7th Street, surrounded by his small collection of stuffed animals. He's too young to read, but the first *Harry Potter* book lies on the bed beside him. The current Ben hasn't opened a book in years. The toys are different, too—shoes, electronics, magazines, clothes. In attempting to fill the shoes of both parents, has Jonathan only succeeded in spoiling him? Or did the problem take root even earlier, when Maddie was still alive, and they were one big, unhappy family? Ben has stopped talking. Is staring at his father with the same blameless look on his face.

"Ben, you promised to find a job," he says. "Like we all agreed."

"Dad, I've been looking, I *swear*. I sent my résumé to a bunch of places last week."

"Right. That's my point. *You have no job,* but apparently you have thousands of dollars lying around in the closet. Not to mention the rest of it," he adds, letting the implications sit between them. Of course, he can't be certain the bag did contain money. But he has a pretty good idea. Now, tellingly, Ben is silent. "Ben, this is your chance. Come clean, and I promise, we'll figure it out together, as a family," he prompts. "Laura is *not* happy about all this. I mean, for goodness' sake, I'm trying to protect you here!"

Whatever would Mahoney make of this amateur interrogation? It's supposed to come across as some kind of implicit warning. Instead, it sounds like Caleffi and Connor doing one of their good-cop, bad-cop routines. As for consigning Laura to the latter role in this scenario, what choice does he have? She's the one making him force the issue. Ben gazes up at him with a wounded expression.

"Dad, I don't know what you thought you saw, but I haven't done anything wrong," he says. *Deny, deny, deny.* Your children are meant to be a source of pride, aren't they? Of joy, not shame.

At the periphery of his vision, in the street below, something moves. He goes over to the window to get a closer look. Nothing. The street is empty. A change in the light. A random shadow, he decides as a weird chill flitters upward from the base of his spine.

"Dad . . .?" Ben looks bemused. "What is it?"

"What? Nothing. I . . . I thought . . ." Probably just coming down with something, he decides. Best take some vitamin C and get an early night.

"This . . . and the rest of it . . . the *money* . . . it's . . ." Jonathan turns back to his son, but can't remember what point he was about to make.

"Dad? Are you OK . . .?"

All of a sudden, he feels so exhausted by the conversation, and so distracted by everything else, that all he can feel is annoyance at Laura. Would it hurt her, he thinks, to give his son the benefit of the doubt for once? She wants him to read Ben the Riot Act, but then what? What is he expected to actually *do* about the problem? Call the cops? Easy for her to say. Once you got into it with someone, there was always the risk one of you would say—or do—something that could never be taken back. Once you started, in other words, it was not so easy to stop. Ben appears to be waiting for him to say something.

"Get a job," Jonathan says. "Hold up your end of the bargain."

"I promise, Dad," Ben replies solemnly.

"Make sure that you do," he snaps. *Idiot. I sound like a fucking idiot.*

He leaves the door slightly ajar—*it's my house, isn't it?* The kid isn't stupid. Scratch that. He's not even a kid. Ben may be blatant and brazen and a million other unsavory adjectives that, as a parent, Jonathan doesn't care to dwell on. But is he guilty? He goes into the bedroom, sits down for a moment to calm himself. *Loser.* His own son is taunting him. Daring him to say something. As if he knows his father doesn't have the guts to challenge him.

Slum

2000

"All set?"

It's an order, not a question and, as is her habit when she calls, Cindy doesn't bother to introduce herself.

"Yes, ma'am," he says into the phone. His agent can be kind of intimidating, but she "love, love, loves" his book, and he knows the drill. For tomorrow's launch of *Dark Tide,* she says, Jonathan is to read out no more than three *short* extracts from his book and do a *brief* Q and A.

"Give 'em too much," she warns, "and you'll look desperate."

"Do you want to be one of those losers with an unfinished novel in the back of a drawer?" Cindy had said when they first met. Or rather, that's what he had taken from the conversation. Early on, he'd understood that being published, amazing and unbelievable as it was, came with certain responsibilities. Public speaking was one of the most daunting, though for some reason, it is also the one he's most looking forward to. Still, more than once since signing with Cindy, he has had to remind her that his wife's disappearance was barely four years ago. That the loss is still extremely raw and that he can't see a day when he'll be ready to discuss any of it in public. Meanwhile, after years of toiling alone, he has had the utterly new experience of a whole team of people seemingly

captivated by his work, with nothing but flattering things to say about it. Cindy asks what he's planning on wearing.

"Maybe . . . a blazer?" he ventures. "And some khakis?" On the other end of the phone there's a more or less approving grunt. "I hope I can meet all of their expectations."

"Just make them like you," she snaps, before hanging up.

He wanders into the kitchen to marvel once more at his new espresso machine and gaze into his fully stocked fridge. Incongruous sights in his tiny kitchen, with its peeling paint and scratched Formica surfaces. He experiences the familiar pang of sadness: that his wife can't be here to witness any of it. And again, that sense of being an impostor. The nagging suspicion that he doesn't deserve any of it and that, sooner or later, someone will call him out as the fraud he surely is. The hefty advance is more than his father made in ten whole years, and there are days when he wonders if the whole thing isn't some elaborate joke.

He measures out a small cup of espresso beans, pours them carefully into the grinder, and ponders Cindy's parting advice—not "Be yourself," but "Just make them like you." It is all a little terrifying. With Ben in school, there is the unexpected luxury of deciding how to spend his day. On a whim he tips the beans back into the bag and decides to go get coffee out instead. Why not? He can allow himself this one little treat. Scooping up his backpack from the chair, he plucks a notebook from his brand-new stack of them and, from the collection he keeps ready on the desk, a fresh black Sharpie. At the last minute, he decides to bring his Filofax—a very fancy version in brown pebbled leather—and is out the door. Jay laughs every time he catches sight of it. "Woah! Put that thing away!" Maybe it is a bit old-fashioned, Jonathan will admit, but he's always wanted one. He heads down toward Soho with some notion of taking himself for coffee—and lunch—at

Jerry's. There's nothing better than sitting in one of the booths with an extra helping of fries. Except—he remembers now—his new personal trainer has told him that he needs to lose thirty pounds. If there's time, though, he might treat himself to a popcorn-less movie, or even a massage.

Cindy has suggested a name change, to *John Dane*, which she has declared "more manly." He wasn't sure how to feel about that. "Dane" will take some getting used to. Also, as a freshman in college, he'd started calling himself "Jon," because it sounded cooler without the "h." But he hadn't dared argue with her.

On Broadway, he drops into a Starbucks and spends a contented few hours practicing his new John Dane signature and, though he's no idea what anyone will ask, rehearsing his answers for the Q and A. Cindy already has him working on a sequel.

"What's the sequel about?" she'd asked after he handed in his first book. A sequel?

"How many mysterious murders can there be in one town?" he'd joked.

"You're kidding me, right?" Cindy shot back.

Two weeks later, he'd managed to submit an extremely rough outline for *Kill Her with Kindness,* the continuing story of his two crime-busting cops and their quest to rid Ocean Falls of all its murderers, drug dealers, and lone drifters bent on making mayhem.

He heads back to the apartment, stops by the local deli to pick up some milk, and gets stuck in line behind a couple of international students. The guy leans into the girl, mutters something.

"Well, how would I bloody know?" she replies.

As her clear English accent seems to reverberate around the store, a sick dread crawls over Jonathan and he drops the milk on the counter and runs outside. He leans panting against the wall. The eyes of passersby settle curiously on him for a moment, then look away. *Pathetic.* What the hell was he running from? *Success,* according to his new therapist. They have yet to delve fully into his wife's disappearance, but he has told her about the anxiety attacks. Mopping his brow with the sleeve of his jacket, he continues home, milk-less.

At the door to his building, he takes out his key and performs the usual mime of pretending to unlock it. He's given up trying to get the landlord to make any repairs. Cindy has already threatened him with her real-estate broker, and if she could only see him now, Jonathan thinks, she'd absolutely die. Unsurprisingly, there's another envelope from her in the mailbox. Another single photocopied sheet.

FOR SALE. Rare opportunity! Historic townhouse est. 1869 located on a picturesque block between Bleecker and West 4th Street. Four bedrooms, three-and-a-half bathrooms, five fireplaces, fully refurbished kitchen on garden level, French doors, HUGE landscaped backyard, very private. Four-story family residence featuring all original architecture.

Scrawled across the top in Cindy's signature red ink: *"MOVE OUT OF THAT SLUM ALREADY!!!!"* These exhortations are averaging about two a week at this point. His living situation isn't ideal, he'd admitted, but one book didn't mean he could go on some gigantic spending binge. What if his book didn't sell? What if he never finished the second one? What if he got writer's block?

"What if, what if . . ." Cindy had mocked, waving her hands, puffing out her cheeks. "Gimme a break. You got a three-book deal. You're rich and successful. Now act like it."

At long last he'd given in his notice at the restaurant. Each night, once Ben is asleep, he puts in a few more hours at the typewriter. He's been meaning to buy a computer, but for now, this seems good enough. He's about to get in the shower when Laura calls to wish him good luck on tomorrow's launch.

"You've come a long way," she says. "I'm so proud of you." It's true. Writing has given him his life back. This time last year, Laura would regularly have to come get him after he'd passed out at the local bar, where they had her number on speed dial. After he showed up drunk and puked in the lobby of her building, Laura had mopped him down with a "Hon . . . It's OK . . . It's not your fault." Like Matt Mahoney, she has been a real support. He offers his congratulations on her own good news, a glowing restaurant review in this week's *New York Times*. Like him, Laura is finally coming into her own. Her restaurant, C-Salt, has opened right around the corner on Avenue C, with two partners and a bunch of investors behind it, including Jay. People are literally lining up to throw money at it, and he couldn't be more delighted for her.

"Cindy permitting," he says, "I'll try and come by after the launch tomorrow."

"How is Cindy?" Laura asks. "Behaving herself?" It was Laura who'd said it wouldn't be long before someone of Cindy's caliber recognized his talent.

"Same as ever." He laughs and adds that she's still bugging him about moving.

"Uh-huh." There's a short silence.

"What do you think . . .?" he says. Another gap, in which he senses Laura weighing up how to respond.

"Jon, *you know* that I am so, *so* thrilled for you . . ." she begins.

"Thank you, but I hear a 'but' . . ."

"And that you deserve all your success."

"Yeees . . ."

"But it's not helping you, still living there."

"I know . . ." Is it, he wonders, some masochistic desire to punish himself? To force himself to continue living in the same home that he and his small family had once shared? It was interesting, his therapist had observed, that he spent as much time as possible out of the apartment, writing longhand in coffee shops. He shares this with Laura, who asks how he's finding therapy.

"I'm not a total convert," he tells her. "*Yet.*" Insane as it would sound to anyone who truly understood his situation, he thinks, the sessions do leave him feeling like a less terrible person afterward.

"It feels a bit self-indulgent, going on and on about yourself," he confesses. "But I kind of like it. Does that make me a terrible person?"

"Hmm . . ." Laura replies teasingly. "What do *you* think? What does *terrible* mean to you?"

He laughs. Laura seems to have a knack for injecting light-heartedness into a situation, of bringing him back to reality in the gentlest possible way.

"Seriously, Jon," she says, "you can always talk to me. You can trust me with anything, you know that, right?"

"Don't worry," he assures her. "In six months, I'll either be broke or cured." They chat for a few more minutes, agree to meet Saturday at their usual time to shop at the Greenmarket.

"By the way," Laura says, "there's a photography show up at the Schomburg Center. I've been meaning to check it out all year. 'The Gaze Shifted,' everyone says it's really wonderful."

"I was thinking about seeing that as well," he says, though in truth, he's never heard of it. There's an awkward pause.

"So, would you be interested in going to see it with me . . .?" Laura says finally.

"Sorry, yes. *Absolutely*," he replies, not quite sure what he's agreed to. "It's a plan!"

Scrabble

2019

"How can you be a writer and not love Scrabble?" His sister appears almost offended.

In the end, she bribes him with a large glass of rosé and they sit outside on the deck, arranging their plastic letters on wooden racks. After a morning spent at various farm stands (trout for himself, grass-fed beef for everyone else), Laura is inside, with Saul pressed into service as reluctant sous chef. The Catskills are a faint, blueish-purple tinge in the background, and the afternoon feels lazy and bucolic. Sighing, Jonathan arranges his letters into some kind of half-hearted order. Heather consults her phone.

"Ugh, can you believe it? Ninety-seven in the city today." Their group has spent the morning gleefully exclaiming about the heat index back in the city, agreeing that it's not the heat but the humidity, and so forth. What with climate change, Saul had assured them over breakfast, being able to escape the sticky hell that was the city in July was "hardly a luxury anymore."

"On the contrary," he'd gone on, gesturing toward the flung-open windows, "it's environmentally responsible." Annoyingly, Jonathan tells himself the same thing. The lake house is an absolute hideaway that neither he nor Laura can imagine doing without.

"Your turn," Heather says impatiently. He has the letters to form the word *soggy*. Not a *terrible* score. Not a great one either. He places them on the board. Another insult, apparently.

"Is that it?" she says. He shrugs. "Ten points? That's your best effort?" He raises an eyebrow.

"Chess?" he offers.

"Yeah, right . . ." Heather scoffs. "Like you even know how to play chess."

Jonathan takes a sip of his rosé, watches Jay down by the pool, tinkering with the barbecue. *A place in the country.* Years ago, after *Dark Tide* took up permanent residence on the *New York Times* bestseller list, suddenly there was money to burn. He'd asked Laura whether she'd mind driving up with him to take a look at the place. A modernist structure with interiors that were spacious and spare, he liked the contrast with Heather and Saul's stuffy-feeling second home.

When the broker had left them alone for a half hour "to take a look around," Laura had wondered aloud whether the guy thought they were a couple. They had taken a walk into the woods and come upon an ice-covered pond. She had pointed out a large boulder and, before he could stop her, had lifted the thing, staggered toward the edge, and heaved it a good way out onto the ice. He was astonished. It was almost bigger than she was. In the late-afternoon woods, the sound as it hit the surface was as sharp as a gunshot, the cracks spreading rapidly outward.

He watches Heather slowly moving her letters around. "I can see what you're doing," he tells her, as another thought—unexpected, inevitable—drops on him from nowhere: that there is something hollow or deeply predictable about the scene. The middle-aged siblings tamely playing Scrabble. The spouses dutifully chopping. The obligatory best friend tending the grill.

"You're cheating!" Heather says.

"You wish," he replies.

With the exception of Saul, they all look pretty good for their age. Laura does Pilates and hot yoga, and worries about her hips. Jonathan trains hard at the gym and worries less about his weight these days than his schedule. All are fulfilled in their chosen careers. All able to travel where and when and how they want, to eat and drink the best of everything. They enjoy the privileges that—as Heather loves to point out—they have "worked their asses off" to earn. Now, his sister narrows her eyes, switches out her letters for a new set. A movement catches his eye, out past the boundary of the property, just inside the tree line. Squinting, he tries to see past the sun's glare.

"You're cheating again!" Heather protests.

Whatever it is, it is too far away and was moving too fast. A local hunter, he decides, barely discernible against the dappled green canopy. A shadow steps into the light.

"Wow, you guys really killed that wine!" He looks up to see Laura holding out a bottle of IPA.

Smiling, he reaches up to take it from her. "Thanks. I was just about to get my butt kicked," he says.

Heather, he sees now, has managed to leave the table without him noticing, and now stands down by the barbecue, chatting with Jay. "How's the prep going?"

"Pretty good. Saul hasn't complained in at least ten minutes." Laura perches on the edge of the table, cocks her head to one side. "You doing all right? You looked miles away."

"Just figuring out this gig later."

"It's the local bookstore, right?"

"Exactly. Country bumpkins."

"That's not what I meant."

"Whatever, I guess I'm just not feeling in the mood."

Show up, smile, ten-minute Q and A, sign a few books. *Done.* He could do it with his eyes closed. Laura appears to study him for a moment, as if considering her next words.

"OK, big shot." She consults her watch. "I should go check on my sous chef. Lunch is up in forty." *Bumpkins*—was that her problem? For goodness' sake, it's a harmless joke. If Saul has accused him of being a snob, Laura has always defended him.

"Oh, and Jon?" She turns back. "I brought your jacket up. It's in the bedroom, if you want to try it on for size."

"*Yes*, ma'am," he promises. "Right after lunch. *Absolutely.*"

He takes a slug from the bottle. The beer is satisfyingly cold, provides a pleasant jolt. He glances over toward the tree line, and only then remembers that it isn't hunting season for a few weeks yet. Which didn't mean it wasn't a deer. It wasn't as if the creatures were like themselves, migrating en masse someplace else for the summer. After all, what else could it be?

"Twenty-four hours, eight waterproof matches and one Pot Noodle!"

Saul, who has apparently escaped from the kitchen and is down by the barbecue, loudly recounting his latest "wilderness adventure" to Heather and Jay.

Twice a year, his brother-in-law takes himself off for what he calls a "solo"—hypothetically, a solo retreat in the middle of nowhere. *Hypothetically*, since this "wilderness" happens to be located in the woods a perfectly pleasant and leafy fifteen-minute stroll from Heather and Saul's country house. Jonathan knows exactly where it is and it is literally in their own backyard. It's hysterical.

"Wait, that's where, exactly?" Jay inquires, and Saul switches the topic to the nearby Zen monastery, which holds public meditation sessions.

"You should give it a try," Saul says. "It helps calm the 'pain body.'" Maybe he's right.

After lunch and a short nap in the hammock, Jonathan goes up to the bedroom and finds the jacket hanging on the closet door. Sweaty from his afternoon in the sun, he holds it away from his torso. The arms have been altered to the correct length, but the midsection appears too narrow. Whatever, there's no need to put the thing on to see that it doesn't fit. He stands sideways to the mirror, lifts his T-shirt, sucks in his stomach, lets it out again, sucks it in . . .

"*Jon, car's here!*" Laura, calling him from downstairs. Really, he decides, she simply can't expect him to figure this out now when he has a gig to get to and hasn't even showered or decided what to wear. He replaces the jacket on the door. He'll take care of it later. And Laura will just have to understand for once, won't she?

Menace

2019

Paranoid? Or perceptive? An old conundrum, and one that right about now Jonathan could use the answer to.

Baseball cap pulled low over the brow, eyes a bar of darkness; the man is moving steadily closer. It was the jacket that first caught Jonathan's attention, the type worn by hunters and amateur snipers—khaki, with a bunch of pockets. One of which, he sees now, bulges disturbingly. Isn't that where they keep all their knives and their ... *ammo*? A pleasant, fifty-something woman in a long purple skirt approaches the table, but all he can see is his would-be assassin, seven places away. He knows better than to pay the man any obvious attention. His publicist couldn't be bothered making the schlep up from Brooklyn, but she's supposed to handle this stuff. Positioned somewhere behind his left shoulder, unobtrusive yet obvious, ready to fend off any weirdos or lingerers. Even in an out-of-the-way venue like this one. *Especially* here, it occurs to him now, recalling the shadowy figure in the woods behind the house. He is acutely aware of his own fear, attempts to calmly acknowledge it, as per his therapist, and let it wash over him. But it's too late for that. The next person steps up, introduces her grandson, a small boy with a mop of blond hair, and plunks down five identical copies of his latest book, all brand new. Is she planning to sell them?

"The family are all big fans," she explains. "I'd love if you could sign all of them. Just your name, though," she adds. "No personal message." *Definitely selling.* Normally this would irk him, but tonight, with one eye on the khaki-jacketed stranger, he produces a fresh Sharpie and takes his time working through the pile.

The woman gathers up her signed books and is replaced by two students. Khaki-vest Man moves one step closer. "Lotta crazies out there," had been Mahoney's view on the strange, badly spelled letters that were sent to one of the newspapers shortly after Maddie's disappearance. (He'd often wondered whether Ragione was behind them.) "Always some joker ready to crawl out of the woodwork," was the cop's verdict.

Jonathan's story had been in and out of the newspapers— *and that's a good thing, right? Jog some memories. Make people think.* He'd appeared on prime-time local news, plastered in thick orange pancake makeup, and given "tips" on how to look like the grieving husband. It was insulting. For the first minute, he'd felt numb and dry-eyed. They'd made him do it a second time. By the third take, appealing—*begging*—Maddie to get in touch, he had found himself breaking down. Watching at home later, he discovered that they'd kept the cameras rolling the whole time. Still, memories were short, and the news caravan had moved on. No crazy person had shown up, no one ranting and raving or waving a hunting knife—*until tonight.* And tonight, he is on his own.

One of the students wants him to sign the book to his mom. Jonathan stalls for time, asks how to spell her name, inscribes it slowly and deliberately, keeping Khaki-vest Man and any sudden movements firmly in his peripheral vision. His heart is pumping almost out of his chest . . . *Can no one else hear it?* Sweat trickles down his back, begins to soak through his shirt. What can he do? *How will he get away?*

He signs books for two women in diaphanous flowery shirts—"We didn't like it as much as the others"—and one for a man in a loud Hawaiian-print shirt—"Gee, you're awfully short in person." Khaki-vest Man moves one place closer. A bespectacled girl offers him a copy of *Tick Tock Kill* and, glancing up, he sees—*how has it happened?*—that the man is right there, the very next person in line. The eyes are visible, darting and small under the stained rim of the cap. One meaty hand fingers the . . . whatever it is—a brick? A knife? A *gun?*— concealed in the bulging khaki pocket. Other pockets will hold different horrors. Hand grenades don't take up much room, do they?

As the bespectacled girl smiles, the waves of menace coming off the guy are palpable. *Does no one else see what's going on?* He tries to see past the man's head, to an exit, to the stockroom— anywhere. Sweat cascades down his back. The instinct to rise from the table is unbearable. How far would he get? The top of the stairs? The cookery section? He is a sitting duck. As the girl snatches the book out of his hand—"Awesome! Thanks!"— and moves off toward a group of friends, he is gripped by the urge to call her back—"*Don't leave me!*"

Too late. The man is coming right at him, his body an immense shadow, filling Jonathan's vision, looming over him. For a moment everything seems to move in slow motion as, reaching into the largest pocket, the man thrusts an object at his chest . . .

"Could you sign it," he whispers, "to Tommy, my cat?"

Jonathan, who has so far managed to avoid making any eye contact, registers the cover of his latest book, and looks up in astonishment. Its owner is blushing bright red.

"My cat . . .?" he says uncertainly, looking down at his shoes. "Tommy . . .? Is that OK?"

Jonathan, who wants to weep with gratitude, flashes his biggest, warmest smile. "Sure!" he says. "You bet!" The man beams, the relief in his face surely mirrors his own.

"Tommy's a big fan of the TV show as well," he goes on. "He can't get enough of Danielle and Jim on Thursday nights. Sits right in front of the screen. Won't even come for his dinner . . ."

Jonathan's body is coursing with adrenaline, and he finds himself babbling gratefully at the khaki-coated stranger—"I love it, that's hilarious!"—who, beneath the vest, has on a cheap-looking black polyester button-up and a heartbreaking little bow tie in some indiscriminate polka dot pattern. "That's really great to hear!" he says. "And that's . . . T-O-M-M-Y, right? What a great name for a cat! And what's your name again? *Sam?!*" he continues manically. "Wow. *Great* name! Superb choice. I love that name. A real classic . . ."

"We follow you on Facebook . . ." Sam tells him, clearly overwhelmed by this show of enthusiasm.

"The more the merrier, that's what I say!" Jonathan trills meaninglessly. Sam can't believe his luck. He looks ready to bust a gut with happiness.

For Tommy, he writes, grinning up at Sam, both of them dizzy with gratitude, as with an extra flourish he adds an unprecedented, *XOX.*

Chill

2019

Jonathan finds them all in the den. Jay is emptying a family-sized bag of chips into a bowl. Heather and Laura are curled under blankets on the couch. Saul—typically—has installed himself in Jonathan's favorite armchair.

"Hey, how was your thing?" Jay asks as Jonathan places his bag on the floor. It's late. *The Big Chill* plays on the TV, a depressing movie from the eighties whose appeal is lost on him.

"It was fine," he replies. Even before the false alarm of the khaki-vested stranger, a strange atmosphere had prevailed at the event—bored, restive, hard to put a finger on. During the Q and A, someone had asked where he got his ideas.

"Inspiration can strike at any time," he had answered. "Overhearing a snatch of conversation on the crosstown bus, while doing laundry, or even cleaning out the cat's litter tray," he'd added—a line that was guaranteed to get a laugh. A scruffy young man in the front row had immediately raised his hand.

"Do you actually even do your own laundry, though?" he'd drawled with an air of false innocence as several audience members tittered.

On the TV, a tense scene plays out in the kitchen. Jonathan gets a glass of water, sits down in the only vacant chair, and attempts to let go of his irritation. The habitual drone of Saul's unasked-for running commentary isn't helping. Kevin Costner played the dead friend, Saul informs them, as he never fails to, practically levitating with smugness. But his footage ended up on the cutting room floor, he goes on, which is why you never see him.

"Oh yeah? Never heard that before," Jay offers sarcastically, shoving a handful of chips into his mouth.

The room stinks of weed. Being "out in the boonies" makes Jay antsy, Jonathan remembers, and when he does show, he seems to take particular delight in getting everyone high as kites. In Saul's case, this makes him even more insufferable than usual, though admittedly this is quite an achievement.

Laura asks whether Jonathan's hungry and he tells her he's lost his appetite. Jay reaches over and offers him a drag off the pipe.

"Take the edge off."

"No, thank you. I'm going to bed," he says, standing up.

"OK, babe." Laura smiles over at him. "Get some rest."

"Yeah, *lighten up*," Jay calls as Jonathan goes upstairs.

He changes into a pair of old sweats and goes to brush his teeth. From the den downstairs, a volley of gunfire goes up, followed by loud giggling from Jay, who will no doubt have persuaded the others to switch out *The Big Chill* for something dumb and violent. A noise comes from outside and, startled, he looks up to see Laura standing in the doorway, the pipe in her hand.

"Sorry, didn't mean to scare you. How's it going in here?"

"Fine," he replies, putting his toothbrush away. There's a pause, as if he's supposed to elaborate in some way. As he goes back into the bedroom, Laura follows, sits on the bed.

"So, what happened earlier?"

"With the event? Oh, you know . . . *mobbed*." A thin smile from Laura, who doesn't laugh. "You know, *the usual*," he adds, in case she missed their joke. *Nothing*. Again, that sense of a tense, faintly chilly atmosphere. As if they're stepping carefully around one another.

"And you're doing OK . . .?" she says.

"Yes, why wouldn't I be?" *Let me count the ways . . .*

"You seem kind of tense. And you looked really pissed when you got in just now. You barely said hello."

He shrugs. What to say? The events of this evening aside, life no longer feels normal. Hasn't since the day he sighted his allegedly dead wife in their local Barnes & Noble.

"Did something happen?" Laura asks, taking a small puff from the pipe.

"Aside from Jay being a total dick?" The perpetual note of concern in her voice is beginning to get on his nerves. "If you must know, tonight was kind of a tough gig."

"Oh?"

"Not worth going into."

"O-K . . . Well, I'm sorry to hear that. I mean . . ." Another toke from the pipe. Eyes closed, pipe in midair, her voice trailing off, as if choosing her next words. ". . . That's too bad."

He has never liked it when Laura smokes. How it transforms her into some laid-back, hippy-chick version of the eminently practical and reassuring Laura he signed up for. He dislikes it. Dislikes *her*, he realizes, when she's like this. He opens his laptop.

"I'm sure you're right," he says. Can't she just leave him alone? As she regards him in some coolly appraising manner, it strikes him that the drug also makes her tough to read.

"Help you relax?" she says, holding out the pipe, and against his better judgment he finds himself taking it. He draws the smoke into his lungs. Manages to hold it there for only a second or two before being overcome by a fit of coughing.

"Lightweight," she laughs. "You sure you won't come downstairs? We're watching *Tropic Thunder*. It's super funny, actually."

He catches her glancing briefly at the jacket, a dark shadow looming, suspended in the corner from its hook. Has it finally dawned on her that the thing will now reek of weed? Getting up, he takes the jacket into the bathroom and, aware of Laura's eyes on him, makes a big deal of hanging it from the shower rail.

"Thanks, but I need to get some work done," he says, closing the bathroom door behind him. After Laura goes back downstairs, he tries to write out a few ideas, but his concentration is shot. *Maddie* . . . In his mind's eye, the letters of her name seem to sprout leaves, flower buds pulsing and turning, like a fast-motion sequence in a nature film.

Giving up, he gets into bed and turns off the light. After a few minutes of trying to get comfortable, he is just reaching for his glass of water when he notices that the door to the bathroom is open. Wasn't it closed? Didn't he close it himself? He distinctly remembers doing it. Right at the top of the house, their bedroom has always felt like an aerie, safe and perfect for sleeping. Except, something about the open door . . . the gap in the darkness, is making him feel deeply uneasy. All he needs to do is get out of bed, walk across the room, and close the damn thing. *Simple*.

He tries to distract himself with other thoughts. A documentary about a tribe located somewhere in Africa. Children who dreamed of tigers, who were taught to conquer the fear within the dream itself. *Tigers? Africa?* That doesn't sound right.

Allowing himself another furtive glance toward the bathroom, he is aghast to see that, in the half-minute since he last checked, a tall oblong of darkness has appeared in the space between the door's edge and the wall. Just a shadow from outside, he thinks desperately. Car headlights casting random shapes. Tree branches. Except the blinds are down, and out here there are no cars nearby or lights of any kind. He watches, transfixed, as the oblong appears to shift and coalesce into something solid and three-dimensional as, from the bathroom itself, a steady drip-drip of water starts up. Moaning, he curls his knees up and hugs the pillow to his chest. Which of therapy's stupid tools can possibly help him as he cowers here in his own bed? Fearful, helpless—he *hates* that he feels this way. The patch of dark is no longer an absence, but threatens to become an actual *thing*. A tall, vaguely person-shaped thing. Frozen in fear, he watches as it appears to detach itself and move toward him. He attempts to construct a "logic tower" in his mind. Apparently, it is made of matchsticks. Down it tumbles, he watches it fall. He wants to dive under the comforter, but if he closes his eyes, he'll only open them to find the shape standing next to the bed, dead, white fingers reaching out to touch his ... *drip, drip, drip* ... The noise becomes louder, a steady gush. And it is this, and the mundane anxiety that he has left the faucet running, that causes him to take action.

Before he can change his mind, he reaches across the nightstand and flips on the bedside lamp—*click*. And sees that— how can it be?—the door is *closed*. Confused, he sits up. Could he, in some agitated state, have misread the shape of dark and light in that part of the room? *Drip, drip, drip* ... The noise is real enough, but with light flooding the room, the shadow— and the fear—has vanished.

Getting out of bed, he tiptoes to the bathroom and puts his ear to the door. A faint swooshing sound—the toilet running again. He opens the door and turns on the light. The faucets are in their off position. The water in the toilet bowl is mirror-still. The jacket is right where he left it, and the shower curtain—*thank God*—is open, so there's no ghastly moment when he is forced to pull it back. But still. A sound in the hallway. A woman's voice, very faint, almost a whisper. He listens. *Silence.* A deep silence in the house that he has never noticed before.

Is the film over? They only just put it on, didn't they? The voice comes again. Laughter—muffled, covert. "*Jonathan . . .*" it says. And again, more quietly—"Jonathan." Paranoid? Or perceptive? *Ridiculous,* he decides.

Egged on by Jay, the others are playing tricks, for their own sick reasons, doing this to him on purpose. He goes to the door and finds it locked. A moment of panic, before he remembers he'd locked it himself—*who knows why*—after Laura left. He's no longer scared, but angry. Really angry. He makes his way downstairs, punching on lights as he does so, and marches into the den, ready to demand what the hell they're all playing at. Pictures flicker silently across the TV. Chocolate wrappers, empty tubs of ice cream, the half-eaten bowl of chips and guacamole, lie abandoned on the coffee table. Saul, asleep in the armchair, chin on his chest. Laura and Heather, curled up on either end of the couch like bookends. Jay passed out, snoring quietly.

Flab

2019

". . . Yadda yadda yadda . . ." Rings flashing, Cindy waves a hand over the remains of her perfectly roasted wild salmon.

Telling Jonathan to come up with a new character is only one of a whole bunch of other unwelcome ideas she's hit him with since the moment they sat down to lunch.

"Nothing extreme. Just someone more interesting or off-beat," she adds, forking up a last mouthful of fish. "Something more . . . *modern*. More *now*. Maybe a, a nice"—she waves her knife in the air—"a nice, *whatever*. You know . . . someone more *diverse*."

Who does she think she's talking to? Does she think him as shallow and cynical as she is? As Cindy likes to remind everyone, her grandfather sold women's undergarments on Orchard Street, so she doesn't "sugarcoat" her opinions. But telling him what to write is not her job.

"Don't get me wrong, your detectives and all, they're terrific," she continues. A waiter comes to remove their plates and Cindy orders herself an espresso, and a latte for Jonathan.

He thinks back to the many happy afternoons he has spent listening to her badmouth other authors. Make that "authors." In recent years, Cindy has developed a small true-crime division. Filling it with assorted warlords, despots, felons, gangsters, tin-pot dictators, celebrity murderers, and Wall Street swindlers on the lam, aka her "bad boys," as she indulgently refers to them. "A bit of a shockeroo," she'll remark, each time one of these jokers commits another heinous act of violence or corruption, frequently from the confines of their prison cell.

"How's the next one going?" she asks.

"Definitely getting there," he says and watches her attention shift past his left shoulder as she nods hello to yet another important someone at a neighboring table. It is always a shit show when Cindy chooses the restaurant.

"What's it about again?" she says, turning back to him. Can't she even pretend to remember? He gives her the briefest outline. "OK, and what else?" *What else?*

"Is that what this is to you?" he says. "Me pouring out my heart and soul on paper?" He offers this half in jest, but Cindy sighs.

One long fingernail taps at the side of her e-cigarette. The gum-snapping cashier at his local Duane Reade is the same way, Jonathan recalls, drumming her long acrylic fingernails on the counter before he's even handed over his loyalty card.

"Well," he begins, "let's see. A property magnate's mistress is murdered. And Detective Connor's dealing with a divorce. His brother has joined a, a drug ring . . . so that's, uh . . . a big problem." As Cindy waits, he attempts to ignore the waves of impatience emanating from across the table. "And Caleffi is having issues with her work-life balance and thinking of quitting." He pauses. Silence. "But *then* . . ." he improvises. "A young teaching assistant is kidnapped. So . . . there's *that*." If this book has been progressing slowly, he is thinking, that's nothing to be concerned about, is it?

"And lemme guess, in the end they rescue her."

"The . . . the girl? Yes. I mean, *sure*." Where is she going with this? *Tap-tap-tap. Tap, tap, tap. Tap-tap-tap*—a Morse code of impatience. "Well, that's the plan so far!" he adds, in what he hopes is an upbeat tone. "Though since you ask, it's kind of close, because they only get there in the nick of time." Cindy picks up her fourteen-dollar Sanpellegrino, regards him over the edge of her glass, minus the usual flirtatious gaze.

"I have some thoughts," she says, "but go on." What does she want him to say? Her 15 percent cut of his income has yielded her literally millions. *Millions.* Including that tacky mansion of hers in Fort Lauderdale. He's never told her how much he despises the place, the interior of which calls to mind the old joke about not having realized how much cash you could drop in Woolworths. Or Walmart, as it would be nowadays.

"Jon, look," she says. "I'm not saying your work is"— another smile at someone over his right shoulder—"is *stale* or anything." *Stale?* He looks at her in genuine astonishment. It is as if she has plucked a steaming turd from a stinking pool of scum and set it down in front of him. "But it sounds to me like it's . . ."

". . . The same as the last one?" he cuts in. "Is that what you're trying to say?" Has any sleepy ocean hamlet and reluctant murder capital, he thinks, contained more excitement than Ocean Falls?

"I did *not* say that, Jon," Cindy replies huffily. Flawed-but-mostly-law-abiding cops Danielle Caleffi and Jim Connor have solved countless murders, and always get their man. And they *are* all men, he thinks guiltily, recalling the hulking figure bent over the murdered girl in last Friday's TV episode of *Ocean Falls*—Season 13: "The Reckoning." Husbands, brothers, creepy male neighbors . . . is that Cindy's issue? *Has she decided to become a feminist?*

"Look, Cindy . . ." Her ring finger, the nail reflecting a hard, electric blue shine, hovers threateningly. "I'm not sure what you're implying, but my readers expect some kind of consistency. They're not idiots."

"If you say so," she says. "Anyways, in your last one, when those girls got kidnapped, and what's-his-face . . .'"

"Detective Connor."

"Yeah. Her"—*him*, but he lets it pass—"When she goes climbing up on that roof or whatever, to get them down?" In *Murder Included*, Caleffi's dying father was held hostage by a Mafia kingpin, and she and Connor had had to race against the clock. As with the other books in the series, events in the final chapter were genuinely touch and go.

"Cindy, what's your point?" he says. "Because I'm having a hard time seeing it." With exquisitely bad timing, the waiter appears with their coffee and—without first checking whether Jonathan would like anything else—Cindy requests the check.

"Look," Jonathan offers, "maybe the series has plateaued . . . or gotten a little played out or . . ." *Jesus*, he thinks, *I can't believe she's making me say this.* Cindy holds up a hand.

"Sweetie," she says. "Your work is great. *You're* great." As he offers her his chilliest stare, she smiles past him and he realizes that, once more, her attention has been pulled elsewhere.

Other writers complain about their agents. The impossibility of getting them to return a call or a simple email has spawned a thousand jokes. He has always regarded these stories with faint amusement. Now that the shoe is on the other foot, Cindy's inattention is—undeniably—"a bit of a shockeroo."

"Your sales are OK," she says. "But they're not increasing. We'd expect your backlist to be selling more, but that's not moving either. Basically, your numbers aren't getting better, and we need to figure out *why*."

Is that all he is? Some drone producing work to order on a conveyor belt? With Cindy positioned at the far end, squeezing, sniffing, discarding, like the firefighters who periodically swarm the produce section of his local Trader Joe's. He regards her in stony silence, but she doesn't seem to notice.

"I'm thinking . . ." She downs her espresso in one go, replaces the cup noisily on its saucer. "I'm thinking . . . and this is just a little idea for you, Jon, so don't take it the wrong way . . . that maybe you need to get with the times and whatnot."

"*Excuse* me?" With her eighties shoulder pads and "nude" pantyhose, he thinks, how dare Cindy try and lecture him on being up to date?

"This is your last one, correct?" Jonathan doesn't reply. "For this contract?" It's the intense way she's peering at him, he decides, as if he's a mere specimen. An insect pinned beneath a jar.

"Correct," he says. *What more does she want?* For him to take his knife and open a vein? Or stab himself through the heart over the zabaglione and mixed berries he'd been looking forward to ordering?

"It's the truth, darling," she says, reaching into her bag. "I'm not saying we kill off your career. Hell, haha, why would I kill the goose that lays the golden egg? But frankly"—she swipes some lipstick across her mouth—"you need to think about where you want to be five years from now." *You*, not *we*.

Jonathan pretends to take an interest in the disintegrating milky heart shape that dapples the surface of his cooling latte.

"Listen to me. You think these people give a damn about your creative development?" He looks at her. "Yah, sure, they sweet-talk you and blow smoke up your ass and all that crapola. But all they want is for you to keep churning them out. One after the other. *I'm* the one . . ." she goes on. "I'm the one who actually gives a shit about you." Wasn't Cindy the one, he thinks, who said that his literary ambitions were a waste of time?

"You're telling me I should be writing something more . . . more *literary*," he says.

Cindy guffaws. "Fuck, no!"

He stares hard at her, to no effect.

"You really want me to spell it out?"

"Not particularly."

She goes ahead anyway. "When we first met, I saw something in you. Call it an *edge*. You had that edge, Jon."

Had?

"*Sweets*." Cindy smiles, showing all her teeth. "We both know that you're far more interesting than you let on."

"If you're asking me what I think you are, it's never going to happen. And it's not up for discussion," he adds quickly. "Now or ever."

Cindy sits back, takes a delicate sip from her water glass.

There's no way he's going to write her some lurid true-crime tell-all about his wife's disappearance. Cindy studies him for a moment, smiling enigmatically. Which is concerning, he thinks, because Cindy doesn't do enigmatic.

"Okey dokey, smokey," she says finally. "I thought you might want to get your story out there. But excuse *me* for thinking about your future. I guess you'll figure it out on your own . . ." *Was that a threat?*

Before she can waylay him with any more "shockeroos," Jonathan reaches across the table and snatches up the check. Normally Cindy's the one who pays, and this feels like a way to assert himself, to claw back the control. As she exchanges air kisses with some other important someone passing their table, the waiter glides over like a shark and, without bothering to look the check over first, Jonathan smoothly hands over his credit card—*power move*. Jay would be proud. A minute later, the waiter drops the slip on the table, but there's no pen—leaving him to fumble indecorously in his jacket, a writer who has nothing to write with. He locates a dried-out Sharpie, scratches out his signature as Cindy looks on with a pitying air. She stands and heaves her bag over her shoulder.

"Walk me out," she says.

Outside on the sidewalk, he finds himself falling back into their regular routine—waiting as Cindy rummages in her giant handbag. Out come the Marlboro Golds. Two big puffs, the smoke blown up toward the building behind them, the rest flicked into the gutter—an action that in that moment feels horribly symbolic. She asks what he has on for the rest of the day.

"*Work*," he offers sourly.

"All-righty." She looks at her watch. "I have to run." She's off to meet a new client ("a natural storyteller . . . so authentic . . . so 'now'"). "Think about what I said," she tells him. And then, kittenishly, leaning forward to squeeze his arm, "See you later?"

Since first meeting all those years ago, they have attended the same party together twice a year, every year. It strikes him now that the last one had felt like kind of a chore. Too many social climbers, he had told Laura afterward, and not enough of the old crowd.

"I'll check my schedule," he tells her. As Cindy makes for the waiting town car, he finds himself scurrying over to open the door, watching her dive into her bag again, spritzing perfume on her wrists and neck—an overpowering, cloying eighties fragrance that he's personally never cared for. As the car moves off into the thick traffic on 54th Street, she waves her e-cigarette out the window.

"Don't forget," she trills, "you're the best!" He doesn't bother to wave back. Cindy herself is still the best in the business. Not the most well-liked—well, *obviously*—but one of the most respected. But what of himself?

He flags down a cab, thinks about his old life—living hand-to-mouth, check-to-check, barely scraping out a living. And his current lifestyle—the endless *bougie* rounds of country weekends, far-flung vacations, fancy dinners out four nights a week. Has it caused him to lose it, this "edge" or "authenticity" or whatever it is Cindy's accusing him of having mislaid? Physically, he's never been in better shape. Which begs the question: Has the flab accumulated elsewhere?

Telltale

2019

Joyce has died.

The message waits for him on the office landline when he gets home. It's midevening in the UK, but he calls back immediately. A tired-sounding administrator answers and Jonathan listens to the clicks of her keyboard as she brings up Joyce's records. Years ago, with his first royalty check, he had paid for an upgrade in her care and set up a direct debit. Now he's informed that although Mrs. Morgan passed away two weeks ago, they can't stop payment until he removes all her belongings. *Two weeks?*

"They did send you several emails," the administrator adds sternly. He doesn't appreciate her attitude, or being made to feel guilty. He lies and tells her that he's been away on vacation, asks instead about the funeral.

"I believe that was all taken care of," she replies.

"By *whom?*"

"We don't give out that sort of information, I'm afraid. Not over the phone." How can that matter, he thinks, at this point? An idea occurs to him and he asks whether he's still registered as Joyce's only family member. After a few more grudging taps, she tells him that there's nothing showing up on the computer. When might he be able to collect Joyce's belongings? she says. And he remembers that there are, of course, a couple of items among Joyce's possessions that he wouldn't mind taking a look at. Ideally before the facility has had the chance to mislay them. In the next few weeks he has to be in the UK as part of his book tour. It would be easy enough to fly into London and take the train down to the coast one day. Since he is still being charged for her room, he tells the administrator, perhaps they won't mind leaving everything in the room as it is until he gets there.

"If we really must," she replies.

Not going with Cindy to the party feels faintly rebellious. He messages Laura, who has the night off, and suggests a quiet evening in.

Playing hooky from the boring work party? she replies. *You've got yourself a deal. XOX.*

When she walks in later, he is down on his hands and knees with an old toothbrush, scrubbing the kitchen floor.

"Babe . . . ?" Laura places her bag down, turns on the radio—"*. . . but wasn't that conclusion long ago proven erroneous?*"—and turns it off again. "You know the housekeeper's here tomorrow?"

"You don't smell that?" Walking into the kitchen earlier, he'd discovered the dishwasher spewing dirty water onto the floor.

"Smell what?"

"Like . . . a weird, rancid smell. Like something's gone bad." Laura removes her sunglasses, sniffs the air.

"Huh . . . like . . ." She sniffs again. "Like a kind of weird, rancid smell, *right?*"

He nods.

"Nope."

"*Funny . . .*"

"The machine probably needs servicing," she says, leafing through the mail. "I'll reach out to the repair guy tomorrow." They both know this isn't the best use of his time, Jonathan thinks, as she heads upstairs. But working the bristles into the little spaces between the tiles offers focus and space to think. And when he's done, a momentary sense of accomplishment.

He resumes scrubbing, puts aside the puzzle of Joyce's funeral for a moment to dwell on Cindy and the lunch from hell. He refolds the towel under his knees, pulls the bucket toward him, wrings the excess water from the sponge. Exactly how worried is she? He runs a fingernail along the rubber seal of the dishwasher door, peels away a long sliver of black slime in one satisfying layer. Bringing it to his nose, he sniffs cautiously. There is no suggestion of the mildly fishy odor he detected earlier. He dips the sponge in the bucket, wrings it out, gives the underside of the machine another squirt of bleach from his special squeezy container.

Last night, he'd had an old dream about Maddie. For a while everything had appeared normal, just like it used to be. Then at some point he'd noticed something odd, some element that was jarring or out of place.

This is a dream, he'd told her. Maddie just laughed. Like it was the funniest thing.

Touch my hand, she'd whispered. *I'm real.* This is the point where he does—inevitably—reach out to touch her. And always wakes up. A mercy, he decides, considering the alternatives.

"Jon . . .?" Startled, he looks up to see Laura standing over him with damp hair, clearly already showered. *Didn't she only go upstairs five minutes ago?* She peers down at him. "Everything all right?"

"Just trying to fix the problem," he replies. As the atmosphere in the room drops several notches, he continues to scrape at a stubborn patch of dirt staining the edge of the door. Laura picks up a small pile of laundry, bras and under-things in down-to-earth cotton fabrics, and goes into the laundry room. He listens to the click of the washing-machine door, the series of beeps as she sets the dial to the delicates cycle. Evidently, he's not the only one doing the housekeeper's job.

"So how's your week been?" she says, coming back to stand over him. They haven't spent much time together since the lake house last weekend, so this feels like a loaded question.

"Sorry. I guess I've been trying to make my deadline."

Yesterday, after an entire afternoon spent, quite literally, reorganizing his sock drawer, he'd spent three hours at the gym in a bid to burn off his self-loathing on the treadmill. Regardless, doesn't Laura trust him? He should probably let her know about Joyce, but it's not as if the two of them had ever met, and really, he doesn't feel like getting into it all. Not to mention he'll be tempted to get into the whole funeral mystery, which for obvious reasons would be a mistake. He gets up, goes over to the wine fridge, and finds it locked.

"Where do we keep the key again?" Laura sits at the island with an overly patient look, like an official at an arms summit.

"Still in the everything drawer," she replies. He finds the key, selects a few bottles that look ready to drink, and holds one up to her.

"Didn't we have more of this? The 2009?" He places two glasses on the island, wondering whether the locked fridge has something to do with Ben.

"Listen, Jon, I—"

"I had the—" he begins, as they both speak at the same time.

"You first," Laura says. He fills their glasses, pushes one toward her.

"I had the *worst* meeting with Cindy today," he tells her. "Just brutal."

He waits for Laura to ask what happened, but she appears absorbed in something on her phone.

"With Cindy?" he adds. "My agent?" The words, Jonathan realizes, contain an unpleasant echo of "Tommy? My cat?" Then again maybe this does make a dismaying kind of sense. If he'd been unreasonably spooked by that encounter, he'd had a breakthrough on the incline treadmill that would have made his therapist wet her pants: the guy had reminded him of himself. The unsophisticated, doughy, socially anxious self of more than twenty years ago, that is.

"Sorry." Laura looks up and smiles. Finally, he has her attention. "Brutal, how?"

He recounts the entire incident, from soup to nuts. How he'd felt pressured to plead his case, the humiliation of Cindy's talk-to-the-hand response. "And right after," he tells her, "she had the *nerve* to start gushing over some *other* author she's got on the hook."

"Oh no," Laura replies. He can't tell what she means by this half-hearted response to his distressing day. Between small sips of wine, she has punctuated his story with little nods and uh-huhs. But still—his news doesn't appear to have surprised her.

"Poor you," she says now. *Poor you*—her go-to response with her tiresome, perpetually unemployed brother. Laura had encouraged his writing from the get-go, he thinks. Has read every single one of his books, from cover to cover, and loved them all. Or so she claims. As she gazes back at him with some version of a sympathetic "unhappy face," he's overcome by a wave of irritation and it's all he can do not to reach out and slap it off her. Then, as if to prove her total lack of interest, she changes the subject.

"Have you seen Ben?" she asks.

He picks up the wine bottle and scrutinizes the label. He has a bad feeling about what's coming. "I saw him this afternoon," he replies shortly. "You sure you ordered three of these?" He turns the label toward her. "I feel like we only got two." Laura sets her glass on the counter, takes a breath.

"The apartment's listed on Airbnb," she says. "And he's pocketing all the cash."

"What?"

"Ben turfed his roommates out. I overheard him boasting about it on the phone, so I went online to check." She holds out her phone for him to see. He ignores it. "It's definitely his apartment."

"When was this, exactly?" How could she have kept this from him?

"Right before the weekend. I wanted to tell you, but it never seemed like the right time."

"You can say that again."

"Sorry?"

"Last weekend? The *weed*? It didn't exactly help." The ordeal with the bathroom, the hearing voices, and general weirdness—it was like Laura had knowingly let him smoke the kind of weed that made people paranoid.

"Really?" She looks surprised. "I'm sorry, why didn't you say? No one else said anything . . ."

"Is that right?"

"Yes, of course. Why would I lie?"

He shrugs. "You tell me."

Laura looks down at the floor for a moment.

"You know what?" she says. "I am trying *really hard*. And though I am more than happy to discuss . . . *weed*, or whatever it is that's on your mind lately, right now, I need you to focus on something that's important to both of us. And not to change the subject." After the whole "go-nowhere" confrontation with

Ben, Laura had made him promise to check in with his son again. And check in with her after that. He's done neither, of course. "I read all the reviews," she continues. "They're not great."

"Excuse me?" For a moment Jonathan thinks she's talking about his book reviews.

"On Airbnb. The reviews aren't great, but nobody's complained about the plumbing." A pause. "And his whole attitude is kind of off lately," she says. "Haven't you noticed?"

"He's got exams coming up. I expect he's just tired."

"I expect he is."

"What's that supposed to mean?"

"Jon, don't be so naive."

Jonathan picks up his own glass, takes a sip to buy himself a moment.

"Kids experiment," he says. "They *party*. If you're imply-ing drugs are involved, I'm sure Ben's being smart about it." *Just like the bad weed, hon,* he stops himself from adding. "Didn't we all do coke in college?"

"Not me," Laura replies tightly.

"Then if you've never done it," he says, "how do you know that's what it is?"

"Give me some credit . . ." She's right, of course. Her indus-try is awash with the stuff. "I'm not saying I know for sure. But he's exhibiting a lot of the signs."

"And I'm not saying he's perfect," Jonathan counters, "but he's making an effort. He's going to school."

Laura shakes her head at him. *You're pathetic*, it says. "Jon, how many times do we have to go through this? You cannot be that oblivious. This Airbnb thing for one. And I *see* him. He sleeps half the day, goes out with goodness knows who all night, claims he has class but never takes a single book. How does that make any *sense*?"

Jonathan brushes at some dried flecks of cleaner on his jeans.

"Welcome to the twenty-first century," he says.

"Right. Except—in case you haven't noticed—he never takes his laptop, either."

Jonathan stands, goes to gather up the cleaning materials, starts lining them neatly inside the box tidy. Laura waits in silence. He can feel her eyes on him. Is she right? Ben has been in and out of college for years, switches his major virtually every other week, and still hasn't earned enough credits to graduate. Part of him wants to rise up and accuse her of spying. Of being insecure, jealous, controlling. Of trying to get at him through his son. In the past he has lashed out in anger. That's not something he's proud of. As his therapist likes to remind him, a child is not an extension of yourself.

"That's not all," Laura says. "Remember that day when I got home and had this feeling someone had been snooping around in our bedroom?" Last week. He'd brushed her off then as well, he remembers. After suggesting Ben was likely just looking for some clean socks, he'd banished the incident from his mind. "That gorgeous vintage Cartier you bought for me last Christmas?"

"What about it?"

"I was just looking for it, and it's gone."

"You probably left it up at the lake house."

"Nope." An emphatic shake of the head. "I almost never take it up there. You know that."

Jonathan goes to the fridge, takes out a bottle of Fiji Water.

"Thanks, I'll take one of those," Laura says.

"Sorry." He gets a second.

Not that long ago, he remembers, Laura had secured Ben a weekend job as a busboy in a friend's restaurant. A few weeks later, they'd gotten a call to say Ben had been caught stealing, so Laura had convened a family meeting. A misunderstanding with the credit-card machine, Ben had explained. New to the job, too nervous to ask how it worked, he must have pressed the wrong key. This seemed like a perfectly reasonable explanation and, after Laura made a call, the restaurant had taken him back. Only for the same thing to happen again. This time the general manager had gotten the police involved, and Jonathan was the one reaching for the phone, having Mahoney pull some strings with an old cohort in the 6th precinct.

"I'm so careful with it," Laura is saying. "I always put it back in its box."

"Right, but it belongs in the safe," he says. "Why didn't you put it in there?" *Victim-blaming.* The towel is still wrapped around her head. Little tendrils of hair have come loose, graying here and there. Against her dark skin it's an attractive contrast, if another reminder that neither of them is getting any younger. Perhaps sensing his scrutiny, she quickly pushes the strands back underneath.

"You know, he doesn't even use my name anymore," she says. "He calls me his *stepmother* . . ."

"Come on, I've never heard him call you that . . ."

"Well, I have," she says, blinking back tears. "I've heard him talking to his friends. 'My *step*mother.' *God* . . ." She shakes her head. "I never realized what an ugly word it is." She takes a large gulp of wine.

"OK, but technically you soon will be, right?" Jonathan says cheerily. "I expect he's just getting a jump on the wedding." Laura shakes her head. "It's kind of flattering, if you think about it," he adds.

"You weren't there," she says. "I'm not his mother. And I get that, believe me. But it's the way he says it. In this super scornful voice . . . like, like I'm the wicked witch from hell."

Jonathan had been explicit about not wanting more children. Either way, finding yourself a parent to someone else's kid couldn't be easy. But Laura had been like a fairy godmother to Ben. Throwing herself into the role, taking an active part in his son's welfare and education. It was a thin line. And Laura, he reminds himself, had walked it with compassion and grace.

"But you guys have always been close . . ." he says.

"Not anymore. I feel like . . . I don't know . . . Ever since we announced the wedding, he's been so strange and distant."

"Don't you think you're being a little hard on yourself? Ben adores you. And he's a kid. He's probably just going through a phase."

Laura shakes her head. "No, Jon. He's *not*. He's a grown man. That's what you refuse to get."

All the glib, sincere, *improbable* explanations he's been fed whenever he's asked Ben about the apartment or the never-ending repairs. Or anything else, for that matter. The non-answers, the overexplanations, the wide-eyed *absolutely*s and *definitely*s. And yet, he reminds himself, whatever Laura believes, there is no actual proof, no real evidence of wrongdoing.

"We were lucky all those years," she is saying. "He was wonderful. A great kid. But something had to give."

Once, a long time ago, Jonathan had tearfully confessed to Laura the concerns he used to have about Maddie. How with her mood swings and unpredictable outbursts, he used to fear for Ben when he was in his mother's care. Now, with this comment about luck, it's not clear to him whether Laura is referring to this, or to the simple fact of the child having lost his mother at such a young age.

"I never hit my children," he'd overheard his mother inform his aunt one time, "because I'm scared that once I start, I'll never stop." His father, of course, had felt otherwise.

"What happens the next time?" Laura is saying. "And the

next? And the time after that? He acts out, we get pissed, you forgive him. Wash, rinse, repeat. How do you think this is going to end? *Jail?*"

She has a point. Ben has been cosseted and indulged. Fancy vacations aside, he has little notion of the world beyond Manhattan. He doesn't even pay for his own phone.

"Handing over money and asking nothing in return, it doesn't serve anyone. Least of all Ben."

"Maybe it's my fault," Jonathan says.

"Hey, bud"—that's the extent of their communication these days; the words grating and ingratiating, even to his own ears. He's never been a real father, more like someone playing a "dad" on TV.

Laura lays her hand on his back, moves it in small, soothing circles. "I don't mean to be harsh," she says. "He's your son, and you love him. *We both do.* But this can't be good for him, this turning a blind eye."

When Ben first got in trouble, he is thinking, hadn't Laura, too, looked the other way? He could argue that this situation was just as much her fault. (Maddie, he thinks, would say it was his.) He hears her take a breath, quick and shallow.

"There's something else," she says quietly. "I feel weird saying this . . . but sometimes, when I know he's here . . . it's not that I feel . . . *scared* or anything. But there's this atmosphere in the house that doesn't feel right." Jonathan stares wordlessly at her. "Do you know what I mean?" In just a few sentences, Laura has voiced his own fears. For different reasons, hasn't he found himself locking the bedroom door? Peering around corners as he moves through the house? Feeling that he wasn't alone? Just the other night he'd heard the toilet flush all by itself.

"I'm sorry," he tells her, "but I can't say I do."

★   ★   ★

His woes continue in the shower, which sputters, thin and lukewarm, then blasts him in the face with a jet of scalding water. He fills the basin from the cold tap and fetches a washcloth, holds it to his burning skin. Laura has suggested they try "one last time" to sit down and discuss the Ben situation as a family—the very next time they can both catch him at home, that is. Meanwhile, she will take one more look around for the watch. And if it doesn't show up, they'll take the matter up with the insurance company.

He examines his face in the mirror, the skin tight and painful, like a bad sunburn. *Is a criminal born,* he thinks, *or created?* Nature or nurture, the eternal question. Whether the blame lay with the parent, or within the child itself. One more question that, right now, he's not sure he wants the answer to.

He fills the basin a second time, resoaks the washcloth. As Ben's father, was he fooling himself? The money, the multiple pairs of fancy sneakers, the casual references to restaurants even he and Laura would think twice about dropping cash on. He pulls the plug, watches the water swirl and vanish into oblivion. *Red flags.* All the telltale signs have been there. Once you got away with one thing, once the people around you have proven themselves gullible and blind, it was like one of Ben's video games: What was to stop you moving up to the next level?

He recalls Ben in the park as a small boy. Laura had asked whether he remembered playing hide-and-seek with his mom. "*I remember everything like it was yesterday,*" Ben had replied somberly. Father and son hadn't always had the easiest relationship.

Jonathan finds a clean towel, dries himself down in the bedroom in front of CNN. Magazines, restaurants, designer clothes—there is not only a shadow side, but a distinctly shallow one to Ben. And yet, underneath it all, he senses an inner resolve. A steely, almost cold-blooded resourcefulness. *"How do you think this is going to end?"* If Ben did end up in jail, he thinks, with an inward shudder, his son would find a way to survive.

He rubs the towel harder across his shoulders, down his legs for a second time, but can't seem to get dry. He sniffs at the skin on his arm. That funky salt smell again. He goes to the sink and scrubs at it. How much does Ben remember about the first years of his life? He was barely four when his mother went missing, yet the boy remains fiercely loyal to her memory. As for himself, wrapped up in work, high on his newfound success, he had not always been the best parent. There's a look he's been getting from Ben recently as well. Something in the eyes that he can't name, and doesn't like. Some spark of secret knowledge Jonathan doesn't have the courage to delve into. But for Laura, he can tell, it's now or never. His own last chance to step up and call his son out on his actions, without pussyfooting or backing down. And if he challenges Ben? He sits down on the bed for a moment. Will Ben bring up the past, with its difficulties and cruelties and all the impossible choices that his father was forced to make? In other words, what will Ben say in return?

"... It's not that I feel scared ..."

If only he could say the same.

Sabotage

2019

Jonathan wakes to find raised welts extending across his entire left cheek, a sight that brings with it a slew of uncomfortable memories.

In the fridge, he finds an ice pack and presses it to his face for a few minutes as the espresso machine heats up. There is no sign of Ben, save for a half-eaten bagel and a scatter of crumbs, and he can't help but feel relieved. He posts a response to a dog picture one of his Twitter followers has tagged him in—*What an adorable pic! I'm so glad he's a fan!*—then worries whether the exclamation marks make him look feminine or desperate to be liked. Or worse, *illiterate*. He closes the app, washes and dries his cup, then arrives at therapy ten minutes late and mentions none of this. He does mention his discussion with Laura, though. Observing the marks on his face, his therapist inquires gently whether things had become heated.

"Goodness, no," he replies, taken aback that she would even suggest such a thing. To be honest, he continues, there were moments when he'd had to fight the impulse to tell Laura to "hold that thought" and run upstairs to make notes—bits of dialogue, the light in the room, what each was doing with their hands, and so forth.

"The conversation about your son, it was painful for you," the therapist observes, doing that empathetic thing with her face. "Isn't that part of the problem?"

"You tell me," Jonathan quips. *Self-sabotaging.* Some days he can't help himself, finds it hard to take the whole *process* seriously.

There was the steep "arc" of his professional *journey*, and the rather more shallow arc of his personal one. The former had reached its zenith one day around ten years ago when, slumped in the waiting room in some mire of self-pity, he'd watched the door open and a famous actor emerge. Was that when it happened? When he knew he'd truly "made it" and could afford the services of life's winners? Seeing Jonathan stare, the man's posture had taken on that absurd "hunted" look celebrities wear—so ridiculous and unnecessary in New York, where everyone prides themselves on pretending neither to know nor care how famous you are. None of which had stopped the whole experience being completely validating, as he has never told his therapist.

He manages to spend the remaining thirty-five minutes of their session discussing Cindy, after which, with time to kill before the gym, he decides to take a stroll through Soho and get the 6 uptown. Except in emergencies, traveling to and from the airport, after late-night social engagements, or when he's exhausted after a workout, he never takes a car. It's a privilege he's never been comfortable with. Even with a regular old yellow cab, the whole driver-passenger inter-action feels fraught with awkwardness. Naturally, when he was struggling to make a living, these were precisely the kind of luxuries he'd pined for. And naturally, once the option presented itself, the idea had completely lost its appeal. No doubt this too is "part of the problem." He continues down Sixth Avenue, briefly considers whether this cab refusal serves any real purpose, or is merely a smug badge of pride, akin to the type of showy self-denial he associates with Saul.

The tourists are out on Prince, the sidewalks a mass of legible T-shirts, unflattering shorts, and white sneakers-with-socks combos. People heap scorn on Soho, but he doesn't mind it, especially in the mornings. The stall owners laying out their wares—the amateur paintings, the cheap silver and turquoise jewelry.

Preparing for bed last night, he'd confided to Laura his real concerns about the impending book deadline.

"But you can't expect to be inspired all the time," she'd said. "And they can't expect you to write on demand, can they . . .?"

With its requirement to be "creative," but not too creative, she'd continued, Jonathan's career was a lot like her own, so she could certainly sympathize. Was she serious? he'd thought to himself. For Laura, the pressure was not nearly as intense as it was for him, and the stakes not nearly so high. He'd found himself feeling obscurely angry at her.

He continues on to Spring, always a risky choice, the challenge being to breeze right by Balthazar Bakery without looking in the window. Now, the violent, almost chemical craving for an almond croissant is too much, and he finds himself ducking inside. Doesn't he deserve it? "*Be kind to yourself,*" his therapist likes to say. Maybe it's time to take her advice.

On the sidewalk, he takes one bite of the delicious pastry, and then another . . . and then, as a tourist family gapes at him, tosses the rest into a nearby trashcan. He gets lucky with a train and finds an empty seat. A dark-haired man sits opposite. Well-cut suit, forty-ish, elegantly European, with a trombone case balanced between his knees. Next to him an elderly woman is dressed in the uniform of an Italian *nonna*—white streak in her hair, absorbed in knitting a long, shapeless garment in thick, black wool. A few seats away a man is humming opera. All reason enough, Jonathan decides, to favor the city's decrepit, failing subway system over a taxi. For its strange flora and fauna, its random happenings, and unexpected characters. At Astor Place, an unkempt-looking guy gets on and fixes his attention on the man with the trombone.

"*Yo*," he says, "you gonna play that, or what?" Trombone Man smiles faintly and ignores him, so the guy tries his luck with the opera-humming man, who appears happy to oblige. As the latter starts up in a deep baritone with "Beautiful Dreamer," an atmosphere of contentment takes over the car, as if its passengers are being sung a lullaby. At 33rd Street the singer is just launching into "O Solo Mio" when Jonathan happens to glance out of the window and his heart almost jumps out of his chest. *No.* It can't be. But it is, without a doubt—*Maddie*. There is no mistaking her this time. Walking rapidly along the platform, heading for the turnstile, her face in three-quarter view.

They are pulling out of the station, the train picking up speed, the platform already a blur of people. With some notion of yanking the emergency stop he jumps up, realizes just in time that this will only leave the train stranded between stations. As they take the curve and glide into Grand Central, he is ready at the doors.

Even as he elbows through the waiting passengers, runs up the steps onto 42nd Street and sprints down Park, he knows it's hopeless. Barely four minutes later, lungs bursting, he runs his Metro card through the turnstile at 33rd. He runs along the platform, looks behind each pillar, checks all the faces. Too late. Always too late. Of course it is. He searches east as far as

Bellevue Hospital, south as far as Madison Park, back to 33rd. *Nothing.* Soaked in sweat, bent over with his hands on his knees, he stands panting in the middle of Park Avenue, feeling lightheaded and crazy.

Glitz

2019

Taco Tuesday is a tradition they've kept up since college. Tonight, their food sits uneaten on the table between them, because Jonathan has just blurted out to Jay the very thing he's been trying to avoid. Jay is nonplussed—"*Jesus . . .*"—and calls immediately for the check. The news requires an immediate "walk and talk" and a drink at one of Jay's regular watering holes.

As they track their way up through the West Village, Jay listens in devastating silence as the whole story comes pouring out.

"Look, I get that you *want* it to be true," he says, when Jonathan's done, "believe me, I get it." They arrive at their destination, a brutalist-style building that straddles the High Line. Jay hustles them past the unsmiling doormen—"Hey, my man!"—in a manner that makes Jonathan feel rather embarrassed. The feeling is soon forgotten as the elevator whisks them up to the eighteenth floor, where an exceptionally attractive hostess seats them at a table by the window.

"Fuck. I forgot. Gotta be out of here in thirty," Jay warns, as Jonathan takes in their surroundings. The room really is spectacular. Ersatz seventies, or thirties, perhaps. A golden light reflects down from the ceiling, bestowing a flattering, selfie-friendly hue to the faces of the already rather beautiful patrons that surround them. A waitress glides over, tall and sulky-looking, clothed in what appears to be a small gold handkerchief—prompting a guilty image of Laura in her stylish but sensible ensembles from Cos and Eileen Fisher.

"Whistle Pig Manhattan," Jay instructs, with a glance at the shiny new Rolex Submariner on his wrist. The latest addition to a burgeoning collection Jay keeps at home in a special, velvet-lined drawer. ". . . and a Tito's and soda. Thanks, babe."

"This place is pretty cool," Jonathan says.

"Told ya," Jay says proudly. "Better than a sharp stick in the eye." In college, Jay moonlighted as a club doorman, he remembers, and still claims to know "everyone that matters." Jay leans in. "Dude . . ." he says. "What's up with your face? Are you wearing . . . *makeup?*"

"Just some concealer," Jonathan says quickly. "A thing with the shower."

"Uh-huh."

When they emerged from the elevator just now, someone had stopped them to ask how to get to the rooftop swimming pool. In an effort to change the subject, he asks Jay about this.

"Yeah, that's the other room," he replies. "Way less cool than this one."

Jonathan smiles to himself. Wasn't there always another room? A more rarefied level of exclusivity to be attained? This is a whole side to his friend's life that he hears about, but rarely enters. Their drinks arrive, and he takes a grateful sip. It's excellent. Admittedly, it does feel good knowing they're sitting at the very best table in one of the most exclusive rooms in Manhattan. Besides, isn't this why he'd fled his hometown? Leaving behind a colorless suburb outside of Rochester to arrive—finally—in the place where he knew he belonged. For a proud Jersey boy like Jay, being here is about status. Like showing up at the Monaco Grand Prix each spring. The girls, the glitz, the drugs, the yachts . . . does Jay even watch the actual race? He's never asked. Formula One was one of Maddie's passions. They drink in silence for a moment, each perhaps reflecting on Jonathan's news.

"So how are things with you?" Jonathan asks finally.

"Can't complain. Busy."

"How's . . . I'm sorry, I forgot her name." It was hard to keep track of Jay's dating schedule.

"You and me both." Jay grimaces. "Couldn't deal with her. Totally out of her mind." Always the same story, he thinks to himself. Laura's opinion was that Jay simply liked having the upper hand. Until he didn't, and got bored.

"Remember how we used to go out together, all of us?" Jonathan says.

At the next table a group of twenty-somethings flirt and laugh, passing their phones around. No one is paying the two of them the slightest attention.

"Yeah." Jay removes his jacket, lays it carefully over the back of the seat next to them. "And about that," he continues. "Maybe it's not my place, but this . . . this *whatever* it is . . . you think you saw? If you ask me, you're just getting cold feet about pulling the trigger."

"With Laura? You think I should feel guilty about marrying her . . . ?"

"Yeah, *right*." Jay snorts. "I'm saying it's no biggie, getting second thoughts. That's what guys do. But what *is* a big deal is you flipping out and thinking this stuff is real." Jonathan says nothing. "Look, have you reported it?"

"To the police?" Jay nods. "I mentioned it to Matt Mahoney, but—"

"Wait, you spoke to Matt about this? When?"

"I don't remember," he says. "Recently." If Jay is going to be unhelpful, so can he. "Why?"

"No reason." Their waitress appears, asks whether their drinks are OK. "Everything's awesome," Jay replies.

"Actually," Jonathan says after she leaves, "since you're so interested, Matt acted kind of cagey about it when I told him."

"Why, what did he say?"

"It was more about what he *wasn't* saying . . ."

"Cops," Jay observes. "All the fuckin' same." And after a pause, "So you planning on telling me what he actually said?"

"He said the same as you," he sighs.

"Yeah." Jay takes a slug from his glass. "Well, maybe you should listen." Jonathan recalls the opera-singing man, the knitting needles clicking as the train picked up speed. The windows dirty, his view blurred, the crowd of fast-moving commuters . . .

"She's my wife," he says. "And I'm telling you it was her."

"*Was* your wife, Jon." Silence for a moment. How can Jay be so indifferent? How can he not want to know what happened to Maddie? His friend looks away, toward the large plate-glass windows. *Subject closed.* For whatever reason, it seems Mahoney isn't the only one being evasive.

"By the way, I almost forgot . . ." Jay says now.

"What?"

"You look like shit."

"Thanks. You're a loyal friend."

"Aww, c'mon . . . Big month coming up for you, right? Got your grand European tour and all."

"Ugh," he says. "Don't remind me." He has an event out in New Jersey this week. Then the tour, the talks, the interviews. Plus, he's booked to deliver a masterclass on creating charac-ter. The timing really is bad. *Is that what she wants?* says a small voice inside him.

"Gotta get out there and suck some dicks, right?" Jay punches playfully at his arm. "Right? Am I right?"

London . . . Copenhagen . . . Rome, the living mausoleum that is Paris. The endless hotels and unsatisfactory room service and answering the same questions about the same things, over and over. Just thinking about it is enough to bring him out in hives.

"Yes," he agrees, rubbing at his arm. "Thank you. You win the prize."

There's a lapse in the conversation—companionable, part of that ease and comfort they've always enjoyed. Jay nods toward the windows, huge and dark like immense mirrors. Nighttime Manhattan is laid out below them, glittering and impassive. To the west, faint little lights are winking from boats on the Hudson. On the Jersey side, figures can be seen moving along the promenade.

"You wanna hear something funny?" Jay says.

"Sure. I could use a joke."

"I'm here all the time, but I've never got why anyone would want to come up and watch the sunset over freakin' Jersey."

"You're right," Jonathan laughs. He attempts to locate the immense black oblong of Central Park, but from where they sit, there is no view to the north and the park is invisible. At night, it is like the dark heart of the city, like a grave awaiting its occupant. He and Maddie spent so many summer afternoons there. Not always happily, it was true.

"How're things at home?" Jay asks.

"Pretty good. Laura's back and forth to the West Coast. Busy with the new place."

"Yeah?" Jay regards him carefully. "Well, she's worried about you." *Great,* Jonathan thinks. The people closest to him have known each other for years, and from time to time they have also been known to compare notes. He's not thrilled about this—who would be?—but their intentions are good, and with so much history between the them, it feels churlish to complain.

"Look, I haven't told Laura about any of this," he says, in case Jay gets any ideas. "And I'd rather you didn't, either." With all the work and travel he and Laura have ahead of them, Jonathan continues, he sees no need to freak out his fiancée with news of his dead wife.

Jay is silent, signs the check with his right hand, picks up his drink with his left. It was Maddie, he remembers, who'd first noticed this quirk after seeing Jay wield a baseball bat. Who had wondered aloud whether this ambidexterity indicated some kind of ambivalence or duality in Jay's personality. Jonathan remembers being amused that it was she—not himself—who was overthinking something for once. Jay beckons the hostess over, hands over the check, which includes the tip—three twenty-dollar bills—tucked neatly underneath. Until now she has limited herself to the disdainful, model-y expression he imagines is company policy. Now she reveals a wide, surprisingly toothy grin. "Wow, thanks!"

"You're welcome, sweetheart," Jay tells her. A minute later she returns with some kind of chocolate dessert and two glasses of vintage port. "On me," she says, with a flirtatious wink.

"Sweet girl," Jay remarks when she glides off again. "Dumb as a bag of hair." The dessert sits between them. Neither makes a move.

"After you," Jonathan says, and Jay laughs. Around them, the din in the room has become louder, the crowd at the bar thicker. As he watches Jay swirl the remains of his drink, he feels a yawn coming on.

"How's it going with Ben?" Jay asks.

"Not great, actually. We're having some issues."

"Oh yeah . . .?"

A twenty-year-old memory comes to him. Their old gang—himself, Maddie, Jay, and Laura—one night after class, bombed out of their minds. Someone—it could only have been Laura—had asked Jay how many kids he planned on having. "Kids?" Jay had guffawed. "Kids are like one big mouth, gobbling up hundred-dollar bills."

"Hard to say. I suppose . . . I suppose I expected more from my own kid. You know? It's just . . . *dismaying*."

"I hear you," Jay answers sympathetically. "And hey, if there's something I can do, or you want me to talk to him or whatever? Just say the word."

"Thanks. I may take you up on that." Ben seemed to like Jay, whose lifestyle of glitz and glamour was presumably more impressive to Ben than his father's. Though for that same reason, he decides, his friend is hardly the best role model.

"So . . ." Jay says after a long pause. ". . . How long has it been?"

"Sorry?"

"Since she . . . since . . . you know."

"Almost twenty-three years," Jonathan replies.

"Long time."

"Doesn't always feel like it—but yes, I suppose it is." For so very long, the answer to this question had been "like yesterday." Waking up each morning to those first few seconds, not knowing where, or even *what*, he was, but understanding that something was terribly wrong. Years later, it was almost possible to believe that the events of the past—even Maddie herself—had not been real. Now, his dark mood has returned with her.

"So, if it was her," Jay is saying, "if she's somehow . . . *come back*, here's the thing: Why the hell would she sneak around in the background?" *Why, indeed?* The question he has asked himself a million times.

"I guess that depends," he replies, wrinkling his brow, "on a few things."

"...*Well?*" Jay says finally.

Jonathan looks over, confused.

"What do you think she wants?" Jay stares at him, waiting for an answer.

Eighteen floors below, a car alarm goes off, and with it a stark realization dawns on him. One that—incredibly—Jonathan hadn't considered until now.

"I don't know," he lies.

Drunk

2019

The rain isn't helping. Or rather, it is. Hammering hard on the roof like movie rain, it provides just the excuse Jonathan's been looking for. After canceling his therapy session, he has shut himself in the study with the idea that he's doing valuable research. He sets up a folder on his computer—labeled *Unpack_workflow_2.1* to deter snoopers—then performs searches for *security, personal protection, self-defense.* And reads the results on his screen—*judo for women, bodyguards (armed or unarmed), discreet adult diapers.*

For one outrageous moment, he considers calling Laura or Ben to ask for help. But this would involve explaining himself, wouldn't it? Explaining his own insanity. Regardless, something about the process of at least checking his options makes him feel safer. Less out of control. Which in itself, he thinks, is arguably its own species of madness. Another night of tossing and turning has left him seriously sleep-deprived. *What does she want?* Hasn't he sensed the answer himself? The fear, seeping through the excitement and the uncertainty? Seeing her from the train, he had noticed the set of her jaw, a determined hardness that had almost faded from his memory. If Maddie has returned, he had realized speaking with Jay last night, the only reason to conceal herself was because she plans to do some kind of harm.

And he's about to marry someone else—would she try to hurt Laura? In his mind's eye he is once again on the subway. The train moving fast, her face glimpsed momentarily through the mass of moving bodies. As he's learned through his *actual* research, mistaken identity is a common enough occurrence. Offered a hazy sketch or suggestion of a thing, your brain will fill in the gap for itself. Magicians, for example, depend on this. *Stagecraft, deception*—a glimpse, a flash, misdirection accomplished with a flick of the hand, and the illusion is complete. *Or* ... he lets his eyes close—is he, in fact, going mad? Seeing what he wants to see. Trying to make an illusion fit the facts. He picks up his coffee, sips thoughtfully at it. No, he decides, it was definitely her.

In which case, does she know where they live? Had she tracked him from here, through Soho, and onto the train? She'd got off before he did. Did that mean that she wanted him to see her? Doubtful. He'd looked up only by chance. It's hard to know what to think. He promises himself ten more minutes on the internet, then back to work. After anxiously scrolling through old emails, deleting, archiving, tidying, he gets caught in an endless series of YouTube videos—a snowboarding Jack Russell, a wine-tasting tutorial, a TED Talk by an FBI profiler on how to lie with confidence.

By the time three o'clock rolls around, he's in serious need of a break. He calls Jay, but he's not picking up. His old crime-writer friend Bill has left several messages, and always provides a welcome distraction, so in a conscious effort to relax, Jonathan prepares himself a snack and settles on the couch with the phone. Bill answers after ten rings and launches immediately into a long diatribe. Twenty-five minutes on, it's still unclear what Bill is talking about. What is clear, is that Bill is extremely drunk.

"Just as well I'm not prone to insecurity, huh?" Bill is saying. "What about yours?"

"Sorry," Jonathan says through a mouthful of sun dried tomato and triple cheese focaccia. "My what?"

"Your Amazon reviews. Haven't you read them?"

"Well, no . . ." he says, surprised that Bill would read his.

"My publisher actually takes them seriously, if you can believe that," Bill continues. "I mean, it's outrageous what's happening these days. It's gone too far. Completely out of control. *Authentic* voices, whatever that means—and don't get me started on all this . . . *true-crime* crap. You *literally* can't make it up anymore!"

As Bill talks on, though it's still light out, Jonathan finds himself patrolling the downstairs rooms, checking doors, closets, windows. The task feels easier knowing he has someone on the phone. Even a drunk someone, who seems to be acting very out of character.

"*Please . . .*" Bill spits. "It's not goddamn Hollywood, is it?"

"Sorry, what isn't?"

"You know," Bill answers impatiently. "Being a *real* writer."

Isn't it? Jonathan thinks. The book tours, the interviews, the appearances. Once, he'd even been asked to cut the ribbon for a new shopping mall. At times, his face ached from smiling, even for radio or podcasts because—as he had learned early on—it made you sound more "relatable."

In the kitchen, he sorts through the mail, puts away plates, a coffee mug—*Best Dad in the World!*—a Father's Day gift from Ben. From a few years ago, obviously. There's been little sign of his son since the discussion with Laura. If Ben comes home at all, he sneaks in late and leaves early, before anyone can catch him.

"Course . . ." Bill slurs. "We can't all be like you, can we? Still tossing out two books a year. I do truly admire you for that, Jon." *Was that a dig?* He has always admired Bill, who's a household name, with books that sell in the millions. Sure, they always gossip about other writers, who doesn't? But Bill has never taken a shot at Jonathan himself.

"Everything OK there, Bill?" It occurs to him that he should have received a review copy of Bill's latest book, but there's been no sign of it. "How are things going with the new one?" On the other end, there's a lengthy silence.

"Not too well, as a matter of fact," Bill says dejectedly. "They gave me the old heave-ho last week."

His agent, Bills explains, has dropped him. As has his publisher. Jonathan doesn't know what to say.

"That's that, I guess. I'm old news." A sigh. The sound of ice clinking in a glass. "I should have seen it coming," Bill says.

Jonathan pulls a half-bottle of Pinot out of the fridge and brings it up to the study. Plucking a selection of his own books from the shelf, he lays them down on his desk, side-by-side and face up, like playing cards. He turns over the first, reads the back cover.

Face of Sand
   When a young dog walker is found brutally murdered in an old trunk that washes up on the beach, it's anything but an open-and-shut case. Then six more young women go missing, and it's apparent that anyone could be next. Is a disgruntled "dog mom" to blame? Or is there more to this story than meets the eye?
   Once again, dauntless Detectives Caleffi and Connor must pit their wits against an unknown and implacable foe. But as the clock ticks, one frightening question dogs their every move . . .

Jonathan tops off his glass. *Poor Bill.* He feels bad for him. Of course he does. Then again, Bill's books have all gotten rather the same recently, haven't they? The last one he'd guiltily speed-read while watching *America's Next Top Model*.

Above him, there's a loud "clonk." Ben—who must have crept in while he was on the phone with Bill. Laura isn't home, so thank God there's no need to get into some *talk*. Still, he wouldn't mind knowing what his son thinks he's up to, skulking around with the lights off. He goes upstairs, but finds all the rooms empty. Nothing appears amiss. No book fallen from its shelf. Nothing lying in pieces on the floor. Without investigating further, he goes back down to the study and locks the door behind him.

A Knack for Killing
When the dismembered corpse of a popular party planner and rising star of the high-school PTA is found on the local golf course, it appears that no one has seen a thing. Then hours later, the slaughtered remains of the local book club are discovered in the middle of a deserted cabbage field, eyes gouged bloodily out, and Ocean Falls' favorite crime-fighting partners are on the case once more. But as Caleffi and Connor find themselves trying to outwit a pitiless killer, their own lives are about to get a whole lot more complicated . . .

When Bill spoke about his readers, it was with fear—as if watching an angry mob rush the castle gates brandishing pitchforks. Did he expect Jonathan to put in a good word for him with Cindy? In that case, Bill would have to start "tossing out" a book every six months, wouldn't he? Obsessing over reviews, badmouthing other writers, drinking at three in the afternoon . . . Really, it's just *sad*, is what Bill is.

Lay Her Down with Poppies

When the badly mutilated bodies of the local cheerleading squad are discovered in a dumpster behind the local 7-Eleven, the town is left reeling in shock. Soon after, a lone drifter is arrested and charged with murder. But in a stunning turn of events, he too is found slain, and when a celebrity yoga group receives threatening letters, it's clear that far more powerful interests are at stake.

In a twisting tale of drug trafficking, Hollywood intrigue and cold-blooded murder, Detectives Caleffi and Connor must grapple with one unspeakable secret …

When you get right down to it, Jonathan decides, it's Bill's attitude that stinks. The self-pity and blaming others, it's the kind of pathetic desperation people can smell. No wonder Bill's career has tanked.

He picks up his glass, is surprised to find it empty. *I'm not saying we kill off your career.* Cindy's words, repeating on him like a bad oyster. His phone buzzes—a text from Laura, who's in a cab home. Never has he been more glad to hear from her. *Great!* he types in and, in an afterthought, splurges on a clapping-hands emoji. There's a cold sensation trickling into his veins, which has nothing to do with the house. Or Maddie. Or Ben. *I'm not saying your work is stale or anything.* The truth is staring him in the face. He knows it. So does Cindy. When will his readers figure it out?

Talent

1992

"*I* have a red shirt. You have a *red* shirt. I have a red *shirt* . . . *You* have a red shirt!"

In the other room, Maddie and her acting partner have been passing this same phrase back and forth for what seems like hours. Confined to the bedroom, fearful that the clacking of the typewriter will disturb them, Jonathan's gotten nothing done save for scribbling down a few notes. Any minute now, they'll switch to some other meaningless phrase, working themselves up until their voices become loud, angry, anguished . . . The most successful rehearsals, Maddie has informed him, end with one or both participants bursting into tears. There's a pause as the women discuss technique.

"I mean, if you want the audience to believe you," Maddie begins bossily, "you have to believe what you're saying in the moment that you say it."

"Oh, OK . . ." comes the reply. This month's partner is a homely-looking girl with the demeanor of a shy librarian. She seems content to let Maddie lead their rehearsals and dole out unsolicited advice. He knows the feeling well.

Last month the acting school had put on a special one-night-only performance. He'd offered to write Maddie a monologue, but apparently her teacher already had something picked out. Heather, Saul, and Laura had shown up in support. And when Maddie first came out on stage, it took Jonathan several seconds to even realize it was her.

"Your girlfriend is a very talented young woman," Saul had informed him warmly in the bar afterward.

Coming from Saul, he'd told Maddie later, this was praise indeed. "He knows *everyone!*" he'd added.

Maddie seemed unimpressed, launching into a cruel but fiendishly accurate impression of his brother-in-law that had Jonathan in fits of helpless, guilty laughter.

"If you want to work in film, you need to be in LA," Maddie is telling her acting partner.

LA . . . She has been talking about the place more and more. Keeps a running tally of how many of the school's graduates are Oscar winners. Not that he doubts her convictions. Or her potential to be a success. Quite the opposite. Which is why recently he has started to wonder what he's supposed to do when she takes off for Hollywood to make her fortune. Maddie had that magnetic charm. She had *star power*. Even Saul thought so. Once she got to LA, it would surely be only a matter of time before she met someone else. Someone better looking and more successful than himself.

"Don't start," she'd said when he broached the subject the other night, before getting her coat and leaving for one of her long walks.

He's always played the straight man to her "crazy gal." And that's fine. It's yet another reason they're so perfect together. She had once remarked that his parents were joined at the hip. And though this seemed like a bit of an exaggeration, he has tried to give her the freedom she craves.

With rehearsal over, he finds her sitting alone in the kitchen, smoking a cigarette and making notes with her signature black Sharpie. She keeps a bunch of them in his old mug, mended just as she promised. There's a whole feature in this past weekend's *New York Times*, he tells her, about the Shakespeare Garden up in Central Park.

"We could take a picnic?" he suggests. "What do you think?" What she doesn't know is that he's already prepared one. Sneaking out earlier to East Village Cheese to purchase a selection of fancy foods, and then to Veniero's for her favorite cannoli.

"Mmm ... it's four degrees out." Her head is bent, she barely looks up. True, he says, but he thought it'd be fun, wrapped together in a big blanket, with a hot flask of coffee? She puts her pen down. "Didn't we just hang out in the park yesterday? Really, I'd love to, but I've got an *improv* class," she says, "and some other stuff to take care of."

"Like what ...?"

As usual, Maddie smiles, but doesn't elaborate. For all her energy and enthusiasm, she can be maddeningly self-contained. Meanwhile, she's not the only one with "stuff" to get done. He's way behind on a paper. It's hard not to feel envious of her self-discipline.

If only she weren't so weird and secretive about this part of her life. They are both writers, after all. The other day she mentioned carelessly that she'd started writing a novel—a *novel*! She wouldn't let him see it. And—since the humiliation of the yawning incident—she has not seen any more of his work, either. It's like another barrier between them.

"How about tomorrow, before my shift?" he asks.

"Can't. Have an appointment."

"Rehearsal?"

"No. Something else." This is vague, even for her. But some sense or intuition tells him to push, not to let her off the hook.

"Mads ...?"

"What?"

"Are you all right?"

A pause.

"I missed my period," she says finally. "I have an appointment at Planned Parenthood."

"Wait . . . What!?" He can scarcely believe it, but it makes complete sense. She has been acting so "off" lately. With her class, with rehearsal schedules that changed from week to week, day to day, hour to hour. More and more he has felt confused by her. Mystified by her behavior. The way she'll go off on some unpredictable tangent—mentally, intellectually, physically. Now he understands why: *hormones*.

It's a relief to have a reason. To know that everything's going to be OK. More than OK. As he moves in to hug her, a number of certainties go through his head in quick succession: they will get married. If the news is unexpected, as a couple it's exactly what they need. They're young. They have their whole lives ahead of them. They have time to figure it all out. He moves toward her, arms open. She holds up a hand.

"I don't need you to come with me."

He looks at her in surprise. She is literally holding him at arm's length.

"This . . ." she says, looking down. "It's not something I want for my life. Never have, never will."

For a moment, he doesn't understand. And then, the light-bulb goes on, stark and unforgiving. "Mads . . . *no*. Come on. You don't mean that. I know you don't." It's like she wants to cut out a part of himself.

"Jon, it's not about you. Or us." Her eyes look into his. "It's not enough. It's not what I want for my life. You know that."

He doesn't know at all. They've never properly discussed it. Or rather, he'll bring it up, and she'll change the subject. Surely, he thinks to himself, someone with whom he has such a deep connection must feel the same way he does?

"You're just panicking," he explains. "Which is totally understandable. It's a big step." But if she takes a moment to reflect, he goes on, she'll realize that it's the *right* next step, and that they both want the same thing. "I'm sure a lot of women feel that way," he says, as she regards him, stone-faced. "When the time comes, you'll feel completely different. Just ask my mom." He laughs, a half-hearted attempt at a joke. What would his mom say if she could hear his girlfriend talking like this? "Honestly, she'll tell you. It's just what happens," he adds. A horrible silence.

"*Is it?*" Maddie says finally. "Is that right?"

"Look . . ." he says, desperately. "I've put in for the general manager position at work, so we'll have some cash saved up." They'll be the kooky neighborhood family, he tells her, like in that old David Bowie song she likes. "What's it called again?" he asks, and receives a scowl. "I know that it might seem a little early in our relationship. I get that. But Mads, why not? Why *not* now?"

"Because *I* don't *want to*, Jonathan." She looks hard at him. "Not *ever*. It's not even a decision for me." She returns to her notebook. "Though it is mine to take," she adds quietly. "And the money's taken care of. I don't expect you to pay for it." She doesn't have a job, he thinks, she doesn't even have a bank account—how can she afford it? A procedure like that must be hundreds of dollars.

"Maddie. *Please*. It's the next step for us." He's begging now. "I *know* it is. Can't you trust me? It's only a few years earlier than we planned."

"*Planned?*" A grim laugh. "*You* planned. *I* didn't plan anything." She gets up from the table, re-lights her cigarette from the stove. "Why can't you be happy with what we have?" she says. Long spirals of smoke float up toward the ceiling. He's given up asking her to smoke outside.

"I don't think smoking is a good idea," he says gently.

"I'm sure you don't."

"*Mads* . . ."

"*Jon*. You're not hearing me. There are things I want for my life. And I'm sorry . . . but this isn't one of them."

"Like what? What do you want?" It's a genuine question.

"It doesn't matter," she sighs.

He has an idea.

"Look, I'll be done with college next year. Then, what if we moved to LA?" She looks up sharply. "All of us, I mean . . ." he adds quickly. It sounds crazy, he thinks, but it's no crazier than half of Maddie's harebrained schemes. The apartment feels very quiet. As if the outside world has disappeared.

"And how's that supposed to work? Where would we live?"

He doesn't have an answer.

"The main thing is that we *love* each other. That has to count for something . . . right?"

"Isn't it pretty to think so," she murmurs, tossing her cigarette into the sink. It's not enough, he thinks. What he's offering isn't enough for her.

He has told her about his plans for after college. That his degree will ensure security and a good salary. She lights another cigarette, goes into the bedroom. He follows, unsure what to do or say, or where this leaves them. He tries to think. Racks his brains for what he can offer her. She sits down on the bed, flicks ash into a small, leaf-shaped green dish she keeps on the nightstand. He remembers buying it for her in Chinatown, at Pearl River Mart.

"LA," she says, "you're just saying it. Telling me what you think I want to hear." Their relationship, it's so new, he thinks, yet already so precious, so essential to his life. He must give it his best shot, or regret it forever.

"Actually," he says. "I have a plan." A frank look from her—cynical, disbelieving. Almost pitying. He composes his features into a serious expression. "Listen to me, Mads. I didn't want to say anything until I was sure ..." He waits as she takes another long drag of her cigarette, glances moodily at him. "One of my bar regulars at work, Josh? Really nice guy. He and his wife, they have this ... apartment in Los ... in *LA* ... that they don't use. And they can't sell it right now. He says it's a pain in his ass, if you can believe that!" He laughs. No response. "It's in a good neighborhood, but ... I guess, you know ... he's been searching for caretakers. They want a stable, responsible couple to live in and watch the place. In exchange for free rent." Sometimes, Jonathan thinks, it seemed like the whole world was full of people who owned beautiful things they didn't appreciate.

"I'm sorry, who is this person again?" She's not buying it, he can tell.

"*Josh.* The banker guy, don't you remember? He got us front row seats to *The Iceman Cometh* that time." Too late he remembers Maddie had hated every second of it. Said afterward she couldn't believe that he too hadn't spent the entire three hours counting the decorative tiles above the stage to prevent himself from screaming. He keeps going. "Anyway, I checked in with him the other day," he says, "and they're fixing the outdoor terrace or something. But it should be done right around the time I graduate."

"Where in LA?"

"Maybe ... gosh, somewhere ..." He wrinkles his brow, his mind racing with possibilities. "... Near the Hollywood sign? I'm pretty sure that's what he said."

"That's near *Griffith Observatory* ..." Her pupils have grown huge, the rim of black around the green irises intense and vivid. Her eyes have always captivated him. The way they seem to change color, depending on her mood or the time of day.

"He told me whoever took the job would be doing him a huge favor," he continues, hitting his stride. "Knowing Josh, he might even throw in some cash on top," he adds blithely. She looks back at him. Has he said too much? She looks so grown-up. So stern and unforgiving. She'll make a great mother.

"This guy," she says, scrutinizing him, "this *Josh* person. You don't even know he's for real."

"But he works for Goldman Sachs . . ."

She seems to find this funny.

"Come on, Mads, why else would he offer? I can't exactly ask him to write it all down like some contract. That would be rude. All I can tell you is he's some kind of big honcho there."

"Doing what?"

"I don't really know. He explained it to me once. 'Derivatives' . . . Sales something?" Jonathan gives her a weak smile. "Honestly, I don't really understand it, but he makes a ton of money. And trust me, he's a stand-up guy. Think about it," he says, "if we got married, you'd be able to work here. Legally, I mean. In film or do whatever you want. I know my parents would loan us some cash to get us started. We'd be a family, and we'd live in Hollywood. It'll be brilliant!"

Stubbing the half-finished cigarette into the dish, Maddie takes her coat and goes out into the yard. He makes himself stay where he is, and thinks about what he has just promised. The general manager position? A loan from his parents? *The Hollywood sign?* Josh's apartment was real enough, save that it happened to be in Aspen, and Josh hadn't offered it. OK, so he'd improvised. Told the tiniest of minor white lies. Told them, for Maddie's sake. To save their relationship and have the amazing life they deserve. She's so flighty and impulsive, and motherhood could be the making of her. Offering her the focus she so obviously needs. Strange, he thinks, sitting down on the bed. Though he'd had no idea what he was going to say, somehow the right words had come. And, in the moment he'd said them, he'd believed every single one.

Merch

2019

"My wife was buried with all your books. She died reading them."

The speaker is a rumpled-looking middle-aged man, dressed in what Ben would call a "dad" sweater. Jonathan signs his copy of *A Tender Killing* with extra care.

"Thank you," he says, handing it back. "That means so much." For once it's true. It's probably the nicest thing anyone has said since he arrived in New Jersey two hours ago.

A combination of cocktail hour and book signing, his job is to circulate and chitchat with readers while limiting himself to polite sips of Pellegrino. At a long table piled high with "merch," publishers' interns busy themselves with credit-card machines. Here and there a number of smaller tables have been set up, places for people to put their drinks or have Jonathan sign their book amid a scatter of Ocean Falls and John Dane branded pens, cup holders, and all-weather dog jackets. Right up until the end, the man in the dad sweater says, his wife never missed a post on Facebook.

Jonathan doesn't have the heart to say that he doesn't even look at Facebook anymore, let alone write his own posts. Not in the last three years anyway. Or is it four? *Five*, he realizes. When his followers hit one million. Five years and three million sales and countless network TV seasons ago.

"Actually, I do a bit of writing myself," the man is saying, when they are interrupted by a plump-faced woman, the official representative for the local book club, who stand arrayed behind her like courtiers. She asks whether he could tell the group where he gets the inspiration for his characters. He smiles. Questions like this are among his very favorite. Generally speaking, he replies, authors take inspiration either from their own lives, or they conjure characters and events from their imagination.

"I happen to fall into the second category," he fibs, glad Mahoney isn't around to contradict him.

Across the room, a tall, slim blonde comes into view. A flash of recognition, a burst of heat coursing through his body . . . then she turns . . . and he breathes out. How many false alarms has he experienced recently? He should be used to it at this point. As he moves his attention back to the group, he can't remember what he was saying.

"Yes . . . so, uh . . . as I mentioned . . ." he begins, drawing a blank and settling on, "your characters live in the details"— possibly a bad omen, since it's one of Bill's lines. The group nods in happy agreement.

A man in the back suggests that his fictional detectives behave badly.

"The police do an incredible job," he smiles, "with limited resources, under very difficult circumstances." His ethically compromised cops may bend the rules on occasion, Jonathan thinks, but they weren't as bad as some of the real-life ones you heard about. Connor wasn't sitting in his squad car beating off, or out on the Long Island Expressway getting blowjobs from drunk housewives.

When the group at last moves off in the direction of the drinks table, he lets out a sigh of relief. Having his readers clamor for a piece of his wisdom, seeing them hang on his every word, gives him a warm tingle of reassurance. Not tonight, though. Tonight he feels oddly exposed. A good-looking couple approach, the woman in the upmarket suburban uniform of Lululemon and Chanel bag. "We can't even tell you how important your work has been to us," the man says. "Our son has ADHD, and Ocean Falls was a real stepping stone to having him read real books."

"Thank you," Jonathan gushes. "That's *great* to hear!" *Just make them like you . . .*

Gritting his teeth, he continues to circle the room, charm switched to "high," nodding and smiling like a visiting foreign dignitary. The event organizer steps up to the podium, thanks everyone for a great turnout. 10:15 p.m. *Almost done.* Absently, he straightens a collection of pens and napkins on the table nearest him. Next up the local police commissioner with an impassioned speech, and the usual aside lamenting "a few bad apples." He ends by thanking Jonathan—with not nearly enough enthusiasm, he decides, considering 100 percent of tonight's proceeds are going to the Police Benevolent Association. If he weren't in such a wretched mood, he might find this all rather amusing. Jay had shown up earlier. Now, pasting on a bland smile of appreciation, Jonathan tries to calculate the chances of dragging his friend from whichever intern he's hitting on and being home by midnight. People are looking in his direction and smiling. "Thank *you*," he mouths, inclining his head as everyone claps. (He's yet to succumb to the false modesty of making that annoying "praying" motion with his hands.)

Not long afterward, he's collecting his jacket from one of the event staff. Jay is still MIA, so he looks for somewhere to stand. The room is already being dismantled. Tables, glasses, and discarded canapés cleared away by a small

army of white-shirted young men and women. He positions himself in a shallow alcove near the exit and takes out
his phone. People generally take the hint. A long, incoher-
ent message from Bill—he hits delete—and nothing from
Cindy. This morning they'd had their first real conversation
since the ill-fated lunch. She had asked whether he had any
thoughts.

"Actually, yes," he'd replied carefully, "but nothing I want
to share right now."

What else could he say? They have a good relationship, but
he's under no illusions: to Cindy he represents an
investment.

"No rush," she'd replied. "I can't do lunch next week, but
we'll catch up soon."

No lunch? That's a first. Was she preparing to give up on
him? Keeping him on the hook until . . . *until what?*

"You're the best!" she'd trilled.

Am I? he'd thought. *Am I, though . . .?* And yet, it had worked
last time, hadn't it? All those years ago, Cindy's words had
provided exactly the push he needed—*the kick*. He considers
this for a moment. Was Cindy the catalyst? Or had the real
kick occurred with his wife's disappearance? Fast forward a
few years, and he was loved by literally millions of people,
most of whom he had never met. How many authors could
say that? Nearby, two women with expensive hair chat in low
voices. Concealed in his alcove, he's been only half listening to
their sober debate on whether to save or trash all the "dick
pics" on their phones. The brunette, who has an undeniably
shapely behind, plucks *Kill Her with Kindness* from her bag,
proffers it to her companion.

"Read it?" she says.

"Nuh-uh," the friend replies. "Definitely not. I'd remember
the cheesy cover."

He checks her out as they walk away—barrel-shaped torso, no waist. *Bitter*, obviously. Cindy never said he had to like them back.

"Tough crowd, huh?" Friday night and traffic is bumper-to-bumper. The Lincoln Tunnel is a mess. Of course it is. *Who didn't see that coming?*

"Like you'd know," Jonathan replies. He's not in the mood for Jay's snarky wisecracks. If Jay had been there, he goes on, instead of in a bathroom stall fucking one of the interns, he might have noticed the weird note of hostility running through the crowd. Through almost every conversation he'd had the misfortune to have foisted upon him, in fact.

"You weren't down there," he continues. "It was a *bloodbath . . .*"

Jay snorts with laughter. "Seriously? You're killin' me. It's a dumb promo, not fucking Fallujah."

"Thanks again," he replies tightly. "I appreciate your support."

"Man, you are *unreal*. But hey, that's why they pay you the big bucks, right? You're great at imagining shit." As Jay playfully nudges him in the ribs, it's all he can do not to punch him in the face. What had he been thinking, agreeing to this stupid event? He'd had a bad feeling about it from the very start. Then again, these days he has a bad feeling about a lot of things. He turns his gaze to the window.

"Jon . . ."

"*What?*"

"You're all bent out of shape over a few wackos. You do know that, right? You need to learn the difference between a wackadoodle and a wack job." Jay turns toward him. "Is this about that *thing* we talked about? Are you still on that?" How could he *not* be? Jonathan thinks. Merely the thought of her.

That she could be close by. The fear that he has either found her. Or only thinks he has. And has therefore lost her all over again. The fear that she has found him . . .

"Don't be ridiculous," he replies. For the next few minutes, there is silence in the car. "It was like they were trying to trip me up," he says finally. "You really didn't pick up on it?"

There's a pause.

"Not really, Jon, no."

"Fine. Have it your way. But if you can bear to cast your mind back," he adds frostily, "I think you'll find that I've never had all of these so-called 'wackadoodles' in one room." The knowledge that no one believes him. The possibility that he is going mad . . . *I need to sleep*, he thinks. To *not* think. To *not* answer dumb questions. To be in bed, blissfully unconscious. To sleep, and *not* to dream.

In the last day or so, his back has been acting up. Last night he spent half the time up and down to the bathroom, trying to figure out whether he had prostate cancer. He's not even fifty, for Christ's sake. Sickness and infirmity, like an unwanted perfume sample thrust upon you in Bloomingdale's—cheap and very nasty indeed. Until recently, he has always thought of age as time propelling you forward, but maybe the years are more like a steady accumulation of weight. Barely noticeable at twenty. Manageable at forty. And by fifty . . . sixty, beyond? The weight increasing until it buckled your limbs, stopped your heart, drowned you in your own lungs—or worse. He stares out of the window, at the grimy walls of the tunnel crawling past. Because the end could be so much worse, couldn't it?

Nausea

1997

The news arrives in the early morning, right as he's getting Ben ready for school. Jonathan hears it from the bathroom, the local TV news anchor cutting in. "*... A body has been sighted in the sea off Southampton ...*"

He leaves Ben to finish brushing his teeth, runs into the living room and turns up the volume. Against a backdrop of ocean, helicopters, and rescue craft, a reporter stands on a beach. Behind her, several bystanders can be seen, faces scrunched against the wind, excitedly pointing out the scene to others.

"*That's right, Jim,*" she is saying. "*Coast guard and marine control have been scouring the area, hoping to locate the unlucky victim of a possible tragedy that has gripped this tiny ocean community for the past twelve hours.*"

Jonathan's knees give way and he finds himself sitting abruptly on the floor. Fighting off a wave of nausea, he manages to dial Mahoney's number. The cop sounds surprised to hear from him.

"Probably nothing," he says reassuringly. "Stuff in the water. We get reports like this all the time. And Jon?" he continues. "It's been a while ... if you know what I mean." Jonathan does know. He thinks of little else.

In the awkward gap that follows, he gazes toward the kitchen, at the bars stark against the dirt-streaked window.

Weeds have sprouted in the yard, pushing up through a rusted bedframe someone has dumped against the wall. She had wanted to plant flowers, he remembers. To create a little garden. And he had told her no.

"You're right," he replies. "I wasn't thinking. I'm sorry for wasting your time."

"Don't sweat it—you got me on my day off. So it's either shoot the shit with you or mow the lawn." Mahoney sighs. "If you catch my drift." *No pun intended.*

Though he's yet to learn much about the cop's private life—where he lives or whether he has any children—at this point Mahoney feels like a friend. And once you got him going, Mahoney liked to talk. In the background there's the faint chatter of a TV, the rattle of crockery. Farther off, a dog barks. Suburban sounds. The kind of life he long ago turned his back on. Mahoney checks in regularly, updates him on their progress, or lack thereof. Jonathan asks whether there have been any developments. Nothing significant, comes the reply. "You need to stop beating yourself up," Mahoney continues. "Focus on your kid. That's what your wife would have wanted, right?"

Would she? he thinks. Is *that* what Maddie would have wanted? He's grown so tired of everyone's advice. Well-meaning friends telling him what his wife *would* or *wouldn't want* for *his* life. For Ben's sake, he has no choice but to move forward without her. But it's not been easy. Work, subway, grocery shopping, work. Going through the motions—feeling empty, angry, hopeless. Her absence always present. His thoughts scattered, concentration shot. How can she be nowhere? he thinks, walking into the empty apartment after a long shift, when there are so many things he wants to tell her.

"I feel so responsible," he confesses to Mahoney. "I keep thinking . . . if only I'd done things differently."

"*Listen to me,* Jon. People do all kinds of stupid shit. In my job, I know that better than anyone. No disrespect, but the actions that full-grown adults take? That's on them. Not you."

Like all married people, Jonathan thinks, he and Maddie had had their problems. But these have paled compared to the problem of his wife being dead. *You're here, you're alive . . .* he had said to her in a dream last week. *And you're dead.* She'd smiled. She was not wrong. Waking to reality was like being hit by a tsunami. *And yet . . .* as the wave of loss receded and he'd gone about his day, he had found himself brought inexorably back to all the hurts and bitterness of the past.

"If it was my wife," Mahoney is saying. "Sure, I'd beat the hell out of myself over it. That's a fact. But I sure hope someone would let me know it's a waste of my damn time."

Before they hang up Mahoney suggests meeting next time he's in the city. "I'd like that," Jonathan replies. Nothing more to do, Mahoney says, except wait and hope. *And pray,* he adds, though Jonathan knows this won't help either.

Setting off to walk Ben to school, he reflects on this advice. All this time, traveling out to Long Island, putting up posters, pestering the locals. *Permission*—is this what he's been waiting for? For someone he can trust, someone in charge, like Mahoney, to tell him it's OK to cut himself a break? They cross Tompkins Square Park, past people relaxing on benches, workers busily raking the flower beds. On a precious evening off, Jonathan could sit here and write freehand. "Could," because right now it feels inconceivable that he ever used to do such a thing. He's started using alcohol to sleep. And to get up in the mornings. And to get through his shift at work, where he's resorted to stealing bottles and sneaking them home in his bag. He owes money all over the place. Even to Laura, who's not exactly swimming in cash herself, but insisted he accept a small loan. If he can finish his novel, if he can make the rent, if he can pay down his debts, cut down on his shifts . . . The future is like a black hole of nothingness.

After dropping Ben at daycare, he goes straight home and turns on the TV. The reporter looks colder, her coat is tightly buttoned, but otherwise the scene appears exactly as it did an hour ago.

"*It's a fluid situation, Jim,*" she is saying.

He paces back and forth in front of the screen. He's heard about it, this lack of closure after a loved one goes missing. How it can tear you apart. *I just need to know.* Mahoney has implied that there's no chance that it's her, and he's probably right. It has, after all, been a while. A long time for someone to be in the water. What if he's wrong, though? What if it is his wife? Would he be expected to identify her . . .?

As the camera pans across the beach and sweeps out to sea, excited onlookers pose for photos as horrible images run through his mind. Two teenage boys mug for the camera— "*Hi, Mom!*" A lone helicopter buzzes ominously. He can't seem to tear his eyes away. As the camera roves back and forth across the ocean, he goes into the bathroom and splashes his face with cold water. All the times he has pictured the scene— he and Maddie on the beach, happy and excited . . . as the car moves stealthily across the bridge, rounds the corner into the parking lot, and waits, engine purring.

Out there, somewhere, was the person who had taken his wife from him—the person who was responsible. *Was it a stranger? Someone they knew? Someone they'd both met randomly somewhere? Did it just happen, or was it planned?* Thoughts that leave him desperate to crawl out of his own skin.

There's another feeling as well, that hums steadily in the background. Unsayable. Unspeakable. *Rage*—it drops on him out of nowhere. It's like being crushed by great flanks of meat, dripping hot blood, and trying to claw his way out from underneath. So many times he has had to fight the urge to lash out, to put his fist through a window or scream at some idiot blocking the subway doors. Tortured by the thought that he should have known what was happening . . . but didn't, and so did nothing. *". . . The actions that full-grown adults take? That's on them. Not you."* Did Maddie bear some responsibility? Once more his mind scrolls through a rolling list of all the things he wants to say to her, but never can. *Cheated.* He has imagined himself, lying face down on the grave she doesn't have, digging at the soil, the tragic hero in his own cheesy movie. It frightens him, how real these moments seem. When not playing out all the conversations they will never have, his mind comes up with bargains. What would he give? What *wouldn't* he? He has imagined every sacrifice, every possible scenario—a thumb, a hand, an arm, a leg. Both legs. Heather, struck down by cancer. His mother under a bus. Whole cities wiped away in a flood. The entire population of California nuked. Plague, locusts, fire . . . until, with shameful inevitability, the ultimate bargain—*God help him*—of something happening to their son. Of sacrificing Ben. All to have her back.

Long hours later, with the day almost gone, he's leaving to pick up Ben when the phone rings. Mahoney, with four simple words: "It was a log."

Enemies

2019

"*Really?*" he complains to Cindy. "*Really?*" The crap he'd had to deal with in Jersey. The unwanted "feedback." The sheer variety of weird, nasty, ill-thought-out remarks he'd had to endure. Cindy is no help. Then again, Jonathan thinks, she's never been good at sympathy.

"Remember, you're the best!" He can practically hear her laughing at him through the phone.

After they hang up, he gulps down another double espresso and goes to work off his angst at the gym. True, his trainer resembles a psychopath who gets off on torturing people. But the beauty of these punishing thirty minutes is that they leave no room in his head for anything else. Not work, not Laura, not Ben—and not Maddie. Calves, hamstrings, deadlift, squats—he's taken through an intense lower-body routine until his legs literally give out from under him. But for the first time, he can barely concentrate.

"Focus, please," instructs his trainer as Jonathan picks himself up off the floor. A few seconds' reprieve as the stopwatch is reset, numbers noted down on a clipboard.

If it is *her*, he is thinking, where is she living? Is she stalking him, following him around the clock? What is she planning? And *when* is she planning it? Each day before leaving the house, he scans the street outside, repeats the action as he steps onto the sidewalk. He checks for suspicious vehicles, for anyone turning their back to gaze in random store windows. Earlier, in yet one more outlandish movie moment, he'd considered leaping onto the train at the very last second, right before the doors closed. Imagined staring at her out of the window as she stood on the platform, gazing after him. Instead, he had taken his time. He wants her to show herself, doesn't he? At least, he thinks he does.

As they move to the treadmill, he realizes that he doesn't have any kind of plan for this outcome. Has no idea what he would do or say. His trainer punches the setting up to its steepest gradient. Down again. Up again, over and over, for ten of the longest, most agonizing minutes he can remember. His calves are like burning bricks, his quads like someone is repeatedly stabbing them with a white-hot screwdriver. During the final ten seconds, he thinks his chest might explode. And then, just like that, it's all over. Gratitude toward his torturer, but no sense of elation this time.

"Where *were* you today?" he is asked sternly. Luckily, he's too out of breath to answer.

Arriving home, he's physically exhausted, but the feeling of unpleasant nervous energy is still with him. He'd spent an awful lot of time during the night being aware of being asleep—or so it seemed. Images had formed; not quite dreams, they changed shape, merged into events from his past. His parents, vital and alive. And *Maddie*, never far away, waist-deep in the ocean, beckoning to him, lips moving silently. When the alarm went off, he'd had to kick hard to escape the pull of it, like the swirling sand and seaweed at the bottom of the ocean. He thinks about calling Mahoney and leveling with him. Saying that he honestly believes his wife is alive, and . . .? *And what?* That he creeps through the house, startled at shadows, fearfully anticipating

the next turn of the stairs, like a scene from *Mission: Impossible?*
Jay is right. He sounds completely out of his mind.

He prepares the obligatory protein shake and, recalling
Bill's words, decides to take a quick peek at his reviews. *Why
not?* He's been fighting the urge for days. For years, in fact.
Sure, he could call up his accountant. Request a look at his
incomprehensible financial statements. *Or* he could simply
bite the bullet.

*Engaging characters, gritty and real. One of the best books of the
year, bar none.*

The *New York Times* seemed like a safe place to get his feet
wet. Maybe too safe. Their new crime reviewer is a friend and
her review practically radiates approval. Jonathan's hand hovers
over the keyboard—really, what the hell is he scared of?—types
in the URL for Amazon and heads to his author page.

Headshot (serious, but accessible). Cover shots of the
Ocean Falls series arrayed colorfully underneath, along with
an ad for the new season of the hit TV series. Not obsessing.
Market analysis. All. Perfectly. Normal. Behavior. He clicks on
Dark Tide. 4.8 stars. Way above average for a first novel. He
waits for the comments to load and reads the first two:

Come on, JD, write faster! ;)

Riveting! A masterful plot. Can't wait for the movie!

Encouraged—*what took him so long?!*—Jonathan keeps
going, fast-forwarding through his career. 4.8, 4.8, 4.9.
Reaching book twelve, however, he discovers something
disturbing. His average sinks to 4.5 stars. He moves to book
thirteen . . . 4.1. Book fourteen—3.8.

This can't be happening. It's not a nosedive, exactly, but more a steady tailing-off. Heart in mouth, he checks the rating for his latest book. A career-destroying 3.4. He sits back in his chair, stunned. Literally stunned. He'd had no idea it was that bad. Why hasn't anyone said anything? Why hadn't Cindy told him earlier? He stares at the screen and, though he knows it's a stupid idea, starts to read the comments.

Phoning it in
Dane phoning it in again with this one. Plot thin. Ending predictable and insulting to people who buy his books IMHO.

Don't waste your time
I have always loved this series because it's realistic and isn't afraid to show the violence. But I'll never get back the hours I wasted waiting for something to happen with this shoddily writ-ten book.

One particular (1.5 star) review pierces him like a bullet to the heart:

So disappointing
*I'm no prude, but all the sex stuff in this book is disgusting. What kind of person thinks like this? I'd like to recommend this book but I won't be doing so now and neither will my husband. **Very** disappointing.*

He wants to vomit. It is as if someone has thrust their hand into his chest and ripped out his heart. All those hours he put in studying The Bad Sex Award nominees and trusting that he had avoided their mistakes. As early as book two there had been subtle, but unmistakable, sparks of attraction between his detectives. Later, after a bitter divorce for Connor, the pair were at last able to start exploring their feelings for one another. And if the mountains of Ocean Falls "fanfic" were anything to go by, people loved it. He's frequently asked how he feels about these tributes. The steamy, floridly written encounters in the backs of squad cars, at gory murder scenes, with or without bondage or their loyal spouses along for the "ride." It certainly is flattering, he replies. Privately, of course, it is deeply unnerving. Like being made to watch your pets or close relatives have sex.

He keeps scrolling. On and on it goes, comments rising up from a seemingly bottomless pit of spite and hate. What is he supposed to do with this information? His books are already out there. It was like looking at someone's wedding photos and telling them they looked fat.

People rate him poorly for things that are beyond his control. *This book did not arrive on time. Also the packaging was damaged.* Writing from the point of view of New York's finest, his sympathies are assumed to lie with his vulnerable female victims. Permanently subdued by husbands, colleagues, lone drifters, and jilted boyfriends, they remain necessarily silent as his detectives go about delivering justice on their behalf. Some commentators appear personally insulted by this. *Where are all the women?* complains one, going on to compare his work unfavorably to some up-and-coming young writer he's never heard of. He checks out her author page. Four thousand positive reviews. A solid 4.9-star average. Fine, Jonathan thinks, but have *her* books been translated into more than forty languages? Getting up, he goes to the window, watches the passersby—dog walkers, deliverymen, NYU students—going about their happy, carefree, critic-free lives. That unpleasant churning in his stomach is back, a sensation he associates with school, with being found out or unfairly accused in front of others. It all makes sense now, the feeling of insecurity settling over him like warm gravy. The persistent ripples of hostility he's been sensing at events. Not his imagination at all. Worse, as he has been *tossing them out,* others are threatening to take his place in the spotlight, and at this rate will soon leave him in the dark. He gulps his tepid coffee, swallows too fast and chokes. He could—and should—simply step away from the computer, he thinks, mopping at the spillage with his sleeve. Go for a run or do something productive, instead of poring over this stuff. And yet, for some perverse reason, a part of him finds the experience mesmerizing.

His phone vibrates—therapist. He hits ignore. Would she say he was "acting out?" Self-sabotaging? Then again, his therapist isn't the one facing a shallow dive into literary obscurity, is she?

He goes into the bathroom, fills a glass from the faucet, and brings it back into the study. It tastes salty and rank, and he spits it out into last night's wineglass, which—he is mildly surprised to notice—sits discarded on his desk alongside one from the night before. Down in the kitchen, he is just passing the glass doors to the terrace when he catches sight of a menacing figure outside—middle-aged, haggard, hair askew—and jumps—and sees his own face react in surprise. *Day drinking. Is this what it's come to*? With everything going on, he's been treating himself to the little nightcap he deserves. And very occasionally, a tiny sip of something to get him started in the mornings. Apparently, this is not helping. Rattled, he sits at the island with an ice cold bottle of Fiji Water and attempts to organize his thoughts.

If his work is "just a formula," Jonathan reminds himself, it's a page-turning, addictive one that over the years a whole boatload of people have done extremely well from. Now, like children, everyone seems to want different things. A thought comes to him—could it be that he's been asking the wrong questions? Asking what everyone else wants—his readers, Cindy, Laura, Ben, and God help him, Maddie . . . instead of asking what is it that he, Jonathan, wants? For so long he's been itching to write something new—but what? He gazes longingly at the wine fridge. It is practically calling out to him. Restless, he goes back upstairs and paces the area in front of his sticky-note wall, trying to settle the queasy, lurching sensation in his stomach. Cindy is right. Somewhere along the line, his readers have become his enemies.

Crude

2000

"Everyone says my life should be a novel," his barber had revealed. "It's just a formula, though, isn't it?" his accountant had remarked, during a meeting about how to manage Jonathan's newfound income. *Dark Tide* has hit number one on the *New York Times* bestseller list, and people can't wait to put in their seventy-five cents. Friends who have never expressed a shred of interest in writing, or reading, or even books in general, have let him know they themselves have written a book. Or were going to. Or almost had. Or would have—if only they had the time—"It's just a hobby really, isn't it?"—since they had "real jobs" to attend to. Never has Jonathan been the object of this much envy and attention—and it is the most amazing, *incredible* high.

There were still days his success made him feel like an impostor or a fraud. And yet, somehow here he is—at his new desk, in his new study, in his new home, in his new neighborhood. Like so many New Yorkers, he had long coveted a townhouse in the West Village, but never dreamed he'd actually possess one. Wandering through the light-filled rooms, marveling at the high ceilings, at the polished handrail and the sensation of the smooth American oak under his fingers, curving up, and up, *and up* . . . toward the impossibly distant top floor—for only the second time in his life, it was love at first sight.

"I'll take it," he'd joked to Cindy's broker. It was one of those corny, hokey lines, like "Follow that car!" that he'd always wanted to toss out. His whole street is so ludicrously pretty and clean and *picturesque,* it's almost like living in the suburbs. And just one more reminder of how, against all the odds, he has managed to turn his life around. Ben's "progressive" public school is right around the corner, its students drawn from affluent local families, including those of a few celebrities. Jonathan has noted the SUVs lined up outside, the faces discreetly shielded behind dark glasses. Who could have predicted that his own child would be taking finger painting and "musical expression" classes with the sons and daughters of movie stars? *If she could see me now,* he'd thought. *If she could only see me now . . .*

Saul arrives back with Ben. They've come from the car show at the Javits Center, Saul informs him, eyes taking in the hallway as Ben scampers upstairs to his room. Jonathan asks if Saul has time for coffee, or a tour of the house. Saul looks at his watch—"Another time, perhaps"—and asks whether the house isn't very noisy. It's true, Jonathan admits, that weekends brought the "Bridge and Tunnel" crowd, gunning their cars along West 4th and Bleecker, windows down and music blaring.

"But honestly, compared to my old apartment it's like living in a church!"

Saul casts a withering look toward the living room and says he needs to get back. Afterward, Jonathan wonders whether it was something he'd said. Saul is originally from Queens. Had the phrase "Bridge and Tunnel" come across as offensive? Next to Saul, it is easy to feel crude and stupid—like the village idiot, lumbering along the street with a pickax. He orders in pizza for himself and Ben, watches the child eat, his nose in a book of fairy tales. This wasn't the only chilliness he'd sensed lately from his brother-in-law who—now that he thinks about it—only seems to act friendly when Heather's around. A short while ago, Cindy had approached the producer of Saul's show, *Making Waves*, with an eye to having Jonathan as a guest, and gotten mysteriously stonewalled.

"I'm not worried," she'd assured him. "They'll be back."

But for once, Cindy was wrong. He gazes out of the window for a moment at the backyard, beautifully landscaped and bordered by strategically planted shrubbery, and makes himself a promise: *I'll never get used to this.* Never become jaded, or take for granted not having to worry about debts and bills.

Ben asks for more juice, and he gets himself another cappuccino too, listening with pleasure to the hiss and tap of the glossy red machine. He'd made sure to consult coffee-expert Mahoney on which model to buy. Then as a thank-you, sent the exact same one—in blue, naturally—to the cop's precinct out on Long Island. Was it too much? After putting in the order, he'd had second thoughts, worrying that the gift might be seen as inappropriate or too generous. Or, God forbid, as some kind of bribe.

After dinner, he puts Ben to bed and goes down to the study to gaze at his antique art deco desk, a find from the 26th Street flea market that Laura helped pick out. He'll never tire of its sleek lines. Sitting down in his new ergonomic chair, he takes a moment to enjoy the sensation—childish and satisfying—of the wheels rolling smoothly across the rubber mat. Tomorrow, he and Ben are meeting Laura for ice cream. For most people, kids spelled baggage. Not Laura. She's so good with Ben and provides the kind of loving support that Ben's own mother wasn't always so great at. They have, he supposes, been spending what might look like rather a lot of time together. In fact, next week Laura will be traveling with him to an out-of-town event. He still finds these rather terrifying.

"Act like you're talking to a friend," Cindy had said. The secret, she had explained, being to say just enough true things about yourself to come across as authentic. He'd replied that this sounded a little cynical. "And if you didn't spend so much time thinking about prizes," Cindy had shot back, "maybe I'd take that comment seriously."

Cindy—his pushy, wily stage mom. Sure enough, in interviews and appearances, audiences have seemed to take to him. As he'd mentioned to Laura, he couldn't have been more surprised—or more relieved.

"You obviously have a talent for it," Laura had said warmly, her hand coming to rest on his for a moment.

He turns his attention back to the screen, cues up the plot outline for his next book and reads it over. He has big plans for his detectives, and for the small, unsuspecting community of Ocean Falls. Young women in peril—throats slashed, beaten, strangled, imprisoned, chopped into pieces, thrown into ditches. Crimes that, in his version, will always be solved, no matter what. In which murderers—husbands, boyfriends, lone drifters, and unassuming neighbors—are brought swiftly to justice. To anyone else it would sound terrible, Jonathan thinks, but for him the prospect is strangely cathartic.

Status

2019

The manager of the bookstore has called again. He has in his possession another item, something very private that Jonathan must have forgotten, and far too personal to messenger over.

Jonathan waits for the guy on the top floor, where copies of *Gold-Plated Murder* are piled next to the cash register. Except the spines have been turned inward, obscuring his name.

There's a sound like a firecracker—*crack-crack!* And again, closer this time, *crack-crack-crack!* There's a fire exit ahead, and he makes a run for it, slams his body against the heavy metal door, takes the stairs three at a time. Left hand hits the rail at the bottom of each flight, holds fast as he spins around, almost in midair, down to the next. The gunman is right behind him, so close Jonathan can hear his breath. Five flights, six flights, down and down and down. Any second now he'll reach the bottom, find the way out.

The breaths become louder. The stench of gas fills the air. *Not breath*, he realizes. *A car*. And someone gunning the accelerator. He can see it now, two flights above, tires bumping and juddering obscenely down the stairs. Water is splashing at his feet. The farther down he goes, the deeper it gets. Eight flights, nine . . . *Nine?* No. That can't be right.

The car is right behind him. More water, putrid and foul, sucking at his shoes, swirling around his ankles . . . his knees . . .

his waist. Lights move crazily over the walls, the engine roars. *This is it,* he thinks. *This is where it ends.* There is no other choice. He turns to face the car. Sees it crouched at the top of the stairs like an animal, throbbing and ticking. And then, the engine revs and it charges toward him like an angry bull, and at last he sees the driver's face—and she is smiling.

Wide awake, he runs to the bathroom and retches into the sink, runs the faucet hard. In the mirror, his own face gazes back at him, frightened and pale.

He finds Laura in the kitchen, unloading groceries.

"Hey, sleepyhead . . ."

She would have been at the market by 6 a.m., but looks way fresher than he feels. He sits down, pours himself some coffee.

"We just got a bunch of new investors," she says, "did I tell you? I can't believe how well it's all taking shape. Milk?"

"Great. Thanks." His mind is still occupied by the nightmare, waiting for the car to run him down.

"And the guys had a wonderful idea for the cake," Laura continues over the din of the milk frother. "So they're going to bring samples for dessert tonight." Jonathan looks blankly at her. Her business partners are coming for supper, she reminds him. "Tell me you didn't forget . . ."

"You're right," he says. "It totally slipped my mind." While both men are perfectly lovely, Jonathan thinks, their restaurant talk can get somewhat dull and repetitive. Rather generously, he suggests that he take himself out later instead. "Let you all talk business."

Laura smiles. "No need." He watches her lay a neat spiral of scallops on a paper towel. "By the way," she adds, "I've been meaning to ask, what's going on with your Facebook status?" This is dropped into the conversation in such a deliberately off-hand manner that he knows immediately what she's referring to. For herself she doesn't care, Laura goes on, *obviously*. But her family finds it a little odd. "No biggie, but would it be an idea to update us to 'engaged'?" she suggests lightly.

"Actually," he replies, "I find the question a little odd." She glances across at him. "My Facebook is really nothing to do with me. Some intern at my publisher handles that stuff, you know that."

"Uh-huh." She moves to the sink, refills the water jug.

"It's not exactly my own personal outlet," he continues as she takes a tub of olives from one of the brown bags and looks around as if wondering where it belongs. "Did we forget something . . .?"

"The yellow alpine sea salt? I texted you yesterday. Where did you put it?"

"Sorry. I guess I was busy." Not to mention preoccupied with an extremely important deadline, he thinks to himself. Laura seems pretty relaxed, but he doesn't have a lot of free time and isn't exactly available to perform errands for random cookery ingredients. "I guess I could run to the Yoga Center," he says. "If you need me to."

"Good luck with that."

"Sorry?"

"It closed."

"Oh. Right."

The demise of their local yoga-cum-health-food place— another thing he's neglected to recall. Likely on purpose, seeing that the issue of beleaguered mom-and-pop stores was the subject of a hectoring sermon at Heather and Saul's last Sunday. *Predatory entities . . . bullying the small and vulnerable . . . blah, blah, blah.* During a recent visit to the store, he'd purchased a last-minute chocolate bar at the register, only to see the item pop up on the receipt as "impulse chocolate." As if the store had access to his inner thoughts, or his equally dubious eating habits. Tracking, watching, keeping tabs—everyone was doing it. Even the hippies.

"You know," Laura is saying, "if you installed the app I told you about, we wouldn't have this problem. I mean, we're both running around so much . . ."

The way she keeps opening and closing the cabinets, he thinks, is making him feel very antsy. And she seems very fired up about this tracking app, which has come up in conversation a few times. It knows exactly where you are, Laura explains now, as if this is a good thing and not some form of voluntary surveillance. As if it's not bad enough, Jonathan thinks, that they have all those buttons stuck to their fridge, ordering stuff on their own.

"Sounds complicated," he says.

"Heather and Saul love it."

"Well, there's a recommendation." Granted, he is taking what his mother would call a "tone." But why is she acting so insecure? What with everything going on, and all the pressure he's under, he's not in the mood for being prodded and hassled by Laura, of all people. "Why don't you have the fridge order salt?" he says. *Wiseass.*

"Oh, please. You're on your phone *all the time.* And we both know you use all kinds of taxi apps. I just don't get why you're so opposed to this one."

"Don't you trust me?" he fires back.

Laura turns, surprised. Flipping things around on your partner is bad practice in any relationship. His therapist will be very disappointed when he tells her. *If* he tells her, Jonathan thinks. *If* he ever goes to stupid therapy ever again. "You don't trust me," he repeats, sensing he has the upper hand. "Is that it?" Laura is holding a can of umami paste. For a moment, he wonders if she's going to throw it at him.

"Well, since you mention it, *I don't know,* Jon. Like, recently? When I want to know where you are, but you won't pick up the phone? When you say you're going to the gym but you're gone for hours? And when you *swear* you'll speak with your son and make no effort whatsoever? I mean, you complain about him all the time, and Lord knows I get it, but *you?* Your son is *hurting,* he needs help, but you refuse to properly address anything with him."

He feels the blood rush to his face. "Fine," he says. "Fine, OK, so tell me this: if the red dot stops in the middle of the street and stays there, what am I supposed to think? That you've been hit by a car?" And then, because he's in a hateful mood. Because he has wasted another fruitless morning on the internet. And because Ben is the very last problem he wants to get into, he lets her have it: "What if it *disappears? How about then*?! Is there some way this *stupid app* of yours can tell me whether you've been kidnapped or killed in a mass shooting? Does it tell me when to call 911?"

Laura regards him across the kitchen island with a shocked expression.

"Is this about—?"

"I am *not done*!" he yells. "Seriously, do you even hear yourself? You're picking a fight and we're having this totally *pathetic* argument about *nothing!*" He marches over to the fridge, yanks open the door, pulls out the nearest bottle of wine. "Literally *nothing!* Unless you're pissed at me for not finding the stupid yellow alpine sea salt. Which—*FYI*—the last time I looked, doesn't even exist! Seriously . . ." He makes sure she's looking in his direction, then shakes his head in disgust. "Seriously, I can't believe you're doing this."

The other night, he'd felt Laura nudging him awake. Groggy, mired in a feeling of dread and foreboding, he had thought there was a fire or some kind of emergency. *"No,"* she'd murmured, *"just talking in your sleep again."*

"What was I saying?" he asked.

"I couldn't tell," Laura replied. But now he wonders.

Meanwhile, she looks pissed. Has he overplayed his hand?

"Look," he says, relenting. "How about I run up to Trader Joe's and see if they have it?"

She looks down at the floor. "Actually, Jon, you know what? Don't bother. You're not exactly a pleasure to be with these days and I need to talk business with the guys later. So why don't you go out? Call Jay or take one of your precious walks. Just go deal with"—she gestures impatiently, twirls her fingers at him—"... your *stuff.*"

And just like that, he is off the hook.

Venom

2019

Behind him, a shadow moves, and Jonathan almost jumps out of his skin. He turns. Ben, smiling in the kitchen doorway.

"Hey, buddy, I didn't hear you come in . . ." Jonathan says. "How have you been?" He keeps his tone easy and conversational. Laura is on the West Coast for a few days, so luckily this isn't the right time for a confrontation. Though part of him can't help wondering whether Ben somehow knows this, and whether his appearance is deliberately timed.

"Doing OK," Ben says, heading for the fridge.

"I'm having lunch at Uncle Saul and Aunt Heather's in a while," he says. "I don't suppose you'd like to join us?" His son will have plans. He always does. But it never hurts to ask. "I know they'd love to see you," he adds mildly. "And Jay said he might drop by."

"Yeah, Uncle Saul already texted me."

Saul had confirmed with Jonathan as well, which is unusual. As was Jay promising to show up, especially on a Sunday, when he's either at the game or sleeping off the night before. Then again, after last week's conflict over the yellow alpine sea salt, he wouldn't put it past Laura to have asked the others to keep an eye on him during her absence. They've exchanged a few messages since she left on her business trip, all perfectly

241

pleasant. To his surprise, Ben says he wouldn't mind coming to lunch. "That's great, son," he replies, and means it.

As they walk to the subway together, chatting easily about Ben's plans for next semester, he decides that in all ways this can only be a good sign. Maybe it was for the best that Ben had kept himself out of the way for a while. He likes to think a child of his would have *some* sense of right and wrong. And with time to reflect, he has considered whether he and Laura had overreacted. Whether the situation had gotten somewhat hysterical and overblown. The insurance company is going to replace the watch, and when the damned thing shows up at the lake house or wherever, Laura will feel terrible about it. As for the stuff with Airbnb, he hasn't had time yet to check the listing. But if they are renting the place out, no doubt Ben's roommate Jamie would have talked him into it. What was it people said about trying to prove a negative? That it was basically impossible? There was no proof the shopping bags *didn't* belong to Jamie, or that the gym bag *wasn't* actually full of textbooks. And if it *was* money, he decides, it made sense Ben may only be trying to cover for his friend there as well. The latter came across as a perfectly nice kid, but perhaps a little *too* perfect? A little too obliging and too polite? Bad guys always pose as the good guys, after all.

They arrive to find Jay already there, for once not absorbed in his phone, but exchanging war stories with Heather about high-maintenance clients.

Saul accepts Jonathan's excellent bottle of Riesling and suggests iced tea. They all sit in the living room, which is stuffy and smells unpleasantly of boiled chicken, chatting about the weather, the news and—inevitably—Saul. As Heather pours from a large plastic jug, Jonathan is struck by how dismally provincial it all is. How . . . *American*. Saul clears his throat.

"I expect you're all wondering why I've brought you all here today," he begins importantly. *Time to renew your vows—again?* "Unfortunately, we need to discuss a very worrisome issue."

Jonathan steels himself for a lesson on inclusiveness, personal responsibility, gender discrimination, whatever. *Why did they all put up with it?* This incessant preaching to the choir? It's not as if they don't all read the fucking *New York Times* and pass around the relevant YouTube clips of Trevor Noah and Stephen Colbert, like everyone else. *Truly,* he thinks, *I want to die.*

"My Platinum AmEx has been used online," Saul continues grandly. "Might I add, without my permission." He looks around the room, pushes his glasses farther up the bridge of his nose. "The fact of the matter is . . ." Saul pauses, as if expecting someone to tell him. "The fact of the matter is, I understand that a number of rather concerning *issues* have come up with Ben recently."

Jonathan feels everyone's eyes on him. "Excuse me?" he says.

"With finances and so forth," Saul replies, with a nervous look in Ben's direction. *Was Saul kidding?*

Jonathan asks to see the credit-card statement. Saul hands it to him. Running his eyes down the column of charges, he's shocked to recognize brand names from his son's shopping bags. He looks over at Ben, who is staring intently at Saul, as if willing him not to say more. The card was used right around the last time Ben was here, Saul says now. An uneasy glance at Jonathan this time. Ben was in the study using the computer, he goes on. The card was sitting on his desk. It's like a hideous game of Clue, Jonathan thinks.

"I don't mind the loans," Saul says, "but this is completely unacceptable." His brother-in-law has been giving Ben money? *Since when?*

"You've got Uncle Saul *giving you money?*" Jonathan says, but Ben won't meet his eye.

At first, his son is indignant. Then, once it becomes clear this strategy isn't working, with depressing inevitability Ben changes tack.

"But *Dad,*" he is saying, "it wasn't my intention to actually *charge* anything. I told you, I needed books for school. They asked for a credit card for security or ID or something? And then, like maybe I went on some other sites and put in the wrong card."

"Ben," Jonathan says carefully. "I'm not a complete idiot. Whatever it was you were doing, it clearly wasn't for school." Each word that comes out of his son's mouth is so disappointingly, wretchedly *predictable.* His therapist maintains that good people can make bad choices. That they make mistakes. How about when you make the same one over and over? "Mistake"— Ben's excuse from the very beginning. A "mistake" with the credit-card machine. A "mistake" with the check. Calling a wrong number or misreading the instructions when putting together some piece of Ikea furniture—that's what qualified as a "mistake." *Like having a child that Maddie didn't want,* whispers the quiet little voice inside him. A child who had chosen to embarrass him in front of a sanctimonious asshole like Saul. Furious, he rounds on Ben.

"Do you even go to class?" he says. "I asked you! *Weeks ago,* I asked you. I gave you the chance to come clean. And you've chosen to squander it!" He gestures toward Heather and Saul. Saul, he remembers, who has summoned them all here to rub Jonathan's nose in his bad parenting. "You've *embarrassed* yourself in front of your uncle and aunt. You've stolen from them when they've done so much for you."

"Dad, honestly, it was never my intention to . . ." Ben begins tearfully, his tone unctuous and ingratiating.

"Don't bother," Jonathan snaps. "Just stop with the goddamn excuses already." The promises, the assurances, the *crying*, for Christ's sake. His son means none of it. Has never taken responsibility for his actions or shown even an ounce of remorse.

"Uncle Saul's lying," Ben says now. "He's a liar!"

His son, Jonathan decides, is not some teenager exhibiting temporary bad behavior. He's a criminal. And not a very talented one, either. The second time the restaurant accused Ben of stealing, didn't Heather say that a report to the police would teach him a lesson? Give him a fright? If only he'd listened. Ben is an adult. A complaint made now will create a criminal record. And then where will they all be? How will Ben ever get credit, an apartment, a mortgage . . . a job? That he doesn't even care about covering his tracks. That he took Saul's credit card and went straight to White-Off, or Superior, or whatever the hell it was, then strolled casually up the street and dropped another few hundred at John Lobb. Does his son feel entitled to the things that he takes?

"You know what, Ben?" he says. "*Sorry*'s fine. Just say *fucking sorry* for once, and mean it."

"But Dad—"

Jonathan steps forward. Ben takes a step back, fear in his eyes, looks wildly around the room as if searching for an escape route. "Dad, *look,* no . . ." he says.

"Jon, take it easy." Jay steps in, positioning himself between them.

"*Stay out of this*, Jay." Jonathan turns back to Ben. "I don't even know who you are anymore," he says. "But I do know there's only one liar in this room. And that's you."

"You're overreacting . . ." Ben bleats, as another surge of fury moves through Jonathan's body—Ben is *exactly* like her. He reaches forward, grabs Ben and shakes him violently.

"Who the fuck *are* you!?"

"Jon, take it easy!" Hands on his own shoulders. Jay, restraining him. Meanwhile, his actions have brought about a tremendous change in Ben. He looks defiant.

"You're the asshole," Ben says, voice dripping venom. *It speaks. The mask has slipped.* "I hate all of you. I wish I'd never been born!"

That makes two of us, Jonathan thinks. And then he sees Ben's face, and realizes that he must have said it out loud. There's a shocked silence. Ben leaves the room. Jay, Heather, and Saul stand as if rooted to the spot as, from the direction of Saul's study, comes the sound of drawers opening and closing. Then Ben returns, holding something in his hand.

"Is this what you've been looking for?" he says, holding the object out to the room with a sideways leer at Saul. "Check it out, Dad." He does, and his mind reels. A woman's scarf. Electric blue, with a vivid red flower pattern. *Unmistakable.* His gift to Maddie their very first Christmas together.

"Where did you get that?" Jonathan says quietly.

"This old thing?" A nod toward Saul, who looks like he's seen a ghost. "He keeps it in his desk. Oh, *wait*, you didn't know?" *Was she wearing it that day? Was she wearing it on the beach ...?* His thoughts race. He can't remember. Can't be sure. His mind is a black sheet of rage.

"*You* ..." he snarls, lunging at Saul, who is still staring open-mouthed at Ben. He knows he should stay back, be smart about it. But he can't: the scarf is akin to a guilty plea. Saul skitters backward into the wall, almost tripping over his own feet.

"It was an *accident*," he bleats, echoing Ben, holding up his hands. "A *mistake*. It just happened."

In the next few seconds, everything seems to happen at once. As Jonathan reaches for Saul, Jay leaps forward and grips Jonathan firmly by the upper arms. Saul makes a grab for the scarf, but Ben hangs onto it. There's a sickening rip, and the scarf hangs in two pieces. For a moment, Jonathan doesn't understand what it is, the high-pitched, piteous noise that fills the room, like an animal keening. Even Ben looks stunned, lets his half go. As it flutters to the floor, Saul drops to his knees, weeping—groveling and snatching at it. Heather gapes. Saul, coming to his senses, abruptly drops his half and scrambles to his feet, looks behind him as if assessing his chances of escape. The whole scene is theatrical, unreal.

"*Both of you*," Jay says. "Quit it now."

Saul cowers against the wall with an anguished expression, looks gratefully up at Jay, and scuttles into the hallway. A few seconds later, they hear sounds of a heavy piece of furniture being dragged across Saul's study, and wedged against the door. Dazed, Jonathan looks around. Heather, slack-faced, standing woodenly in the doorway. Jay, arms held at his sides, ready to leap into action. And Ben, gazing at his father with a triumphant expression Jonathan's never seen before. Of a job well done, perhaps.

As Ben leaves, slamming the apartment door, he takes a few steps toward the study, ready to kick the door down. Once more, Jay's hand closes around his arm.

"Jon. *Listen to me*. It's not what you think." Jay looks over at Heather, a look passing between them.

"*Isn't it?*" Jonathan spits. "Are you all fucking kidding me? You're *protecting* him?" Why is no one calling the police?

"Come on, let's get you out of here. Heather? You too."

"No, I . . ." he begins.

"Jon, you gotta trust me on this." The adrenaline is wearing off and suddenly he feels awfully tired. He allows himself to be steered firmly toward the front door, Heather following—but not before stopping to pick up both pieces of the scarf and stuffing them into his pocket. As he makes his way unsteadily across the room, he sees Jay pick up a chair he only vaguely remembers knocking over.

Chopped

2019

In the elevator down, all three are silent, absorbed in their own thoughts. *Respond,* Jonathan is thinking, *not react.* With his mind still in turmoil, he needs to figure out what's going on and how to handle it.

"Both of you," Jay instructs, when they get outside, "go get coffee or something. Heather? Sorry, but you need to tell him. It's time." Heather nods, face a white mask.

Before Jonathan can ask what this means, Jay has flagged down a passing cab and is gone. *Respond, not react.* It is only once they're a good half-block from the building and its prying doormen that he can see how angry his sister is.

"Oh God, I'm gonna be sick . . ." She runs for the gutter, clutches at her stomach, takes a few deep breaths before finally recovering herself. Then, as they continue on, out it all comes.

Never has he heard her so free with her expletives. Pedestrians stare and hurry by. In any other circumstance, it would be hilarious. No one is laughing, though. He lets her vent—for so many reasons barely able to believe his own ears.

"Fuck him. Just *fuck* him. Sure, the East Coast fucking *elite* assholes all know his name, but compared to me he makes chicken feed."

Standing in line at Starbucks to order their drinks, Heather is still not done. Jonathan is in awe, watching as twenty years of rage pours out. When she at last takes a breath—a sob more than a breath—it's a mere interval between items on a long list of insults and injuries.

"*I'm* the breadwinner," she is saying. " *I* bust my ass working sixty hours a week. Not him. The apartment is in my name. The house, *my* name. *Not* his."

He glances around them. Heads buried in phones, eyes glued to screens. Oblivious.

"And the Audi? That's mine too. I paid for it . . ." Another ragged breath. "I had him sign a postnup—you didn't know that, did you?" Jonathan admits that, no, he had no idea there even was such a thing. She had her lawyer draft it when they renewed their vows, his sister says. "Saul made me feel like a complete *bitch* for even suggesting it, but I did it anyway. 'You fuck someone else?' I told him. 'You get nothing. *Nothing. Not a cent.*'"

Their drinks arrive and they find an empty table and sit down. So far he has said very little, doesn't even know what to say.

"All those late nights at the radio station," Heather says. "She was always pestering him to read her work. I should have known when he offered to 'mentor' her—what a joke! He said she was deluded, practically *stalking* him. That it didn't *mean* anything, and he felt nothing for her. Oh, *God* . . . every cliché in the fucking book." Jonathan stares, literally lost for words. "Yeah. Well, I guess things aren't always how they seem, are they?" Heather says.

You got that right, he thinks savagely. *Saul* . . . that pious, supercilious, self-righteous *prick*. Where did they do it? Hotels? Saul and Heather's apartment? *His* apartment? There's the fact that Jay knew. Jay, his best friend, had said nothing. More betrayal. *It was you,* he had screamed at Saul. *As if.* Not for a moment did he think Saul had killed Maddie.

But he was happy to let the rest of them think so. *I know kill-ers,* he'd wanted to say. *I wrote the book on killers. I've researched and written about killers and their crimes for twenty years. And* you, you piece of stinking shit, *you don't have the fucking balls!* It was a close thing, but somehow he'd managed not to go there.

Maddie, called out for late-night rehearsals, taking hushed phone calls at odd hours. And himself, working endless shifts to support her and Ben. Telling himself that they weren't like other couples. That they were artists, living intensely, with passion and truth—and freedom. *Idiot.* How did he not see it?

"You think you know someone . . ." Heather is saying.

He had spent a great many years thinking about the person who had driven his wife away from him. Not for a minute had he suspected that the person who'd *actually* taken her was someone close. *Saul.* A member of his own family. *Saul.* Of all people. "*A sad little man. The poor man's Napoleon.*" Another sick joke. One that was on him, apparently.

"He told me he didn't love her," she continues. "And I believed him." A humorless smile. "You must think I'm such an idiot."

As his own feelings begin to settle, Jonathan finds himself able to reflect on what just happened—Saul's desperate grab for the scarf, his howl as the fabric was ripped in two. How, in that moment, it had all come together: his brother-in-law was in love with Maddie—and still is.

"*He's* the idiot," Jonathan says supportively as a realization comes to him that his therapist would be proud of. Saul, with his unquestioning devotion to Maddie, is a mirror image of himself. Or rather, the person he used to be. Is that what Maddie had seen in Saul? Someone she could control—save with one convenient exception: that Saul was more successful.

Now, he thinks. Now all the pieces fall into place. Now it all makes sense.

Saul had tried to break it off, Heather continues, but Maddie wouldn't listen. And then, after she went missing, Saul got freaked out and confessed everything. "He'd just won the Pulitzer, remember?"

How couldn't I? Jonathan thinks. Like the perpetual references to fucking Harvard, Saul has never let Jonathan or anyone else forget it.

"Vaguely," he replies.

"He was terrified of the scandal," Heather says, pausing to take a first sip of her coffee. "He had his . . . *reputation* to uphold." *Reputation*—he can hear the bile in her voice. The bitterness. The word virtually spat out onto the table between them—an echo from the moment of discovery that doubtless his sister is not even conscious of. In Heather's world of law and lawsuits, a cheating spouse wouldn't have looked good for her either. The gossip, the outright pity from friends and associates—his sister would have hated it. More patrician than pretty, by her early thirties, Heather was a high-flying associate, traveling frequently with the senior partners—to Latin America, Asia, Europe. Likely she could have had affairs. Almost certainly she had chosen not to. Instead, she had stuck by the nebbish Saul who, when his own chance arrived, had quite literally grabbed it with both hands. It's despicable.

"When he told me," Heather says, swallowing hard, "I swear to God the first words out of my mouth were, '*Her?*' That shallow, pseudointellectual, undermedicated—sorry, no offense, Jon—airhead *bimbo*?" She takes a breath. "You were too good for her. You know that, right? We could all see it."

Too good for her? I'm too good for all of you, he thinks. Though up until the very end, with Maddie he'd been convinced that it was the other way around. Not cultured, not worldly, not exciting enough.

"She told him it was over between you, and that it had been for some time," Heather continues mercilessly. "Said she was scared to tell you because you'd freak out, or some bullshit excuse. She had this idea they were going to just run away together, right after Christmas. To Hollywood or someplace. Had it all figured out, apparently. I mean, for goodness' sake, she used to cut her own freakin' hair!"

After Christmas. Would they even have been back from their round-the-world trip by then? Numbly, he tries to remember what their plans would have been for the holidays that year. Take Ben and spend it at his parents' depressing ranch house in Rochester, probably.

"She thought they were *in love*! Give me a fucking break. It was so *obvious* that she was using him."

When, and where, and how had it all started? And *who* started it? He feels he knows the answer to that one. *No*, he thinks. *I can't. I won't. That way, madness lies.*

"I should have known when he told me how *'multitalented'* she was," Heather continues.

And what was I, he thinks, *chopped liver?* A meal ticket? Apparently, you didn't have to trek to some glamorous or exotic location to have an affair. You could meet someone on the local bus or in the laundromat. Or—in Saul's case—right in your own metaphorical backyard.

Motive, more than opportunity, provides the engine of an affair. Opportunity merely cracks the door a little, gives you a tantalizing peek at what you are missing. But that didn't mean you had to open it all the way. Had Saul hesitated? Had he even stopped to wrestle with the implications of what he was doing? Or had he jumped right in? *Come in, the water's warm!* That his brother-in-law was the last person you'd suspect, he decides, is what made it all so . . . *tragic*. Was that the word? And tragic for whom? How happy Maddie had appeared that last weekend. And now Jonathan knows why. In her mind, she was already gone. Her escape was already planned. She was happy, but not for the reason he thought. *It's . . . taking something that isn't actually true . . . and imagining it for yourself. And then, if you do it well, for the audience it appears true.*

"Honestly, I just couldn't imagine her being *abducted* by anyone," Heather is saying. "The idea of *her* not being able to defend herself. And suicide, *please.*" A bitter laugh. "That girl was way too vain to kill herself. I figured she ran off to stupid Hollywood or found some other patsy to take care of her."

You can stop twisting the knife now, Sis, he thinks.

"Yes," he says. "I can understand why you'd think that." Saul must have lured Maddie in with promises he couldn't keep, or why else would she have taken up with him? As for his own relationship with her, had it merely been some elaborate *trap* all along? And was he, Jonathan, just the poor sap who'd fallen into it? The only one dumb enough to make it official? Maybe she had him pegged from the get-go. The very night they met. Someone to wait on her, hand and foot. Someone to pay the rent, leaving her free to concentrate on her "art." A rest stop en route to Hollywood. Then Ben came along. And that changed everything. Marriage—how willingly the rebel artist and unconventional "free spirit" had said yes to *that* idea. And with it, naturally, the small matter of a Green Card . . .

"Deep down, I must have known, right?" Heather repeats ruefully. His sister will torture herself with this thought forever, Jonathan thinks. Once you took a ride on that carousel, it is almost impossible to get off. "*People let you know,* isn't that what they say? It's always the assholes you think you can trust."

"It wasn't just you," he reminds her. "We both got played."
Had they laughed at him behind his back?

"Yeah, well, fool me once . . ." Heather rearranges the cream-colored Hermes scarf around her neck. An unconscious attempt, perhaps, to reclaim some dignity.

In the silence that follows, he watches her pull at her hands. It's an unconscious gesture she's used since they were children. Signaling embarrassment, reluctant admissions. A quick sidelong glance into the room, as if to check who's watching. Knowing? Nervous? Neither of these? He can't tell. He knows all of his sister's facial expressions, and this isn't one of them.

"I'm sorry," she says. "There's something else you should know." *God help me*, he thinks. What fresh hell could possibly lie in wait for him now?

Heather leans forward, lowers her voice as if to invite him to participate in a conspiracy. "*Laura*," she says.

"What about her?"

"Laura knows."

There was the shot, he thinks. And then there was the chaser. No wonder Jay took off in such a hurry.

"I was upset, and after Maddie went missing, I guess it slipped out. But, you know, Laura was Maddie's friend, so she already knew."

There's something else Heather's not saying. He can tell. "*Spit it out*," he says.

She sighs, shifts awkwardly in her seat. "Laura told Jay," she says, "and he was *pissed*. He wanted to tell you about it, but she made him swear not to. Jay's argument was, if there was Saul, maybe there were other guys in the picture as well. So he agreed not to tell you, but he insisted on telling the cops, just in case."

Mahoney, he thinks. Mahoney knows. It is death by a thousand cuts.

Heather places a hand gently on his. "I know you're upset," she says. "And you have a right to be. But you don't remember how you were. You were in such a bad way, Jon, and you didn't need more bad news. We were all so worried about you." She pauses. "Whatever we thought of her, it was a terrible thing that happened and . . . I was worried you were never going to come back from it."

How many other people know of his status as a cuckold? Question and analyze your thoughts, his therapist says. Catch them as they occur. Observe them with interest, not emotion. But most of all, *do not act on them.* For almost twenty-three years, he has tried to cultivate this habit, to live by its principles. Taking an amused, tolerant approach to his thoughts and feelings—*Isn't this all just so amusing?*—a tolerant parent, a Buddhist monk at a raucous dinner party. And, save for minor hiccups, he's mostly succeeded.

"We didn't set out to deceive you," his sister is saying, "but we all talked it over and this seemed like the only way."

All the waiting, all the wondering and not knowing. The perpetual sick feeling in his stomach. Simultaneously dreading and hoping for the sound of the phone. How could Heather possibly understand what that was like? All the times he'd wanted to disappear himself. The nights and days of despair spent with his head in a bottle. Knowing that he could so easily have stopped it all from happening.

"We all care about you, Jon," Heather is saying. "You know that. And if it's of any comfort, we all promised that we would never discuss it with anyone, not even with each other."

Please, he thinks, *just shut up now.*

"*She'd be so proud of you,*" Laura had said when his first novel was published. Had she meant it? Or, like the others, had she just said it to make him feel better? The notion of the people he's closest to pitying him, discussing him, whispering

256

about him behind his back. They would never admit it, but there would have been the undeniable thrill of a secret that concerned him, and that he himself was not privy to. What else weren't they telling him?

"You didn't leave," he says.

"What?" A ripple of irritation crosses her face. "No, I didn't leave my husband."

How about now? he wants to say. *What's the statute of limitations on cheating?*

"Why not?" It's a genuine question.

Heather places her cup on the table. "Because that's what people do, Jon. When they love each other."

"Please, Heather. Don't lecture me about love . . ."

"Look, Saul made a *mistake*." *That again.* "It doesn't mean I don't care about him. It doesn't mean he's a bad person." *Denial.* Apparently, it was quite popular. He watches her mouth twist, as if trying to get it around something difficult.

"Actually," she says with a small cough, looking quickly around the room. "Actually, we went into couples' therapy."

Despite everything, he almost laughs.

"You're joking, right?"

His sister is hardcore, with little patience for what she calls "new-age BS." She won't even go with Laura to Pilates. The day is full of surprises.

"*No.* I'm not. Aren't *you* in therapy?"

"Sure. But I go alone. That's not the same thing." Couples' therapy signaled the death knell for any relationship, everyone knew that. As for himself, you couldn't exactly call it "deep" or traumatic, the so-called "work" that he and his therapist did together. Not with a straight face, anyway. Basically, he pays four grand a month to bitch and moan about his agent, his publisher, and his schedule, in that order. That this leaves little time to complain about his friends and family is, he supposes, just as well.

"Well," Heather says shortly, pulling herself upright. "It worked for us."

Jonathan refrains from the obvious retort. Can barely imagine how much it must have cost her—emotionally and reputationally—to even show up to therapy in the first place. To discuss with a complete stranger the humiliation of having your husband fuck someone else, over and over, while sitting on the couch right next to the self-same piece of shit. *And she's still going!* Unbelievable. Marriage—committing to one another, in sickness or in health. Forsaking all others via an ironclad contract, never to be broken. You "worked" at your relationship. You turned the other cheek. You dealt with your "issues" like a grown-up. *Yadda yadda yadda.* Marriage was a spark of optimism, but that's all it was. It took an effort of will to trust someone . . . which made it so much worse when that trust was betrayed. When you discovered that, for the person who was your whole world, it was all a performance. A game of "Let's pretend." *Poor Heather.* Two decades of emotional revelation and mutual vulnerability and "how do you feel about that?" and sharing with your partner every single trivial thought or passing insecurity that went through your head, only to . . . *God, does he really want to put himself through all that again?*

"I don't even want to look at him," Heather says, pushing away her coffee cup. "Jon, he kept her fucking *clothing!* It's sick."

"Yeah," he says. "I get it."

Questions are still cascading through his mind like a series of falling dominoes. If Saul had had the balls to leave Heather, would Maddie be with Saul now? And where would Jonathan be? One thing's for sure. If they hadn't been at the beach that weekend, his wife would still be alive. His mind is bursting with these if/then conundrums, some of which he can share with Heather, and some he can't—obviously.

As they lapse into silence, the sounds of the coffee shop seem to magnify around them—the clatter of cups, the sharp hiss of the espresso machine, the surly barista calling out orders. Frenetic activity in stark contrast to the nearing-middle-aged man and woman, sitting with their cold cups of coffee amid the tired wreckage of their personal lives. How is Heather supposed to come to terms with this double betrayal? He watches her dig for something in her bag, take out her phone.

"It's him . . ." she says, glancing at it. "I should go back." She produces a large pair of sunglasses and sets them carefully over her eyes.

"You look very Jackie O," he remarks.

"Thanks," she says with a wan smile. "I guess."

He remembers something he's been wanting to ask since they sat down. Jay had told the cops about the affair, but was Saul ever properly questioned by the police? Or, for that matter, threatened with a lie detector? Not to mention bullied and scolded by man-hater Ragione, brandishing her pink handcuffs.

"By the way," he says. "The weekend Maddie and I were out at the beach, Saul was away, right? Where was he, exactly?" Does his sister still believe Maddie got into a car with some other man she was seeing, and drove away to a happier life? Or is that simply what she needs to tell herself? Resolve the cognitive dissonance with self-deception. He knows how that works.

"I told you," she replies. "He was at a conference." Too late, he has already seen it. A millisecond of hesitation. His sister is nothing if not thorough. She would have dotted the *I*s and crossed all the *T*s. But the question has spooked her. Today's revelations have been a shock to her too. And maybe even she is having doubts.

"And you know that for sure?"

"You think I don't know my own husband?" *Clearly not.* Then again, he doesn't know his own sister as well as he thought. Or his own wife. Or his own friends.

"He was at a conference. The police know that." She pauses. "Fine. Look. If you must know, he got back that Friday night and left first thing Saturday to go upstate to the house." A big sigh. "But I told them he spent the whole weekend here with me in the city."

"You lied to the police?"

"Oh, knock it off, Jon." Heather rolls her eyes. "We're not all besties with the cops. You'll forgive me if I didn't want them poking their noses in our private life. Not with everything we had going on. Honestly, I didn't need to deal with one more damned thing."

"Uh-huh . . ."

"He was definitely up at the house. On one of his ridiculous adventures in the woods. I told you that at the time, you don't remember?"

"Under the circumstances," he replies, "you'll forgive me if I don't."

Another huge sigh as she picks up her bag and stands to go. "You know what I think?" she says. "I think she tricked him into the whole thing."

"I'm sure you're right." *The lies we tell ourselves . . .*

"By the way . . ." As she turns back, there's a crooked little smile on her face. "He thought you did it."

"What?"

"Saul. He was utterly convinced that you'd . . . I don't know, *done* something to her."

"*To Maddie?* Jesus . . ." There's a pause. "Like fucking what, Heth?"

She shrugs. "No idea. I don't think he had that part worked out."

"Why didn't he tell the police?"

"Oh, he wanted to, believe me. But I reminded him that making accusations would only bring his own sordid mess out into the open."

"Makes sense," he sighs. How typical of Saul to want to pin the blame on him. And that his holier-than-thou brother-in-law would rather a would-be murderer go free than soil his precious reputation. Truly, you couldn't write it.

There doesn't seem much else to say, so they agree to speak soon and Heather leaves.

Watching her walk out onto the street, it strikes him that her whole posture has changed. As if something inside her has broken or given way. As his big sister, she has always been there for him. Before Jay, before Maddie, before Laura. They'd had their differences—what siblings didn't? But whether defending him from high-school bullies or covering for him with homework, she had always been his protector. And as an adult, sparing him the bad news about Maddie's affair, she had attempted to do him a kindness, even as the knowledge had taken its toll on her. Well, that was one way of looking at it. Because this so-called "self-sacrifice" was also—undenia-bly—self-serving. Lying had allowed her to preserve her own reputation and her dysfunctional marriage, and to carry on as if nothing had happened. Worse, she had provided a false alibi to the very last person who deserved one.

He watches her, standing at the crosswalk on Amsterdam Avenue, as she takes out her phone. There is something slightly dishonest, he thinks, about observing people who have no clue that you are doing so. It places them at a distinct disadvantage. Once Heather is out of sight, he gets up and walks thoughtfully out into the late-afternoon heat. What they hadn't touched on, he realizes, was Ben. Which is interesting. How long had his son known about the scarf? And that his uncle has been holding a torch for his mother?

Meanwhile, something else has been bugging him since the showdown at the apartment. Something significant, flickering away at his consciousness, almost-but-not-quite coming to him as he'd struggled to keep his wits intact. Now, in a flash of recognition, he sees it. He doesn't know how he knows it, but it's so obvious he can't believe he's missed it for so long. When Ben called Saul a liar, Saul looked as if he were going to burst into tears. And when Ben appeared with the scarf . . . *God* . . . He almost feels bad for the guy . . . the expression on Saul's face, the bewilderment, the disbelief. An expression he himself understands only too well: that of a betrayed parent.

Locked

2019

After another sleepless night, Jonathan calls the locksmith. Ben hadn't come home, and that was probably for the best. Resisting the temptation to address Ben in his own language by firing off a "GTFO," he instead sends a text that conveys calm and control. When Laura gets back from her trip, he says, they will discuss the apartment and Ben's future.

At around eleven-thirty, the doorbell rings. Ben stands on the stoop, no "Hey, Dad," no ready smile.

"I need to get my stuff," Ben says, without looking at him. Jonathan waits in the hallway, paces back and forth while Ben goes upstairs and gathers his belongings. He is making this far easier than anticipated. Then again, there is very little to say. Nothing *he* needs to say, at least.

Does Ben suspect that doting Uncle Saul may well be his father? Quite possibly he has no clue. Saul may be cowardly and deceitful, but he isn't stupid. And by all accounts, he has a keen sense of self-preservation. The risk of being subjected to a paternity test, quickly followed by the loss of his marriage and his reputation, would not be in Saul's interest. Not then, and certainly not now. God . . . how sordid and disappointing it all was. Like one of those cheesy daytime talk shows he'd never dream of watching. He had found himself chewing over the various scenarios during the night. Considering that if what Heather said was true, and Saul *had* tried to end the . . . affair, Maddie could have said the child was his. (Though this could also have been a lie to gain leverage.) After all, in the unlikely event Saul had himself demanded a paternity test, she could have refused and threatened to blow the whistle on the whole sorry situation. There is some comfort in this hypothesis. In realizing that he, Jonathan, was not the only idiot.

Somewhere above, Ben's footsteps thump to and fro across the floor. It's true people remark that Jonathan and Ben look alike. But, so what? People see what they want to see. Or more likely are just being polite. Heather never once mentioned Ben yesterday, which in itself was deeply odd, until you assume that she too believes Saul is the father. And, though Jonathan has no actual proof, and has absolutely no intention of taking a paternity test either, he is choosing to believe it too.

At last, he hears Ben's suitcase being bumped down the stairs. Jonathan had made his own way in life, hadn't he? Now it was Ben's turn. Let him see what it is really like out there. In fact, throwing him out will be doing him a favor. He opens the front door, waits until Ben—stranger, impostor, changeling— has walked through it, and locks it behind him. Some people, Jonathan decides, were just born rotten.

Last week, in a fit of paranoia he'd taken back their spare house keys from their guy at the corner deli, who normally keeps them on hand under the counter. He now needs to get the new ones to Laura and, whether from Ben having left or the events of the day before, he finds himself dropping them off at the deli again and feeling fairly relaxed about it. Likewise, walking to the parking garage, though it hasn't entirely dissipated, there is less sense of being followed or pursued.

Taking the car, he drives up to the midtown tunnel. He has always avoided book engagements out east, and it's years since he's been back, to the town or anywhere near the Hamptons. One reason he's been able to build and maintain a friendship with Mahoney is that he and his family live in Queens. Today, however, requires the element of surprise. And that means showing up in person at the dock where Mahoney keeps his boat—and not letting him know beforehand.

Arriving in the town a couple of hours later, he's faintly surprised that it doesn't resemble Ocean Falls. Of course, the fictional hamlet is his own creation—its homes, main street, stores, bars, and restaurants cribbed from other towns, from films and Google images and—like a few other things—his own imagination. His fictional town is smaller and more hidden than this one. You'd drive right past the sign for Ocean Falls on Highway 27. That is, until the city people discovered it. Which is when all the trouble started.

He passes the police precinct, looking as dreary as it did twenty years ago. Old paper. Stale coffee. Bleach. It probably smells the same as well. He won't be going in to find out.

Locating the boatyard, he pulls into the parking lot (*For our trusted customers only*) and places his PBA card on the dash. He finds Mahoney on the deck, untangling some fishing line.

"Jon . . . hey . . ." Mahoney looks up, startled.

"Surprise." Jonathan smiles.

"That you are." Mahoney gets to his feet and flinches as he does so. "Knee playing up again," he sighs. "Not like you to show up without telling me. Everything OK . . . ?"

"I was in the area," he replies, "just doing some research. You're always telling me to come out, so I thought I'd drop in and say hello."

"Well, I'm glad you did." Mahoney grins. "Welcome aboard."

Jonathan steps gingerly across the narrow plank connecting the boat to the dock. Gesturing to a plastic table, Mahoney pulls up two crates for them to sit on. "Whaddya think? Pretty fancy, huh? Get you a beer? My brother-in-law left a couple bottles in the cooler."

"No, thank you. Maybe later."

For the next few minutes, they exchange the usual pleasantries. Mahoney asks after Laura and Ben, and Jonathan replies that everyone's doing great.

"Hey, how about coffee?" the cop says. "I got a new machine." Jonathan asks for water, and Mahoney disappears into the boat's little cabin. In the harbor, people tinker contentedly on their boats or sit gazing out into the middle distance. What on earth did any of them like about it? The perpetual bilious rocking, the oily water, filthy and insinuating. The air holds the faint odor of gasoline—of rancid dead things. Mahoney returns carrying a plastic jug of water and two mason jars.

"So, what's new with you?" he asks Jonathan.

"Nothing too much." And, after a pause, "Just something I wanted to run by you."

"Sure. Shoot." Mahoney squints into the sun for a moment, rolls up the sleeves of his shirt, relaxed and content, enjoying his retirement. Diving right in, Jonathan asks about Maddie's case, how many people the investigation had taken in, and how thoroughly they had all been looked into. Mahoney looks bemused. "Is this for your next book or something?"

"No, not really."

Across from them, a number of boats sit raised on stilts, wrapped in what looks like shrink-wrap. *A Shrinking Violet* features just such a boatyard. It's where Caleffi discovers the killer's third victim, sealed and concealed. He'd included a number of cheesy jokes between his detectives about "wrapping up the case," and the like. But as he'd learned the other day on Amazon, this hadn't gone down so well with some of his readers.

"OK . . ." Mahoney says, clearly still mystified. "As you know, we checked out every lead we had. That's standard operating procedure." Jonathan lets the silence linger. "What's your concern, though? You think you've seen her again . . .?" He shakes his head. Mahoney, visibly relieved, looks curiously at him. "Anything you wanna share . . .?"

"Not right now, no. So you're saying that you checked out everyone?"

"Yep, you betcha."

They have shared a lot over the years, Jonathan thinks. He has heard it all—the cop's thoughts on marriage, his tough blue-collar upbringing. Mahoney has often remarked on what a great listener Jonathan is. "That's the writer in you," he had observed early on. Not that their conversations haven't been interesting. On the contrary, they have been immensely helpful. And Mahoney is right. He is all ears, always. If not always for the reasons people assume.

"What about people closer to home?" Jonathan asks.

"Like who?"

"Family members." Mahoney blinks twice rapidly in succession, chooses this moment to top off their already full glasses from the jug on the table. *Gotcha.* No accident, Jonathan decides, that Mahoney takes this opportunity to reposition the jug as well.

It now sits directly between them, blocking Jonathan's eyeline. Using the excuse of taking off his jacket, he shifts in his seat, re-establishing eye contact.

"I think I'll have that beer," he says now, "if you have one lying around." Historically he has abstained from alcohol when they meet up because it seems rude to indulge when someone else doesn't.

Mahoney goes below deck and he hears the crack and hiss as the bottle is opened. His friend is not the only detective on board. As a writer, Jonathan has made it his business to uncover people's foibles and failings. Including one key piece of information Mahoney has never shared. That many years ago, he was investigated for alcohol-related misconduct.

"You sure you won't have one?" he asks innocently when Mahoney returns with a rather dusty-looking bottle of super-market beer. There's a beat. Mahoney clears his throat, looks a little thrown.

"No, I'm good, Jon. Thanks." His eyes move away for a moment. "About your wife's case," he says. "There were rumors. Gossip. I can tell you that for sure. Stuff happens and people have a lot to say. You know what I'm talking about?" Jonathan nods. *Sure do.* "Always some knucklehead with an ax to grind, ready to talk shit or shoot their mouth off. People get off on the attention. Makes 'em feel important."

Not for the first time Jonathan is struck by how, even during his most difficult moments, some part of his brain is always noticing, observing, taking quiet little notes. Body language, gait, gestures, facial expressions, verbal qualifiers, uncon-scious tics and traits. How a person might sigh at particular times; at others raise a hand to their mouth. *How readily people betray themselves* . . . If you know what to look for, it is laugh-ably obvious, the tiny, barely perceptible things that underpin and reveal an individual's character. Most laughably of all, perhaps, being his own. Of all people, he has long understood the value of getting it right. People may see what you want them to see. And yet, try as you might to conceal it, the truth leaks out in other ways. The *invisible obvious*—missing what is right in front of you. And here it is, Jonathan thinks. Right in front of him. *Et tu, Mahoney.* His best friend, his fiancée, his sister, her husband. And now Mahoney. Traitors, all. He thinks of Ragione, that malicious smirk. God, he'd wanted to slap it off her. Would do it, as well, if he ever got the chance. He had expected more of Mahoney, though.

"How're Saul and Heather doing these days?" the cop inquires every time they meet up. As another keen observer of human behavior, Mahoney prides himself on being one of the "good guys." So it's hard to believe the cop can't see the contempt seeping out of him. Or does he? Does he, in fact, smell a rat? Briefly Mahoney tugs at his ear—the cop's particular "tell." *Tacit knowledge.* Information people possess that they don't consciously realize they have. Mahoney senses something amiss, but hasn't yet identified what it is.

"As far as I recall . . ." he is saying, as if testifying before congress, "everyone checked out." *Truth,* Jonathan thinks darkly, but not the spirit of the truth.

Evidently, in Mahoney's view, they don't know each other well enough for that. Already the cop is defending himself. Covering his own ass. Petty criminals caught in the act, regular people caught in a bad place; rats in a cage. In the end, they all try to find a way out. In the end, almost all fail. Jonathan takes a lavish swig from the bottle, smacks his lips, smiles encouragingly.

"It was a question of limited resources," Mahoney continues uncertainly. "It wasn't worth wasting our time—or yours—on hearsay or gossip. Information comes up . . . that . . . we need to know . . . but isn't . . ." The cop appears to be having trouble finding his words. He would, Jonathan thinks, be terrible at improv. ". . . our business," Mahoney goes on. "We check out the information we're given, but we don't get into your personal life any more than we need to. You get what I'm saying?"

Jonathan nods. Mahoney can talk, but he is never this wordy. He's beginning to sound desperate.

"We share the important stuff, that's all I can tell you." As Mahoney sits back and crosses his arms, Jonathan balls his hands into tight fists under the table and counts to ten, as his therapist has taught him.

"Standard operating procedure," Mahoney repeats, almost to himself. "Not our business unless it impacts the case," he adds, looking Jonathan in the eye this time. *Too much eye contact,* he thinks, *is as bad as not enough.*

As Mahoney tries again to fill their already brimming-over glasses, Jonathan thinks about the email exchange he had with Cindy this morning. He had asked whether she'd consider letting him take a break from the Ocean Falls series to write something else.

Memoir? had come the reply. *Let's talk!*

No . . . he'd written back. *Maybe a standalone.*

About?

Not sure yet, he'd replied, which to Cindy, he realizes, would have come across not as tantalizingly opaque, but disappointing and indecisive. They both know he would need to properly wind up Ocean Falls before attempting anything else. Then again, things didn't always end the way you wanted them to.

As Mahoney gets up on some excuse of refilling the water pitcher, an idea comes to Jonathan. Mahoney's nephew—was the child ever found? This information has not been offered and, knowing how it felt, he had not wanted to pry. The incident could offer an interesting plot point for a final book of one of his fictional cops' family lives. Not that this hadn't occurred to him already, obviously. As a writer, there weren't a lot of lines he wouldn't cross, given the chance. And exploiting a family tragedy would certainly cross one. As of now, however, this rule no longer applies to Mahoney.

Jonathan can envisage exactly how the story will play out. The utterly mundane setting of the mall. The child snatched, quick as a flash. It's the moment all parents fear and can identify with—not least Connor, Mahoney's fictional counterpart. Next, the panic, the search, the tense aftermath as the mother disappears into a gin bottle and another child goes missing. Ending with all the players pulled into the action for the glorious, gory finale. It'll translate even better in the TV version. Taking out his phone, he makes a quick note before it slips his mind. His readers will love it. And if they don't? Just another bridge he'll burn when he comes to it. Mahoney returns with the pitcher.

"Work stuff" Jonathan smiles, putting away the phone. "Where were we?" Mahoney is looking so discombobulated that in spite of himself Jonathan almost laughs. Water, coffee, soda. Never anything stronger for Mahoney. You had to admire it. He himself can't even give up chocolate for Lent. Still, once an alcoholic, always an alcoholic. As with Saul and his lost weekend in the woods, this wouldn't be an issue until some career prosecutor dug up a series of disgruntled ex-colleagues. *"Always some knucklehead with an ax to grind, ready to talk shit or shoot their mouth off."* Happens all the time. Or, as Saul himself has (for once) correctly observed: *People can be so unforgiving . . .*

Mahoney leans toward him, as if desiring to cement something they've established between them. Jonathan can smell the stink of stale coffee on his breath.

"You and me," Mahoney says. "We go back a long way, don't we?"

"We certainly do," he agrees. In his mind, they are sitting opposite one another in that miserable interrogation room. The passage of time has wiped much of the episode from his memory, but he has never forgotten how it made him feel.

The shock, the terror, the blind panic. Now the tables have turned. And Jonathan has turned them.

"You think there's some reason we need to reopen the case?" Mahoney is saying. "I'm askin' because if you have something you think needs looking into . . . I'll do whatever it takes to help, Jon. You know that."

"Thanks. That's good to hear. I just needed to get some clarity on a couple things." Make that *one* thing. There had been zero need to trek all the way out to his least favorite place on earth to discuss his brother-in-law, or anyone else. It was Mahoney he had questions about. And Mahoney who, without realizing, has just answered every single one of them.

"I appreciate your time, Matt," he says, and sees Mahoney visibly relax.

"Anytime, Jon. How about you sleep on it, whatever's on your mind? And give me the heads-up when you're ready."

"I wouldn't have it any other way." He smiles.

Trust

2019

In the car, Jonathan jots down a couple more notes about his excellent nephew-themed plot idea. Then, instead of heading back to the highway, he decides to make a small detour. It's been a while. But it feels like something that needs to be done.

He drives slowly past the coast-guard station, across the bridge and down toward the long beach road. Setting out from the city hours ago, he'd reminded himself to check at intervals in the rearview mirror for any cars on his tail, but found himself forgetting. Pulling off the road into the parking lot, the place appears less isolated than he remembers. The plethora of trash cans is new. As is the dog-poop station, surrounded by discarded, excrement-filled plastic bags, as if people were filled with good intentions, but couldn't bring themselves to walk the last few feet.

There's the tiniest chill in the air and, as he takes the familiar path through the dunes, he buttons up his jacket. *Maddie* . . . to be in love with her had been to experience happiness he could never have imagined. At first, that is. The rest of the time he'd spent in a state of perpetual terror. Terrified of losing her. Convinced she would be mugged, raped, or taken from him by some pitiless disease. And then, one day, his fears had all been realized. How many years has he spent as the grieving widower? Mourning his wife, trying to come to terms with what happened. Now Saul has been added to the mix. And that changes everything.

He steps onto the beach, doesn't bother to remove his shoes. His chinless, gutless, quite possibly dickless brother-in-law—whatever had she seen in him? Saul had trotted out the "just sex" excuse with Heather, as if that made it more palatable. Not that love, *real love* (whatever that was) made it right . . . but love, he remembers, could force you into doing desperate things. Things you could never have imagined. And in that way, perhaps love made your actions more honorable.

As before, the tide is going out. The ocean is a flat, pallid green. There is no sign of the jetty, which he supposes has had twenty-odd more years to crumble into the ocean. According to Heather, Maddie believed Saul's connections to people in the media would help her career. *Was* Saul merely her ticket out? Away from Jonathan, and from the child she never wanted? Or did she—repellent as the notion was—actually love the guy? He can't decide which is worse.

In the fraught aftermath of his mistress's disappearance, Saul had shown up puffy-eyed more than once, as if perpetually on the edge of something. If Jonathan had thought anything of this at the time, he'd have written it off as Heather and her relentless organizing. Making his way across the sand toward the water, he experiences a mild shiver of unease. He turns, but there's no one there. Of course there isn't. He moves parallel with the water's edge for a while, decides Heather was right about one thing. Saul almost certainly did spend that entire weekend alone. Scampering around in the trees behind their backyard. Doing yoga or meditating or indulging some pathetic little fantasy of being rugged or masculine—all things Saul will never be. And while Jonathan has no reason to disbelieve this story, others may not be so generous. Tracing his path along the sand, aware of the gentle swoosh-swooshing of the waves, for the first time in weeks, he feels less anxious, almost relaxed. As for the scarf, what was Saul thinking? Why on earth had he kept it around? Deep down, had he wanted to get caught? It was not uncommon among criminals. The more probable explanation was that, like his probably illegitimate son, the scarf was the only thing Saul had left of her. Baseball games, trips to the museum, tours of the radio station—Ben and Uncle Saul had spent an awful lot of time together over the years. In fact, Ben is one of the few human beings his brother-in-law has seemed willing to go out of his way for. Which brought them back to the present day. Saul, betrayed by his own son, had ratted him out. In retaliation, Ben had revealed the scarf. Where did that leave the men's relationship now? As shredded, Jonathan imagines, as the scarf itself.

Ahead, a thirty-something couple in matching red T-shirts jog side-by-side along the surf. A kite bobs and ducks in the breeze, a vision of tranquility. Over the years, Saul would have told lies about Jonathan, while painting a picture of himself as the benign, kindly helper, gradually turning Ben against him. *Mission accomplished.* No wonder his own relationship with Ben was so poisoned and dysfunctional. That Saul actually thought Jonathan had had something to do with Maddie's disappearance . . . he certainly hadn't seen that coming. That he had neither the guts (nor the evidence) to go to the police hardly bears thinking about. As he himself admitted to the cops from the outset, he'd had his own part in the whole tragedy. And that's something he's had to live with every day since. Heather thought Maddie had skipped out on them. Saul thought Jonathan had murdered her.

"*Always some knucklehead with an ax to grind, ready to talk shit or shoot their mouth off.*" Everyone had their opinion. "My wife left me," he'd begun telling people at some point, a statement that shut down the conversation nicely. He'd been saying it for so long that by now it is—*almost*—how he thinks of it.

He digs the toe of his shoe into the sand, kicks a shower of particles into the air. All their youthful plans . . . none of which they'd accomplished. Not together, at least. He had allowed her so much freedom. And asked for so little in return. And what had he got for his trouble? *More trouble.* For Maddie, he was just another role. A means to an end. She had never wanted a child. And it was only after Ben was born that he realized he didn't want one either. *I wish I'd never been born.* If Ben had never existed, might Maddie still be alive?

He passes a group of teenagers laughing and joshing, not a care in the world. Even as a baby, Ben had little notion of boundaries. Like her, he never knew when to stop. And as with her, Jonathan had tried so hard to make things work. He wasn't always proud of how he'd handled things with Ben. But he had been pushed, hadn't he? Pushed so very, very hard, to a breaking point. It wasn't as if Ben's mother had ever tried to discipline the child, either. Instead cosseting and spoiling him. So what choice did that leave Jonathan? As the child grew into an adult, other troubling elements had made themselves known: the secretiveness, the manipulative nature, the moodiness, the countless betrayals of his trust. Like mother, like son. Whether through her son or her ex-lover, Maddie was still making her presence felt. Nowadays, when Ben strolled through the door, all Jonathan felt was anger and disappointment. The memory of Ben's lies fills him with outrage. His useless, impostor-son. The untalented Mr. Ripley.

Though Ben, who never took responsibility for his actions, would presumably have convinced himself he'd done nothing wrong.

In the past, he had asked himself whether it was possible to *un*-love someone. Or to force yourself to love someone you didn't. Because Lord knows he has tried both. Well. He now has the answer to at least one of these questions.

Walking on, he half expects to see his wife emerge from the ocean, eyes ablaze. In a few days, he'll once again find himself in the seaside town where she began her life, where he'll pay his respects to her mother and perhaps find some answers. Is she still out there, somewhere? Again, that lack of her, of that recent sense of her being close by. Looking out toward the empty horizon, it occurs to him that perhaps she never was.

The parking lot is as deserted as before, containing just one car—his own. He unlocks it, sits sideways in the driver's seat, and takes off his shoes. For people who knew him, his career success had been part of the tragic narrative—because Maddie hadn't lived to see it. Would the life he has built finally meet her standards? Would it be good enough for her—even now? And would he have achieved all his success in the first place, if not for her absence? A difficult question that leads to another, even more thorny question. One that has haunted him in recent weeks. One he has not dared ask himself, let alone answer.

Another discovery—both good and bad—from the past twenty-four hours is that his friends had all been witness to his wife's bad behavior. Maddie was no saint. And it turns out he wasn't the only person who knew it. He thinks about his own conduct these last weeks—the paranoia, the hearing things, this patently absurd notion of being tracked and followed. Jay and Mahoney were right. What with the wedding, the stresses of family and work, not to mention his burgeoning midlife crisis, he's created in his mind a presence that doesn't exist. Regardless, in their way, the revelations of the past twenty-four hours have been a gift. The real Ben has been revealed. The real Saul. *The real Maddie*. The truth laid bare, in all its raw ugliness. And thus revealed, Jonathan thinks, perhaps she—or some spirit of her—has delivered its message, leaving him free to move on, without her. "*The actions that full-grown adults take* ..." The nagging sense of guilt, the conflicted feelings, the painful, perpetual background throb to his life—for the first time in years, they have vanished. And in their place there is ... *what*? He upturns each of his shoes, watches the sand make patterns on the ground. Liberation? Acceptance? *Except*, he thinks, for one small detail: *Saul fucked my wife*. That would never change. And that was going to take a long time to heal.

He digs into his pocket, takes out the torn remnants of the scarf. That was real enough. She used to wear it all the time. It was around her neck in all the missing-person posters, in the photo he'd given to the cops. In all the panic at Heather and Saul's, he'd struggled to recall exactly when he'd last seen it. Now it comes to him. The scarf had been inexplicably "lost," Maddie had announced, showing up late and flush-faced without it one night after one of her seven-hour walks. Whether she had freely given it to Saul, Jonathan decides, or Saul had taken it like a serial killer desiring a keepsake, hardly mattered. He experiences an unexpected stab of pity then for the hapless Saul, in thrall to her—to the myth of her—after all these years. Well. He knew how that was, didn't he? He holds the fabric up to his nose for a few seconds. Nothing. Not a trace of her. And yet, in so many ways, an item of clothing bore the imprint of a person, did it not? Their DNA, for one.

He puts on his shoes, pulls out of the lot, and heads for the bridge. Aside from himself, who else knows that his wife couldn't possibly have been wearing the scarf the day she went missing? *Only Saul.* And Saul—as everyone knows—has every motive to lie.

Distance

2019

He arrives home to a haze of cigarette smoke in the hallway. Clearly, Ben has returned and found a way to break in. Going straight downstairs, he prepares himself for a scene—only to find Laura sitting alone at the kitchen island next to an over-flowing ashtray. He'd totally forgotten she was flying back today.

"Where have you been?" she says without looking at him. He tells her that he met up with Mahoney, got caught in traf-fic on the Long Island Expressway. And that after dropping off the car, he'd stopped for a quick drink at the Jane. All true.

"You smoke now?" he asks, getting a bottle of water from the fridge. In an empty takeout container, a cigarette has been unceremoniously stubbed out.

She hasn't brought up the subject of Ben, and that's surpris-ing. They had exchanged one or two texts. He'd let her know about the new keys, said only that there had been another incident and that he wasn't happy with how things turned out. He'd expect her to ask what happened. Instead, Laura is silent.

"How was your trip?" he says, seeing her take another drag from the cigarette, inhaling stiffly and self-consciously like the smoker she isn't.

"Trip was fine," she says. What to make of her behavior, aside from one more element in the unending puzzle and mystery that was other people? Curious, he pulls out a stool and sits down. Her cigarette goes out and, as she snaps half-heartedly at the end of it with the lighter they use for the outdoor stove, he obligingly gets back up, goes to the "every-thing" drawer, rifles through it, and returns with an old book of matches from Raoul's.

"It's a problem?" Laura says.

"Sorry?"

She points to the crumpled remains of the pack of American Spirits. Two left, their tips poking out.

"Not really," he answers. And it isn't. Not in the scheme of things. Or rather, not as much as it should be. He's about to suggest they go up to the roof, talk things over there. Just in time, he stops himself. What the hell is he thinking? *Maddie—she* was the one with whom he spent all those hours on the roof. Looking out over their city, "shooting the shit," as she loved to say.

"Remember in college," Laura says, with a sad smile, "I was one of those girls who smoked at parties?"

"So you were." In truth, he doesn't remember. He has few memories of Laura from then, her face blurred into others around campus until he bumped into her out with Maddie one night. Maddie used to make him lie on the roof in the rain, he remembers, watch the lightning strike the Empire State Building as she sucked down clove cigarettes, a habit she claimed to have picked up in India. *Had she even been to India?* Everything about her was so sexy and daring and cool, and the person he was then hadn't thought to question it.

"She smoked, didn't she?"

"Who?"

"Even when she was pregnant." They both know who and what she's referring to. But Heather's recent broadside against

Maddie has left him feeling weirdly defensive of her. Ironically, even a little protective.

"I don't recall."

"*Yes,*" Laura insists. "You remember. I know you do. You just won't admit it."

To Laura, Jonathan thinks, a cigarette would feel transgressive. She's slightly drunk as well, having trouble enunciating her words. Seeing her like this is unsettling, but also perversely thrilling, like walking into the house and discovering a room that wasn't there before. It occurs to him that if he doesn't remember the exact moment he and Laura first met, then perhaps he's never tried to. But he does remember the first time he saw *her—Maddie.*

Jay had been working the door at some club, and Jonathan had gone down after class to say hi. Emerging from the crowd of revelers was Laura, who called him over and pointed to a tall, remarkably striking girl dancing on a nearby table. "That's *Maddie!*" she had yelled over the din. "She's from *England!* She's the *craziest* girl you'll ever meet!" Next to them, a group of freshmen were gazing up at the girl with rapt attention. "She just came to New York to hang out for a while," Laura went on. "Isn't that *wild?*"

"Yes," he'd agreed. "Wild." For Laura, he could tell, the friendship was a badge of pride. Laura was pretty, but next to her friend . . . this extraordinary creature, stomping across a line of tables as people chanted and banged their glasses together . . .

"She said I'd be a much better mother than her," Laura says now. "Did I tell you that . . .?" She frowns, looks uncertain.

"I think so," he lies.

Had Maddie actually said this? Probably. If so, when? Before Ben was born? *After . . .?*

"Can I get one of those?" He nods at the pack of cigarettes. She pushes it toward him. He shakes out the remaining two, lights both, hands one to her. A last cigarette—was it time for the blindfold as well? There is a heavy-hearted, almost futile sense to their exchange this evening. A little flat, a little dead. And the impending arrival of a conversation that they've needed to have for some while. As Laura stares out toward the backyard, he studies her profile, thinks about all their years together. With success, he'd started to feel better about himself. Hadn't needed her to hold his hand so much. By then they were living together and he'd gotten comfortable, settled into a relationship that felt safe and offered a measure of predict-ability—perhaps too much. Laura, he realizes then, has always been more of a mother to him than a lover. Maybe his thera-pist was wrong. Maybe, to do work that really mattered, what he needed wasn't safety and security, but to feel relevant and alive. To feel that sense of danger, of existing on the glittering edge of something.

"Hey . . . I'm talking to you . . ." Laura looks annoyed.

"What?"

"I said, you don't listen." She looks hard at him, as if wait-ing for a response. "You never look me in the eye. You tell everything to . . . to *Jay*, or your precious *therapist*, and leave me in the dark."

In his therapist's neutrally appointed office, he thinks, but can't be bothered to point out, there are no outbursts or accu-sations. No one to judge him. No one to nag him about "communicating." Then again, the whole *therapy* thing has likewise begun to feel rather too controlling and codependent recently. Another pause, another gap he assumes he's supposed to fill. But with what?

"If it's about who I think it . . ." Laura begins, but appears to stop herself.

"What?" He's not letting it go this time. "*What were you going to say?*"

284

It was true when lazy writers likened the crackle of tension between people to electricity, he thinks. To the minutes before a storm.

"You think it's worth it?" Laura slurs, glass in her hand. "*Her.* Worth it . . . all this *shit*?" There is the tiniest beat as he thinks about how to answer. In which he is aware of the kitchen island between them, a solid wall of protection.

No secrets. Isn't that what they'd promised? There had been a special sting in discovering that his fiancée had knowledge of the affair. That she, too, had chosen to keep it from him. To betray him.

"*You need to stop fucking talking,*" he says. The words come out more forcefully than he meant them to.

As he registers the expression on Laura's face, it is as if he is watching himself, watching her. Seeing her take the wine bottle and slop the last of its contents into her glass. Then get up and go to stand on the opposite side of the room, next to the doorway, as out of nowhere, one of Maddie's terms comes into his mind: "The murder side"—her name for the side of the bed closest to the door.

"You think people don't talk?" Laura says, swaying slightly.

That's when it dawns on him. *Laura knows.* For the second time, Saul's betrayal has punched a hole through the center of Heather's life. She would have called Laura the moment she left the coffee shop to pour out the whole scarf story. And in her emotional state, likely his sister wouldn't have thought to leave out his own reaction. He looks Laura straight in the eyes.

"You wanna lecture me about people not communicating? Go ahead. I'm all ears." He sees the uncertainty in her face, but to her credit, she isn't backing down.

"You talk about her all the time," she says. "You don't even know you're doing it. Even when you're sleeping. And believe me," she adds bitterly, "I've listened to enough of it." He waits. "She was my *best friend*. I missed her too."

"'Missed' ...?" he repeats harshly. Faced with the truth, how else to defend himself? With contempt, naturally. Another relationship "don't."

He puts his focus on his breathing, in . . . and out. Slow and steady.

"Jon, she did dumb, *reckless* things . . ."

"Yeah?" he says. "You should try it sometime."

They both know there is no danger of Laura careening off the rails or doing something crazy. Unlike *her* . . . he thinks, the woman who had flung herself at things (Saul) or professed to despise them (Saul). As if to prove his point, Laura doesn't dignify his comment with an answer.

"She's *gone*," Laura says. "And she's not coming back. *We* have a life. *You and me*. This is our life now." *This is our life now*. The voice of doom. The words seem to reverberate like the sound of the prison doors clanging shut.

"You're obsessed," he says, shaking his head in disappointment. "I don't even know what to say to you."

"Me?" She laughs, and in it he detects an edge of hysteria. *"That's women for you,"* Jay once said. Hysteria, drama, passive-aggression. *"Can't live with 'em, can't kill 'em."*

"This . . ." She gestures around the room, to the empty wine bottle, to the chaos of takeout containers littering the counter, as if they have something to do with him. "This isn't us . . . this fighting and . . ." He tunes out the rest, draws the smoke into his lungs. He thinks of the suit jacket, hounding him for months. Pursuing him through the house like some remorseless, shape-shifting monster in a horror movie.

"What is it that you want from me, exactly?" he says. She looks at him in astonishment.

"What? *You.* You're what I want." And when he doesn't reply: "You have *nothing* to say to me?" The cigarette should taste disgusting, but as he draws in a last lungful of smoke, all he can think is how good it feels.

"You're right." He sighs, stubbing out the butt in the remains of a box of jasmine rice. "And it's good you're bringing this up now. Because I've been thinking . . . I'm not sure that now is really the right time."

"The right time for what?" The book, the tour, the rewrite—any would serve as an excuse. Those or the fact that half the time Laura's out on the West Coast, three thousand miles away.

"I don't know what to tell you," he says.

"Wait, *what*?" Laura sets her glass down. Firmly this time. Without a shake. As if his words have brought the abrupt return of sobriety. "What just happened? You're canceling our *wedding*?!" A violent downward movement of her head. "Jesus. *Jesus* . . . I knew you'd do this . . ." And another desperate little drag from her cigarette. "I fucking *knew* it." How like Heather she sounds.

"I just don't think we should rush into anything, that's all. I mean," he adds, "you're super busy with the new place . . ."

"Are you saying it's *my* fault? Seriously, I don't even know what you need from me anymore!"

He lets out a sigh. *Getting hitched. Tying the knot.* Phrases that are no accident.

"Honestly, what I need right now," he tells her, "is to pack."

As she turns her back and goes up the stairs, he stays where he is. He listens to her moving around. Closet doors opening and closing, her voice on the phone to the parking garage. It seems Laura is choosing to pack up and leave before he does. Fifteen minutes later, she comes back down carrying her overnight bag and plucks the car keys from their hook in the kitchen.

"It's late," he says. "And you're drunk. You shouldn't be driving alone."

"If I wanted to feel alone, I'd stay here, wouldn't I?" Her eyes are red, but defiant looking. He opens his palms.

"Where does this leave us?" he asks.

She laughs, but there's no mirth in it. "You're asking me?" She throws the keys into her bag. "You're something else. I don't even know who you are anymore." Another woman, he thinks, driving out of his life. Except this time, there is nothing to say. Nothing to be done for now, save to take the out and let her go. At the bottom of the stairs, she turns back for a moment.

"You know what?" she says. He watches her face contort. "I used to think you were too good for her."

Out of habit, he begins his recent room-checking routine, but can't summon the energy—or the anxiety—to finish the job. On the top floor, he half expects to find Ben lounging on the bed, headphones on. The room is empty. And in some indefinable way, it's true, he thinks, Maddie really is gone as well. He brushes his teeth and gets ready for bed. In six hours, the pigeons will be awake, gathering noisily on the window ledges. At 5:15 a.m., the car will arrive, and after that he'll be winging his way to London.

Jay calls.

"Heading out to Carbone," he says, "then the Garden for the fight, but I wanna—"

"Sounds good," he cuts in. "I need to run. Catch you later."

They haven't checked in since Heather and Saul's, and Jay will want to "debrief." Though it's not difficult to guess what Jay's defense will be: *Zero upside in telling you. I made a judgment call. And I'd do it again.* They can patch things up later, Jonathan decides. For now, he badly needs to put some distance between himself and everything that's happened.

And—though he should probably call Laura and issue a groveling apology or try to smooth things over—from pretty much everyone in his life.

Taking his roomiest Rimowa suitcase down from the closet, he gathers clothes and toiletries. In the bathroom, the jacket hangs from the door like a funeral outfit, a fresh note attached, without the smiley face this time. Jay, Laura, Mahoney—the very people he had kept closest, each in their own way unworthy of his trust. And himself, the patsy, who never saw it coming. In the case of his light-fingered, counterfeit offspring, nature—not nurture—was to blame. And there is relief in understanding this. And vindication. Ben, the briefly sweet child whose personality had been replaced by a calculated, curdled brand of charm that—*yes*, he decides, snapping open the locks on his suitcase, surely he's allowed to admit it to himself now—sickens him. Though considering who Ben's parents were, all of this makes complete sense. Jonathan stops. Why on earth is he wasting his energy still thinking about this? There is no longer any reason to feel responsible for this person who he's fairly certain has nothing to do with him, and who wants nothing to do with Jonathan, either. *Who is anyone?*—the question is posed, but rarely addressed, in Ocean Falls, every time a vicious killer was discovered living in the midst of the tranquil seaside hamlet. If there was one takeaway from this past week, it was that relationships are perilous. That they place you at the mercy of the very people who know you best, who are privy to your insecurities, your little fears, and weaknesses. With Laura gone, hoping it's not too late in the evening, he sends a quick text to their housekeeper to ask her to feed the cat. He checks for each of his things: passport, currency, credit cards. Gathers notebooks, a fresh batch of Sharpies, and enough clean shirts for six weeks on the road, and then some, in varying European climates.

Then he begins the task of untangling assorted wires, head-phones, and chargers, before losing patience and tossing the whole mess into his hand luggage. He can take care of it on the plane.

A stale waft of cigarette smoke has drifted up from down-stairs and he opens the window, looks out over the street, and breathes in the damp city air. No eerie play of light or ominous shadows—just a neighbor standing under a streetlamp, star-ing down into his phone, waiting for his dog to finish its business.

Had she ever really loved him?

Getting into bed, he pops a Xanax and half an Ambien, and turns out the light. Sometimes it was better to remain in the dark.

Funk

1996

More bruises. Only as he is getting Ben into his pajamas does he spot them, the series of small but vivid marks on the child's upper arm.

"Liar!" Maddie's voice comes at them through the bedroom door. She's been screaming bloody murder nonstop for the last hour. "You promised! You *promised* me!"

Jonathan comes out, carefully closes the door behind him.

"Please, Mads, keep your voice down—you're making him upset again."

"*Me*!? That's rich, coming from you, you fucking hypocrite!"

"We've been over this," he says. "The apartment got tied up in Josh's divorce and went to his wife. One day. One day we'll go." An angry shake of her head. "OK?"

"When?" This is yet another issue between them. Why can't she trust him? He'd hoped to have been making a steady income by now. But what with taking care of Ben, and Maddie's shifting moods, building a real career has been a challenge. It's not that he doesn't think about their plans, he tells her. But they were made three years ago, and they weren't exactly footloose and fancy free anymore, were they?

"And who's fault is that?" she says.

He has tried to detect some pattern in her behavior. Before Ben was born, he'd been able to discount or laugh off her occasional moodiness. God help him—how was it possible?—if anything, it had only made him fall harder for her. More and more now he can't tell what is right and reasonable. What is a normal response. And what is overreacting. No, his wife is not easy, but nothing worth having ever is.

"It's never been the right time," he explains. "You know that." She leans against the wall, folds her arms. "There isn't the money. And what about my parents? They aren't getting any younger."

"Neither am I," Maddie says flatly. Silence in the apartment. She turns away in disgust, sits on the couch with that terrible thousand-yard stare.

In the bedroom, he takes Ben's teddy bear from the dresser, puts it in the child's arms, tries to get a closer look at the marks. Something shatters in the kitchen—a plate or a glass. The bruises . . . it isn't right. Of course it isn't. It isn't the first time, either. But it was hard sometimes, trying to quiet their son. Now Ben pulls away, eyes wide and fearful, shrinks farther back into the pillow. Last week, the administrator at Ben's daycare had called. Ben was sick—could someone come get him? That someone was Jonathan, naturally. And naturally, the woman had asked about the bruises.

"We're in the playground a lot," he had explained. "Boys can be so clumsy at this age, and he gets into all kinds of scrapes. You know how they are."

"Is everything all right at home?" she had asked. He hadn't known whether to laugh or cry.

"We're all doing fine." He'd smiled. What else could he say?

Ben is crying now. Long, heaving sobs rack his small frame. "OK, buddy . . . I'm so sorry. I really am. I know it hurts."

Best leave it for now, he decides, and check more closely in the morning—before school, when Ben's mother is still sleeping off her temper from the night before. For her sake, he has taken on the burden of caring for the child. Getting him into his clothes each morning, teeth brushed, off to school, and ready for bed at night. Maddie spends most evenings with him, reads him poetry or whatever, but that's hardly the same, is it? Jonathan has—literally—been left holding the baby. And yet, the more he does, the more difficult Ben becomes, and the farther away his mother drifts. It's as if they both want to punish him. *"A girl like that . . . a girl like that could really make you feel like someone."* Or no one, he thinks savagely. Nowadays, he rarely has to wonder what mood she'll be in. Brittle. Hysterical. Spitting nails. And frequently all three. The most innocuous comment or suggestion sends her spinning into a rage. All he can do is cling on, and hope.

Quietly, he closes the bedroom door and tiptoes into the living room where Maddie now appears to be sleeping peacefully on the couch. He sits at his makeshift desk. Around them, the neighborhood is gentrifying; older buildings being demolished, newer ones rising, creeping eastward. Their own street isn't there yet, but once it is, the landlord will raise the rent and who knows where they'll end up. It's been an unusually cold early fall, and the building has turned off the heat again, and whether from this, or from the trials of the past few hours, he finds he can barely lift his fingers to the keyboard. Always walking on eggshells, always waiting for the next outburst, always ready to hustle Ben outside or into the other room. Days when his own existence feels like an unbearable burden. *If I don't sleep, I'm going to cry,* he thinks, and feels his ability to go on, to put one foot in front of the other, drain away. Is this how Maddie feels when she stays in bed all day? The hopeless crying, the storming out? Is her anger an effort to throw off some kind of … postnatal depression? An aunt had suffered from it, had tried—and succeeded—in drowning her own baby in the bath, and herself with it. He has tried to broach with Maddie the subject of the bruises, in a careful and low-key manner. To say that he only wants the best for her. To explain that maybe, when she gets upset, she doesn't always realize what she's doing or remembers after she's done it. He wants so badly for things to work, for them to be honest with each other. To have no secrets.

"Don't you dare fucking gaslight me!" she had screamed.

For a while, they had—just about—maintained a satisfactory physical relationship. But she is not—he tries to conjure the correct word—*friendly*. His wife is not friendly. She is not warm. They have sex, but they don't make love (a phrase she claims makes her skin crawl). How tenderly she used to kiss him. Now everything feels hostile and cold. Last time, searching out her face in the half-dark, something in her expression had scared him. Indifference? Scorn? It was hard to put a name to. Now, he feels her tilting away from his touch. In his most fearful moments, it's like watching her speed away from him into the distance.

He gazes at her sleeping figure and wonders what it is that she wants. What *he* wants, and needs, is to give up trying to figure her out. He knows this. Has tried to un-love her, because loving her was like being caught in barbed wire. The more he struggled, the more tangled and hooked he became. His thoughts race with conversations. Ones they've had, ones they would or could, or *might* have. If only he had the courage. Certainly, they both know by now what Maddie didn't want. "*It's not what I want for my life.*" Too late. Though she had given it her best shot. Several of them, if memory served. As late as six-and-a-half months, he'd come home to find her comatose on the couch, a bottle of cheap vodka lying empty on the floor.

Beset with mysterious ailments, she barely eats and refuses to see a doctor. He'll wake to find her scrawling maniacally in her notebooks, or pacing the room like a caged animal plotting its escape. And frequently she does escape, vanishing for hours, leaving him alone with Ben. No wonder it all gets too much for him sometimes. After a long walk, she always comes back in a better mood. But it never lasts. Last week he offered to get her a pager, just so they can keep in touch. A perfectly innocent suggestion, but one that had made her accuse him of spying on her. Now he finds himself watching her sleep like a prison guard on suicide watch.

And yet, for all the misery and uncertainty, as he listens to her breathing, there is one thing to look forward to. One bright promise shining in their future. In six days, it will be Maddie's birthday. That weekend, he's arranged for Ben to stay at Heather and Saul's, and they'll take a trip out to the Hamptons with Laura and Jay. Walks on the beach, lazy mornings in bed, barbecuing in the yard—he can hardly wait. What Maddie doesn't know is that for months he has been saving whatever he can from his meager wages. And that, last week, without breathing a word to anyone, he'd gone up to the airline ticket office opposite Grand Central and purchased two round-the-world plane tickets. A small fortune, but, to his mind, a crucial investment. A last attempt to snap his wife out of this inexplicable funk she's in. He listens as she sighs in her sleep. It'll be so worth it. A break from it all, to guide her back to her real self—and to him.

Bones

2019

He wakes seconds before the alarm to a sound like small bones being crunched underfoot—the remnants of a dream that has already faded. Getting dressed, he finds that he has almost no memory of last night's conversation with Laura—what he said, what she said, how she had looked, how she had looked at him—or indeed, how he had felt in those final few moments before his possibly soon-to-be ex-fiancée had packed her bag and left. Once again, he has managed to check out of a significant moment in his life—though too much therapy has at least enabled him to recognize this.

Meanwhile, he's not the only one up early. There's a terse message from Heather, announcing that she's throwing Saul out and filing for divorce. No more hateful Sundays on the Upper West Side, Jonathan thinks, taking his suitcase down the stairs. No more tedious pretheater drinks. No more morally improving lectures and self-dealing compliments from the hypocrite Saul.

Good for you, Sis! he replies, glad she isn't headed into another futile bout of couples' therapy.

Heather will need space and time to figure out her life without Saul. Which will—he hopes—make what's coming next a bit easier for her to cope with.

After a short detour to drop a package with the doormen at

297

Jay's building, Jonathan's car is speeding toward JFK through the vast, blurry stretches of cemetery that seem to make up half of Queens. He can't wait to be away from the city—the frenzied activity, the crowded sidewalks, the perpetual expectations. To fly, fly away from everyone and everything, and head for a place where, whatever happened later, he had found himself briefly happy. His phone rings. Jay—also up—asking about the package. Jonathan explains what he needs done with it and lets Jay talk for a minute or so.

"Scumbag," is Jay's verdict. "It's the first rule: Don't shit where you eat." Jonathan says nothing. "Look. I get that you're mad," Jay continues. "But here's the deal: I figured I'd tell you one day. When you were ready. But then you got with Laura, and it never seemed like the right time to piss on your cornflakes. Zero upside, you know what I'm saying?"

"Uh-huh." He lets the silence hang there for a moment. Meanwhile, Jay is clearly pleased that he's being trusted with the package. "That prick," he says. "I'll take care of it, Jon. It'll be my fucking pleasure."

"They're calling my flight," Jonathan lies, as the car moves along the expressway.

Ending the call, the phone pings again. *What now?* A lengthy text from Laura. Nothing about their fight or talking things over. Instead, she tells him that the embittered Saul is pressing charges of grand larceny against Ben and won't be persuaded otherwise. There's something about finding a lawyer, which he skims over. Way more interesting is the fact that in her own text, Saul's future ex-wife, Heather the lawyer, had managed to omit this crucial piece of information.

Call me when you get this, Laura says. *We'll figure it out.*

Or not. Never has he felt more glad to be leaving the country.

★   ★   ★

There is one last person he needs to speak with first, though. Where relationships are concerned, he has often told himself that he has developed a more "evolved" perspective. That time has rubbed smooth his sharp edges and eroded away his anger. And until the day before yesterday, this was, arguably, more or less true.

At the departure gate, he keys Mahoney's number into his phone.

"I didn't want to believe it at first . . ." he tells the cop, injecting the appropriate tremor into his voice. But considering the circumstances, there's no other explanation, and it all makes complete sense. A friend of his will be in touch later today with a key piece of evidence, he explains. Like Jay, Mahoney sounds overjoyed to be asked for help. After taking down some notes, he tells Jonathan to leave it with him.

"And Jon?"

"Yes . . .?"

"Don't feel bad. Seriously, you don't want to blame yourself for any of this. You couldn't have known."

"Thank you," he sighs. "That's good to hear. I'll do my best."

Six-and-a-half hours later, his plane touches down in London and he wakes to Mahoney's short voice message: "You were right," he says. "I'm sorry. Looks like we missed this first time round. I'm gonna dig into it and get back to you."

It's late. Almost nine in the evening local time. Having flown in a day early to acclimatize, Jonathan takes a cab into the city and checks into his usual suite at the Lanesborough. By chance, tomorrow is Maddie's birthday. So it seems right that in the morning, he'll make the journey to her hometown, where he's booked himself into a nice hotel on the oceanfront. With the countryside spread out behind it, the wild rockiness of the beach and the light summer evenings, he has good memories of the place.

"It's Hove, actually." The hotel's concierge smirks, as if making some kind of joke. Jonathan looks blankly at him.

After checking out of his London hotel at some ungodly hour to catch the express train to the coast, it seems Joyce's facility is not even located in the same town. *Hove,* he thinks to himself. Even the name sounds depressing. Like another word for death.

"You could walk it," the man goes on. "It'll take you about half an hour."

During the interminable journey down, the train had gotten stopped outside one dismal suburb after another. *"Delays,"* the voice on the PA system had intoned uninformatively, *"are caused by earlier delays."*

Once they'd pulled into the station, he'd found rain and wind and a large group of people in line for a cab, making it to the hotel in time for the last dregs of breakfast. From a table by the window, the only guest in the dining room, he'd watched the doormen grapple with giant umbrellas as sea spray blew across the street in huge sheets. The ocean . . . he'd listened to it hammer at the window, and realized he had forgotten its power.

"I don't think that's going to work for me," he tells the concierge. "Can you call me a cab?"

"A *taxi,* sir?" Another withering stare. "Right away, sir."

Fifteen minutes later, he's dropped outside the Peaceful Lea Nursing Home—a Victorian-era building set back on a tree-lined, residential street. He gives the receptionist his name, and she taps a bell on her desk. A friendly looking woman emerges from the back and introduces herself as Sandra.

"I'm new, so I didn't really know Mrs. M," Sandra explains, leading him along a carpeted corridor. The air carries a stifling institutional combination of boiled cabbage mixed with anti-septic, under which lurk more human odors. They pass a kitchen and a small waiting area lined with beige-colored soft furnishings. Joyce's home had been similarly uninspired, he remembers. And recalls the first freezing-cold night sleeping in her spare bedroom, when Maddie informed him that her mother did indeed have central heating but preferred to keep it turned off. Like the overcast skies and the biting wind, at the time, he had thought this quaint and romantic.

"Are you staying locally?" Sandra says.

"At The Palace Hotel, on the oceanfront."

"*Oceanfront*," she repeats. "Oooh. I like how you say that. Sounds so much grander than our tatty old *seafront*. It's meant to be very nice inside," she goes on, "the Palace. So I've heard."

"Yes." He smiles. "Very nice." Three times he'd had to call down to the reception desk. Twice about the nonflushing toilet, which itself involved a recessed plastic button into which you were obliged to insert your index finger and push. It was beyond disgusting. And once about the drapes, which had simply collapsed in a heap on the floor after he tried to close them against the lashing rain.

"She passed quite suddenly, did Mrs. M from what I understand," Sandra is saying. "A mercy, really, when they don't improve . . . it's so difficult with the Alzheimer's, isn't it? You don't even know who's in there half the time." *Gallows humor.* Presumably this was what you resorted to in order to get yourself through the day here without going completely insane.

His phone rings. "Excuse me one moment," he tells her. An update from Laura saying Saul may be open to dropping the charges, provided Ben goes into rehab. Rehab? For what? Kleptomania? *Have fun with that.* Ben really is shameless.

"I meant to ask," he tells Sandra. "I was a bit confused about Joyce's funeral. Do you happen to know who organized it?"

"Might have been prepurchased, but I can ask Matron," she replies briskly. "A lot of them do that these days. When they don't have much in the way of family." Joyce and Maddie didn't have the best relationship, he thinks, but if Maddie were alive, would she really not have gone to visit her mother? Though in Joyce's state, who knows if she would even have recognized her daughter.

"Can you find out if Joyce, *Mrs. M*, had any other visitors?" he says.

"Oh, you needn't fret. Mrs. M wouldn't have passed on alone. Not here." God, it was like pulling teeth. "They do a nice Catholic mass in the chapel up the road, and they make sure one or two of the staff and carers are in attendance. They're good like that."

Was Maddie a Catholic? *Doubtful.* She didn't think much of the pope.

"That's good to know, thank you." Did the staff always refer to Joyce as "Mrs. M"? he wonders. Or has Sandra simply forgotten her name?

They have stopped outside a white-painted door. Sandra unlocks it, turns on the light, the same vicious LED-type lighting as in his hotel room. Under its harsh glare, he sees a single bed, a built-in closet, dresser, nightstand, and a chair in the same beige fabric as elsewhere in the building. Here and there, various ugly metal and plastic bars have been screwed into the walls, presumably for those "guests" who have trouble hauling themselves around. A large window offers a faraway, barely discernible view of the sea, but is pointedly nailed shut.

"All her bits and bobs should be in here," Sandra continues. The place recalls the bathroom in his mother's care facility, he thinks; everything relentlessly minimal so that it could be hosed down with disinfectant. The only thing missing is the drain in the middle of the floor.

"Very popular it is too, this room. Has a waiting list and everything. And a proper view." Sandra gestures out of the window in the manner of a real-estate broker. Her accent and her way of speaking really are beginning to grate on him. "Oh yes. Must be nice, seeing the sea every morning." *I don't know about that* . . . Jonathan thinks. "Not that you can see a thing on a day like this. Disgraceful, all the rain we've been having, isn't it? I expect it's nice and sunny where you're from."

"That's right."

As she moves around the room, opening and closing drawers amid various noises of disapproval, he tries to imagine the other rooms, the photos of dead parents . . . of dead spouses, propped up in cheap frames. Of neglectful sons and busy daughters, who rarely called and spoke impatiently when they did. He shudders. Each room would contain its story, and each one would be soul-destroying in its own way.

"Now, that *is* strange . . ." Sandra puts a hand to her chin. "I could've sworn there was another box in here, with all her photo albums in. She opens the closet to a jangle of empty coat hangers, peers suspiciously inside as if checking for burglars.

"Could someone else have been here before me?" he inquires. Joyce would have had to edit down her belongings when she moved into assisted living. Regardless—he can't be sure why—it feels as if there are things missing. "Maybe a young woman? I mean an older one," he corrects, realizing his mistake. "Somebody around my age?"

"I really couldn't say. It's hard to keep all the names and things straight. So many of our residents are in and out. Mainly out, of course, poor dears." Sandra permits herself a chuckle. "Feet first, most of them."

He stares hard at her.

"Oh well, I'm losing my own mind, I'm sure. No offense," she adds hastily, and gestures to a heap of plastic shopping bags stacked up on the dresser. "I expect you'll find most of it in there. Feel free to go through any of the cupboards and suchlike. Take whatever you fancy. Anything you don't want, we'll find a use for or donate to the charity shops." There's a pause. Is he meant to tip her? They're not so big on tipping over here. Then again, judging by the hotel's lackluster break-fast buffet, they're not so big on service either. "Well, I should be getting on. I'll leave you to it, shall I?" she says.

"Yes. Thanks again." He smiles.

Joyce has left pitifully few things. He discovers a collection of hideous porcelain figurines and sundry other knickknacks, thrown into a box amid an assortment of hard candy wrappers, bobby pins, and an empty bottle of cough syrup. Under a dusty wreath of plastic flowers is a modest, neatly folded pile of skirts and sweaters in dull, inoffensive colors which give off the cheesy, unwashed odor of an airline blanket. Twenty minutes later, after a thorough search through a trove of items best left to Sandra and the charity shops, he at last finds what he came for.

Fallen behind the dresser, wedged between it and the wall, they have been tossed inside an old plastic shopping bag, along with a bunch of yellowing gas and electric bills. *Sad to leave so little of yourself,* he thinks. If not as sad as if he had actually liked Joyce when she was alive. Meanwhile, there is no sign of the precious photo albums, which is puzzling, though really he could care less about them. On the way out, he bumps into Sandra, who tells him that the facility doesn't keep records of visitors once a resident has "moved on." He thanks her anyway, feeling foolish for even entertaining the notion that his dead wife was wandering around alive and well, let alone organizing funerals.

"Oooh, where did you find that, then?" Sandra points to the object in his hand. "Peculiar thing for an older lady to have, isn't it?" *Sexist,* he thinks to himself. "I expect you'll be taking it back to America for your kids, won't you?" *And nosey.*

He smiles. "Actually," he says, "I don't have any children."

Milk

2019

Outside, the rain has stopped and the street, with its ugly paved-over front yards, appears almost pleasant. He stands for a moment, reflects on his last exchange with Sandra, how the words had so easily tripped off his tongue. And why wouldn't they?

With jetlag kicking in, he decides to walk the half mile back to the center of town. Perhaps he'll explore the pedestrianized maze of streets behind the hotel and give one of the local restaurants a go.

During his last visit here, they had left Ben with Joyce and taken a walk down to the ocean. The weather had seemed warm, but by the time they arrived, a cold wind was blowing. Sun, mist, rain, all in the space of a few hours. He'd never known weather so changeable, he'd told Maddie as they made their way onto the beach. Just then, the sun had come out, and the sea had taken on a shimmering, silvery beauty. It had seemed like a good omen.

He passes a young family. Parents with despairing faces, the child, one fat hand reaching out of the stroller, screaming and screaming. All parents do their best, he thinks. But in her absence, trying to scrape out a living for himself and Ben, he couldn't handle someone else's tears. And when Ben had screamed, he had wanted to scream back. It wasn't as if

Maddie had ever lifted a finger to teach her child how to behave. Or instilled in Ben any sense of right or wrong. As for himself, he wasn't a bad father, a bad guy. But, very occasionally, he had ended up having to play one.

Crossing the coast road, he reaches a series of wide, featureless lawns, beyond which he discovers some kind of tarmac boardwalk. *Oceanfront?* Sandra was right. It was laughable, far too grand a term for whatever this is.

One hour later, he finally locates the restaurant recommended by the hotel concierge. The place is empty, so he claims a solo table next to the window, stares at the gaggle of waitstaff chatting around the cash register.

At 2 a.m., he had found himself staring glassily at his phone, poring over yet more vindictive, disappointed reviews. Was this how you destroyed yourself? One review at a time? Going back to pick at each one as you would a scab? Too much sex . . . not enough sex . . . too much gore . . . not enough . . . too much . . . not enough . . . too much, not enough. No edge, no daring—*no surprises.* Cindy wanted some cheesy misery memoir. Famous author's secret sorrow, and so on. "*We'd have a bestseller on our hands,*" she'd said. *If only she knew* . . . You told your story and hoped for the best. If you thought yourself a master manipulator, in the end, people possessed free will and free speech. A right they got to express all over the internet, apparently.

His phone dings. Another dramatic-yet-opaque message from Heather. She probably thinks her phone's bugged. It probably is. *CALL ME ASAP. Too bad, Sis.* He deletes it. *You reap what you sow*—one of her husband's trite sayings that Heather might have considered before she lied for him.

As for his own relationship, having told Laura he wants to delay the wedding, he wonders whether it's an unconscious effort to appease his wife, even now. To mollify her ghost. He flags down a reluctant, cranky-looking server, offers his most apologetic smile. "Could I be terribly annoying," Jonathan says, charmingly, "and get an espresso with whipped cream?" Sometimes, he thinks, watching the man hurry off to fetch it, it is almost too easy. Masking your true feelings. Saying your lines. In the beginning it had felt impossible. On a number of occasions he'd almost come unstuck. His old self—appalled and disbelieving—had cowered behind the words. First with the cops. And then with everyone else. At what precise moment had it become easier? Automatic? A pleasure? *A thrill.* Because there was that too, wasn't there? Once he knew he was safe. *"What appeared real,"* she had said, *"is real. Work your as-ifs."* Only then were you permitted to say the words.

"Please," he had sobbed in public on the local TV news. "Please, Maddie, please come back."

No need to conjure any *what-if*s in that case. Nor the sense of being cheated. Or the not knowing—the unbearable, hour-to-hour hope and fear that, against all evidence to the contrary, his wife might still be alive. Because the feeling was real, and it was right there. Along with his grief, his guilt—and his hatred. Over the years, the feelings, and the words that went with them, had begun to spring up on command. A few more years and it became almost impossible to recall the real version of events and, on occasion, the real version of himself. Well, not really. But still. His coffee arrives, delivered with a smile. It is creamy and good. Deliver your lines, and let the audience fill in the gaps. That was the key to good storytelling. *"It's a formula, really, isn't it?"* More than that, Jonathan thinks, it's a habit, built from the ground up until it flows naturally. It was yet another thing he could be proud of. In private, at least.

Next to him on the table he has placed the notebooks, doubtless unread by the tragically vacant Joyce or her equally vacant carers. For the last hour, he has been putting off looking at them. Now, leafing through their pages, he discovers that they read more like journals. And that they do indeed contain a few of his wife's deeply unfair thoughts about their relationship. And yet, undeniably these are woven together with such cleverness . . . with dialogue and character sketches gleaned from her travels in and around the city . . . The thing could use a title, but it was real, the novel she had taunted him with. An entire world, elegant and complete. Who knew? Her writing totally blows him away. From his bag, he takes out the object Sandra had remarked on, feels the solid weight of it in his hands. He'd expected to have gotten a few of the details wrong, but examining it now, it is exactly as he described it.

Around him, restaurant staff are laying down new place settings in hopeful preparation for the evening shift. He gets the check, gathers his things and tosses some change on the table. On the way out, he stops in the bathroom to wash his hands and is promptly scalded by a vicious stream of boiling water. Separate hot and cold taps—another inexplicable feature. The servers that don't serve, the heat that doesn't heat . . . *How did these people ever control an empire?*

Mask

2019

The town's famous pier is a rusted iron structure extending out beyond the stony beach some distance into the water. A yellow-curtained booth marks the entrance, inside which the mechanical figure of a fortune-teller beckons stiffly. On the flight over, he'd read a terrifying and feasible-sounding short story about this exact same pier, which described the whole thing collapsing into the sea in a jumble of bloody flesh, wrought iron, and abruptly amputated limbs. He'd enjoyed it immensely. Giving the fortune-teller a wide berth, he passes through the gates and steps cautiously onto the pier's planked wooden surface. *What is it that he expects to find?* Directly behind him is the beach where he had watched a barefoot Maddie pick her way easily across the hard little stones and dive straight into the freezing ocean.

"Swimming team!" She'd laughed as he'd looked on, horrified.

It turned out that, before her dad died, they used to take the "polar bear plunge" every Christmas, diving into the freezing waters of the English Channel as part of their holiday celebrations. And yet, he thinks now, watching the tide swash beneath him, don't they say it is always the best swimmers who drown? On that day, just like the last day, he'd believed that she shared his happiness. In the end, even this golden, carefree time was to be snatched from him, revealed as an illusion. A *deception*.

He makes his way along the pier, past the cheap stalls and ice-cream parlors, picturing that other beach, the one where he'd had to abandon his old self. Nothing was the same after that. How could it be? He used to think he had brought out the worst in her. But in the end, she had brought out the worst in him. Made him someone he wasn't.

On his phone, he sees now, another voicemail has arrived from Mahoney.

"Jon . . . I asked them to look back into the case files and they spoke to your sister. Looks like she definitely gave her husband a false alibi. Though I gotta hand it to her, she came clean about it. At this point, it's gonna be tough to ascertain precisely where he was," Mahoney continues. "But what we do know is no one can account for his whereabouts that day. And the clothing you sent over? It's with the judge, but that's not lookin' good for him, either." A pause, in which he can hear the cop breathing. "I'm sorry, Jon." Uncertainty. A note of fear? "We screwed up, but I'm gonna make this right."

Three minutes later the phone rings again, with a call from Heather, which he doesn't bother answering, followed by another all-caps text. He powers down the device, tosses it in his bag, and decides to cut through the video arcade. He's not happy with his sister, but he is proud of her. Her honesty will make her culpable but, though she may not yet realize it, she is exacting her own revenge. And Heather's smart. In digging two graves, as the adage goes, he's confident she'll have the strength to dig herself out of her own, while leaving Saul at the bottom of his.

After being outdoors, there's a strange thrill to be had in the noise and clamor of the arcade—the slot machines, the pennies falling, it's like a miniature Vegas set on the waves. A heavily made-up woman stares at a screen, mindlessly feeding in coins and pulling at the lever. A scrum of gleeful teenagers take turns thumping at the Whac-A-Mole machine.

As Jonathan weaves his way through, it strikes him that one of the new feelings bubbling up in himself is gratitude. Gratitude—after all this time—for Maddie and her treachery. For without it, where would he be? Never in a billion years would he have gained the fame and the riches and the life that he enjoyed now. Never would he have experienced the rage, the urge to revenge himself, over and over—and have it all play out on other young, careless, albeit fictional, women. True, he had tortured himself with visions of the life they would never have together. But how would that have worked out in the long term?

As he exits at the far end of the arcade and emerges into the fading daylight, he contemplates the prospect. What would life have been like, dealing with her whims and unpredictable moods? With her, his precious energies would have been squandered. With her, he would never have met Cindy. With her, never would he have been able to cast off the old Jonathan, so timid, so fearful to ask for more.

He gazes out at the sea, at the jagged choppiness of the waves. *With* her, he'd be like every other graying, pot-bellied middle-aged dad. Eking out a living in some drab, colorless suburb, in some ugly ranch house that was modest and appropriate to their status. *Without* her, he was living in the best city in the world and was unbelievably successful. Without her, he has found his place. In his mind's eye he is able to catch small glimpses of her now, as she was then, and as the others would have seen her. Like a million girls arriving in the big city, head full of chaos and impossible ambitions that were ill defined and changed daily. Maddie ... so beautiful and so broken. And so determined not to be ordinary that she succeeded only in making herself as mediocre as all the rest. And yet, he reminds himself, somehow she had managed to write something extraordinary . . . Does he still love her? Laura seems to think so. And in a twisted kind of way, Laura may be right. Even in death, it is as if Maddie is still manipulating him.

He's been keeping half an eye out for the red-and-white striped booth they'd come upon during their last visit. *Punch and Judy.* Some little puppet beating up his wife. He'd found it bizarre and disturbing, but as Maddie laughed and laughed, he'd found himself unable to look away. Punch and Judy, man and wife, together forever, come hell or high water. He had kept the faith. She had not. *And now?* If she were here, what would she want? *Revenge* . . . The idea had come to him as if there were some reason for it. But really, who was the real victim here? For so long, he has focused on her suffering that he has almost forgotten his own. If she were to walk right up to him now, what would he do? What would he say? For sure, there would be a reckoning. And at last, he'd get to say all the things he's been burning to say. And yet, all those conversations he's played out over the years, all the angry words, they now feel oddly redundant. After all was said and done, he and she are even. Fewer people now. The shuttered rifle range. The smell of oil fryers fading, the mineral tang of the ocean acute and invigorating. *Yes*, Jonathan thinks, he would be considered a fortunate man. "Blessed," as they say in Hollywood. At the end of each book tour, he gets to look forward to being home. To his routine of gym, therapy, writing, and dinner with Laura. Sitting up in bed together watching the late-night talk shows, tapping away on their phones. The his-and-hers nightstands, the reading glasses, the books neatly stacked. "*This is our life now.*" If he let things stay as they are, what then? One year hence, five, ten . . . *Gym, therapy, writing, dinner.* Like one of those deathly Midwestern marriages, his remaining years mapped out for him. *No edge. No daring. No surprises.* Mist swirls around him, damp and cold. With their repetitive adventures and banal domestic problems, it seems his cops' lives are as stale as his own. He is keenly aware of the notebooks, the solid weight of them against his body. This delusion of Maddie coming back to taunt him, maybe it is best seen as a reminder of who he was, and what he might be capable of in the future. Because he can go so much further, and achieve so much more than this. After all, if you wanted to go after the important awards and prizes—the ones that *count*—you had to come up with something genuinely new. To pull a hat out of a rabbit. Can he do it? There will be the thrill of once more casting off his old skin, of being rid of the old story and replacing it with something fresh and exciting.

Glancing back toward land, he spies a thin figure moving down the beach. Its movements are slightly unnatural, like an animation or bad CGI. The more he focuses on it, the more it recedes, until finally it merges with the background and vanishes. Was it even there in the first place? He shivers, raises the collar of his jacket, imagines for a second her restless spirit drifting furiously through the empty streets, along the desolate oceanfront. His feelings are real, but she is not. He understands that now. Not that she had respected his feelings. Even when she was alive, she had never taken him seriously. Left him to toil away at a job he hated and care for a child that wasn't his. Making him feel bad to the point where he'd considered destroying his work. Now he has hers—and hasn't he earned it? Doesn't he deserve a piece of the story for himself? After everything she put him through, doesn't she owe him? Once this tour is done, he can take some time in Europe. Rent an apartment, toss out the last Ocean Falls, and put his own little spin on the notebooks. *His* story, not hers. Picking up his pace, he feels stronger and more alive than he has in years. The blood sings in his ears. He feels the adrenaline powering his mind. Ideas fizzing and sparking. *Award* . . . such a boring and worthy word. Whereas *prize* . . . *prize* is pure glitter.

Magic

2019

The sun waits for him on the horizon, glows at him with an orangey-pink intensity as a few last wispy clouds trail themselves across the sky. Cotton-candy zoo animals—elephants, tigers, zebras. Somewhere, carried faintly on the wind, a radio plays tinny pop music. It is almost dusk. Ensnared by slot machines and junk food, few people made it out this far. Shadows close and flit through ornate filigree archways. A lone attendant leans against a line of empty bumper cars, pulls on a cigarette with an expression of bored detachment. Unseen, Jonathan ducks under a railing and squeezes through the small space between the swing ride and a construction workers' hut. Seconds later, he finds himself at the farthest point of the pier, the secret spot where she had brought him, all those years ago. Alone together, up against the railing, no one watching . . .

"*No one can see us,*" she'd murmured into his neck. Droplets of sea spray mist his face, the sea the color of the sky, the sky already growing dark. How lonely and exhilarating it is, like being perched on the prow of an ocean liner. Yes, he thinks. *Yes.* He has missed it, this feeling. Giddy, vertiginous, elated. Like love—it sent you out of your mind. Love, he remembers, which made you want to do everything, know everything, gobble it up like food. Always hungry, always desperate. Powerless and insatiable. To anyone who hasn't had the experience, it sounded insane, this need to consume and memorize every detail of someone's life—their favorite films, their likes and dislikes, their childhood experiences, all their quirks and endearing little habits, the names of each and every beloved childhood toy ... Love made you foolish, it was true. But one day, if you were very, very unlucky, it all came in useful.

He takes the toy car from his bag, cradles it against his chest for a moment. Improv was always her favorite class. The one she most enjoyed lecturing him about. *Improv.* Even the word was annoying. If his own story was improvised, if it wasn't the literal truth, it was in the spirit of the truth, was it not? Faced with an impossible situation, he had panicked and reached for ... something. *Anything.* And suddenly there it was. Appearing as if by magic. The little car, pulling up in his mind like Cinderella's golden carriage. Arriving right when he needed it. It was—as Ragione had somewhat accurately observed—as if the car were waiting for them.

"It's an E-type," Maddie had informed him. "From 1961."

They were sitting in Joyce's garden, looking through old photo albums under what he remembers as blazing sunshine, but almost certainly wasn't.

"Her father gave it to her for her ..." Joyce had begun, the sentence trailing off into the ether.

"For my tenth *birthday*," Maddie said. About half the size of a shoebox, the model car was a perfect replica of a real one. The detail was astonishing. How the doors opened and closed, and the trunk lifted open, too. How even the tiny steering wheel turned. The car was old, a little beaten up, as if it had been loved too much and a little too hard.

"They're much more common than you'd think," Maddie had continued, rubbing tenderly at the shiny red paintwork with her sleeve. "Even over there. It was the best one. Brilliant to drive."

"Don't you want to bring it home with us?" he had asked, understanding that the car was a treasured possession. Now, it is almost as if he hears her voice, with him again, at the end of the pier.

"No . . ." she had replied. "No, it's safer here." Had she known? Had some part of her known? That she too would have been safer if she'd stayed right where she was? Interesting how life worked out. How many times had he wished her back again? All his lost limbs . . . all the people that he has mentally sacrificed. And again, that thorny question he has never asked himself, let alone answered. For in all that time, he had never once offered up the very thing her absence had made possible: *his success*. In the distance, a cloud appears to lower itself onto the water. The effect is otherworldly. Exactly twenty-three years later, his own version of their last day together only feels more real—not less. Their perfect weekend and his last-ditch attempt to salvage what remained of their once-perfect relationship. His wife, running down the sand, happier than he'd seen her in a long time. Almost her old self again. The first time in months that he could recall her laughing. Excitement, anticipation, the plane tickets burning a hole in his pocket. Waiting for the right moment. Wanting to say the right words. He'd thought he had it in the bag. He couldn't have been more wrong—*Surprise!* He turns the car over in his hands. Uncanny how precisely he'd managed to describe it to the cops. The fender dented in two places. The front head-lamp busted out. The duct tape curled and peeling—a nice touch, that last part, he decides, and permits himself a smile. "Brilliant" how these details had lent his description the ring of truth. That when he had found himself grasping at straws, he had remembered the car so vividly and managed to improvise. He strokes his fingers over the smooth red enamel of the hood—the "bonnet," she'd called it. Adorable. At the time. The notebooks are stashed safely in his bag. He'll need to get rid of them eventually. But not yet. *I dare you* ... Does he have the courage of his convictions? Does *he* dare? How long has it been since he threw caution to the wind? Or took a risk? Too long. Not since that day.

Far below, gray-green waves slap against rusted metal girders, seaweed flows around them like mermaids' hair, appearing and disappearing between slender fingers of curling mist and sprigs of foam. *Seafoam* ... or was it *chartreuse*? Either way, it was certainly a long way down. Even if you survived the fall, you'd be dashed against the pier's iron struts and carried far out to sea in no time. "*I dare you,*" he whispers. The time has come to be done with it. To put it—and her—to rest. On the back of his neck there's a prickle, the hairs abruptly rising. He spins around. No one there. Just a raindrop. On the western horizon, a storm is brewing, clouds threatening, dark and heavy. Yes ... she is out there, somewhere. If not in the way he had hoped, and feared. Like the hapless victims of Ocean Falls, his wife will remain forever silent. He opens his fingers, feels the weight of the car leave his hands. A brief flash of red as it turns in midair and hits the surface—*plop*—and he watches the water take it.

Happy Birthday, Maddie. You got everything you deserved ...

Love

1996

"Oh, *Jon* . . . Oh, you shouldn't have . . ."

He had thought they were tears of joy. Now, he can't believe what he's hearing.

"It isn't working," she repeats, "you must have known."

All he knows is that, for the longest time, his wife has been unhappy. And that the tickets are meant to make her happy again. *We'll drop Ben off with his grandma in England,* he had been about to say. And then, it'll be just the two of us. Two whole months together, roaming the globe, free as birds. Going wherever we want, when we want, how we want. *Just like we used to.*

"But it's what you wanted . . ." he stammers as she shakes her head. What she wants is a divorce.

"It's too late," she murmurs. "Look . . . I didn't want to tell you like this . . ." Below them, the waves lap higher around the jetty, white tips made foamy by the wind. "We didn't plan it . . . it was a mistake. Honestly, it just happened . . ."

We . . .? he is thinking. What is she talking about? She bites her lip and looks away.

"Who is it?" he says. "Tell me."

She refuses. Even now, as he continues to plead with her, he's waiting for the catch. Waiting for her to laugh—*Haha, oh my God, you should see your face!*

321

Instead, she looks out toward the ocean, won't meet his gaze. "It doesn't matter," she says. "It doesn't matter who it is. But if it matters to you, for what it's worth, I'm truly sorry." Each time she opens her mouth, it's like another punch in the gut.

"What about Ben?" It's all he can think of, but it's precisely the wrong thing. Her lips move but the words are lost on the wind. Or perhaps he can no longer bear to hear what she's saying. The expression in her eyes tells him all he needs to know. He may be standing right here, but she no longer sees him. She is looking at him and sees *someone else*. Or wishes he were someone else. He has been rendered invisible. Who, who, *who?* He begs, but she won't say. Instead, she holds out the tickets.

"*Here,*" she says. "Take them. I'm sorry. Maybe you can get a refund."

This is the moment. The moment when he knows that there is no going back. When he understands, with unbearable, devastating clarity, that she is lost to him. It's the look on her face, the expression of pity, that makes him do it. He strikes her. Hard. Full in the face with the flat of his hand. He's been wanting to do it for ages, he hadn't realized how badly until now. Or known even that he could—and has. For one slow-motion moment she seems to hover, balanced in midair, her expression one of utter surprise. And then she tumbles backward and hits the jetty. He hears it, the sickening crack as the side of her head meets the concrete. Her eyes flutter closed, then open—before closing again.

"Maddie?" She doesn't move. *Playacting.* It's the only explanation. "*Maddie . . .?*" No answer. No movement.

He's terrified of touching her. Doesn't want to, but forces himself. Tentatively, he extends a foot toward her. No response. It's unreal. There's his foot, he thinks, resting gently against his wife's hip, as if they are on the couch together watching TV. He listens to the waves slap indifferently against the jetty. They might have come here again, spent hours together lying in the sun. Except that nothing is simple or straightforward anymore, is it? Everything is ruined. And she has ruined it. *How could she do this? How dare she?* He prods again with his foot. The feel of his bare toes against her lifeless body makes him want to gag. Unaware of what he's doing until it's done, he pushes hard with the ball of his foot, and watches her body tumble slackly into the water below. *Did I really just do that?* Disbelief, revulsion. He stands there, transfixed. Maddie, floating face down in the water, her body bobbing serenely in time with the waves.

At that moment, it is as if there are two of him. Two Jonathans. The one who watches in horror. The other calmly observing the dead body of his wife. Time seems to collapse: he's back at their apartment, watching her, over and over, slam the door and leave. Ben yelping in pain as Jonathan grabs him firmly—too firmly—around the arm: "Why can't you *ever* just do as you're told?" He had tried to save her. To warn her. To rescue her from herself. She wouldn't listen.

He glances back toward the shore. The beach is empty. What should he do? Claim an accident? He could say that she dove into shallow water. Or that she slipped and fell. No. The skin on her cheek bears the imprint of his hand. Would it fade? When, though? He has no idea. Dark clouds crowd the horizon. The wind gusts harder, the waves whipping up at an alarming rate. He checks the beach again. Empty, not a soul to be seen—looks back in time to see her dress billow out grotesquely for a moment, like a balloon. A human sailboat.

She had surprised him, Jonathan thinks, but it was her face that bore the expression of surprise. And he was the one who had put it there. Now, there are no surprises left. And no words. Only the current swirling fierce and fast and out to sea. *Her. And not her.* No more than a minute can have passed, but her body is already moving away, moving out into the water, drawn out by the tide with shocking rapidity. Right below the surface, his own surface, underneath the horror and disgust, the rage still burns. He can feel it, white hot in his veins as her body glides away from him, turns slowly, obscenely, almost lazily, onto its back, and drifts serenely out to sea.

He gets his sneakers and socks and makes his way back to shore with the peculiar sense of being outside his own body. He has no idea what to do next. Almost any decision risks making the nightmare real. Shivering and lightheaded, he finds himself sinking abruptly down on the sand. *How could she do this to him? How could she?* A low rumble of thunder and it starts to rain. He gets himself up and scans the ocean. Nothing. No sign of anything . . . untoward. It is as if they were never even here.

He tries to think. What he needs is a plan. A *story*. One that, like the real one, is just unbelievable enough to be believable. Detail, but not too much. And detailed in the right way. A story that even she would be proud of. Before he can even consider leaving, or saying anything to anyone, he will need to get every piece perfectly clear in his mind. Better to stay right here, in the freezing rain, for as long as he can bear, than risk getting it wrong. He needs to report this. Not *this*, obviously. But *something*. The local police station is just a few miles away. They had passed it on the journey in. Could he plead some kind of an accident? Again, no. The mark on her face—testament to all his double shifts and all his sacrifices. To all the going without and his long-stored-up excitement and anticipation. And to her callous rejection. It wasn't only her coldness, but the thing that sat behind her eyes. A look of scorn, of triumph. He looks at his watch.

Weird, that in the split second before it happened, he had pictured himself pushing her. Had understood how unforgivable it would be. And he had gone ahead and done it anyway. Twenty-four minutes. How much longer should he wait? Long enough for the current to do its work. Long enough to come up with a story.

He puts on his sneakers and socks and walks up the beach to where they'd propped their bikes not an hour before. In the deserted parking lot, the rain hits his skin like hard little nails, streams down his face like tears. As he turns his bicycle toward the bridge, vast, jagged streaks of lightning reach across the sky, horizon to horizon.

Like an invisible hand scrawling a message as, in a flash, it comes to him. The perfect story. "*. . . taking something that isn't actually true . . . and imagining it for yourself . . .*"

Rehearsing his lines, backward, forward, sideways, he pedals into the wind.

Epilogue

BRUNCH IN DEPTH:
"*Gone Hollywood*—Talking Trauma, Healing, and Letting Go with Jonathan Sayer, Author of *A Heart Too Soon Made Glad.*"
The *Celebrity Life & Arts* Interview

Jonathan Sayer picks tentatively at his steak tartare and gazes out of the window toward the ocean beyond.

Unthinkingly, I had suggested Samphire for our lunch date, before realizing my faux pas (about which more later). The author was gracious, however, countering with newly opened, celeb-heavy hot-ticket, Shades on the Beach. A clever choice, I think to myself, as we sit down, offering privacy and a bevy of staff who have seen it all.

It seems we are hidden in plain sight. Having done the rounds of the late-night talk shows, Sayer is that rare thing—an author who's recognizable to the general public.

"I didn't think this through, did I?" He laughs, after the third person in as many minutes stops by our table.

"Hope you can drop by the set," says one, before returning to a booth containing an array of famous faces. Barely a week after the publication of his acclaimed and much anticipated novel, *A Heart Too Soon Made Glad*, jetlagged after catching the red-eye in from Tokyo, Sayer looks amazingly well, if understandably a bit glassy-eyed.

Beginning—with a knowing nod and a wink—on the proverbial "dark and stormy night," the book morphs into a different animal entirely, pushing the boundaries of fiction to form a dazzling, transgressive, and wildly experimental narrative. If this sounds like a rave review, I am not alone. With its captivating female protagonist and its colorful, shifting, inclusive cast, reviewers have hailed it as a virtuoso bravura demonstration of twenty-first-century writing at its most emotionally complex.

I ask Sayer about his move to the West Coast. He is only the latest in a storied history of writers who have made the city of angels their home. Though unlike many celebrities, he has chosen to live not high up in the Hollywood Hills, but in a bungalow at Chateau Marmont. Likewise, the launch for his novel was held, not in a trendy restaurant or grand ballroom, but at Griffith Observatory.

"I've worshipped the place since I was a kid," he explains, with a boyish smile. "In fact, moving to LA was the realization of a lifelong dream." Even as the literary world debates the tangled issue of whether writers should "appropriate" other voices, critics have applauded the novel for that of its vivid and persuasively authentic female protagonist. The emotional heart of the novel comprises the young woman's journal, and her life as a kind of modern day flaneuse in rapidly gentrifying 1990s New York. With stunning deftness, Sayer captures the diversity of the people that she encounters—the too-cool-for-school musicians, down-and-out artists and random characters—amid a stunning landscape of the sort some are christening "urban picaresque." A self-described feminist, Sayer clearly *gets* women, I observe.

"That's great to hear." He smiles.

As our starters arrive, I tell him that I was struck by the

undercurrent of emotional manipulation that's visited upon the young woman at the center of his story, in ways both subtle and overt.

"None of us can know what goes on in others' relationships," he says. "But sometimes there's this . . ." He pauses, frowns. ". . . This kind of emotional blackmail that needs to be answered to."

Having attained considerable success as a crime novelist, ditching his birth name, John Dainty, to write pseudonymously as John Dane, *A Heart Too Soon Made Glad* has seen the author assume yet another identity—Jonathan Sayer. It is, I suggest, as if he is desiring to emerge for the first time as his real self. A *sayer* of truths, perhaps?

"I realized only fairly recently," he replies, "that, for decades, I have been trying to work through the trauma of my wife's disappearance by writing about other young women in peril, and of justice being served." As we sip sparkling water, Sayer continues. "Yet, these women were never heard from. Their voices and their experiences were never explored. I'd essentially silenced the female victims at the center of my books," he says. "That was . . . problematic. And that needed to change."

I ask him about the jumping-off point for the novel. Several years ago, he reveals, going through some storage boxes, he'd come across a collection of his old notebooks, filled with stories, characters and ideas he'd long ago forgotten.

"Or had just written off as youthful pretension . . ." He smiles. "But reading through them again really set something off for me."

In the recent Oprah Winfrey special, the author spoke movingly of the unwieldy emotions that he grappled with following the disappearance of his wife, Maddie Morgan. How did he get himself through it? I ask. The question is hard for him, I can tell. His gaze shifts toward the ocean, as if hoping to find the answer there. For an uneasy moment, I suspect that we are both wondering whether he is about to cry. Then he flashes that wide movie-star smile we've been seeing so much of lately.

"Sorry about that. My own emotions still take me by surprise. Some days, the experience still feels so raw. But to answer your question, it took a lot of therapy and a lot of journaling. I began to realize that I had spent 20 years allowing myself to feel guilty for no reason whatsoever," he says. "As a successful author sometimes you have to play the part, obviously. Fake it till you make it, right? But in retrospect, I believe I suffered some kind of PTSD."

I notice that his hands are shaking. We are, of course, dancing around the elephant in the room—Sayer's brother-in-law, Saul Godley. As many readers will be aware, Godley was the much-lauded presenter of the award-winning public radio show, *Making Waves*. Two years ago, an article of Ms. Morgan's clothing was recovered that provided a definitive piece of DNA evidence in her case. At which point, in a shocking development, the Pulitzer Prize winner was subsequently implicated in her disappearance. Godley's widow and Sayer's sister, former high-flying Manhattan lawyer Heather Godley, was herself implicated, having admitted to providing her husband a false alibi. After successfully securing herself a plea deal, her husband was indicted on first-degree murder and kidnapping, with the case due to go to trial this fall.

Sayer has ordered for us both, and our main courses now arrive—the fish for me, and the ribeye steak, rare and bloody, for him. As he smiles warmly up at our server and instructs him to remove the bread basket, I ask how these events affected him. Sayer pauses to top off our water glasses, then answers carefully.

The discovery of a cold-blooded murderer in the family, he tells me, was "a betrayal and an utter tragedy in its absolute waste of two lives."

Didn't Sayer himself post the one-million-dollar bail? I ask, as delicately as possible. "I did . . ." he admits. "And in retrospect, that was a mistake. You want to believe the best about someone, you know?" After an apparent act of suicide (and presumed admission of guilt) Mr. Godley's corpse was discovered by a jogger, hanged in a heavily wooded area, not a hundred yards from his lavish country retreat in upstate New York. Over the months, various conspiracy theories have been peddled concerning the death, but both Godley's case and that of Ms. Morgan are now considered closed. (Although, in yet another bizarre development, the investigators originally assigned to Ms. Morgan's case are rumored to be under an internal investigation for various acts of negligence and alcohol-related misconduct.) Still, it's hard to forget that, at the quiet center of all this activity, remains Maddie Morgan herself, whose ultimate fate remains a mystery.

"We'll never know exactly what happened," Sayer tells me, slicing into his steak. "All we can ever be sure of is that my brother-in-law was someone we trusted and let into our family. And that, unbeknownst to us, he was a wolf in sheep's clothing." Investigators have spoken of a vulnerable, impressionable young mother. Of an obsessive, jealous, and controlling predator who emotionally manipulated and fatally preyed on a naive young woman going through a period of emotional instability.

"His suicide cheated us of all knowledge, all closure," Sayer tells me. I circle us back to Ocean Falls, his bestselling crime series, brought to a notorious conclusion with his two lead characters and their entire families meeting their demise in bloody and spectacular style. Regarded at the time as a wanton act of literary suicide, it's become clear that this was a necessary prelude to an act of rebirth. I ask how the loyal followers of Ocean Falls have greeted this move toward a more literary oeuvre.

"My fans are wonderful," he says. "Just really willing to come along on that ride with me."

And what a ride it is. Tipped for the Booker Prize, lauded here and internationally, even Sayer's TED talk, "The Illusion of Authentic Self and the Creation of Character," is riding high, garnering even more views than Joe Smith's "How to Use a Paper Towel."

Having spoken candidly about Maddie Morgan, the author is less forthcoming about some of his other relationships. In an interview three years ago, he is on record talking about his plans to be married again—"happily hitched," he phrased it at the time. Today, word is that his relationship with Manhattan-based chef Laura Stead, owner of Manhattan's C-Salt and its recently shuttered LA outpost, Samphire, is over. His publicist has declared this topic strictly off limits, however, as is that of his rumored-to-be-estranged son, who last month emerged from a lengthy stint in rehab and is said to have adopted his mother's last name, Morgan.

In happier news, this past year Sayer founded a charitable foundation, Maddie's Room, dedicated to supporting and empowering—through acting and theater, with a particular focus on improv skills—those left behind after a loved one has gone missing. In fact, today marks the twenty-sixth anniversary of his wife's disappearance, while this weekend will see the author return to the East Coast and head out to the Hamptons for a star-studded Maddie's Room fundraiser.

Why acting? I ask. "It's about finding the emotional truth of your character," Sayer replies. "And fully and deeply inhabiting them. It's that kernel of you, playing you. And making that work—not only for yourself, but for others. An act of creation is an act of hope," he adds. "And creating stories has literally saved my life."

I nod in agreement. At this point, film rights to the novel have been sold for an undisclosed seven-figure sum and Sayer finds himself one of the wealthiest authors on the planet. While more uncharitable souls have suggested that the foundation is a convenient tax dodge, I ask whether giving back has had a positive influence on his life.

He breaks into a grin. "*Absolutely!* Gosh, I'm probably too passionate about it," he says. "It's like having a child, you know?"

We're interrupted by the owner of the restaurant, proffering dessert menus. Tanned and toned, Sayer politely declines, but tells me to please go ahead and order for myself.

"You know, we never found her body," Sayer tells me softly. "And for a while there, I was in this really bad place where I used to see her. On the subway, in the street, wherever." He takes a breath, swallows hard. "Until the very last, her killer showed no remorse and refused to own up to what he did. He refused to tell anyone what happened. How she had died, or where he left her. That was the hardest thing for us, as a family." He pauses. "Maddie wasn't a writer herself," he goes on. "My wife was far too much of a free spirit to put pen to paper. But she always supported my craft, and you could say that she speaks through me."

How so? "I believe my hallucinations were some manifestation of her spirit, telling me it was OK to let go," Sayer replies. "To dare to write the book I was always meant to write. And share it with the world."

Being open about these painful personal circumstances is incredibly brave, I observe.

"That's great to hear." He smiles, drawing his hands into a

prayerful thank-you. "Success is something I have to live with every day of my life. But you have to earn the confidence to be humble, and I feel truly blessed."

As is the tradition with *Brunch in Depth,* I finish by asking Sayer about his biggest fear.

"Sharks?" He laughs, at which moment we are once again interrupted.

"Hello, Jon." An older woman stands at our table, bedecked in an extraordinarily large array of rings and gold jewelry. Sayer looks taken aback, but appears to recover. Though judging by the stilted exchange of pleasantries that follow, I realize this can only be Cindy Straub, Sayer's longtime literary agent, with whom he rather publicly split after abandoning his Ocean Falls series. A new author of hers has just completed a true-crime memoir, Straub informs us, a real-life story of survival against the odds. As Sayer looks at his watch and lets out a conspicuous yawn, she gestures toward a booth in the far corner of the room.

"We just had a celebration lunch for her birthday," she says, as I look over to see a striking forty-something blonde in a gorgeous green dress, nonchalantly applying lipstick. She looks up and smiles directly at Sayer, clearly recognizing the famous author. After Straub takes her leave, I turn back to my guest, curious to know whether he has any comment on this encounter with his ex-agent. However, Sayer appears not to hear me. His attention is still fixed on Straub's table, where the women are now being helped on with their coats. All the color has drained from his face. He does, I realize, look positively unwell.

"I'm so sorry, was it the steak?" I ask, worried that the food has disagreed with him, and am not surprised when he asks to terminate the interview. As I watch a clearly agitated Sayer get to his feet and head rapidly toward the fire exit, I wonder whether I have delved too deeply into his life, triggering his trauma and PTSD. In the rapacious, cut-throat world of book publishing, it's no easy feat for a seasoned author to take on a radically different voice. All the more impressive, then, that with his literary debut Sayer has reinvented himself. As I pay the bill, I cannot help but wonder about the mysterious new author whose name we never learned. Then again, with powerhouse Straub on her side, it can only be a matter of time.

Acknowledgments

A shocking number of people are involved in getting a book into shape and out into the world. These include my fantastic editor in London, Myfanwy Moore, who took on Birthday Girl and helped improve it no end. Likewise, Bea Fitzgerald, Lisa Gilliam, Rebecca Miller, Christina Maria Webb, Will Speed, Rachel Southey, Alice Morley and the whole team at Hodder & Stoughton, and Giuliana Caranante at Mobius. Another massive thank you must go to my agent Alexa Stark at Trident Media in New York, for not only having the best GoT name ever, but for believing in the novel from the very beginning. And a special mention to Trident's Adrienne Santamaria for all the transatlantic hours she put in on my behalf.

I am indebted to Giulia dR and Des GM for giving me a place to write. And to CydCharise, D–King, Gaby, Giulia, Jason, John 'Taxi' T., John W., Jonathan E., Laura, Lia, Liam & Mark and Ricky, Lina & Jeff, Margaret MT, Naomi, Paul, Pepe 'AK', Rachel, Rick, Sean, Sharon, Shawnee B., Steve B., Tom and Team Y for their friendship through dark days.

Thanks to Max R. for his inspired 'tankcopter' concept. To Chris C. (FBI, Ret.) who got on the phone one day to confirm my wildest notions about the criminal mind. And never forgetting NYPD officer CJB, who sat with me during much of the writing of this book, and occasionally consented to my interrogations. Needless to say, in support of the plot, I have taken

some factual liberties regarding the police and their proce-
dures, and any inaccuracies are mine alone.

Speaking of which, regular visitors to a certain bookstore in
Union Square may notice that I have taken some poetic licence
with the 'down' escalator. In reality it faces the back of the
store, with no view of the exit . . .

This book is dedicated to my lovely Violet – velvet-eared
canine asset, dog of dogs, and a true friend who was only ever
herself.

About the Author

Niko Wolf was born in London and her first novel, *The Favourite*, was published in the UK in 2017 under SV Berlin. Long listed for The Authors' Club Best First Novel Award 2018, it was also chosen as an ELLE Book of the month.

Most recently, she was a Screenwriter and Story Editor for independent movie *A Son of Man*, selected as an official entry in the foreign-language category for the 2019 Oscars. Wolf works in artificial intelligence, and lives in Manhattan.

Birthday Girl is her first thriller.